T0137676

CHATEAU PACIFIC

By John McCraw

Cover Artwork provided by
Ronald Dykes of Art of the Eye

Order this book online at www.trafford.com
or email orders@trafford.com

Most Trafford titles are also available at major online book retailers.

Printed in the United States of America.

ISBN: 978-1-4269-5930-1 (sc)
ISBN: 978-1-4269-5931-8 (hc)
ISBN: 978-1-4269-5932-5 (e)

Library of Congress Control Number: 2011902956

Trafford rev. 03/31/2011

 www.trafford.com

North America & international
toll-free: 1 888 232 4444 (USA & Canada)
phone: 250 383 6864 ♦ fax: 812 355 4082

CHATEAU PACIFIC

By John McCraw

Cover Artwork provided by
Ronald Dykes of Art of the Eye

Order this book online at www.trafford.com
or email orders@trafford.com

Most Trafford titles are also available at major online book retailers.

Printed in the United States of America.

ISBN: 978-1-4269-5930-1 (sc)
ISBN: 978-1-4269-5931-8 (hc)
ISBN: 978-1-4269-5932-5 (e)

Library of Congress Control Number: 2011902956

Trafford rev. 03/31/2011

 www.trafford.com

North America & international
toll-free: 1 888 232 4444 (USA & Canada)
phone: 250 383 6864 ♦ fax: 812 355 4082

CHATEAU PACIFIC
TABLE OF CONTENTS

STARR COUNTY

From my point of observation, I could see both upstream and down without fear of detection. The live-oak I'd chosen was perfectly positioned on the river's edge, and still carried enough autumn foliage to conceal a man in camouflage. The subdued black nylon spook suit that covered every square inch of my 6 ft. frame was both comfortable and functional, but it was my 9mm Smith & Wesson, snugly holstered in the small of my back that provided the majority of my personal comfort and well being. Without a doubt, the cool breezes coming up from the Rio Grande also helped a lot. "November in the 90's!" was a great slogan for the Convention and Visitors Bureau, but the reality was hell on us working folks. At least this was a night gig.

Downstream, the moonlight danced and glittered off the ripples of the swirling and churning river. Upstream, however, the reflections were smooth and glassy, so if there was going to be a crossing, and JJ was certain there would be, this was the perfect location. Crossings were commonplace from El Paso to Brownsville, but tonight was going to be different. Very different. It just so happens that the Sheriff of Starr County was expecting a very special delivery from his collaborators across the border, and tonight fit his schedule perfectly. Swimmers had been gathered at various points up and down the river as diversions for any unwanted observers from the

Border Patrol, or other fellow officers, but the payload would be crossing here. JJ was certain of that. Very certain.

"Detection means Death!" Our topkicks at infiltration school took special pride in drilling that phrase into us. The Army definitely has a way with words when they want to emphasize a point, and covert assignments in Southeast Asia and Central America proved them to be absolutely correct. For some strange reason, people involved in clandestine activities have a tendency to shoot first, and then ask questions. Collecting evidence on one of the most powerful men in the region, who also just happens to be the County Sheriff, only heightened the danger factor. To return fire on a cop, even a dirty one, is still a death penalty in the eyes of his peers.

Jonathan Jamison Walker, former classmate and now operative for the CIA, was somewhere across the river observing the Mexican connection to this party. Being partners all the way through spook school, we became good friends. Testing and proving our skills under fire together made us best friends for life. Years later, he still calls when he needs a second pair of eyes, or someone to cover his back. Trust is the word he uses to describe our relationship. Being a born-again adrenaline junkie, I look forward to these sorties with the unexpected. My assignment tonight is to view and record the crossing with a Sony Digital minicam equipped with night vision and telezoom. In accordance with my orders, identifying the principals was only secondary to recording the specifics as to how and where.

The night itself seemed eager to participate, and added its own special twist to the mystery and suspense. High level atmospheric winds were blowing the billowy cumulus clouds in and out of the moon's pathway, thus causing periods of eerie darkness intermixed with times of brilliant moonlight. The auto-iris of the night-vision zoom lens was being taxed to its maximum capabilities, but seemed to be holding its own. It was during one of these blackouts that I saw the first swimmer enter the river. The AK-47 he carried was easily identified as he held it above the water while he swam. Once across, he reconned the landing area, and then signaled his accomplices to follow. Another armed soldier immediately entered the water, then a third, and fourth. I hoped JJ was safely observing all this activity, because if I was less than fifty yards away from the action, he was probably much closer.

I lowered the camera to readjust myself against the upper trunk when the skin on the back of my neck began to twitch. Taking a moment to scan my position, I looked straight down and saw a human form crawling right under the tree I was hiding in! I could literally taste the adrenaline as my heart began pounding in my chest and my pulse rate elevated. I easily identified the Remington 700 sniper's rifle he carried, but couldn't make out any insignias on his camouflage uniform. He spoke Spanish into a small communications device as he continued to watch the crossing through the scope on his weapon, and within seconds, two more uniformed snipers appeared beneath my tree. They conversed briefly in Spanish, then the two new players moved into position in front of me. How many more of them were there? Were they behind me, too? I didn't dare move or my questions could be answered by a silent bullet. I could feel myself really starting to sweat, so now all I needed was the urge to pee!

I shifted the Sony into my left hand and withdrew the 9mm with my right. Shaky pictures or not, I had to be ready for the worst-case scenario, because eyewitness testimony is only valid if the eyewitness is still alive! Scanning between the viewfinder and my close counterparts, I watched the deadly game unfold as a group of four swimmers entered the river carrying a container designed to float. Slightly larger than a steamer trunk, and obviously of significant weight, the resemblance to a coffin was both ironic and unnerving. Once into the river, one of the men attached a guide rope and then quickly swam across. I could see at least three people on the opposite shore, three in the river, and four on my side. Again, the one question racing through my mind was how many snipers were involved in this production? To think all of the perpetrators were within eyesight was asking a bit too much for my luck. In my gut I knew that every second brought me closer to being a participant rather than just an observer.

The swimmers were about halfway across with their package when all hell broke loose. At high mag through the viewfinder, I recorded and watched as the swimmers were blown to pieces by the heavily silenced magnum rounds. Panning from side to side, I observed as people on both sides of the river were being systematically gunned down. Suddenly, both sides of the river erupted in automatic weapons fire as the targets began to shoot back. Through all the noise, I could actually hear the man below me laughing as he continued to blow away whoever appeared in his cross-hairs. I tried to keep on filming, but with the container now free and floating right towards us, the action was getting way too close for comfort. Suddenly, another uniformed assailant appeared next to my downstairs neighbor and began talking into his communicator. The two assassins in front of me made their way back to my tree while the other two continued to go about their grizzly business. And then, it was all over, and an eerie silence fell over this stretch of the Rio Grande. There was no gunfire, no screams of death, no nothing. Just laughing! Those sorry mother-fuckers below me were lighting cigarettes and joking about what they'd just done, so I zoomed in for tight face shots of each of the perpetrators as they described what they had seen through their scopes. I also figured the emblems now visible on their uniforms would make for interesting conversation when the powers-that-be got to analyze my video.

All four men were sitting right below me when the one closest to the trunk of the tree leaned back to take a long draw off his cigarette. His eyes were closed as he drew the heavy smoke deep within his lungs, but as soon as he raised his lids, I felt our eye contact immediately.

"Meda pariba! Meda par . . ."

Two quick shots to the face abruptly ended his sentence. Using two-shot bursts, I worked my way down the line of assassins with surgical precision, but when I lined up the fourth, he had drawn his revolver and was ready to shoot. We fired simultaneously. My round caught him right below a protruding Adam's apple while his exploded into the branch I was standing on, sending fragments of wood and lead straight into me. I grabbed my left thigh in reaction to the immediate pain, and lost my balance. Falling out of a tree is bad enough, but falling after being shot leaves a lot to be desired for technique points. I plummeted to the ground, landing on the first assassin which forced the air from his lungs, smelling of smoke and death. I tried to move, but the shock from the fall, and the pain in my leg made me immobile. I tried to roll off, but that only made more blood and smoke ooze from the holes I'd put in his face. The harder I tried, the more entrapped I became in the macabre scenario. I was trying to roll from side to side, anything to get free . . . .

"Jeffrey! Oh, Jeffrey wake up! Please, Honey!"

My eyes flew open like rolled shades. I saw blond hair, blue eyes, and a very concerned expression.

"Oh, my God. You're soaking wet!" she said, then hugged me anyway. "Where were you this time?"

"I'm OK, Angel," I replied, wiping my face with the driest portion of my wet T-shirt. "Whew, that was intense!"

"You scare me to death when you do this," said the beautiful little blonde I share my home and life with.

"Me, too, Honey."

I stood, exchanged my wet T-shirt for a dry robe from the standing rack, and then walked into the upstairs game room. I was still shaking and my heart pounding as I stood and looked out of the large Bay window

onto the rainy street scene below. Legal or not, times like this make me wish I still had some smoke around. Anyone who denies the medicinal functions of marijuana has never had nightmares. At least not like mine! Nightmares! Yeah, right, just keep telling yourself they're only nightmares. I moved my left hand inside my robe and touched my outer thigh. The scar tissue was still there. Same spot, same leg. Same nightmare! Oh yeah, they'll go away. Sure they will.

HOME SWEET

Houston traffic really has no slack time. If you're in a hurry, there's traffic! I saw an opening, made a snappy lane change, then kicked the Mustang in the ass. The big V8 responded by slamming me back into my seat and leaving the Obamamobiles behind to duck the flying asphalt. Speed limits were irrelevant. All that mattered was getting home to Terri, and our uninvited guest. Not unwanted, necessarily, just completely unexpected.

I had planned a slow, casual day in the computer room getting caught up on all my classic black & white printing while Ruby, my associate photographer and worthy assistant, had a full day scheduled in the camera room shooting kids. I was ecstatic not to be involved in that screaming endeavor, and was geared down to spend the majority of my day in front of a monitor when the call came in.

"Hey, Mac! Stop banging the hired help and get your ass home!"

"JJ! What the . . . ? Are you really at my house?"

"You tell me. I'm looking at blonde hair, blue eyes, and a hefty rack on a 5'2" slender frame. Sound familiar?"

"Her name is Terri, and I'm on my way."

"I know you are."

I made the relaxed 20 minute drive from my studio to my house in 12. Turning down my street, I was surprised to see the gray Ford Taurus parked in my driveway. JJ has a passion for Porsches, so the domestic sedan threw me. I had barely turned off the ignition when my gorgeous roommate came bouncing down the sidewalk with a mischievous grin on her face. Terri threw her arms around my neck, rubbed her chest into mine, and kissed me passionately. Being typically male, I grabbed her ass with both hands and kissed her right back.

"Hi, Angel," I said. "What's going on?"

"You're taking me to Mexico, as if you didn't know." She was smiling from ear to ear, and obviously somewhat tipsy. "You're such a sly little bastard! How could you keep this from me?"

I just shrugged my shoulders and shook my head. I had no fucking idea what she was talking about, but I figured I'd find out soon enough. "Where's JJ?"

"Opening more wine, of course."

"Of course!" I could feel every one of my internal alarms going off all at once. When JJ resorts to bribery, the prospects of an easy assignment start to dwindle rapidly. The last assignment almost got me killed, and I hadn't laid eyes on him since. He called a few times to check on me, and to tell me to lay low during the trial, but never does he make social calls. This had to be another assignment!

Arm in arm, we walked into the house and straight towards the den. Looking more like a Baptist preacher than a CIA operative, there stood my former partner-in-crime wearing a designer suit and pouring expensive wine. He smiled a warm and sincere smile, shook my hand, then gave me a real manly hug.

"Hey Mac! Looks like you're no worse for wear," he said, then patted me on the shoulder. "Great rug," he smirked, obviously referring to Terri.

"Very comfortable, old man. What brings you to town?"

"I came to see my friend, the world famous photographer, of course," he replied, then handed me a glass of wine.

"Of course." Chassange-Montrachet. Oh shit, I'm really in for trouble now!

"Sit down and relax, you two," Terri said then whirled about. "I'm going to get some goodies to go with the wine. Be right back!"

We sat on opposite ends of my antique couch, then made eye contact. JJ had a real sincere expression when he finally opened up.

"Glad everything's going OK, Mac. I've got a girl in research who keeps me informed of your exploits with a camera." He leaned towards me and spoke softly. "I especially liked the Penthouse layout!"

Visions of an incendiary Mexican Ho semi-masturbating on the back of a chopped Harley passed before my eyes. I only did the shoot as a favor for an old friend who went ballistic over the photos and insisted I send them to a magazine. Not anybody's style at Playboy, Penthouse was my next alternative, and they bit. Checks quickly exchanged hands, and we got published. I wasn't particularly proud of the pictures, but what the hell, their money spends just as easily as anyone else's.

"Was she as hot-n-nasty as she looked? Of course you had to sample something that luscious!"

"She's not into guys, JJ!" I paused for effect, then continued. "Her 200 lb. girlfriend was standing behind the scenes screaming, 'Come for me, Bitch!', 'Fuck me, Baby!', 'Where's my dildo!', and other such pleasantries. Poor Ruby was so intimidated by the two of them, she had to leave the room, and damn near quit. The whole ordeal was over in less than an hour."

JJ looked shocked. "But she was so gorgeous!"

"Only on the outside, my friend. I prefer my women with class and charm, not tattoos on their ass and arms. Need I say more?"

Terri entered the room with a tray of goodies from the kitchen. We both got the full effect of her French-cut T-shirt when she bent over to set the tray down on the coffee table.

"I think that says it all," was his only reply. He refilled our glasses, then held his up for a toast. "It ain't Lowenbrau, but here's to good friends."

We all clinked glasses, then sipped the golden nectar. The suspense was killing me, so I had to break the congenial mood. "So what's the deal with Mexico?"

"I'm glad you asked!" JJ set his briefcase on the table, opened it, then passed me a large manila envelope. Just to piss me off, he reached for a canapé, sipped his wine, then paused for effect. "Oh yes, Mexico. I've arranged for both of you to shoot a swimsuit catalog at one of the newest, and most exclusive resorts on the Pacific coast." Again, he paused for effect, then tossed a very familiar catalog on the table. Terri and I instantly knew what it was because she was on the cover. The Private Edition Lingerie catalog was our first big success, and the first of many of their publications featuring her beauty and my photography. "When I told them I could guarantee both model and photographer in one package, they ran for their checkbook."

"Whose swimsuits, JJ?" Terri was really getting excited.

"A new design group out of San Diego called Sunset Limited. I have an 'in' with their marketing executives, and decided to return a favor for my good friend. Your reservations are for a ten day stay at Chateau Pacific, beginning in eleven days."

"Eleven days!" she shrieked. "Holy shit, I've got to lose some weight, get a tan, get a haircut, do my nails, get a facial, ..."

"Try these on first, OK." JJ tossed two suits wrapped in plastic on the table. "Sorry about the short notice, but they need this catalog ready-set-go in less than 90 days. I promised them you'd get right on it."

Terri's face lit up like a five-year old at Christmas. I really love the enthusiasm and fire that drives her. To be totally honest, I really do love everything about her. Beauty, brains, passion; what's not to love! She slid into the kitchen, and was back in less than two minutes wearing an exotic floral print 2 piece thong, perfectly made for her classic figure. I could tell JJ was impressed because all he did was nod and stare.

"You mentioned something about a check," I said to break his concentration. His attention was diverted only long enough to pass me an envelope from his vest pocket. Inside was a cashier's check, made out to me, for $15,000. I held it up for Terri to read, and she grabbed it out of my hand.

"Holy shit!" She pounced on me and started kissing me all over my face. Check and all, she dashed back into the kitchen to change.

"So what do you think?" asked JJ.

"I think we're going to Mexico," I replied, then looked him straight in the eyes. "When are you going to tell me the rest of the story?"

Before JJ could respond, Terri came back wearing the tiniest swimsuit I'd ever seen. The triangle-patch top barely covered her nipples, and the G-string bottom left nothing to the imagination. Absolutely nothing!

"It's a good thing we like me slick," she said with a sneaky little grin. This time, we both just stared and nodded.

"I think this deserves a celebration!" JJ stood and downed his wine. "Darlin', how long does it take for you to get dazzling?"

"She's standing there almost naked, and you want more!"

"Public dazzle, asshole."

Even in her state of undress, Terri had composure and sophistication. "Do you want a ten minute dazzle, a thirty minute dazzle, or the whole one hour dazzle?"

"I want to take both of you out to the most outrageous seafood restaurant in Houston. You must know of some classy joint with fresh fish, good wine, and a little ambiance for cool folks like us."

Terri and I looked at each other and said in unison, "Amerigos!"

"The thirty minute dazzle should be sufficient." Terri walked over, purposely bent over at the waist, and kissed me. She knew I would be starring at her gorgeous breasts, and loved every second of it. Me, too!

I opened the third bottle of Montrachet and poured as JJ tried to compose himself. He loosened his tie and unbuttoned the top button of his shirt, then sat back into the comfort of the couch.

"Live and in the flesh, she's one of the most stunning women I've ever met. Where did you find her?" he asked.

"Actually, she found me. I was late getting back to the studio after a fashion shoot downtown, and there she was, sitting on the hood of her Mustang, just waiting for me. I won't say it was love at first sight, but it certainly was love at first session. The camera seems to bring all her inner beauty to the surface. I was literally overwhelmed! I broke my Prime Directive about dating models, and we've been inseparable ever since." I paused until he returned my eye contact. "So what makes you think I'd endanger her by taking her along on an assignment. This is an assignment for you, isn't it? Time for the truth, JJ."

"Truth is, this is really a legitimate photographic assignment for Sunset Limited. Everything can be checked out, completely and totally, without any connection to me or the Company. My 'in' with the marketing group is strictly second hand. Your assignment for me is only to check out the club." He gestured me to open the large manila envelope, then continued. "Chateau Pacific is one of those exclusive resorts for the rich and infamous. Any known agent would get caught in their intensive security checks. I'm proud to say, both Terri and you came through with flying colors and no red flags."

"Security checks and red flags! Why doesn't this sound right to me?"

"That's what we want to know, Jeffrey. Surveillance has reported some world class players in the international black market hanging around the club on two previous occasions, and we now have an inside tip that another meeting is going to take place."

"Let me guess, in eleven days!"

"Exactly. It took some serious negotiating to get permission from the asshole owner to allow the photos. I had to agree to his extortion of $5000 cash as a Professional fee paid directly to him. The GM was agreeable from the get-go, and asked if you would be available to shoot some stuff for the club, which I agreed to immediately."

"What kind of stuff, JJ?"

"Anything they want, buddy boy. The more access you have around the club, the better our chances of finding out what's going on. We need to know who's involved and what's the purpose of these gatherings. Other than that, just have a good time and shoot some outrageous photos. I repeat, this is a legit assignment for Sunset Limited, and they really want both Terri and you. I specifically did not give them exclusive rights to all photographs, so maybe you can make a little extra in some other publications. I suggest you get as many staffers and guests involved in the shoot as possible so you can pick their brains while photographing the rest of their bodies."

Speaking of bodies, Terri walked back in wearing her Athens outfit. While we were in Greece, almost every beautiful woman was wearing a tissue thin v-neck cashmere sweater over a black leather mini-skirt. The way Terri had her hair and make-up done, combined with the motion of her body as she moved towards us, the second pair that captivated our attention had to be her eyes. By the time her entire package had been encompassed, testosterone levels were on a rampant surge.

"Thought I'd go Greek tonight," she said, then made a 360 so we could enjoy the view. "Do I look OK?"

"Dazzling!" seemed to say it all

DETAILS, DETAILS, DETAILS

The next morning, Terri was out the door like a flash to start shopping for all the necessities she would need for her first encounter with the social elite of Chateau Pacific. Knowing she would be gone for hours, JJ and I took the long, leisurely approach to our morning briefing for my pending assignment. The large manila envelope had evolved into several folders of various sizes that spread out all across the dining room table. Rejuvenated by caffeine and a few sausage and egg tortillas, we finally settled down to the business at hand.

"You'll have plenty of time to read all this shit later," JJ said with a yawn and a stretch, "so I'll give you the Reader's Digest version while you look over the surveillance photos." He tossed me the appropriate folder, sipped his coffee, and continued. "Chateau Pacific was originally the property of a Saudi Prince assigned to the ungodly duty of dealing with the infidels of Pemex. He built the elaborate, but isolated villa for himself, and had two dozen or so cabanas built for his entourage and subordinates. The airstrip had been completed and the larger bungalows were under construction when he got moved up the ladder of succession and was relocated to Europe. His successor hated the fucking place from the get-go because it was too small and isolated for his party-hearty appetite, and the airstrip couldn't be enlarged to accommodate his personal A-330 Airbus."

"Life's a bitch, ain't it?"

"No shit. Prince Abdullah basically deserted the place and moved onto his 350 foot yacht he brought over to Acapulco. A couple of semi-suave American developers from Los Angeles bought the place with grand illusions of making it a world class resort, but eleven months and about 15 million dollars later, they went belly up trying to be legit with a corrupt Mexican system." JJ stopped, looked at me, then smiled. "This is where it gets interesting. An investment group out of Switzerland picked up the entire property for about 5 cents on the dollar, found a way to circumvent all the Mexican red tape, redesigned and constructed the resort as it is today, and were open for business in less than a year and a half. The group consists of two brothers and a cousin all named Morea. Originally there were five of them, but two were killed back in the sixties when their financial empire was booming. The eldest brother, Henri, is a vintner and wine negociant in France; the younger, Andre, is an import/export entrepreneur in Tel Aviv; and the cousin, Francois, is the investment banker who lives in Geneva. I traced the family back through old OSS files to pre World War II when all of them were in the wine business and living on the family estate outside Beaune. With the exception of Andre, who was shipped off to Palestine with other relatives before the German invasion, all the boys were members of the French Resistance, and each and every one of them is still held in the highest regards by their peers and associates. They amassed a fortune by trading real estate for freedom during the exodus of Europeans trying to escape the Nazi occupation by using the same conduit for people as they did for their illegal wine exports, or so the French government claims. According to one file, they even ripped off a German general by trading him some prime vineyards in the Volnay region for half a million dollars in confiscated gold bullion, then tipping the SS to the deal. The deeds were forgeries, of course, the General got executed by his own people, and the gold was never recovered."

"I'm sure it's enjoying a warm vault in Switzerland these days," I said with a smile.

"Absolutely! With the exception of a little alleged bending of a few import/export laws here and there, all three checked out clean. According to our research, Henri seems to be the one expressly in charge of the Mexican operation. He set up his nephew, Christian, as President, but hired a female General Manager to run the place shortly thereafter."

"Hands in the cookie jar?"

"Probably. Christian Morea has been in and out of trouble with the law, and his family, since he was around thirteen. After Henri's brother was murdered by agents of Yasser Arafat for funding numerous projects and arms deals in Israel, he took it upon himself to raise his nephew and make him a part of the family business. Henri did a good job of diverting any serious legal problems until a few years ago when Christian 'accidentally' killed some influential German tourists with his Mercedes roadster on the Cornice in Cannes. Christian tested positive for cocaine, and his blood alcohol levels were off the scale, so Henri shipped his ass off to Switzerland while he negotiated the blood money with the families and pay-offs to the local magistrates. Six months later, Christian got busted in St. Moritz with over an ounce of cocaine and two fifteen year old Italian girls he had turned into drugged-out sex slaves. Once again, matters were resolved financially, but that's when they acquired the resort property and exiled Christian to Mexico. Over the last year, however, Christian Morea has been identified by our agents in Cali, Ecuador, and even Saigon."

"Sounds like Christian likes to play with the big boys."

"Exactly. What we want to know is who's attending his next little party at the resort. According to our source, the meeting is a positive fact, and since all previous information has proven itself to be true, there's no reason to doubt the latest communication."

"Wait a minute! If you've got an inside source, why the hell do you need me? I don't relish the thought of getting Terri involved with a few drug lords, their bodyguards, and any other maniacs that just might show up."

"Businessmen, Jeffrey. They're just businessmen. It's exactly like going to L.A., only hotter and more expensive."

"We avoid L.A., too!"

"I need eyes down there that I know I can trust. Besides, the photo assignment is for real. This is going to be a sweet deal for you in more ways than one because the club recruits staff by offering 90-day contracts to young starlets who are in between gigs. There's going to be more pussy running around down there than you and I could fuck in a month, so just put them on display in some of those hot little suits, and the boys will come running. The girls will provide the distraction, so all you have to do is make a spectacle of the shoot, then just take a few casual shots of the people in the crowd, and mission accomplished. The resort has agreed to provide a courier to get your exposed film and digital media to the airport in Manzanillo every morning, then it's off to your processing lab in San Diego, and in my hands that afternoon. The only pressure will be on you to come up with some award winning photographs of beautiful ladies in nasty little swim suits for Sunset Limited to use in their catalog and magazine ads. I know you can handle the camera work, and you know that I'd never send an innocent civilian into a powder keg, much less someone as important to you as Terri."

"You're still sending me in uncovered, unarmed, and using both of us as bait. What makes you think the opposition is stupid enough to fall for this scam?"

"They already have, Jeffrey! The president of Sunset Limited has confirmed the assignment directly with Christian Morea via both E-mail and a personal phone call to express his utmost gratitude for his cooperation."

"I'm sure your performance was award winning."

"Absolutely."

"So, Mr. President, what happens in a worst case scenario?"

"You can be pulled out in fifteen minutes." There was no bullshit in his answer.

"How will you know?"

"You'll be able to tell me."

"This isn't another stupid plastic handgun trick, is it?"

"You just won't let me live that down, will you?"

"Where did you expect to find graphite spray in the Nicaraguan jungle, JJ?"

I couldn't help but grin at our private little joke. On the range, the prototype high-tech composite automatics were both fast and accurate, but in the pleasures of a hot and steamy tropical jungle, they locked up like cheap brakes. If it weren't for the weapons we "borrowed" from the soldiers that were trying to capture us, we never would have made it across the border into the safety of Honduras. When we confronted the armorer after our narrow escape, he just looked at us with contempt and asked why we didn't try a graphite spray. JJ and I both burst out laughing, just like we did in front of the armorer, then exchanged high fives and got back down to the business at hand.

DAY ONE

TERMINAL E—6:40 AM Eleven days, thirteen trips to the spa, numerous laps around the subdivision, and an endless onslaught of tasteless dietary cuisine later, the new me was ready for a Bloody Mary. Seated across from me in the yet to open bar, Miss Tone-to-the-Bone looked too damn radiant for this unholy hour. Express check-in had taken less than five minutes, leaving us well over two hours to kill before our non-stop flight to the coastal city of Manzanillo. We found the cocktail lounge, and were just relaxing while watching the mass of humanity trying to get from Point A to Point B in the least amount of time with the fewest number of casualties. Having been up most of the night, I was feeling pretty ragged.

"How do you do it?" I asked my beautiful companion. "I'm wrecked, and you're so glamorous you're glowing."

"Thank you, Honey," she replied with an honest smile, then transformed her face into one of her mischievous grins. "The glow you see is from the fire you lit inside of me last night. My God, Jeffrey, the encore was incredible! This kind of tired I can handle."

"Gee, Angel, when you put it that way, I'm feeling better already."

"Jeffrey, if you felt any better, they'd make you illegal. I get tingly just thinking about . . . Oh my God! Quick, turn around!"

I spun around in time to see the awesome spectacle of Wonder Woman in four inch heels strutting straight towards us. A six foot tall, buxom brunette bombshell in stretch denim and a white lace bustier had the masses parting like Moses and the Red Sea. Her massive breasts and long, thick, curly hair bounced in unison with her loping strides, putting a smile as big as the one she was wearing on every man's face within eyesight.

"She's awesome!" Terri squealed softly. "And look, she's got the same luggage tags as we do." My spunky little companion stood as the raven-haired beauty approached and asked, "Are you going to Chateau Pacific, too?"

"You bet!"

"So are we. Would you care to join us?"

Shocked, but undaunted, our new guest seated herself and offered her hand to me. Her handshake was not of the dainty, feminine variety.

"I'm Roberta Taylor," she said with a warm smile. "My husband, Jack, made a stop along the way, but should be here in a minute."

"Jeffrey Mason," I replied into her golden brown eyes, "and this is my girlfriend, Terri Clark. We made the mistake of being punctual, so now we're stuck here waiting for the bar to open."

"A lousy job, but somebody has to do it," she laughed. "I've spent enough time in airports to come prepared." Roberta leaned over to open her carry-on down by her feet, and I had to stop myself from reaching over to catch her breasts as they came close to tumbling over the top of her bustier. Terri couldn't help but notice, and had to bite her lower lip to keep from laughing. Roberta sat back up and placed a handful of individual pre-mixed Bloody Marys on the table. "Complements of Continental Airlines," she said, then twisted one open for herself. "Jack's not a happy flier, never has been, so I do my best to make it easier on everyone."

Terri grabbed one of the tiny bottles, opened it with a quick twist, then clinked with Roberta's for a friendly toast.

"We women certainly do what we have to for our men."

"Fucked his brains out last night, right?" Roberta's eyes flashed between us.

"Absolutely!" Terri replied, with eyes as big as silver dollars, and a smile her mother would never recognize. All I could do was nod my head up and down in agreement.

"Me, too!" Roberta downed the entire contents in one motion, then reached for another. "Poor Jack got very little sleep last night either."

"And you feel as good as you look, right?" I just had to ask.

"Absolutely!" was their answer in unison, then burst out laughing.

"Ladies, please!" A large man resembling a 6'4" version of Tom Selleck with about a hundred extra pounds of well defined muscle rounded the corner and came to stand behind Roberta. He had an empty Bloody Mary bottle in one hand, a Penthouse in the other, and a warm smile on his face. "I can always count on Bert to find the party." He stuck out his powerful right hand to me and said, "Jack Taylor."

Introductions and pleasantries were exchanged, Jack sat down, and a bartender appeared out of nowhere. Four large fingers went up, and the man began doing his job. Jack seemed content to just kick back, browse the Penthouse, and let his wife carry the load of the conversation for now. I knew the issue he held in his hands, and wondered if he'd notice.

"So what takes you to Chateau Pacific, Bert?" I asked.

"Anniversary," she replied with a smile, then reached over and rubbed Jack's thigh. "Seventeen years ago we met on Lake Travis, and it's been wild ever since."

Jack barely looked up from his magazine, but I knew what he had found.

"She was skiing naked, drank all my Tequila, then tried to break off my dick in the back of my Suburban. If that's not love, I don't wanna know what is."

The rub became a slap, and Jack finally laughed.

"You have to excuse my husband, he played football and got hit in the head too many times." Bert's accent became deeply Southern. "I just can't take him anywhere."

Terri broke the laughter with her usual perky self, "So, did you really play football, or is this an Al Bundy thing."

"My husband played thirteen years in the National Football League, and I'm very proud of him." The words were spoken with passion from a very loving soul. "We'll be able to have anything we want for the rest of our lives because of what he lived through. For now, we're going to celebrate life to its fullest every day, and no one is going to stop us." Roberta sat up a little straighter and looked at Terri. "Do you know those 'people' at Chateau Pacific tried to get us to change our reservations! We've had this sexcapade planned for over eight months, so I told them we were coming, period. Some mealy-mouthed asshole tried to explain about a private party, but I told him we were paid in full and to expect us as planned. Are you part of the private party?"

"I don't think so, are we?" I put the ball in Terri's court on purpose.

"I don't think so either. Actually, we're going there to work, sort of."

"What kind of work, sort of?" The Penthouse was lowered and Jack was really looking Terri over. I watched as his eyes diverted between the Goddess in the magazine, and the real thing sitting across the table from him.

"Page 128?" I asked.

Jack looked at me, nodded his head to the affirmative, then passed the opened magazine to Roberta. Page 128 contained a full page ad for Private Edition Lingerie consisting of a vertical shot of Terri posed on pink satin sheets almost wearing a delicate white lace teddie. Bert did a few double-takes, then started fanning herself with the magazine.

"Honey, you're gorgeous! I wish someone could make me look that good."

"God already did," I answered. "I just get to take the pictures."

"You took that picture?" Jack asked in no uncertain terms.

"Absolutely," Terri replied for me.

The next twenty minutes were spent discussing all the things people talk about while becoming new friends. Jack had played for the Cleveland Browns and Atlanta Falcons as a strong safety and head hunter on special teams. The last three years of his career were spent in Detroit where they tried to move him to outside linebacker to "make better use of his size and speed" and of course, "to better the team". Three knee operations, permanent pins in his right ankle, and a nasty neck injury finally forced Kaptain Kamikaze to hang up his cleats and retire to a less strenuous lifestyle. For the majority of his playing days, Roberta had stayed in Austin finishing her education in business law, then had a lucrative career dumped right in her lap. She had watched as Jack and other players got cheated at the first of their careers by sports agents and other vermin who get rich on the naiveté of their clients, so she decided to change all that by offering them an honest alternative. Her claim to fame was opening an agency dedicated to preserving the financial credibility of her clients so they would never become penniless for the rest of their short, pain-ridden lives. She retired from active duty when Jack did, but the agency still exists, and she remains a consultant for players and their charitable foundations.

Of all their investments, Champions Sports Bar, Inc. was obviously their favorite. They started the first one in a classic old house in the Montrose district of Houston, and haven't stopped growing since. Jack and Roberta attracted the players, the players attracted the girls, the girls attracted the guys, and the cycle was set. Add outrageous Mexican food, ice cold beer, designer Tequila, and a constant party-like atmosphere to the equation, and people keep coming back time and again. All those things, plus the fact that almost every gorgeous lady received a special ID card that allows her to drink for free, made their establishment the hottest ticket in town. Within six months, a certain Yankee lawyer from New York offered a decadent amount of cash to buy into the place, and then set out to franchise it all around the country. Under Roberta's watchful supervision, there are now over two dozen Champion's Sports Bars from coast to coast, and all of them pay a part of their proceeds to the Retired Players Association, as well as Jack and his partner. Like she said, they were set for life.

The girls had taken off on a clothes theme, when Jack leaned over to me and said,

"Hey, brother-in-law, let's take a walk," then he tried to stand up. He did his best to hide the pain and effort it took to reach a full standing position, but to no avail. "Just a little stiff," he retorted, then stretched for a moment and began to walk away.

I winked at Terri and took off after him, but I really had to move because Jack had reached full stride and was putting some serious distance between us. Now I know where Roberta got her walk! At six foot tall, I don't have short, squatty legs, but I had to do some serious stretching to catch up with him as he made his way back to the news stand. Jack walked straight up to the magazine rack, picked up three more copies of Penthouse, then turned to me and smiled.

"Souvenirs," he said.

The young man behind the register was curious as to why anyone would buy three more copies of the same magazine he had just purchased, so Jack ripped open one of the plastic wrappers, turned to page 128, and passed the magazine to the boy.

"This incredible woman is having a Bloody Mary in the bar right around the corner as we speak. If you ask her real nice, I bet she'll sign this for you."

"No shit!" The boy's eyes only looked up at Jack once.

"No shit."

The kid made a quick look around the empty shop, locked his register, then made a dash for the door with the opened magazine in his hand.

"That should keep the girls occupied for a while," he said with a grin. "Come on, I've got something to show you."

To my surprise, Jack led me back to the main terminal where we caught an elevator up to the roof parking area. Without words, I followed him up to a brand new white-on-white-on-white El Dorado, the doors automatically opened, and we got in. The rich leather seat that wrapped itself around me felt more like a personal recliner than a mere automobile device.

"Now this is what I call a car," I said to my host. "This sure beats the shit out of my old Bronco."

"Roberta's anniversary present," he stated. "I was gonna get her a new bass boat, but decided against it."

"Good choice. I assume she hates to fish."

"No shit." Jack reached under his seat and pulled out a pharmaceutical jar full of pills, threw a small handful into his mouth, then washed them down with something orange out of an old Ozarka bottle. From his visor, Jack retrieved a monster joint, lit it, then took a big draw of the sweet smelling smoke. He exhaled a small cloud, took another deep hit, then passed the reefer to me. Not being totally unfamiliar to the process, I accepted, and partook of a tradition dating back for centuries. Warriors have always enjoyed a peace-pipe mentality throughout time, and it also helps the conversation lead to its inevitable topic. Women!

"So, do you really take pictures of naked women for a living?"

"That's a part of the business. Not a lot of it, but some. It's also not as glamorous as it looks from the outside."

"Come on, you can't tell me you don't get off to some babe getting naked and acting sexy in front of you. I've had my share, and it still works for me."

"Jack, brother-in-law, believe me, when a woman gets naked in front of you, she sees a monster-man football player who's going to fuck her brains out. When that same woman gets naked in front of me, she only sees a camera and a career. There is a certain amount of trust necessary to create the kind of images you like to see on film. When I'm up close and personal with a model, she knows I'm only going to rearrange her hair, or a piece of clothing, or do something else crucial for the shot. She may be getting turned on, but it's for the camera, not the cameraman. I've had my share too, but I learned the hard way that I prefer women who don't whistle when they're standing outside on a windy day. Beauty may fade, but dumb lasts forever."

"Yeah, but dumb sure can be fun."

"Absolutely!"

We laughed so hard, it shook the car. The cloud of smoke was getting out of hand, so Jack opened the sunroof, and whoosh, it was gone. I pity the poor bird that happens to fly through that cloud, but then again, not really. A second joint was lit, and our friendship solidified with every hit. Jack was truly just a good ol' boy that made it big the old fashioned way, and now it was simply time to play.

"If I'm not mistaken, Terri is already trying to get your wife involved in our photo shoot. How would you feel if I took some pictures of Roberta?"

"I'd be pissed off if you didn't! Bert's got more guts than most guys I've known. She's not shy about her body, and as a matter of fact, she loves to show it off. She's the first one to get naked, and the last one to leave. Fifteen minutes after we get there, you'll be able to see for yourself."

"So the answer is, you don't mind."

"Fuck no! Oh shit, we've got a plane to catch."

The pills and smoke must have done their trick, because Jack moved quickly from the car to the elevator without a single grimace. We rounded the corner of the main terminal, went flying down the corridor to our concourse, then made a straight shot to the bar. Just as we got within eyeshot, Jack threw out a big forearm that stopped me dead in my tracks. The girls were still sitting at the same table, but now they were surrounded by at least nine worshipping males. Roberta had removed her cropped denim jacket, fully exposing her white cotton bustier and majority of her double D's to her jubilant fans, and Terri had a pile of magazines stacked in front of her to sign. The table was loaded with drinks, mostly untouched, and poor Terri looked like she was developing writer's cramp. Poor Terri my ass. She was loving every minute of the attention, and I was enjoying watching her work the crowd. Jack nudged me with his elbow, then stepped forward and spoke to them all.

"Ladies, do you want to go to Mexico with us and get naked, or stay here with these little dicks!"

I don't know who moved faster, the girls or the guys.

The flight to Manzanillo proved to be neither crowded nor remarkable. First Class was only half full, so we were able to sit across from Jack and Roberta, but the drinks and smoke had kicked in way too much for any further conversation. I had been perusing the various cloud formations for an indefinite length of time when Terri tapped me on the shoulder and whispered something in my ear. I turned to see a huge grin on her face, and trying desperately not to laugh, she softly said, "Roberta." I peered over Terri's head to see Bert fully reclined in her seat, listening to her iPod. She had removed her jacket again, and in her current position, the bustier was just about to lose the war of containment. She must have been listening to something really hot, because her breasts were keeping time to the music, and they were bouncing around like crazy. I leaned close to Terri and whispered,

"Now that's what I call tittie dancing."

Poor Terri burst into tear-soaked laughter, which startled Roberta and spoiled the show.

Upon arrival in Manzanillo, we were immediately sequestered into a private area outside the main terminal under the shade of a canopy. Our bags were passed in front of a bored Golden Lab, then carried over by three young men who were followed closely by an official looking old geezer wearing an even older looking uniform and handgun. He stood and waited until all the luggage was properly aligned in front of him, then said in near perfect Amexican,

"Theese your bag?"

We nodded, he smiled, then turned and marched away. Immediately, a young Mexican in a neat and clean new pilot's uniform arrived and invited us to follow him to our private plane. Around the corner, an ATR 42 stood primed and ready for us to climb aboard. Inside the commuter aircraft, the interior had been refitted for only 14 first class seats, and we were greeted with a chilled bottle of Mumm Cordon Rouge and a selection of cheese and fresh fruit. We were obviously the only people they were expecting, because as soon as our luggage was aboard, we were in the air.

The Pacific coastline going north from Manzanillo is beauty beyond belief, and our pilot knew how to enhance the spectacle of its visual impact. He purposely flew out over the water and changed altitude as often as he deemed necessary to fully emphasize the rocky cliffs, intense vegetation, and pristine beaches. I responded by acting like a tourist and taking lots of pictures of our coastal trek for future enjoyment. The champagne was ice cold and wonderful as well, but just as we finished the first bottle and were ready for another, the pilot asked us to fasten our seat belts and prepare for our landing at Chateau Pacific. I couldn't help but get excited as I peered out the window for my first glimpse of my assigned territory. Reconnaissance photographs and digital topographies have their value, but nothing can replace the impact of the actual visual spectacle of a target area. More than once I've experienced a full body rush when my senses cranked up a notch and raised my level of awareness to the task at hand. JJ says that's when bravado stops and reality begins. After a quick fly-by which seemed to be as much for himself as for us, the pilot took us way offshore to begin his approach from the northwest. What surprised me the most was how small the actual total area of the resort really was. Even a well trained pilot would have a hard time just parking an A-330 Airbus on that runway, much less landing one! We flew into the mouth of the double horseshoe bay and were immediately under the rim of the coastal mountain cliffs. Lower and slower the plane flew as we followed the southern edge of the bay until we finally crossed the shoreline and immediately touched down. Terri grabbed my hand and started squeezing like crazy as the brakes were applied and the engines screamed in a maximum effort to stop the small plane. No wonder they serve champagne before every landing!

When the door to the aircraft finally opened, we were greeted by a beautiful and slender young blonde woman wearing a red floral print halter top and matching sarong. All smiles, she escorted us to an electric cart, and we were whisked away down a concrete path through the jungle. It's a good thing they were able to stop that airplane, because thirty yards of jungle was all that separated the end of the runway from a sheer rock cliff about fifty feet tall. The pathway took us through a narrow passage between two sides of the mountains that create the double horseshoe bay, then onto a lush garden trail that wound its way to the four story main building with a large attached pavilion, just like the aerial photographs had displayed. Our cart made its way to the circular drive that served as the official entryway to the building and stopped in front of another beautiful woman, this one brunette, and dressed in the same flattering outfit as our current hostess. She smiled pleasantly and asked if we'd follow her for some refreshments. The tropical heat and humidity were becoming overpowering, so I hoped the refreshments included some air-conditioning, but they didn't. They did include an outrageous Macon Villages served with some damn fine Havarti and warm French bread. We were halfway through with our second glass of wine when we were approached by another stunning female, around 5'8", with fiery red hair way past her shoulders and a well toned athletic body. Dressed in a tiny little strapless sheath that barely covered her ass, this hot-rod was heart attack material in bare feet. To complete the total package, she had a walk like a dancer who wanted everyone to notice the perfection of her posterior. All things considered, this young woman was absolutely radiant. She stopped at the end of our table, smiled, and looked directly at me.

"Jeffrey Mason?" More a statement than a question, I just nodded. "Hi, I'm Suzan Jacobs, the assistant manager and personal secretary to Janinne Pavie. We're happy to have you both with us, and are excited about helping you on your assignment. If you'll follow me, Janinne is eagerly waiting to meet you in her office."

We bid a fond adieu to Jack and Roberta, and promised to meet them by the pool as quickly as we could, then followed closely as Suzan led us across the lobby area towards some elevators. By no means having a jealous bone in her gorgeous body, Terri grabbed my hand and planted it firmly on her ass as she mimicked Suzan's deliberate sexy stroll. The roar in the background that echoed throughout the entire first floor was unmistakably Jack Taylor.

JANINNE

The elevator doors opened into an air-conditioned office suite brilliantly illuminated by an entire wall of glass windows facing the ocean. Three young Mexican women worked what appeared to be a central command area located between two private suites which were closed off from the lobby by French doors. Every interior wall was glass and every wooden surface was white lacquer. Suzan led us through the French doors to our right into an office filled with warmth and intimacy. The carpet was a pale lavender that matched the same tones in the floral motif that flowed through the cushions, drapes, and accent pieces. Plants abounded, and all tables, including her pedestal desk, were glass. Very stylish, and very feminine. Standing behind her desk, facing the ocean and obviously on the phone, stood our hostess. Another statuesque blonde, I was already impressed with the way her khaki miniskirt accented her slender hips and long legs, and her hair had just enough natural curl to make it look full and thick, like a mane. She hung up the phone, took an instant to compose herself, then turned to greet us. The woman who stepped out from behind that glass table and walked towards us was nothing short of a living Goddess. If Suzan looked like she had just stepped out of the pages of a Victoria's Secret catalog, this woman was the cover of Cosmo and a Playmate Centerfold all rolled into one perfect package. Her full bustline danced inside her print silk blouse as she walked up to me and shook my hand.

"I'm Janinne Pavie, Mr. Mason. Welcome to Chateau Pacific."

Her smile was genuine and her handshake sincere. However, it was her eyes that I couldn't let go of. They were a Hazel color as soft as the Caribbean, and turned up on the ends like a cat.

"Please, call me Jeffrey. Mr. Mason is a retired CEO living on a golf course, taking all those poor other retiree's money at their weekly tournament. This is Terri Clark, my partner."

"Oh, I knew who you were when you walked through that door," Janinne said to Terri, and shook her hand as well. When the girls locked eyes, the first of several similarities struck me. Their profiles were close enough for them to be sisters, and both absolutely perfect for photographs. Rather than shake and release, they held hands briefly after saying hello, allowing the conversation to pause.

"Please be seated," Janinne finally said, then gestured towards the loveseat in the middle of the office. We sat as directed while Suzan and Janinne took up positions in the two matching wing back chairs across the coffee table, where a bottle of Taittinger Comtes de Champagne was properly chilled and waiting with four crystal flutes. "I propose we begin by sharing some of our finest champagne. Suzan and I are here to do everything possible to help you during your stay. I realize you're here to work, and I hope all the photographs will be wonderful for your sake as well as ours, but I also hope you'll have enough time to enjoy all the amenities Chateau Pacific has to offer."

Our hostess was intoxicating, but I couldn't help but notice all the eye contact going on between her and Terri. Something was obviously happening there, but I'm not sure if they realized it, or if I was just still suffering from the El Dorado smoke-a-thon. Suddenly, the French doors flew open with a bang, and in strutted an insignificant looking little man followed by an Arab in tropical attire. Stopping abruptly at the coffee table, his eyes darted from Terri to me, then focused on Terri.

"You have my fee?"

Not hello, kiss my ass, or nothing. Right to the point; how French. Terri opened her purse, passed me the envelope, then glared back at the man who continued to scour her body with his eyes. I stood and passed the envelope on to our host, who diverted his eyes from Terri only for an instant, then just as abruptly walked back to the door. He stopped, turned back towards us for effect and added,

"Stay away from the private residences, and do not bother my personal guests."

Luckily for all, he left, taking his pet Arab with him.

"Mr. Congeniality, I presume?" I asked Janinne.

"My God, I feel violated!" Terri had brought her arms up across her chest and was gently massaging her breasts. "Who was that asshole?"

"That asshole is Christian Morea, heir to the owner, and President of Chateau Pacific." she replied in a calm and dignified manner. "I'm the General Manager, and deal directly with the owner on all club related matters. Christian's affairs are of no concern to me."

"In other words," said Terri, with a glare in her eyes and voice, "he's the resident prick."

"Bingo!" was Suzan's instant reply.

"Time for an attitude adjustment, ladies," I said, and reached for the Taittinger. With the precision of a Gran Sommelier, the foil was removed, the cork popped, and the glasses filled while the ladies reclined and regained their composure. Terri took a long draw of the golden bubbly, then curled up in the corner of the loveseat.

"This is my favorite champagne." she said while rubbing her fingertip around the rim of the flute. "It's hard enough to find in Houston, how do you get it here in Mexico?"

"All of our wines come directly from the family business in France. Legally speaking, because we are an all inclusive resort, we don't actually sell our wines to our patrons, we give it away. Therefore, we are able to bring our wines into this country without the hassles of going through the federal authorities." Janinne was speaking to both of us, but only looking at Terri.

"Sounds expensive, at the local level, of course," I said, with a hint of sarcasm.

"Of course!" Suzan couldn't keep her smile back. "We also hire a lot of locals, so we're good for the economy in a number of ways."

"Of course." I refilled all the glasses then took my spot beside Terri. From my angle of view, I was immediately aware of the major dilemma that presents itself when seated across from two beautiful women sitting in miniskirts that barely cover their behinds when standing. Let's just say that the view was tremendous, and leave it at that. I tried to divert my attention, and look them only in the eyes, but Suzan's pale pink cotton thong and Janinne's lack thereof was more then I could bare. While I still could, I stood up and relocated myself on the arm of the loveseat, next to

Terri. "Speaking of the local economy, how can Terri and I help yours? It's my understanding that you need some photographs for marketing purposes."

"Exactly." Janinne took a slow, sensuous, sip of her champagne, then finally looked at me. "That's why I don't understand the envelope you passed to Christian. I assume it was money?"

"Exactly," I replied. "Five thousand dollars in $100 bills as directed. He called it a 'professional fee' for using his club in the swimsuit catalog."

Janinne could hardly contain herself. She stood and walked directly to her desk, leaned forward on her left hand for support, and reached for a pen. The swell of her breasts flowed with the motion of her writing, and in far too short a time, she had walked back across the room and was handing me a check for the exact same amount.

"You are a welcome guest at Chateau Pacific. Extortion is not a prerequisite to take photographs here." Janinne slammed her champagne, then refilled her glass and sat down.

"The concept of Chateau Pacific is to provide an exclusive getaway for those who enjoy the finest of food and wine in a relaxed, but very sensuous tropical environment. As I stated, all our wines come from the family business in France, and with the exception of champagne, all our wines are from Uncle Henri's private label, which are unavailable via retail sales. In accordance with French viniculture law, the wines are labeled by Appellation d'Origine and vineyard, therefore a connoisseur can request a Puligny Montrachet to complement his grilled snapper, or enjoy our Soliel Blanc with his shrimp enchiladas. That part of the club sells itself, what I want to show is the rest. The ambiance, the romance, the sensual delights; that's what the world needs to see about Chateau Pacific." Her eyes were beaming with pride and joy. This was her baby, and baby was ready for a new coming out party.

"I don't see any problems with that," Terri said, looking at me, then Janinne. I just sat back and let her take the lead. "We've got 53 swimsuits to photograph any way we choose. Combining romance into a shoot is Jeffrey's style, and our specialty. Roberta Taylor has already agreed to be in the shoot, so I don't think her gorgeous hunk of a husband would mind doing some sexy couple shots, do you?"

"I don't think Jack would turn down any sexy couple anything!" I replied. Terri laughed out loud, while the others enjoyed a subdued giggle. "What about your staff? It's my understanding you hire actresses who are in-between gigs to 90 day contracts. As long as they are willing to sign a release form, I can use as many beautiful bodies as we can find." I brushed my hand against her hair, then settled my palm inside her romper on her bare upper back. "Terri is the main focus, but we welcome any help you can offer."

"I think I know another couple that wouldn't mind being your romantic duo." Suzan had a real mischievous grin and made distinct eye contact with Janinne.

"I agree!" she replied.

Janinne continued to look at Terri, even when she was speaking to me. Oh, she'd dart her eyes over to me on occasion, but her real interests were obviously with my partner in crime. Being in the same room with three of the world's most beautiful women was exhilarating, but being ignored by same did nothing for the old ego.

"My initial gameplan is to ease into the assignment by checking out the club for ideas and locations the first day or two, shoot a little every day, then do the crème de la crème the last few days." I had their attention for a few seconds, so I continued. "As long as we don't disturb his private guests, we should be able to incorporate anything you want into the shoot. Boats, planes, offices, whatever you want. When photographing a beautiful woman, the entire world is a prop."

"And speaking of beautiful women," Terri added, "I think it would be a total waste not to include both of you in our assignment. Don't you agree, Jeffrey?"

"Absolutely!" I liked her train of thought. "Including Roberta, there's enough talent in this room to shoot lots more than just this one assignment."

"Exactly my point." Terri sat up a little straighter and leaned her arm on my left thigh. "Jeffrey and I have contacts with both Playboy and Penthouse, as well as the major travel and leisure magazines. We made enough money off of our Greek holiday pictures to go back three or four times. Think about it! If the accompanying article is well written to the style of the publication, and the photographs illustrate the mood, these publishers will be paying you to advertise this resort in their magazines. Hell, there's no reason we can't all be in Playboy! Think of what a sexy article illustrated by some of Jeffrey's outrageous photographs could do for your resort if it were published world-wide through their international division. So please, join us in the shoot!"

Janinne and Suzan looked at each other with smiles ready to burst through their attempted stoicism. I could feel their energy as they looked back and forth between Terri and I, and each other.

"I'm flattered you think I could be a subject for you in this assignment. Quite honestly, I've never really considered myself very camera friendly." Janinne was serious!

"You've never met a man like Jeffrey. He can capture a part of you that you never knew existed, then turn around and create an image of you on film that you thought the world would never see. And I don't mean body parts." Terri leaned her head towards my leg on the armrest. "Look what he's done for me."

Janinne leaned forward in her chair, eyes afire with energy. "I have!"

"The bad news is that the majority of our guests and special staff left today," Suzan stated. "They should be on their way back to Houston in the same plane that brought you to Manzanillo. The remainder of our guests, and most staff will be leaving in 48 hours." Suzan looked carefully at Janinne, then continued. The grin on her face became broader with every word. "The good news is that a private party will occupy only a small portion of the club, so we'll have plenty of time to work with you. Of course we want to be in the shoot! What are you, nuts or something?"

It took both Janinne and Terri to finally calm Suzan down. They hugged and jumped around a little, then settled down to calmly finish the wonderful champagne. This was going to be a dream come true kind of week. Gorgeous women, hot swimsuits, a tropical paradise for location, and heavenly wines. Oh my God, this could almost be a beer commercial! As long as I don't fuck it up, this could be both fun and profitable! Very profitable!

"If I might make a suggestion," Janinne began, breaking a momentary pause. "Why not spend the rest of today browsing around, relaxing, and recruiting, then plan on shooting tomorrow. We're having a sunset beach bash tomorrow around 5 to say good-bye to the remainder of the guests and staff. Perhaps you could incorporate the party into both assignments."

"I don't see any problems with that. Actually, it sounds like fun!" I got up and walked over to the champagne, not only to refresh my flute, but to see the expression on Terri's face. Having been watching Janinne absorb her, I wanted to get a visual on the return image. Unpretentious as ever, Terri was just curled up on the loveseat being her normal, sexy self. "What do you think, Angel?" I asked.

31

"Why not really make it fun. Let's invite all the girls to our place for a pre-party party to try on the suits, and do hair and make-up. I'll do what I can to help loosen things up, and do eyes."

"She does great eyes," I said to my newest victims. "Sounds OK to me."

"We'll supply enough wine and goodies to help with the loosening up, but I doubt they'll need much assistance." Suzan curled her feet up underneath herself in the wingback chair, then continued with a mischievous grin, "Our going away parties are somewhat notorious, Terri. They only start on the beach."

THE 25-CENT TOUR

Janinne led Terri and I across the lobby and down through the dining pavilion towards what appeared to be a large horseshoe shaped outdoor grill, and the main bar. The lunch crowd was long gone, and the crew was already preparing the dining area for the dinner guests. It looked as if they weren't expecting as big a turn out by the way the workers were carting off tables and widening the spacing between those that remained. Even though it was getting into the heat of the day, I was surprised to see the main bar deserted. After all, this is an all inclusive resort, meaning the booze is free!

At the edge of the pavilion, steps led us down onto the sun deck area and main pool. The opposite side of the pool was sheltered by a ten foot wall of thick flowering shrubs edging the deck, providing both shade and privacy for the mere dozen or so people enjoying themselves in the tropical sunshine by floating, flirting, and just hanging out. Literally! The only females wearing tops were the hired help. We followed the edge of the pool towards a waterfall that flowed over a natural rock wall with a pathway above it which led to an arched bridge. The pool continued under the bridge and opened into a secluded circular pool with a swim up bar and thatch-roofed tavern. Reed lattice suspended by the surrounding palm trees provided a soft diffused shade for the majority of the smaller pool, so here is where we found the people. All twenty of them. The ladies

33

floated around on their rafts while the guys sat on the submerged stools and trolled. The designer of this party pit must have done some tedious research, because the water level kept the floating ladies on the perfect plane for kissing. Passionate kissing, I might add. The two couples involved in the floating tryst were discrete enough to stay over towards the enclosed garden side of the pool, but were way too comfortable in their present environment for what was going to occur momentarily. Janinne casually continued her stroll down the steps that led to bar level, walked under the large thatched roof, and stopped at the bar. She looked at me with a childish smile and said,

"That's not exactly the romantic ambiance I wish to project about Chateau Pacific. Our European clientele need a little more intrigue, neis pai?" Janinne then turned her head and shouted, "Kimberly!" She quickly slipped under the bar door and stepped up to the tall blonde who was facing an older gentleman at the far end of the bar. I diverted my attention back to the floating floorshow to see if they had progressed to oral sex, when Terri started tugging at my shirt, begging me to look. I turned back to see Kimberly and Janinne locked up in a passionate embrace, then the statuesque bartender grabbed a handful of thick blonde hair, and leaned Janinne over the icy beer cooler for a full orgasmic kiss. Just about the time Terri and I were picking our mouths up out of the sand, the rotund, balding man opposite them stood on his stool and began ringing the ship's bell suspended above in the rafters. The only thing uglier than an obese old man in a slingshot bikini is the same geezer in a thong, which is what he was wearing. The smile on the old guy's face was so broad, it caused the thick cigar rammed into the corner of his mouth to stand straight up like an erection. The ladies broke their embrace, then began bowing, waving, and blowing kisses to the standing ovation they were receiving from their adoring fans. Janinne grabbed a bottle of champagne from an ice box, then led Kimberly over to us. Even in a full cut one piece maillot, the majestic, sculpted body of the bartender begged to be noticed. Taller than Janinne, this blue eyed Nordic German athlete looked like she could deliver the workout of a lifetime!

"Where do you find all these tall gorgeous women?" Terri asked. "I'm beginning to get a complex!" I couldn't help but recognize her pouty, little-girl look.

"Honey, you've got nothing to worry about," Janinne replied. "You know what they say about dynamite and small packages." She handed Terri a glass of Mumm Cordon Rouge and made distinct eye contact, "And your small package is dynamite."

I just raised my glass and added, "Amen!"

"Kimberly, this is Jeffrey Mason and Terri," Janinne began, while pouring the ice cold bubbly. "Not only have they agreed to do our marketing photographs, we've been invited to take part in their swimsuit catalog shoot. Kimberly is our resident aerobics instructor, personal trainer, tennis pro, and, of course, favorite bartender."

"I can see why!" I said. "Would you mind giving a rookie an explanation as to what just occurred?"

The girls laughed softly and embraced. "That older gentleman is from Cologne, and has been here for about five weeks," Kimberly said, then sipped her champagne. "He sits at the bar, smokes his cigars, and drinks only our private label vintage Port all day long. The first day he was here, he asked me if I kissed as good as I looked. I told her, 'Better!' So he says, 'Prove it!' and puts two hundred dollar bills on my bar. I'm an actress, Mr. Mason, I'll do anything for money. Well . . . . almost! Anyhow, since I had no intentions of kissing him, I pointed out a waitress friend of mine, and said , 'How 'bout her?' The look on his face was classic! I gave Rosie the skinny, then planted her ass on the stool next to him and began the show with one of my long, slow, sultry kisses. Rosie did her share, too, cause by the time he started ringing that damn bell, she had her legs wrapped around my waist, and her top was untied and coming off. I don't know what was bigger, the smile on his face or the bulge in his Speedo's. We took a few bows, split the bucks, and went back to work as usual. Ever since, he's requested at least two performances a day, at the same rate, of course."

"Of course!" Terri said, with a big smile. "Who chooses your partner in crime?"

"I do," she replied. "A willing recipient always makes for a better show."

"Absolutely!" Janinne clinked glasses with Kimberly and slammed down the champagne. She refilled all our glasses, then looked my direction. "Don't you think Kimberly would look good in some of our ads, Jeffrey?"

"Positively! I'd like to see her in some of our swimsuit shots, too."

"Whoa, people," Kimberly said abruptly. "Like I said, I'm an actress, not a model. I don't mind doing something for the club, but I'm too out of shape and have way too many scars to even attempt to romp around in a skimpy little swimsuit. Thanks, but, no thanks. Besides, I'd like to think that my time is going to be a bit occupied for the next few days."

A young Mexican girl in a matching blue floral bandeau top and sarong walked up behind Kimberly and tapped her on the shoulder. The message she whispered brought a huge grin to Kim's face, then she refilled all our glasses, and reached over and clinked Terri's.

"How would you like to make two hundred dollars, the easy way?"

"I thought you split the two hundred," I said, somewhat anxious.

"I'm willing to forgo my fee," Kimberly replied, eyes not diverting from her target.

Terri took a long draw of champagne, reached up and kissed me on the cheek, then slammed down the remainder of the bubbly. She looked at Janinne, then locked eyes with Kimberly. "Let's see how good of an actress you really are."

Terri slid under the bar door and walked beside Kimberly down to the opposite end of the bar. There were easily seven or eight inches difference in height between the two girls, but the differences didn't stop with height alone. Kimberly's rugged, hard body was obviously the result of many well spent hours of training, while Terri's perfectly sculpted shape and sexuality was an absolute gift from God. Don't get me wrong, my angel takes terrific care of herself, but no amount of sweat can produce that feeling of perfection when you hold it naked in the sunlight. Kimberly lifted her up onto the bar, then stepped back a moment to plan her approach. Not willing to be a total victim, Terri reached out, placed her index finger in Kimberly's ample cleavage, and gently pulled the swimsuit towards her. Kimberly responded by putting her hands on Terri's waist and guiding herself into a full contact, opened mouth kiss. Terri arched her back and began her patented slow sway from side to side, gently rubbing her luscious breasts back and forth across Kimberly's hard nipples. I know that maneuver well, having experienced it many times on various parts of my anatomy over the last two years. Janinne leaned over to me and uttered softly,

"Oooh, Jeffrey, she's good!"

"In more ways than one," I replied.

Still kissing softly, Kimberly reached up and cupped Terri's breasts with both hands, when damn if that old bastard didn't start clanging that fucking bell. The girls disengaged, then gave each other a big hug before they started bowing, curtsying, and blowing kisses to the ravaged crowd of satisfied fans. Janinne and I were without a doubt the loudest of them all as we got a little carried away with our applause and shouts of phrase. Nobody, and I mean nobody, was even the least bit concerned with the wet and wild foreplay going on at the opposite side of the pool. Terri and Kimberly had stolen the show.

Terri walked back over and eagerly accepted the glass of champagne I offered. She took a long draw, then eased her back against the bar and finished the bubbly. Holding her glass out for more, she smiled at me and said,

"Whew! That woman can really kiss!" She took another long sip from her freshly refilled glass, then rubbed the cold flute across her forehead. "Damn, Jeffrey, if I had real panties on, I'd probably have to go change them."

"Me, too!" Janinne snickered, then added, "The softest lips and the hardest nips, that's our Kimberly!" She drained her glass of the remaining champagne and smiled at both of us. "I guess it's time to show you to your room." She slid her arm around Terri's waist and the two of them headed off down the main pathway towards the beach.

The club was laid out exactly as the satellite photographs and digital topographies had described. The natural terracing of the land and the lush tropical foliage led to both the splendor and seclusion of the numerous fourplexes, duplexes, and individual cottages showcased in every available nook and cranny along the downhill slope. We continued along the winding path until Janinne stopped and pointed to a small, well manicured garden area at the next bend. A hammock was suspended in the shade of this particular little palm grove, and in it was a woman wearing only sunglasses, taking a very peaceful-looking nap. The lighting was soft and warm, the colors gentle, and the ambiance perfect.

"This is more of what you had in mind, right?" I asked Janinne, then looked at my watch to record the time in my location memory bank. "Put either of you in that hammock and we've got cover-shot material. Hell, put both of you in there, and Playboy will be flying down to Houston with a whole suitcase full of money!"

Terri laughed softly and patted me on the ass at our private little joke. After not being receptive to the possibility of a 26 year old, 5'2" Playmate of the Month, the overwhelming success of our lingerie shots reached the level of a hand-written note from Hef's secretary, asking us to please resubmit Terri's photographs for use as a special feature and possible cover. Negotiated properly, that's easily a $60,000 paycheck from Playboy! Yet another reason I haven't gotten much sleep since the arrival of the note three days ago. We celebrated with French champagne in the hot-tub, then making love on a blanket under the stars.

"I'll have to remember how to find this place."

"That's easy enough," Janinne replied. "All paths lead to one of four major walkways, such as this one. Go uphill to get to the pavilion and pool, downhill to get to the beach, and you'll notice that each walkway is color-coded to match the nylon cord attached to your room keys. The trails and residences are well marked, and illuminated at night, so getting around is usually not a problem. In cases of over indulgence, it also helps us sort out the bodies."

As the girls continued on down the path, I lagged back a little to enjoy the view. They both had a fluid body motion that enhanced their sensuality, and the same classic shape to back up the fantasy. Even the delicate arch in the small of their backs was similar. I was so deep into the hallucination, I could feel the Nikon in my hands and see them framed in the viewfinder when they abruptly stopped and I almost ran into them.

"Going through withdrawal because you don't have a camera in your hands, dear?" We had reached the end of paved trail and were heading onto the sandy beach when the girls stopped to remove their sandals, and I got ripped off for staring at their perfect asses. Men!" Terri said to Janinne. "Sometimes, you can read them like a book."

They turned and walked away towards the water, leaving me standing there, still enjoying the view. Suddenly, Terri just stopped, put her hands on her knees and started slowly swaying her gorgeous ass at me, then began to sing!

"Na, Na Na, Na, Na! No camera, no film. No camera, no film. Na, Na Na, Na, Na!"

Janinne was coming unglued and I just dropped to my knees, arms outstretched, and begged for mercy. They both came back, pulled me up onto my feet, and we all took off running to the shoreline, which luckily wasn't very far. The girls continued on into the calm surf a few feet, but I decided to reprieve my old Nikes and stayed at the waters edge, observing. To my left, the beach ended abruptly into the mountainous peninsula that separated the two sides of the double horseshoe bay and formed both a natural boundary and barrier to the residential portion of the property. Five hundred yards of pristine crescent shaped beach lay to our right, also ending into a mountainous wall of rock. I expected to see the long pier at the far end of the beach, and the boat shop and deck that connected the pier to the mainland, but what caught me by surprise was the large opening in the rockface directly under the building. This resort was truly a smugglers paradise because it had it's very own sea cave that served as a natural boat house for their shuttle craft. How appropriate! The only other building on the shore was a thatched roof beach bar about three quarters of the way to the walkway leading to the boat shop and pier. Counting the people at the bar, there were no more than ten people on this entire exotic beach.

"This is one of my daily rituals," Janinne said from behind, then grabbed my arm and continued walking down the shoreline towards the pier. "I walk the property every afternoon during siesta for a little sand, sunshine, and peace of mind."

"Brainless therapy is what Jeffrey calls it," Terri said. "I've always found getting close to nature to be a very calming experience. Besides, serenity makes me horny."

"Me, too!" Janinne laughed. "Sounds like we have something in common."

"More than one thing, ladies." I decided it best not to pursue any further explanations at this time, so I left their questioning stares to go unanswered. The girls were bonding so easily, I didn't want to confuse the issue with testosterone fantasies.

"The only thing better than a walk on the beach is a romantic walk on the beach with the right companion," Terri stated.

"Companion, as in singular?" quizzed Janinne.

"Well, I didn't want to sound greedy!" answered Terri, with a chuckle.

"Honey, this is an all inclusive resort, so you can have all you want," she replied. "Overindulgence is always in vogue."

We walked past the beach bar, and made a right turn up to the paved trail that paralleled the beach. Crossing the trail, we continued up a pebble walkway that winded uphill through tall majestic flowering hedges and opened onto a clearing which contained a small cottage. The entire clearing was landscaped to perfection with grass, rock gardens, floral bushes and shrubs, and even its own hammock suspended between two palm trees. All in all, it was perfect.

"This was my personal cabana before I moved into the Penthouse. I chose it for you because it has the most privacy, best view, and nicest amenities of all our residences. I hope you like it."

"Holy shit, what's not to like!" Terri squealed.

The cabana was certainly all three; very private, very cozy, and very sexy. We strolled up to the steps on the left front corner of the cottage, opened the screen door, and stepped into Shangri La. The front room was actually a long screened porch that ran the entire length of the building, furnished exclusively in white wicker with large overstuffed pillows and cushions of a pastel floral motif. An arched open doorway led into an intimate bedroom decorated in the same design. I immediately made note of the large tri-fold mirror above the white wicker dresser and the full length bevel cut wicker framed mirror on wheels as potential props for Terri. Skylights were everywhere, and each room had at least two ceiling fans, but the killer of all was the bathroom. The shower looked more like a tropical rain forest encircled in glass bricks that fell into a rock tub big enough for at least three people. The rest of the bath was all mirrors, black marble, and brass.

As we walked back to the porch, I made a visual check to reassure myself all our luggage and gear was A-OK, and Terri also paused for a minute to toss her hair around and check herself out in the full length mirror. I couldn't help but do a little checking her out of my own, which she automatically sensed and winked at me in the mirror while squeezing her luscious breasts.

"Hey, you two, don't get carried away just yet. You've still got company!"

Our favorite sound of a champagne cork popping brought us back to the porch to find Janinne holding another bottle of Taittinger Comtes de Champagne. She filled three crystal flutes and passed out the prized bubbly.

"I'd like to invite you to join me on my private beach in the morning," she said. "Just like this cottage, it's very private, very beautiful, and very sexy! I think you'll want to use it in your photographs."

"Sounds good to me," I replied. "So far, your taste is impeccable."

"Merci'. Well then, here's to a good shoot, good times, and the most outrageous ten days of your life."

"And to new friends," Terri added, with a smile to all.

MI CABANA ES SU CABANA

The champagne went down a little too smoothly as Terri and I went about unpacking all the props, wardrobe, and gear that came bursting from our bags. Private Edition was ecstatic when Terri called, and FedExed us two dozen new designs, a warm hand-written note of thanks from the president, and another check. That same afternoon, a separate call netted six hot new batik outfits from a designer in Florida, and yet another check. Add 53 swimsuits, her personal wardrobe, and a few "goodies" to the mix; and needless to say, the cottage was totally engulfed. She had already tried on all of the swimsuits during our studio session, and marked which ones she liked, so at least the piles were organized. Slowly but surely, everything found its place and we could finally unwind a little. I had opened the blinds and was sitting on the porch, checking out all my Nikon gear spread all over the wicker coffee table, when Terri approached with the last of the Taittinger. She had pinned her hair up, and her blue cotton romper had become a misty rose short silk robe. Knowing me like a book, she had also put on my favorite lipstick.

"Do you realize I'd have to change clothes at least seven times a day to wear everything we've brought?" She plopped down on the billowy sofa next to me and curled up in the overstuffed cushions. "Do you think we'll have any time to enjoy ourselves, Jeffrey?"

I leaned back with my FM, zoomed in for a few gorgeous face shots in the soft natural lighting, and squeezed the trigger on the motor drive.

"Angel, if I get to watch you get naked seven times a day, we'll have no choice but to make time to enjoy ourselves."

"Exactly my point!" She took the camera from my hands, then pulled me down on top of her.

It seemed like I had been in the shower for hours. I had already washed both Terri and myself thoroughly, but just didn't want to leave the soft warm water that seemed to swirl around my body from all the numerous heads and jets. Luckily, the noise of Terri's blow-dryer brought me back to reality before I drown like a turkey in the rain. I reached up and pulled the big ring on the chain, dousing myself with the overhead flood one more time for sobriety before stepping out.

As I went through my drying sequence, I could hear Terri rustling around in the bedroom getting dressed. Into what; I could only guess, but after everything we'd been through today, and our explosive passion on the front porch, a nightshirt and a nap wouldn't be a bad idea. The bright yellow thong bikini Terri was wearing when she returned to the bathroom wasn't a bad idea either. She strutted over to the countertop, stood on her tip-toes, and bent over close to the mirror to put on her mascara. What a beautiful woman! What a gorgeous ass! What a perfect picture! I could see her look back at me through the mirror as I just stood there smiling.

"You are incorrigible!" she said flatly, not missing a stroke. "Have you forgotten our promise to meet Jack and Roberta by the pool ASASAP?"

"ASASAP?"

"As soon after sex as possible," she said with a sly grin, then winked at me before going back to work on her eyelashes. "They probably think you're trying to kill me!"

"I certainly tried, Darling."

"You most certainly did, Jeffrey." She looked me in the eyes all the way over to me, then put her arms around my waist and buried her cheek into my chest. "I know you think I'm pretty, and I appreciate that fact very much. Look where we are today, and think of where we could be going next. Now that you have me hopelessly in love with you, what happens if I can't hold up my end of the deal?"

I reached down and filled both hands with her glorious ass, then lifted her up to face level. She wrapped her legs around my waist, arms around my neck, and kissed me softly.

"Angel," I whispered, "I'll be glad to hold up your end any time. I treasure every single day of my life with you. In the years and years it will take for you to even think about getting less than gorgeous, imagine how rich our treasure will be. Besides, you've got at least ten more years before you reach your sexual peak. Now that's the ultimate scary thought!"

Terri nuzzled her forehead into mine and looked straight into my soul,

"If you're a good boy, Jeffrey, I'll let you kill me some more later."

We followed the main pathway behind the beach bar till we reached the blue sidewalk that matched the cord on our room keys. Just as expected, it led us uphill past numerous residences all tucked away in their own little tropical gardens, and several park-like areas for intimate gatherings. Be it a gazebo, or fountain, or even a wishing well, each had something unique about it. Sure enough, we eventually reached the pool bar and immediately spotted Jack. With a physique worthy of a warrior in the WWF, it would have been hard not to notice Jack Taylor as he stood up from his watery barstool and pointed our way.

"Yo, brother-in-law!" He had that same ear-to-ear smile he had in the El Dorado, so I knew he was ripped to gills, and it wasn't from the margarita he was holding. "Thought you'd fell in and couldn't get out!"

"Couldn't or wouldn't?" Terri replied, then kissed me on the cheek. She sat on the edge of the pool, dangled her feet in the water, and looked around. "Where's Bert?"

"Went to check out the big pool, and get herself a float."

I sat down next to Terri for a moment, then slid on into the waist-deep water. Kimberly wasn't behind the bar, but the young Mexican girl recognized us and immediately brought over a bottle of Le Grande Dame and two flutes, as well as a surprise. On her tray was the new printing of Private Editions Lingerie International in German, a note, and a small bouquet of tropical flowers. Terri opened the note and actually blushed for a moment.

"I honor your beauty with flowers and wine. Please honor me with your autograph. Thank you for indulging an old man's fantasy. Count Von Spengler."

"Sounds like you've won over another heart, Angel."

"I've never even seen this issue, have you?" She was the only one with dry hands, so we could only watch as she flipped through the new catalog. The cover shot was living proof the editors had chosen our most provocative images for their European clientele. Terri does a great "apres sex" look and it was predominate throughout the publication. I couldn't help but smile at the reaction it was arousing in Jack.

"They actually pay you to do this?" he finally asked.

"By assignment and publication," Terri answered. "Hey, there's Roberta!"

I turned to see her swimming under the bridge, heading towards us. About halfway, she stopped, leaned her head back, and then stood straight up.

"Oh, my God!" I gasped quietly at the awesome display of her majestic bare breasts. Totally nude, Roberta hopped up on the edge of the pool next to Terri and peered at the magazine.

"Like I said before, Honey, you're gorgeous!" She looked around at the sparse crowd and grinned at Terri. "You're not going to let me be the only one here naked are you?"

"Absolutely not," she replied, then raised her hair with one hand and turned her back to me. "If you would, please."

The knot released easily and Terri became one with nature. I waded over to the opposite side of the pool to retrieve two floats from the waitress, and also to observe the two girls together. As I expected, Roberta literally overpowered Terri, so using them in unison would definitely be a challenge. The girls eagerly accepted the floats, then cast their nakedness adrift in the center of the pool, champagne and all. I had just seated myself on the edge of the pool next to Jack when over the bridge came Suzan with a tall, slender blonde-haired man. They walked right up to me and squatted down.

"Jeffrey Mason, this is Jean Claude Cortan," she said as we shook hands. "He's going to assist us in the club ads and has volunteered to be my partner in the sexy couple shots."

"A lousy job, Mr. Mason," he added, with a definite French-Canadian accent. "But how can I refuse such a tempting offer."

"You can't! This is Jack Taylor, another victim, and that's Terri and Roberta floating around out there. With the exception of Janinne, so far, we're it."

"Not for long," Suzan said, and passed me a folded invitation. "You are cordially invited to participate in a Jeffrey Mason photographic assignment tomorrow afternoon. Selected photographs will be used to advertise both Chateau Pacific and Sunset Limited Swimwear in their new campaigns. If you are willing and able to sign the proper release forms, please gather around the Main Bar at 3:30. All swimwear will be provided. Goodies, too!" She was beaming at her creation. "I just printed up three dozen of these. At dinner tonight, you can pick out who you want, and Janinne and I will deliver the invitations. That should eliminate any jealous lover problems, don't you think? We've reserved a table for eight with good visibility, so you should be able get a good look at all remaining staff and clientele."

"Very nicely done, Miss Jacobs," I said, with a slight sarcastic overtone. "Are you always this efficient? My suggestion is you sit and relax, get comfortable, have some champagne, and just chill."

One look at Terri and Roberta's state of naked loveliness, and I knew Suzan was not ready to bare it all. Not yet, anyway. She smiled politely, gave a clumsy excuse about the time, and dashed merrily away.

"If you ever need somebody to carry your equipment, or help with the props, call me!" Jean Claude was trying his best not to laugh as he ran to catch up to Suzan.

"You're a cruel dude," Jack said, then put his arm around my shoulder. "You do realize that she will get naked the next time."

"Without a doubt, brother-in-law. Without a doubt."

Roberta and Terri propelled themselves across the pool and joined us for a pre-sunset toast, but I had a difficult time not staring at Roberta's intoxicating breasts as she raised her flute in salute. I heard Jack say something, but listening would have diverted too much attention.

"Jeffrey!" Terri exclaimed. "Jack just asked if we wanted to take a walk on the beach. Are you going to answer or just keep staring at Roberta's breasts!"

"Sorry, guys!" I said. "I guess I just got caught up in the moment."

"After seventeen years, it still happens to me, too."

"Men!" Roberta exclaimed. "Can't you just smell the testosterone! Honey, it's time you and I got our sweet asses out of this pool and get dressed before they hit us over the head with their clubs and drag us back to their caves."

Roberta climbed out of the pool, quickly dried off, then slipped into a tiny black G-string. So much for getting dressed! Terri did the same, wearing only her thong bottoms, and the two of them staggered past the bar for more champagne before heading towards the ocean. Jack threw on a Hawaiian shirt, and we both grabbed another bottle of champagne and two glasses as we followed our topless bathing beauties down the path.

Once alone, Jack paused for a moment to light the monster joint he pulled from his shirt pocket. He took two huge hits, then passed the killer reefer to me.

"Damn, you're resourceful." I took another toke then passed it back. "How did you get this past the dogs at the airport?"

"Got it here at the club," he retorted. "I asked the kid who brought our luggage if he could get me some 'sweet smoke', and five minutes later, he shows back up with two ounces of red-bud. One for me and one for you."

"Whoa, brother-in-law, there's no way I can smoke that much pot in ten days and remain functional. I've got way too much riding on this assignment to fuck it up by being too fucked up. Far too much is at stake."

"Take a little of your own advice, Jeffrey, and chill out. I understand playing under control, but the games don't start until tomorrow, so relax. Hell, just smoke what you want and throw the rest away! It's not like I had to pay anything for it. Just a tip."

"No shit! When they say all inclusive, they really mean it!"

"Absolutely!" Jack winked, then took the biggest hit off of a joint I'd ever seen.

When we caught up to the girls, they were sitting in the sand, watching the gentle ebb and flow of the surf below the beginning twilight of a tropical sunset. We joined them in the sand and Jack immediately lit another joint, then passed it on to Roberta. What surprised me was the fact that their champagne bottle was already empty. We had done some serious damage to one bottle, but the other was still intact and ready to be consumed. Quickly consumed, I might add. And it was.

The soft breeze gently lifted Terri's hair from her face as we walked arm in arm down the shoreline towards the beach bar. Jack and Roberta were just a few feet away, but in the solitude of our embrace, we were alone. All my thoughts had one common denominator; and I was holding her. We strolled along silently, until Roberta hollered,

"Hey, Honey! This is where we get off." She was hanging all over Jack and her nipples were noticeably erect. "God, this shit makes me so horny! Up the red path, second cottage on the right, please."

Jack swept her up into his arms and took off up the trail. We waved good-bye, then continued our stroll back to our cabana. When she reached the top step leading to the porch, Terri stopped, turned around, and kissed me passionately. Being a step below her, it was natural for me to bring my hands up to her luscious breasts and squeeze softly. She caught her breath, kissed me again, then held me as tightly as she could and whispered,

"Kill me some more, Jeffrey."

DINNER WITH A VIEW

By the time we finally showed up for dinner, even God was well into his entree. Terri's Batik mini-dress accentuated every aspect of her classic figure to the point that a silence was easily felt when we entered the pavilion. All smiles, Janinne met us half-way across the room wearing an ultra-mini baby blue silk sheath with a Mandarin collar and stacked-heeled white sandals that accentuated her long legs and runway walk. The girls embraced briefly, then headed off arm in arm to our table of high visibility. Jack and Roberta were joined by Jean Claude and Suzan as they gave us a standing ovation for finally joining the party.

"Better late than never!" Suzan blared out. "We were beginning to wonder if something was wrong."

"Quite the opposite," Terri replied. "Something was absolutely right."

"Amen, Honey!" Roberta squealed, then slapped high-fives with my insatiable partner. "We just got here a few minutes ago ourselves. C'mon, let's get you something to eat. We girls have to keep up our strength."

Jack put his arm around my shoulders and hustled me over towards the buffet.

"If she was any stronger, she'd break it clean off," he said with a laugh. "Back when I was doing lots of steroids, a two or three hour hard-on was no big deal. She'd ride that locomotive all night long, then wake me up in the morning ready to go again."

"Did you bring any steroids for me? I may need some."

"They make you sterile and cause brain cancer," he stated coldly. "I don't think you really want either of those. Here, try the grilled sea bass instead. Nothing like fresh fish for a hard dick!"

By the time we got back to the table, I had one plate with salads and veggies, and another plate full of all kinds of fresh fish. A classy-looking petite seniorita in a gauze peasant dress offered me a wine list, then tossed me a mischievous grin and winked. Obviously, the word was out about the photo shoot, and this was part of her audition. I played along by looking back and forth between the wine list and her sleek physique on display, then tossed her a grin of my own.

"Meursault Les Charmes, please." I paused for a moment waiting to get a response, then added, "What do you look like in a swimsuit?"

"I don't remember," she said with a raised eyebrow, then smiled, "It's been so long since I've had to wear one." She did a classic Loretta Young turn and swirl, then spirited away to fetch the wine.

"That woman wants to fuck your brains out," Jack said quietly.

"That woman wants her picture taken, Hoss. Didn't we have this discussion earlier today?"

"Oh my fuckin' gawd, was that still today?"

The crowd in the pavilion numbered around sixty, and was a rare congregation of flash, cash, and international sophistication. At a thousand dollars a day, the club attracted only the wealthy and their toys, so the Cougars with their stud-puppies, and the honeymooners were the easiest to pick out. Everyone else seemed to fall into the "Life is good, so what the fuck, let's enjoy ourselves" genre. There was lots of mingling, laughing, and good cheer as the people went about their dining pleasures and drinking of Unkle Henri's finest. It was also obvious that some of God's most finest were walking around, too. A beautiful woman is like classic art, possession is not mandatory to enjoy the pleasure of its appearance, and they were appearing all over the place. It didn't matter if they were married, single, gay, or straight, all I cared about was how they might look in a swimsuit. I leaned over Terri's empty chair and spoke to the vivacious redhead in white lace.

"Do you think we have enough invitations?"

"I have one printed for every woman here," she replied, then turned and gave me the ol' evil eye. "Except a few, of course."

"Of course, and thank you." We exchanged snickers, then she handed me a stack of invitations before going back to her grilled pork. I couldn't help but wonder how much of her fire and pizzazz would really come out on film. Girls like Suzan are like a photographer's clay. She is pure beauty that's capable of being molded into an image that far exceeds its original form by capturing a part of its soul, or an illusion of itself. Terri's such a natural to the camera, she's almost too easy to work with. To get the best out of Suzan, and go beyond her obvious charms, I'm going to have to really be at my creative best. Roberta is an exhibitionist, and Janinne, well, in my mind, Janinne is like Miss Universe does Penthouse, but Suzan could actually be the best of the lot if I'm capable of transposing all that flair and zeal of hers onto film.

Terri and Roberta had drawn a small crowd of girls over by the outdoor grill and were obviously having a good time being the center of attention. I was enjoying the spectacle, when I sensed someone behind me. I could smell the fragrance of her perfume before she spoke.

"I have something for you."

I turned to see our luscious wine stewardess standing very close, cradling the precious wine in her arms. She had pulled the top of her peasant dress down off her shoulders, emphasizing her full bustline, and tied up one side of her skirt at the hip, showing off her slender hips and legs. When she bent forward and extended the bottle for my inspection, I couldn't help but do some peripheral inspecting of my own. She quickly twisted the corkscrew into place, then wedged the chilled bottle between her bare knees and yanked that sucker right out with a loud pop! After the ceremonial swirl, sniff, and sip, without saying a word, I smiled and passed her an invitation. Her face lit up like a Christmas tree, then with great restraint, she slowly walked away to show off to her friends the first invitation awarded.

"I think Maria likes you, Jeffrey." Janinne leaned across the table, picked up the wine bottle and looked at the label. "Wonderful choice. Just tell Maria what you'd like, and we'll add it to the selection in your cabana's vinocave."

"What Jeffrey would like from Maria is best served warm, and slightly wet to the touch." Jack smiled at both of us like a six year old that just learned to fart in public. Janinne covered her eyes with her right hand and just shook her head. After a few moments to compose herself, she pointed her finger at Jack and did her absolute best not to laugh.

"You are such a naughty boy!" Janinne then turned to me with a peculiar but new seriousness about her. "Be sure to try the Soliel Blanc. It's young and crisp, and comes from a small vineyard directly behind the family chateau in Beaune. Unkle Henri says his grandfather planted the sauvignon blanc grapes right in the middle of chardonnay country for his grandmother so she could watch her favorite wine, and their love, grow in the sunshine every day through the view from her kitchen window. She personally tended the majority of the vines all her life, until she moved to Israel. Outside of the family, we're the only place you can enjoy grandmother's Soliel Blanc."

I looked up to see Terri and Roberta heading our way with a nasty looking redhead in tow. More Terri's size, this hot little number was decked out in micro-spandex, diamonds, and the prettiest set of implants money could buy. Throw in a little dental work for that perfect smile, and she had all the qualifications of a very high maintenance woman. I gave Jack a friendly elbow, and chuckled, "This should be interesting."

"Honey, this is Cyndi," Terri said with a subdued snicker. "She's agreed to do the beach party shoot, and has a partner who will too."

"Yeah, my friend Beverly is a stone fox," spoke the fiery little redhead in definite Texan. "We're just down here working off our tanlines before we head over to the Costa Del Sol. It was starting to get boring around here, but this sounds like fun."

"Any problems signing a release form?" I just had to ask.

"I'm a free-agent," she stated coldly. "Since my divorce, I do as I choose. Besides, what better way to show off his finest work than in some of your exotic-slash-erotic photographs. Just because he's not allowed to touch it anymore doesn't mean he can't look at it and dream."

"Interesting concept!" Terri whispered in my ear, then sat down, smiling graciously. I poured her a glass of Meursault and kissed her on the cheek.

"Don't get any ideas, Dear." I said softly, then turned to our guest. "So where's this stone fox Beverly?"

"Entertaining the owner!" Wild-eyed and smiling, she put her hand on her hip, shifted her weight into it, and then began a slow bounce up and down. "You know, dinner for two at his place, with all the trimmings."

"I think I'm going to be sick!" Terri sat back in her chair and took a long swallow of wine. "Just the thought of him touching me . . . ."

"He wouldn't live long enough to enjoy it."

Terri made direct eye contact with me, then put her hand on my thigh.

"You really mean that, don't you."

"Beyond all doubt."

"Hey, there's Bev!"

I looked up to see a spunky brunette with an obvious attitude pushing her way through the crowd and heading towards us. Only slightly taller and thinner, her D-cup attributes may not have had the same perfection as Cyndi's, but at least they were real. She stormed up to the table, poured herself a glass of Meursault, then managed to get most of it in her mouth as she chugged down a major slam of the delicate wine. Beverly wiped her mouth with her forearm, then slid the remainder of the golden liquid down her throat. Dressed ready for action, her sleeveless blue floral silk wrap was only tied together by a single knot at the waist, but this woman was thoroughly pissed off.

"Not what you expected?" Terri poured another round of Meursault, then clinked her glass with Bev's. "I met Christian this afternoon . . . ."

"That sorry little bastard only wanted to watch me fuck his ugly Arab buddy!" She pulled a cigarette from an antique gold case and lit it with one of those very expensive gold lighters nobody buys for themselves. "Over Dom and some Peruvian flake, he invites me to stick around for a few extra days to be his 'special hostess' for a private party of international VIPs that starts tomorrow. Next thing I know, Mahmood is standing behind me, and Christian starts telling us what he wants to watch me do to that stinking sand nigger. I took two monster hits of blow, poured myself a glass to go, then told him 'I don't fuck the hired help', and left."

"Good girl!" Cyndi walked up behind her partner and began massaging her shoulders. "Baby, you're tense. Let's go tap some flake, then I'll take personal care of all your little cares and woes. We'll catch up with you guys later at the bar, or in the Disco. If not, we'll see you tomorrow afternoon."

Off they went through the crowd, and disappeared down the steps leading to the pool. Most of the other people were finished with their meals, and were obviously making plans for the rest of the night, so the time to pass out invitations was here and now. The girls were far more critical of any potential candidates than I ever could have been, so I just turned them loose to use their own discretion. The four of them gaily mingled throughout the crowd, passing out the personal invitations to almost every woman in the room, both guests and staff alike. I enjoyed watching the faces of the recipients and their reactions as they read the words on the paper, then as if on cue, couples started leaving the dining area and either congregating at the bar, or slipping away into the night.

"Looks like there's gonna be some serious fuckin' going on around here tonight, thanks to you." Jack leaned back in his chair and sloshed some wine into his mouth. "Think about it, brother-in-law. She's jazzed because she gets to be a swimsuit model, and he's jazzed because he gets to fuck one!"

"It certainly works for me!" Jean Claude was grinning from ear to ear, and very drunk. He saluted us with his wine glass, then tossed a giant gulp down his throat.

We laughed on and off until the girls rejoined us. Not wanting to lose the spirit of the moment, Jean Claude and Suzan were the first to leave, then Janinne said goodnight after reminding us about our jaunt to her private beach in the morning.

"So what's on our agenda, guys?" Roberta leaned back in her chair, crossed her arms above her head, and slowly stretched her back. It's a good thing her silk blouse was tied together, because mere buttons couldn't have handled the strain. "I'm too stuffed to swim, too fat to fuck, and too sober to sleep."

"Let's check out the Disco," Terri said. "I could use some exercise that requires standing up."

We weren't half-way to the main bar when the floor to the pavilion began vibrating to the heavy bass of dance music from below. As if signaled by Pavlov himself, the crowd navigated its way to the staircase that led down to The Cave. The blast of heavily refrigerated and perfumed air that engulfed us at the bottom of the stairwell was a welcome relief from the humid tropical night air, at first. Without the added body heat of people and dancing, it was colder than a mother-fucker down there, so we congregated at the bar and ordered a vintage '63 Port to help warm us up. Running the entire length of the wall behind the bar was a window that looked directly into the main pool. I couldn't help but wonder what the afternoon tryst in the little pool would have looked like from an angle like this.

The club itself was more like a combination of an up-scale European disco and a classy Houston breast bar. A continuous high backed couch lined the perimeter walls, and lots of little drink tables surrounded the half dozen raised platforms and illuminated dance floor. Rotating spots, spinning mirror balls, strobes, and oscillating lasers that all jammed to the beat of the music filled the ceiling, completing the ambiance of a Star Wars nudie bar. As the crowd shuffled in, the DJ kept everybody moving with her mix of jazz, classic rock, and new age dance music. She cranked it up on Led Zeppelin's "Houses of the Holy" and the girls dragged us onto the dance floor. Terri could be a great stripper because she really likes to, and knows how to, emphasize her ass and breasts when she dances. She loves to brush her attributes up against me, then shake them in my face before retreating with the promise of more to come in her eyes. Not to be outdone, Roberta added some fuel to the competitive fire by doing a little dirty dancing of her own. Jack and I were having a great time watching, and being the victim, as they edged each other on, upping the provocation, and increasing their level of tease. The girls had obviously set the standard for the rest of the dance floor, because it was filling up with dirty dancers in various forms of dress and undress. We gave it our all for five straight songs, then bid a hasty retreat to the chilled bottle of Mumm waiting for us in the ice bucket next to our table. It was no longer cold in the club.

After a quick glass of bubbly, the girls excused themselves to go powder their noses, so Jack ordered another bottle of champagne and we settled back to gawk at all the lovely ladies shaking their asses all around us. Suddenly, the main spotlights focused in on a group of girls dancing together in the center of the floor. They were all wearing sheer lace corsets in various colors with stockings and heels to match, and jammin' down to the tunes. At the next change of songs, they each did a U-turn and strutted over to one of the raised platforms. To my complete surprise, the gorgeous nymphet in sheer purple lace walking straight towards me was Maria! She stopped at the foot of my chair, then continued her siren's dance just for me. As she leaned over and unbuttoned my shirt, I became totally mesmerized by the visual delights, scents, and feel of her. She nuzzled herself into me, starting with her hair on my chest, and worked her way up to where I couldn't help but to rub my face into her delicious cleavage. She spun around, sat her bare ass in my lap, then slowly slid down to the floor, rubbing my groin every inch of the way until the damn song ended. Maria stood up, grabbed my face with both hands, then bent over and kissed me with force and passion. Having not kissed another woman in over two years, I surprised both of us with the intensity of my response. Luckily for us all, the DJ cranked up another hard core tittie bar ass shaker, and Maria stepped up onto the platform next to our table and went back to work. I leaned over to my friend with his mouth hung open, and said,

"You may be right!"

The girls were all whispers and giggles when they got back from the ladies room, announced they were ready to leave, so we grabbed more champagne from the bar and headed towards the door. Seated with two youngsters at the end of the bar, Count Von Spengler waved his glass of Port in the air and smiled broadly at Terri. She waved back, rubbed Roberta's nipples with both hands, then blew him a two fisted kiss. We proceeded up a flight of stairs that led us to the sun deck, then Terri and Roberta made a B-line to the pool and started stripping.

"What the fuck are you doing?" Jack said with a smile on his face.

"Entertaining the guys at the bar!" Terri replied, then they shook their tits at us and dove bare-ass naked into the pool.

"What the fuck are you doing?" I asked as Jack ripped his clothes off, too.

"Somebody's got to entertain the ladies at the bar, don't you think!" He fully exposed his X-rated Hulk Hogan physique, then dove in.

"Or at least make them laugh!" I thought, then threw my naked butt into the clear, wet circus arena.

DAY TWO

Pounding . . . . My head? No, the door! Pounding. Maybe both. I slid out of bed, grabbed some shorts off the floor, and aimed myself for the door. I was halfway across the porch, when the front door gently opened and there stood a cutesy little senorita with my breakfast.

"Good Morning, Senor Jeffrey," she said with a perfect little smile, then entered and set the silver tray down on the table. Around twelve, and dressed in a very familiar white pheasant dress, this future heart-breaker was just starting to bud. I grabbed the Nikon off the coffee table and offered her my arm.

"Venga con migo, por favor, Senorita."

I led her outside into the subdued morning light, sat her on the steps, then filled the rest of the roll with her innocence and charm. When the camera stopped, she gave me a quick little-girl hug, then danced her bare feet down the wet path to tell her friends. I couldn't help but smile as I labored my way back into the cabana. My head still hurt, but I sure felt a lot better.

The tray she left held an array of sliced fruits and preserves, two kinds of coffee, all the proper plates and silverware, and croissants that were still warm. I chose the Mexican coffee over the French roast, then ripped open one of the toasty little rolls and filled it with fresh peaches and strawberries. I went ahead and made another, then headed over to the couch, trying not to drop all the proper cups, saucers, plates, and utensils on the tile floor. The coffee was hearty and rich, and the warm fruit filled croissants were to die for. I could feel the champagne cobwebs slowly dissipating with every glorious mouthful.

"You're an animal!" Terri walked over to the table and poured herself a cup of the French house blend. Her untied short silk robe followed the contour of her perfect breasts and barely covered her glorious ass. She brought her cup and saucer over and set it down on the coffee table, then just stood right in front of me. "I had knots in my hair, you Bastard. What did you do to me?"

"You raped me in the shower, Angel, and I have the bruises from the tub to prove it. I simply returned the favor in our bedroom. As for the knots, you probably deserved every single one."

"Bastard!" She leaned forward, nuzzled her face into mine and kissed me on the cheek. I gently pulled her closer and planted my nose between her perfect breasts. She allowed me a few moments of two-fisted indulgence, then grabbed my face with both hands, straddled me with her knees, and sat down. Pinned to the couch, I had no choice but to continue my gentle massage of her breasts.

"Janinne will be here any minute, remember?"

"Sorry, I just got carried away. You know how much I love to touch you, baby. You're just so perfect."

"Geez, Jeffrey! Wake up in there!" She threw my head into the billowy cushion and leaned forward with both hands on my chest. "Janinne is perfect. And Roberta, well, let's just say she's fucking awesome and leave it at that. Me, well, I'm just a short little fuck with nice tits."

I used a quick spin move and slung Terri around onto the couch, reversing our positions. The suddenness of the maneuver left her wide eyed, gasping, and totally exposed. I held her arms down by her wrists above her head, and looked her straight in the eyes.

"You're a very glamorous short little fuck with magnificent tits, Lady. Not everyone is blessed with the magical allurement that film has for you. This is just the first stop on a World Tour for both of us. When its over, we'll kick back, see what we've learned, and decide if we want to go again. For now, our images are being requested and accepted at the international level, but it really isn't me they're ranting and raving over. You're one of the most beautiful women in the world, even if you are just a short little fuck."

"With nice tits," she added with her pouty, little girl smile.

"With magnificent tits!" I lowered myself and kissed her softly on her lips. "I love you, Angel. What they don't know is that you're probably the nastiest short little fuck in the world, too!"

"Just probably?" She pushed me away and tried to look angry. "Think about what you just said while you take your shower, all by yourself, Animal."

"Yes, Ma'am."

The traditional 3 S's took less than fifteen minutes in the cool refrigerated air. Terri must have cranked the a/c, because my bare ass was seriously cold running around in the bathroom. I stepped into the bedroom and was stopped dead in my tracks at the vision of loveliness standing totally nude in front of the full length mirror. Undaunted by the chill in the air, Terri was applying her favorite moisturizer all over her bare skin, at least everywhere she could reach. In three quick steps, I was standing behind her, helping reach all those delicate places like the small arch of her back, or that real sensitive spot between her shoulder blades that makes her quiver, or the baby softness of the underside of her glorious ass. When Terri reached up and grabbed her hair while I was kissing that tender spot on the back of her neck, I couldn't help but completely fill my hands with her luscious breasts, just like she couldn't help but to arch her back and start rubbing her ass into me. She spun around, grabbed me with both hands, and led me pull-toy style over to the bed. Terri laid down on her back, and without hesitation, placed me inside of her and began working her magic. My lover has a unique expression she makes that begins with insertion and carries on and off during the heat of passion. Watching her face is yet another one of the most joyous reasons for making love to my personal little Sex Goddess. Or started to! The knock on the door was like being hit with a cold bucket of water, without the mess. Terri leaped out of bed and disappeared into the bathroom, leaving me to be the host. I grabbed the same pair of shorts off of the same floor, and ran to the door. Pausing a moment for the erection to subside, I tried to compose myself, then opened the door.

"Good morning, Janinne."

"Good Morning, Jeffrey." Too radiant for words, she was wearing a sexy white terrycloth Danskin and a cute little pair of green floral wrap around shorts. When she stepped inside, I couldn't help but notice the way her nipples exploded through the soft fabric at the change in climate. So much for hiding the old bulge in the shorts! Janinne stepped over to the table to set her tote bag down, then immediately began inspecting the china on the silver tray.

"I see you've met Gloria," she said, then poured herself a cup of coffee. "I recognize the china because it comes from the hutch in my formal dining room. Gloria's a precious little soul who adopted me when I first arrived, and takes very good care of me. Looks like she's adopted you, too."

"I think she just wanted her picture taken, which I did, no problem. I'm glad you're not really mad at her, because she's way too cute to punish."

"Who's too cute to punish?" Terri walked into the room wearing a pastel pink two piece thong and sheer white lace cover-up. Only an expert could have detected the gentle softness of her "all natural" make up.

"You are, Honey!" Janinne walked over and kissed her on both cheeks, European style.

"See, Jeffrey, I told you she was perfect." Terri winked at me, then playfully adjusted her breasts in the tiny top.

Janinne looked back and forth between us, then smiled and shook her head.

"I don't know about you two," she said.

"Yes you do." Terri retrieved her beach bag from the bedroom, then walked over to the table and set it down.

"I don't recommend sandals for the journey to Playa del Janinne," she said bluntly. "The rocks are a little tricky in a few spots, so please wear some sneakers with good traction. It's best not to bring a lot of extras with you, either. Don't get me wrong, it's not that difficult of a trek. It's just that the trail gets a little steep in a couple of places and it can get uncomfortable if your hands are full of junk." Janinne looked down at the floor, and actually blushed. "And speaking of uncomfortable," she turned her head and looked straight at me, "don't you need to go fix your shorts or something."

In unison, the three of us slowly panned down to discover that in the haste of the moment, good old Jeffrey had put his shorts on inside-out. We all cracked up to the point the girls had to sit down.

"When did you first notice?" Why I asked that stupid question, I'll never know.

"As soon as the erection went away," she stated coldly.

For the second time in the same morning of the same day, I strode off to the bedroom, dragging my tail along the cold tile floor. I was going to change clothes anyway, now just seemed like the perfect time. Their laughing their asses off only made the moment much more special.

The trek proved to be no more dangerous than described, but much longer. We took the main trail behind the beach bar, and made the last uphill turn to the right before the trail became a wooden walkway leading around the cliffs to the boathouse. Ten yards up the well manicured trail, Janinne led us up a smaller path that continued straight into the jungle when the main route made a veer off to the right.

"Who lives up there?" Terri asked.

Janinne stopped cold, turned around, and looked us both in the eyes.

"The Devil himself lives up there, Honey." She paused for effect, then continued. "That's the main trail to Christian's villa. That sneaky little bastard has secret passages and conduits all over the property so he can get around unnoticed, or spring up out of nowhere if he so chooses, but that is the tourist route to his vile and decadent habitat. There is absolutely nothing up there you need, Honey."

"So that was the Prince's villa?"

"Very good, Jeffrey!" Janinne smiled and gave me a queering look reminiscent of a lady cop I used to drool over. "You've done some homework on Chateau Pacific, I see." She turned back to the jungle pathway and continued our trek while she also continued to speak. "Prince Wafik loved this place. He built your cabana for his youngest, and most beautiful wife, but preferred to live alone in his secluded villa. Rumor has it, he was building the penthouse for his new girlfriend, and was going to sequester his ugly wives and all their children to a condo in Manzanillo so as not to scare off his guests."

The trail made a few dips through eroded drainage ravines, but for the most part, continued uphill through the jungle. Near the apex, we cleared the foliage and had a magnificent view of the bay to our left, and the open Pacific straight ahead. At the end of the long pier leading from the boathouse, a huge motor yacht was now tied up.

"Wow, did the Prince come to visit?" Terri asked.

"More like Princess." Janinne paused briefly and pointed to the boat. "That 65 foot Hatteras Convertible was designed and built for Christian's girlfriend, with her pocket change no less. She refuses to sleep in his villa because it 'smells like whores' up there, and since I won't give up my penthouse, she had her own bedroom designed and floats it up from Manzanillo when she's going to pay us a visit."

"Well, why doesn't she just leave it here and let Christian take care of it? Oops, sorry! Looks like I just asked another stupid question."

Janinne just smiled at me, then took us straight downhill heading towards the Pacific. Again, we were engulfed by the heavy foliage that allowed only a few feet of visual awareness. Downward we traversed, until the trail became sand, and opened onto a small crescent of a little beach, closed on both ends by rock cliffs and open due west into the Pacific. All in all, the whole thing was shaped like, and about the same size as the classic lot at the end of a cul-de-sac. A small thatched roof hut was on our right, but everything else was just jungle, sand, and water.

"Wow, this is just like out of a movie!" Even trying to be subdued, Terri still had all the refreshing enthusiasm and charm of her inner child. She just stood there soaking up the awe of her new found paradise. "Find me a hammock and some running water, and I could live here."

"Promises, promises, promises!" Janinne walked over to the side of the hut, turned a hidden valve, and cool, fresh water spewed from a showerhead mounted on the corner of the roof. "It's not heated, but you weren't specific. I'll have a hammock sent over immediately, so welcome to the neighborhood, Honey."

Subdued from the direct light, yet brilliantly illuminated from reflections off the water, the girls took on a surreal softness that made their complexions almost glow. I fumbled my way into the Nikon bag for my FM, trying desperately not to dump the whole damn thing out in the sand, yet hurrying enough not to lose the candor of the moment. The girls were stunning together, just being relaxed and talking to each other. I finally accomplished my Olympian feat, only to be spotted by Janinne after three or four frames.

"Oh no," she exclaimed. "I really only came here to swim. Please, can we save that for later? Please, Jeffrey."

"As you wish." I put the camera back in the bag, and set it down inside the hut. I also accepted the girl's belongings and hung them up on the numerous hooks, my cool straw hat and Hawaiian shirt included. We were all down to our swimsuits when Janinne looked at us both and smiled.

"I saw you in the pool last night, so I don't think you'll be offended," then she slipped out of her Danskin and handed it to me. Terri dropped her suit where she stood, and the two of them walked hand in hand towards the water. Walked, I say. God bless her! Terri knew exactly how many milliseconds it took me to grab my camera and snatch some awesome shots as they leisurely strolled the secluded beach. Snatch. What an appropriate word. By the time they reached the waterline, I had switched over to my 80-200 zoom and was ready for their descent, when Terri pulled another maneuver exclusively for the camera. She offered Janinne one of those scrunchy things to tie her hair back with, then turned to a perfect 45 degrees between the camera angle and the light, leaned on the leg closest to the camera, twisted slightly at the waist and raised her face to the sun, then slowly grabbed her hair with both hands and tied it back with a pink scrunchy of her own. Well, monkey see, monkey do! Janinne took the bait and not only worked her way into a classic glamour pose, she was standing close enough to Terri to do doubles, yet separated enough to achieve unobstructed individual shots. Totally nude and standing side by side, the similarities of the sculpting of these two women's bodies was almost scary. Even the size, shape, and angle of their breasts were almost mirror images. When they turned and slowly entered the water, my sub-conscious made me utter out loud the only word worthy of the vision.

"Perfect!"

BEAUTY AND THE BEACH

I dove right into the cool, crisp Pacific waters, and was amazed at how quickly the bottom fell out underneath me. Four strong strokes away from the shoreline, and I was in at least fifteen feet of water. The girls were taking a relaxed swim out to what appeared to be a protective reef, so catching up to them was no big deal. To get myself ready for this assignment, I had done a lot of swimming in the confines of an enclosed pool at the gym, so it felt good to flex and stretch in the open water while advancing on my naked prey. I slid beneath the surface to pass them underwater, knowing full well that the saltwater would burn my eyes, but God what a view! Just before I passed out from lack of oxygen, I popped up right between them.

"I guess you want an underwater camera now," Terri teased, then kissed me. She maneuvered herself behind me, wrapped her arms around my neck, then flicked my ear with the tip of her tongue and whispered, "Don't expect me to believe that you were looking at the fish, Jeffrey."

"Guilty as charged, on both counts." I gave Janinne a quick second to get closer, then continued. "No, I wasn't looking at the fish, and, yes, I wish I'd had an underwater camera down there."

Janinne shook her head and laughed, "Men and their toys!"

"Sometimes being the toy can be fun," Terri replied.

"Sometimes . . ." Janinne's smile said it all.

We floated, swam, and just enjoyed splashing around for an easy twenty minutes, then I swam to shore and laid out in the wet sand to soak up some of nature's finest rays. The girls were getting really close, so I didn't think they would miss me, but I wasn't even dry before they joined me in the warmth of the sun. Shading my eyes with both hands, I watched as they came out of the water and walked towards me. Individually, each was a classic work of human art. Collectively, they were any man's, and most women's, ultimate fantasy. Silently, they stretched out on either side of me and began absorbing the warm, tropical sun. With a beautiful woman laying naked on both sides of me, I hoped JJ had the spy satellites working so I could get photo-documentation of this glorious event.

I turned my head to look at Terri, and was emotionally overwhelmed by her innocent beauty. To be the focal point of all the passion and energy that flows through her temptuous body is truly intoxicating. Simply admiring the tiny droplets of water glistening on her firm, round breasts was more than enough reason to get the ol' testosterone running strong again. A gentle smile spread across her succulent lips, and I knew she could tell I was looking at her, which made me smile, too.

I sat up to clear my head, then took a moment to politely admire Janinne. Completely at ease, this woman was totally gorgeous from head to foot. A soft breeze coming from the ocean felt cool on my face, and also made her nipples get rock hard right before my eyes. Enough was enough! I made a quick dash to the water and threw myself in. I counted ten power-strokes towards the reef, then dove down in the cool water to try to relax. Back to the surface, I tipped my head to get the hair out of my eyes, then looked at my bathing beauties on the beach. They had rolled onto their sides facing each other, and were laughing and carrying on about something. Probably me!

"Get a grip, asshole!" I said to myself out loud. "You're supposed to be a professional, not some frat boy with a Minolta and a hard dick!"

They waved at me, then ran to the water and jumped in. The way they were swimming, it looked like a race. I couldn't help but wish I was the prize.

"Ready to take some pictures?" Terri asked when they reached me. "Janinne has to leave soon, so let's get busy. Think you can handle both of us?"

"Sounds interesting." The possibilities were endless! "Let me go get ready, then I'll signal. I want to get the two of you coming out of the water together."

I left them treading water and swam ashore. A quick rinse in a shockingly cold shower cleared my head and helped me focus on my photography. I slipped on my shorts, grabbed my Nikon, and was as ready as I could be to perform.

The ladies were still laughing and talking about something when I signaled them to come ashore. Terri had obviously said the right things, because they emerged from the water like Goddesses from Neptune's harem and gracefully strolled towards me, holding hands. About halfway, their sexy gait erupted into a tomboyish romp as they raced past me to the shower. The chilly water added to their childish playfulness, and, of course, instantly enhanced their abundant feminine charms. Thank God for telephoto zoom lenses! At my request, and with no objections, they became less playful and much more sensuous with each other. As if on cue, just as the girls, and the water, were warming up, I ran out of film.

"Let's do some posing," I said, once the new film was loaded. Janinne had wrapped herself in a towel and was brushing out her hair when Terri slid up from behind and instantly disrobed her.

"No way!" Terri said with a devious little smile.

I positioned them sitting one in front of the other on a large grass mat in the diffused light of the tropical foliage, then tossed Janinne her brush. Terri took the lead by leaning her head backwards, arching her back to emphasize her bustline, and carefully positioning her arms so as not to obstruct the view. Janinne smiled and began gently brushing Terri's hair, but kept darting her eyes over to me. After a few great shots, and numerous miscues, I lowered the camera and approached the two beautiful naked ladies.

"I'm sorry Jeffrey," Janinne said. "I warned you I wasn't camera friendly. I just feel so awkward!"

"Trade places with me," Terri said. "I'll do the brushing and pampering while you just sit there and be your natural gorgeous self. It's really pretty simple, just lean your head back, close your eyes, and stick out your tits!"

"I think I can handle that!" Janinne stood, but instead of walking around, she straddled Terri and stepped over her, gently brushing her labia across Terri's hair. She retaliated with a firm slap on Janinne's ass, then they both made Ooooing noises and began to laugh. I watched the whole thing in total disbelief, then started to laugh, too.

"Now, now ladies," I said when I could talk. "Be nice, or I'll make you kiss and make up."

"Promises, promises, Jeffrey." The mischievous look on Janinne's face was worth as many frames as the motor-drive could shoot. Zooming in to concentrate on the girls, and out to capture the ambiance of their surroundings, I worked in a circular pattern that started and ended in profile of the ladies. I ended the roll by getting Terri to lean over Janinne's shoulder for some tight double face shots. Awards, blue ribbons, and all, I could already imagine the framed 24x30 hanging in my studio gallery.

"Good morning!" The cheery voice from behind me had to be Suzan. She and Jean Claude had come for their morning swim and sun on the private nude beach. Although he tried not to stare, it was easy to see that Jean Claude was mesmerized by Terri. We all stood around the hut and spoke briefly, my ladies completely at ease with their state of undress, and Jean Claude doing his best to look them in the eyes. Suzan had on a hot pink G-string under her lace cover-up, and nothing else. For a fiery red head with blue eyes, she had a really nice tan and no freckles. She let me help her out of her cover-up, but abruptly ended our conversation when I reached for my camera. She grabbed Jean Claude by the hand and made a mad dash to the water, but I still managed to get a few frames off before they jumped in. In one shot, I could almost swear Suzan looked back over her shoulder and smiled at me. Once again, I found myself captivated by her pizzazz.

"She's a real hot-rod," I remarked.

"Absolutely!" Terri grabbed Janinne and I by the arm and continued. "What I don't understand is why she gets so giddy when we're all together. No one with a body and personality like hers should be easily intimidated, so do you think we make her uncomfortable?"

"I don't think we're the problem." I turned to Janinne and smiled. "Newlyweds?"

"Bingo!"

POOL PARTY

We left the newlyweds so they could enjoy some solitude in paradise and followed Janinne all the way back to the pool bar. She bid us a fond adieu, leaving Terri and I stretched out on a chaise lounge for two, waiting to be served. We bypassed the Mimosas and Bloody Marys and went straight into a bottle of 83 Krug. At 10:15 in the morning, a three figure bottle of champagne seemed to be the perfect reward for skipping breakfast and spending an hour and a half on a nude beach with two of the world's most beautiful women. Not wanting to induce any tan lines, Terri had once again resorted to pure nudity, and I got to rub in all the necessary lotions. Top or bottom, front or back, the magical sensations of our touch was the same. We were soulmates, and both of us understood the Utopian environment that existed between us.

Slowly but surely, the areas surrounding the pools became alive with the survivors from the previous evening. Someone, somewhere in this resort was a confidential informant for the CIA. Male or female, guest or staff, it really didn't matter to me. I didn't need to know who they were any more then they needed to know who I was, or am. Going into any assignment uncovered is always the most dangerous for the operative, because win, lose, or draw, when the assignment is over, it's impossible to step out of character when you're only being yourself. If the opposition gets a positive ID, it's a death warrant with no specific execution date. A simple credit check can provide all the necessary information to locate a target at any given time. I slammed down the rest of my champagne, refilled my glass, then rubbed Terri's delicious ass one more time to change my train of thought.

"Unhand that winch, you scoundrel!"

I looked up to see Count Von Spengler standing waist deep in the pool, holding a glass of port in one hand and a cigar in the other. From his angle of view, and the smile on his face, I doubt it was only her ass he was gawking at. Terri discreetly brought her feet together, then made a U-turn on the chaise so she was facing the pool.

"Good morning, Count," she said in her sleepy little girl voice. "Isn't it a bit early for royalty?"

"Depends on what royalty has on his mind, dear," I replied. "Care to join us in a glass of champagne, Count?"

"Delighted my boy, and thank you!" He plopped his fat soggy ass in the chair next to me and polished off the full glass of port in two gulps. Our cutesy little Mexican waitress had both another champagne flute and a new glass of port on her tray when she arrived. I poured his glass first, then refilled both our flutes. He raised his glass straight up into the air and bellowed, "Damn fine way to start the day, don't you think!"

"Amen!" I didn't want to confuse the issue by bringing up the nude beach, or sex, so I just let him go on and enjoy the combined pleasures of the champagne and port. For some reason, the Count looked much younger this morning than he did yesterday. I would have guessed he was close to seventy, but now he looked under sixty. I guess that's positive proof that only women look better to an intoxicated male. Thank God!

"My boy, you're a hot topic both here at the Chateau and abroad. Having dabbled in the arts at a younger age, I understand the principles of your chosen profession." He took a long swallow of the expensive champagne, then continued, "Who represents you? To reach this level, your agent must be damn good."

"She is," I said flatly. I couldn't exactly say my representative was a buddy in the CIA, so I threw him a curve. "Terri handles me very well, thank you."

She rolled over on her side, exposing her luscious breasts to our guest, and gave us both a devious little smile. "I believe what Jeffrey is trying to say is that we take care of our own negotiations, Count."

"My God, you've got to be joking! How did you ever obtain exclusive coverage of an international lingerie manufacturer without proper representation?"

"I guess you'd have to call it luck. I bought Terri one of their hot little teddies to wear for a Valentine's Day portrait ad I ran in Houston. The shot got a hell of a lot more response than the ad did, so I had a 24x30 made for my studio gallery and we sent an 11x14 print to the president of the company with a letter of introduction. A couple of weeks later, a woman named Vicki Simpson just dropped by the studio unannounced and asked to speak with me. When I came into the gallery, she was just staring at Terri's picture with this huge grin on her face."

"Jeffrey paged me while I was out shopping and told me to meet them for lunch. We cut the whole deal over chicken enchiladas and Margaritas at Cyclone's. So far, we've done eleven catalogs, seven domestic and five international, and get our royalty checks every two weeks, as planned. We also get a nice check every time they send us a new batch of clothes to shoot. All things considered, I think our informal arrangement has worked out real well for everybody."

"Especially yours, my dear!" Count Von Spengler raised his flute in salute, and continued. "I applaud the magnificence of your presence, and the mental dexterity that lies within."

"Hear, hear!" I joined in on the toast, then added my 2 cents worth. "Why, just this morning, I was trying to convince her she's more than just a nice pair of . . ."

"Jeffrey!" Her devious little smile had been replaced by something a bit more intimidating. I winked, she smiled, then out came her little girl poutty face. "I thought you said they were magnificent!"

"Hear, hear," exclaimed the Count. He stood, drained both his champagne and port glasses, then staggered off in the direction of the banas hidden in the garden behind the pool.

It was now time to throw myself into the clear blue water for a bit of relaxation and refreshment. Terri accepted my invitation, so we held hands and jumped in together. She followed me under the bridge and into the main pool for a few laps and a view of who was laying around. As expected, the ladies were working on their tans and the guys were trying to recuperate. I guess Jack was right! With the noted exception of the old broad and her stud-puppy, everyone seemed relaxed and very content. We grabbed a couple of floats and headed back to the enclosed confines of the pool bar. The champagne was kicking in and Terri was starting to fade, so it was definitely time to just lay back and chill until lunch.

When we paddled round the bend, Roberta was waiting for us by our chaise lounge. She had on a huge Texans T-shirt, a pair of flip-flops, and was standing up brushing out her long curly locks. The Count must have fallen in, because we were still the only people in the pool bar area. Bert smiled and waved when she saw us, then met us at the edge of the pool.

"Hi, guys," she said, then dropped down on her knees. "So, how was the private beach?"

"Very private," Terri replied. "You and Jack are going to love it."

"No kidding, it was awesome, Bert. Say, where is your illustrious partner?"

"Jack's not having a very good morning. He's pretty sore today. When I left, he was stretched out in the hammock, trying to get comfortable."

"Poor Jack, I'm sorry to hear he's all stiff this morning."

"No, honey, I said he was sore," Bert exclaimed. "If he was stiff, I'd be in that hammock with him!" She lifted her shirt up over her head, tossed it on the chaise, and slid her naked grandeur into the pool. "Sometimes, it's best if I just leave him alone. I'm sure he'll show up right before lunch with a big smile and a bigger case of the munchies."

I offered her my float, which she gladly accepted, then made my way back to the chaise and a dry towel. To photograph Roberta for the first time, relaxed and unimposing was exactly what I wanted. I twisted on my 80-200 zoom and removed the MD-12 for stealth and silence. Bert was lying on her back with her eyes closed when I locked in on her in my viewfinder. Without an ounce of make-up, she was beauty in its purest form. Her skin was flawless, her lips soft and full, and the rest of her was far beyond most men's grandest hallucinations of the ultimate large-breasted woman. With Terri on her stomach, and Bert on her back, I easily finished the roll of film zooming in and out shooting duos and solos. While I was changing film, Terri got Roberta to roll over onto her stomach, then changed positions herself to where she was on her back. Again, I shot a complete series of the girls in candid composure. Towards the end, Roberta had her head resting on her arms and was just floating and relaxing, when she opened her eyes and looked straight at me. Zooming in on golden brown eyes peering over golden brown skin, I fired as fast as I could to get as many frames as possible before her mood changed. To my surprise, all she did was wink and smile at me before closing her eyes and resuming her relaxed aquatic suspension.

"Good for you, Bert," I said to myself. She was ready to progress to the next level. Once again, Terri had obviously said all the right things. I put new film in the camera, reattached the motor-drive, then made one more very obvious pass at the fabulous flotilla before retiring the Nikon for the rest of the morning. The girls responded as I expected they would, getting playful and trying to act sexy, then just laughing their asses off. When the camera finally hit the inside of the camera bag, it was time for more champagne and some serious R&R. My morning's work was done.

I was long adrift in a serious champagne nod when I was brought back to reality by the sweet smell of burning marijuana. I opened my eyes to see Jack sitting in the chair next to me smoking another monster joint. He took a huge hit off of his hand-rolled cigar, then passed it my way.

"Time to get ready for lunch, Little Buddy!" he said. "I figured this would wake you up."

"Little Buddy?" I indulged myself, then passed the joint back to my new best friend. "Can't you come up with something a little more flattering than Little Buddy. After all, we're going to be surrounded by women this afternoon, and I don't want them to get the wrong idea."

"Especially Maria, Jeffrey?"

"Especially Maria!" We passed grins back and forth along with the joint. "You still think she wants to play?"

"No doubt, Brother-in-law. She's got the hots for you and the body to back up the threat. It's only a matter of time."

"Yeah, right. And, like, what am I suppose to do with Terri while we're splattering the walls with brain matter? It's not like I can send her shopping for the afternoon."

"Sure you can!" I spun around to see Jean Claude standing right behind us. He took the joint from Jack, sucked down a big hit, then passed it on to me. "We take both Suburbans into Manzanillo every afternoon after lunch so the ladies can shop and the guys can relax. Are you planning a coup?"

"Not really," I said. "Jack's trying to convince me I need to explore a new venue."

"Damn! And all this time, I thought we were talking about chasin' pussy."

"Gentlemen, please," Jean Claude's eyes dashed around the pool looking for eavesdroppers. "We're attached to three of the finest women on the planet, so why are we discussing the possibilities of an adulterous affair."

"Probably because they're not around to listen," Jack laughed. Just about that time, Cyndi and Beverly came strolling up to the pool from the beach wearing only tiny little G-strings. They pranced around the pool for effect, then took up positions on the chaise lounges directly across from us, and ordered a bottle of Dom. To make sure they had everyone's attention, they slid out of their Gs, then started a slow rub of lotion on their bare breasts.

"You can't tell me you wouldn't want to try to break it off in either one of those," Jack said without diverting his eyes for a nanosecond.

"Or both of 'em," I added. "If you're going to hallucinate, have a good one!"

Uncomfortable to the point of fidgeting, Jean Claude still couldn't take his eyes off of the bodacious buffet on full exposure across the pool. He took a deep draw off of the joint, then just started shaking his head back and forth.

"Sorry, guys," he finally said. "I'm going to have to pull a Clinton."

"Which one," I asked. "Don't ask, don't tell' or 'I don't recall having that conversation."

"Whichever one Suzan will believe," he replied. "Excuse me guys, I've got to go find my wife."

"Speaking of wives, " I said after JC had departed, "Where are Terri and Roberta?"

"They went to lock up your cameras and change into something dry for lunch. Bert said they had to keep up their image and not look like pigs when they eat." Jack took another huge toke, then smiled. "I think it has more to do with trying to wear all the damn clothes she brought."

The bar areas, both wet and dry, were starting to fill up with the pre-lunch revelers. Kimberly had assumed command and was busy mixing Martinis while her two assistants were buzzing around the Margarita machine. Count Von Spengler had also reappointed himself Bar Meister and had assumed his normal position on the end bar stool. Being a voyeur at heart, I was having a great time watching all the interaction and posturing going on between the guests and staff. After all, most everyone would be leaving tomorrow, so if a move was to be made, it was pretty close to now or never. There was lots of talk about the beach party, and who was going to do what to whom before the night was over. All things considered, the next 24 hours should prove to be very interesting.

The commotion surrounding the bar quieted for a moment, then became focused on the pathway coming up from the beach. I had to smile when I saw Terri and Roberta make their grand entrance. Terri had on a blue floral soft silk romper that draped majestically from her magnificent breasts and clung to her perfect little hips. Bert had on a pair of 60's style white hot pants and matching halter top. Neither showed any signs of undergarments, and both had done their hair and make-up just enough to add glamour to their sexuality. Needless to say, the illusion outshone reality because nobody was looking at the totally nude women hanging around the pool anymore. The ladies strolled over to us, but before they could sit down, Jack grabbed Roberta by the belt-loops of her minuscule hot pants and pulled her close.

"Leapin' labia, Darlin', you look good enough to eat. Come sit on my happy face."

"You know how this works, Baby." she replied. "You have to feed me before you can fuck me, again."

"Again?" I asked.

"And just why do you think he was sore this morning, Jeffrey?"

No reply was necessary, only food.

LUNCH MADNESS

The noon lunch buffet proved to be a cacophony of oral delights ranging from a classic paella, thru the traditional Mexican fare, to anything imaginable thrown on the grill. I tried to behave myself, but still wound up with two plates full of goodies and a huge salad. Terri fielded numerous questions on what to eat or not eat before a photo shoot, and was less than brutally honest in her replies.

"I don't have to watch what I eat. Why, do you?" wouldn't exactly be PC, so her usual response was, "Eat what makes you feel good, that's all I do."

Yeah, right! Considering the volume of food they consumed, Terri and Bert should be feeling great for at least three days. The only thing missing from the girl's normal diet was alcohol. Terri feels she gets "snake-eyed" if she drinks too much before a session, so her usual glass of wine had been replaced by bottled water. Ditto for Bert. Jack and I, however, had no such reservations about our appearance, and did our best to balance out our wine allotment. I drank a bottle of Brouilly that was to die for, and Jack consumed at least a gallon of the bourgogne chardonnay labeled Henri's Private Vin de Pays.

Just as with last night's supper, the layout of the dining area leant itself to cheerful grazing. People easily moved about from table to table, talking, laughing, and having an occasional bite of something new or different.

It seemed like everybody was enjoying stepping out of character and just hanging out with some new friends. On the battlefield of life, these CEOs, CFOs, lawyers, doctors, or whatever type of businessmen would probably decapitate each other to be victorious in a business deal. But here at the chateau, everybody had been reborn as a pampered little beach bum, and the only real competition was in the bedroom. Once again, the only exception seemed to be the old broad and her prized pet. For whatever reason, they remained aloof and antisocial. Even the two pairs of honeymooners acted like they were ready to leap out of their cocoon and party hearty with the rest of us. In a way, I felt sorry for the young stallion involved with the Grande Dame. Being kept on such a short leash was killing him, and she was less than discrete in asserting her overbearing influence. No amount of money would be worth being paraded around like some kind of trophy fuck, so my hope for him was blackmail.

"Looks like there's trouble in body builder's paradise," Terri whispered. "I know what she sees in him, I just wonder what he sees in her."

"Money, power, influence, take your pick," I answered. "Whatever it is, she's holding enough of it to keep him under complete control." I paused for a second to grab a sip of water, then gently held Terri's face with both hands and kissed her. "Oh hell, baby, just listen to us. For all we know, they're probably both guys, madly in love, and wondering how an old geezer like me scored a trophy fuck like you. After all, I am ten years older than you are . . . ."

"Jeffrey!" This time, she grabbed my face, and made me look at her. She was grinning from ear to ear. "Trophy fuck? Someday, when we're sitting around the house, playing with our two children, I'm going to remind you that you thought I used to be a trophy fuck."

"You won't have to, baby." I lifted her onto my lap, and wrapped her in my arms. "Nothing could ever change the way I feel about you. Especially not a child."

She held me as tightly as she could and nuzzled her face into mine. "Two children, Jeffrey," she whispered. "Two children created from our love."

"You'll have to marry me first," I replied softly. "Our children should have our name, don't you think?"

"Absolutely, Jeffrey. Any time."

"Good grief! Get a room, guys!"

We looked up to see Jack and Bert standing behind us, holding hands. They looked both full and content.

"We're going to go stretch out and relax a little before the afternoon begins," Roberta said. "I'll be early, Honey, so you can do my make-up and I can get first shot at the suits. I don't want some Bimbo lookin' better than me!"

"Impossible!" was my only response.

"Amen, Darlin'" Jack put his arms around Bert's waist from behind, and pulled her tightly against his chest. She responded by leaning into him, with a slight grind of her ass into his hips.

"Now look who needs a room," Terri giggled.

"Amen, honey," Bert said through a huge smile. "Time to go feed the beast!"

We chose to take a stroll and walk off some lunch before heading back to our cabana, so we headed off along the row of bungalows that lined the pathway following the upper terrace of the property. As these were probably the first residences constructed at the resort, they were all identical in appearance and followed the contour of the terrain to perfection. Each had a semi-enclosed porch as an entry into the living area, and a loft bedroom with French doors that opened onto a small balcony facing the ocean. The back of these units seemed to be butted up against the sheer rock face of the mountain that separated the two halves of the bay. As with the rest of the resort, the landscaping that encompassed the bungalows was exquisite. When we reached the bend in the trail that led straight down towards the beach, we came across another perfect location for photography. Snuggled in the upper corner of the residences was a small grassy area used for an archery range. The background was a vine covered rock face that showed no areas of brilliant color, only various shades of dark green tropical foliage. The range was long enough to allow for a telephoto lens, and the angle of the natural lighting would be perfect for a late afternoon shoot. Once again, I logged all this information into my location memory bank and vowed to return with cameras, clothes, and my beautiful companion.

At the bottom of the trail, instead of walking straight out onto the beach, we made a right turn and took the pathway that paralleled the shoreline. We knew we would eventually reach the beach bar and our cabana, so we continued our relaxed stroll, looking for more photographic locations and just being together. What we found was not only perfect for pictures, it oozed sexuality and begged for a romantic interlude. Enclosed on three sides for privacy by vine covered white lattice, we found a white wooden porch swing suspended from a majestic floral arbor. The illumination was bright enough to

constrict Terri's pupils and make her big blue eyes all the more mesmerizing, yet diffuse enough to soften even her perfect complexion. Add the floral aromas and a little champagne to the formula, and wham, the perfect make-out spot!

"We have to come back here, soon," Terri exclaimed. "No cameras, no schedule, just you and me."

"And a little Taittinger, of course," I added.

"Of course!"

By the time we finally reached our cabana, I was ready for a bath and a bed. I was into my rinse cycle when I heard someone enter the shower behind me. I felt her fingers on my shoulders, her breasts in the lower portion of my back, and her face in between. I enjoyed letting her hold me for a moment, then turned to face the woman of my dreams. Dripping wet, I carried her to the bed and made sweet, passionate love to her.

BEACH PARTY BINGO

I awoke from my blissful slumber to the sounds of giggling coming from the bathroom. Wrapping a sheet around me, I stuck my head through the door to see what was going on. Terri was sitting on the black marble counter trying to put make-up on Roberta, who was standing up facing the mirror. Both girls were totally nude, and neither one could keep a straight face. Poor Terri was attempting to brush on Bert's lipstick, while at the same time showing Roberta how to hold her lips. Picture two naked beauties making pouty faces at each other, then one goes "Ooooh" and they both crack up. I watched until I couldn't contain myself, then snuck off to retrieve my Nikon. I guesstimated the exposure settings, then peered around the doorway and fired off as many frames as possible to capture the moment. Again, they started hamming it up for the camera until we all burst into laughter.

After another quick rinse in the shower, I had all good intentions of relaxing and making some mental preparations for my upcoming shoot. As with all the other best made plans of mice and men, everything changed when I stepped into the bedroom and saw Roberta standing in front of the full length mirror wearing the same tiny little green 2 piece Terri had tried on for JJ and me back in Houston. When she caught me gawking, a huge grin spread across her face.

"I feel the same way, Jeffrey," she said. "I've got to have this!"

"Consider it yours!" The vision was totally awesome! "Let me get some shots first, then you can just keep it." I tried to keep my enthusiasm at a professional level, but an upsurge of testosterone was getting in the way. "Darlin', nobody could ever fill out that suit like you do."

"I know that's right!" She was beaming. All the shades on the windows and skylights were open, so the bedroom was filled with soft illumination as Bert stood on her tip-toes and twisted from side to side trying to check out every angle in the mirror. The only thing left for me to do was frame her image in my viewfinder, focus, and push the trigger on the motor drive. Best of all, she was enjoying the hell out of being photographed.

Terri had set up shop on the porch to finish any make-up needs and give a few helpful hints on how to perform in front of a camera before sending the victims outside for me to shoot. She had wrapped herself in a short baby blue silk robe and was gazing out the window at our lush tropical setting, when I approached her, put my arms around her waist, and gently held her against my chest.

"It's so beautiful, Jeffrey," she said, then pulled my arms more tightly around her. "And so romantic! Everything just feels so good down here."

"I agree, Honey. It's not like you don't feel wonderful in Houston, maybe we're just a bit more responsive to each other in this environment."

"A bit?" Terri turned around and wrapped her arms around my neck. "I want you so badly, I ache."

No reply was necessary. Our lips met, and the temperature in the room climbed 10 degrees.

"Hey, knock that off!" Roberta strutted into the room and joined our embrace. "I certainly don't need any more inspirations from you, young lady. Unless you're planning to share, that is."

"Oh, yeah. What a great idea! If the two of you didn't kill me, Jack certainly would!"

"Only if he didn't get to watch!" Bert whispered, then patted me on the butt and headed out the door.

In the soft shade of a romantic little palm grove, I worked Roberta through a series of standing poses, then asked her to turn around under the premise of shooting the back of the suit. It's amazing how sexy less than half a square foot of green lace can look on six feet of all woman. As if her double-D's and tight little ass weren't distraction enough, twice I caught some motion in the foliage with my peripheral vision. After the second occurrence, I purposely maneuvered myself to my left, putting Roberta on a direct line of sight to the disturbance. I zoomed in over her shoulder and captured a very recognizable shot of Mahmood for JJ's file. That stupid Arab was so absorbed in Roberta's body, he left himself totally exposed to my angle of view. Hell, he even smiled! To make sure everyone got their money's worth, I moved Bert to the hammock, then got her to slide out of her top and into some very sensuous poses, Playboy style. She enhanced the erotic suggestion by playing her expressions into the pose, just like an old pro. I was standing on a ladder, shooting down into the hammock when Bert sat straight up and started fanning herself.

"God, this is exhilarating!" She looked up at me and winked, "If Jack doesn't get here soon, you're gonna be in big trouble, mister!"

"Promises, promises, Mrs. Taylor." I helped her up from the suspended Yucatan netting, then offered her the minuscule top. She just shook her head no, then grabbed my arm and headed me towards the cabana.

"If I don't get inside, all Terri's wonderful make-up will be running down my face."

"I understand, completely!" I had the urge to wave good-bye to the inadequate Arab, but chose discretion and returned my full attention to the bombshell holding on to me. "C'mon Darlin', I know where there's an ice cold bottle of champagne with our names on it. We certainly earned it!"

Roberta leaned over, kissed me on the cheek, then said softly,

"A man after my own heart."

We were halfway finished with the bottle of Mumm, when up drove Janinne in a cart, followed by two young men in white coats driving another. In a matter of minutes, they erected a 10x10 tropical canopy for shade, then set up a full service bar, complete with hors-deurves, and two troughs filled with iced down bottles of wine and champagne.

During the process, Terri rejoined us wearing a yellow on yellow one piece I'd never seen before. We'd already done studio shots of all the Sunset Limited suits, so this new one took me by surprise. A very pleasant surprise, I might add, too! French cut with a thong back, the thin pastel fabric molded itself to her every curve, and was purposely designed to emphasize her breasts and nipples, which it most certainly did!

"Wow, Honey, that's gorgeous," I said when I could talk.

"No, Jeffrey," Roberta retorted. "She's gorgeous, the suit just proves the point!"

"Thanks, guys." Terri held her arms up like a ballerina and did a delicate 360 so we could see it all, then she grabbed a flute from the rack and poured herself a glass of champagne. "I bought this just for you. I know it's not part of the assignment, but what the hell, I thought you'd enjoy something different, with a little added surprise thrown in."

"You mean it gets better?" My curiosity was running rampant with ideas.

"Absolutely! I know this part of the shoot is for everyone else. We'll have plenty of one-on-one time to do our special pictures, so I want to help make sure everybody else looks good and has fun up here." Terri took a deep swallow of the cold bubbly, then gave us both a devious little grin. "Down at the beach party, however, is a different matter altogether. I'll have to live up to my reputation as a supermodel and show-off a little."

"Or a lot!" Bert smiled, then clinked flutes with Terri. "In these suits, Honey, it's hard not to show off."

"Thank God!" I raised my flute and joined in on the toast.

We watched through the window as Janinne finished her inspection of the newly created libation zone, then she grabbed two bottles of champagne and stepped up to the front door and knocked gently.

"Please come in, Janinne!" Terri said. "You know you really don't need to knock."

"Well," she began as she walked over to us, "I just wanted to make sure the coast was clear. I've heard stories about how supermodels get ready for a photo session." She looked down at the floor and almost blushed. "And, well, after this morning, I just wanted to be sure you weren't involved or something."

"Oh, they're involved all right," Roberta exclaimed. "It's the or something we're keeping them from!"

I wanted to stay as far away from that conversation as possible, so I made myself useful by opening the Taittinger and filling our new flutes. They laughed and carried on

about the mating rituals of supermodels, then excused themselves to get Janinne ready for the camera.

"C'mon in here with me," Terri said with a smile. "I've set aside something wonderful for you to wear for your first set of photos, then something a little more exotic for the beach party, but now it's time to get naked."

"All of us, or just me?" Janinne asked.

"I'm sure Jeffrey has something else to do," Terri replied, then led her entourage into the bedroom, leaving me all alone on the porch.

Finally having a moment to myself, I made a quick check of my camera gear, then pulled out my new toy on loan from JJ and Company. The Sony digital video camera was small and compact, and looked normal on the outside to prying eyes. Inside was a different matter altogether, because this camera also contained a little mega-transmitter. The signal quality would be compromised inside a large building, but in an environment like Chateau Pacific, nothing would deter the satellite hook-up direct to the Imaging Center in San Diego, and JJ. This one way communication link was my ace in the hole in case of any unforeseen complications, or, God forbid, all hell breaks loose. When I quizzed JJ on how something so small could transmit all the way to an orbiting satellite, he just laughed.

I heard a commotion outside and looked out to see Jack and Suzan leading a group of about a dozen women up the walkway to our cabana. Like the pied piper, the rock and roll coming from the boombox he carried gave rhythm and beat to the dance-like steps of his followers. I recognized most of the women he was leading, including Beverly and Cyndi, but the one that brought the biggest smile to my face was Maria. Knowing in my heart that nothing would ever evolve from our attraction to each other, I still couldn't help but enjoy the hallucinations of sheer two-fisted lust exploding in my head, and other parts of my body.

"They're here!" I hollered, then stepped outside to greet the new arrivals. Jack was having too much fun dancing with all the girls, so I approached Suzan first.

"I'm sure Terri has something special in mind for you, so why don't you slip inside and change while I address the troops. As soon as you're ready, come on out and I'll do a quick demo with Terri, then we can get this show on the road."

"Sounds great! If I were any more pumped, I'd explode!"

I just handed her my full glass of champagne and pointed her to the door. It took about three steps to replace the bubbly, and then I became surrounded by a familiar perfume.

"Hi, Jeffrey Mason."

"Good afternoon, Maria with the beautiful smile." And everything else! She had on a spearmint green gauze short set that was wonderfully sheer and clingy. In the warm glow of the tropical shade, her complexion looked more Mediterranean than Mexican, and her full gorgeous eyes took on an almond hue.

"I hope you don't mind, but I'm suppose to help out Kimberly at the beach bar for the party," she said, then hooked her finger around the top button of my shirt, pulled herself a little closer and charmed me with her serpentine ocular weaponry, "So, can I be first?"

"No problem." I paused for a moment just to look at her. "I'm just sorry you have to leave so soon."

"We can fix that," she replied, never losing eye contact.

"Oh, we can?"

"We can if we want to." She leaned forward on her tip-toes and brushed cheeks with me. "Talk to me later," she whispered, then released and walked away.

I just stood there, overwhelmed by the mental pictures of what she said and the real-time vision of her walking away. This time, I was the one sweating. I couldn't help but wonder if the proprietors put "fuck me" powder in the water system or something. In all of my, and our, worldly travels, this place definitely has the strongest sexual overtones I've ever enjoyed. No wonder its so fucking expensive!

"OK ladies," I said, when the song on the boombox ended, "We need to lay out the gameplan, so grab a glass of whatever, if you so choose, and gather round for a moment, please." I gave them enough time to get comfortable, then continued, "The name of the game today is volume. The quicker we get finished up here, the quicker we get to party down there. On the bed you will find a pile of swimsuits. Each and every one of them has to be worn by one of you. When you pass final inspection by Terri, she will record the number of the suit on the release form you will sign, and then send you out to me. I promise not to hurt you! We'll be working over by the hammock and palm trees. Excuse me, ah yes, here comes the fab four now!"

From the door of the cabana, out strutted Terri, Roberta, Suzan, and Janinne in all their radiant glory. Suzan was wearing a white stretch 2pc. thong, Bert was back in her tiny green lace, and Janinne had on a bright orange crochet 2pc thong I thought Terri would never give away. When Terri first tried on that orange suit in the studio, she acted just like Roberta did inside, plus a little extra. Thank God we were alone.

"See there, ladies, you have nothing to fear. These swimsuits can make almost anyone look good!" Thank God Terri didn't hear me. "This will be quick and easy. In the coming publications, each and every time a photograph of you is used, you will be paid. Me, too! Please put a findable address on your release form, or at least a phone number where you can get a message, if you want your money. If you don't want your money, please send it to us, we like this place! After all the suits have been photographed, each of you gets to choose your favorite one to wear to the beach party. We'll shoot the fun stuff and group shots down there. Any questions? OK ladies, salute!"

Everyone raised their glass and we consummated the toast to a good shoot. Jack and the girls joined me as I watched Maria and the others file into the cabana to get ready. Terri came straight up to me, put her arms around my neck, and kissed me full on the lips.

"I thought you wanted a demonstration for the recruits."

"This kind of demonstration has always been my favorite!" We kissed again, then held each other in a moment of silent bliss.

"I remember," she whispered.

"The recruits will be OK." I held her at arms length, but couldn't let go. "Besides, I wouldn't want you to give away all your secrets."

She pulled me closer, blinked twice, and looked straight into my soul.

"Silly boy, my secret is you!"

Jack looked surprised and confused when I handed him the Sony video camera. He fully understood the mechanics of the instrument, just not the motivation behind my actions.

"I'm no cameraman, Jeffrey!"

"You don't have to be," I replied. "You're the partyman, so just be my second pair of eyes and record the party, the babes, and the people. Hell, just have fun! What you're shooting is not for anyone else but us." And the CIA, of course, but why confuse the issue! "Don't waste your time taking shots of me, but some candids of the crowd watching us work the beach bar would be cool. I'd love to capture the expressions on the faces of Christian and his VIP's when they watch Terri and Bert do their thing."

"Consider it done, brother-in-law!" Jack looked over my shoulder and a huge smile spread across his face. "Oh my God, you're in for trouble now." And he walked away.

I turned to see Terri and Maria walking straight towards me. My heart bounced off of the pit of my stomach, then returned to its normal position when I saw them laughing and smiling. If this was going to be an execution, at least it was going to be congenial.

"Maria says she has to hit and run, so I decked her out in something awesome to work the beach party in. What do you think about her face?"

Face? She really had a face? The electric lime one piece thong looked like it had been spray painted over her hot Latin body. Side by side, Terri was just about as tall as Maria, and was the more beautiful, but Maria had an animal sexuality that overwhelmed the situation, and had an international marketability that your classic American beauty just doesn't always have. I mean to take nothing away from the true love of my life, but to have Maria in our stable could reap some sizable rewards in our near future. She had every asset to make her the next phenom in female sexuality, or most men's version there of.

"Jeffrey!"

"Awesome, Angel. Just awesome." Maria locked eyes with me, winked, then blew me a kiss with just the slightest pout. "I'm ready to rock-n-roll pretty lady, so come on over to the hammock and let's get started."

"Just relax, and have fun!" Terri gave Maria a quick European hug, then patted me on the butt and headed inside. Jack suddenly appeared on my left and put his monstrous arm around my shoulders.

"On film, just like you wanted. We will look back on this and laugh, won't we!"

Maria grabbed me by the hand and led me over to the hammock before I could respond. She walked straight to the hammock, turned and sat down, then put her fingers through the belt loops of my shorts and pulled me closer

"Why do you look at me the way you do?" Her eyes flickered both questions and innuendo in their fire. "She's beautiful, yet you still look at me. Why?"

"Yes, she's beautiful and I love her very much, but you are so unique. I want to take outrageous pictures of you and spread them all over the world. I know that sounds like bullshit, but considering what's been going on in my life recently, I see no reason not to pursue this, too!" I gently touched her face with my left hand, and made sure we had eye-lock "You're a very sexy woman, and I hope this will be just the first of many sessions together. Any problems with that?"

"Only one," she said, then rubbed both hands up my abdomen, under my shirt. "I'm leaving tomorrow morning for San Diego."

"Then I guess we'll have to work this out pretty quick."

"Can we?"

"We can if we want to!"

I backed away a few steps, then raised the Nikon and zoomed in on her face. Oh yeah, Terri had done a terrific job on Maria's eyes, because they jumped right through the lens and captivated me in the viewfinder. She took direction well as I worked her through a series of very sensuous poses. My favorite shots were when I got her to lay across the hammock on her stomach, then backed off to get a full length view. They didn't show much of the swimsuit, but God what a body!

I knew Jack was around, but had lost track of him until I heard him scream.

"Hey, you sorry mother-fucker! What the fuck do you think you're doing!" He pounced into the brush like a big cat, and returned with a disgruntled Arab in an inescapable head-lock. "This is a private party, asshole. Unless you have an invitation, you'd better hit the ground running!" Jack jerked him around a few times, then slung Mahmood to the turf like a rag doll. The mighty Muslim bounced twice, then bolted into the jungle like a scalded dog.

"Bravo!" Maria exclaimed. "Just because he is Christian's associate, that nijo de puta thinks he can take liberties with the staff and guests. Your actions may not endear you to Mr. Morea, but you are now champion to us all." She bounced over to Jack and gave him a big hug and kiss, then did the same thing to me. "You must be careful," she whispered. "Christian and his friends are very dangerous when your back is turned."

"Thanks, I'll keep my eyes open and my back covered. Now, let's get back to work."

I leaned her against one of the palm trees and finished her session with standing poses. To get carried away and spend too much time with Maria would be unfair to the rest of the girls and could arouse suspicion on the home front, so I chose to cut it short. She gave me another hug and kiss, then headed off to the beach bar to get it ready for the party. I guess she knew I would be staring at her gorgeous ass, because she stopped, looked back over her shoulder, and winked at me. All I could do was smile and wave.

The next hour proved to be a blur of beautiful women in various poses wearing sexy swimwear. It's a good thing Jack was making a video, because things were moving way too fast to keep a good mental picture. Of course, Cyndi just had to show off her tits, then insisted on doing some full nudes, Penthouse style, for her many fans, but she was the only exception. Everyone else played it straight, then dashed back inside to change and do it all over again. Janinne and Suzan were wonderful to work with, and both left any inhibitions they may have had inside with Terri, but the star of the day had to be Roberta. She exploded through a front closure bikini top secured by mere plastic, then finished the session topless and tantalizing, urging Jack on with little suggestions of where she intended to place his penis in the very near future for the ultimate personal massage.

After all was said and done, Jack and I took a stroll to smoke a joint, and naturally I led him to the spot where Mahmood had surfaced. Once we found the right location, recognizing the one-man trail was a snap. JJ had supplied me with a map of secured trails Prince Wafik had made for his solitary walks, and I'm sure this one tied in somewhere, and all of them led to and from the villa on the mountain. After a momentary flashback of a solitary soldier, with only three rounds left in his M-16, stalking an NVA patrol of at least a dozen or more that had ambushed his jump team, I found myself facing the stark reality that this time, I was totally unarmed. No gun, no knife, just a video camera that lets me talk to a satellite. Wow! What a fucking deal!

"Where do you think this goes?" Thank God for Jack! Now, I had to respond.

"If we followed up and to the left, we'd be at Christian's villa," I said flatly. "Up and to the right, I imagine we'd backdoor a few private balconies then wind up close to the pavilion. Twice I've been told Christian has a private conduit of trails that allow him to circumvent the property without detection. This is probably one of them. Jesus, it's not like they're trying to hide them or anything. This looks like it was trimmed with a weed-eater."

When I turned and looked at Jack, he had a peculiar expression on his face. He was looking at me, but he was also trying to look into me.

"You've got a damn fine pair of eyes. Is that what being a photographer is all about?"

"That's what staying alive is all about." For some strange reason, I didn't expect him to understand, but I was wrong.

"Amen!" He held up his big paw, we exchanged high fives, and another warrior's confidential alliance was permanently sealed.

"Hey guys!" We both turned to see Bert, standing on the steps, waving herself out of the tiny green lace top. "We're ready to go party, so get your shit together and let's hit it!

Want to be popular at a beach party? Show up with a case of cold beer! Want to really be popular at a beach party? Show up with sixteen knockouts in nasty little swimsuits! When we made our grand entrance, the applause from the guys and other guests and staff drowned out the reggae music blaring from the speakers in the bar. After some serious touchy-feely with their significant others, the girls kicked it into the next gear and got down to blatant partying. Everybody was dancing and carrying on while I went about my business taking candid pictures of the party, the crowd, and the girls. The fab four stayed real close together, and seemed to be the epicenter of the festivities as the rest of the crowd swirled around them. Even Count Von Spengler displaced himself from his barstool and was dancing around in the middle of everything shaking his booty. Christian and Mahmood were nowhere to be seen, and since most everyone else looked familiar, I concluded the special party of VIPs was yet to arrive.

"Hey, what's wrong with me?"

I turned around to see Mr. Stud Puppie himself in a pair of Speedo posing tights doing an upper body flex. He worked through three or four classic stances, then stuck out his hand and grinned.

"I'm Tony Candola."

"Hi, I'm Jeffrey Mason."

"I know who you are, cause you're the main reason I'm here." He shifted his weight around in what looked like an effort to get more comfortable, then continued. "My agent told me about your photo shoot, drug me down here over a week ago to get primed, and now you're not interested. What's the deal?"

"Did your agent also tell you that this assignment is for a swimwear manufacturer that only makes women's suits?" The look on his face was answer enough. "I've agreed to do some shots for the club, but that was only finalized yesterday." I located the Grand Dame standing at the bar, watching us like a hawk, and made a slight head motion her way. "Is she your agent?"

"She's certainly not my girlfriend! That old bitch has more plastic body parts than a fucking Toyota! Oh well, I guess I should have known better. She fucked me over to get me here, and has done nothing but fuck me ever since." He took a moment to compose himself, then a devious smile spread across his face. "That's OK, she's a real screamer. I stuck my big dick so far up her ass last night, she won't shit again til she's back in L.A. tomorrow."

"Is she the jealous type?" Wheels were starting to turn.

"If it was up to her, she wouldn't let me hold my own dick to take a leak! Why?"

"What do you think of those two hot little nymphets with the big tits?"

"Cyndi and Bev? Hell man, I'd fuck both of them right here, right now, but Jennifer told them 'hands off' in no uncertain terms. You got a plan?"

"Go tell Boss Momma you're in the shoot for the club, then meet me over by the shower. She's gonna be really pissed off at both of us, but, what the fuck, I'm not the one that has to sleep with her!"

Tony made a bee-line over to the Grand Dame, and I went over to set up my strategy with Cyndi and Bev. They were more than willing to volunteer, especially when they realized Tony was the intended target of our little coup. I left them giggling and plotting, touched base with Jack to make sure the video was ready, then made my way over to the bar. Terri, Bert, and the rest were still totally inundated by their worshipping horde, but at least JC was there to run interference if they needed it. I was just about to create a big enough diversion to allow them a moment of peace, but only a moment.

"Hello Mr. Mason, I'm Jennifer St. John, Talent Unlimited, L.A., New York, and Paris." I have to admit, with a body and face hand crafted by the most talented surgeons in the world, this old broad was pretty hot. Whatever deficiencies she may have in the personality department, she made up for with cleavage and cunning. "Tony says you want to use him in some of your photographs, so, do we need to sit down and talk business first. I pride myself on taking care of all my client's needs."

"Good for you. Since I'm not sure exactly where these shots will be used, for now I just need Tony to sign a standard release so we can try to market them. If nothing else, he'll have something new for his portfolio."

"A spec deal?" She got a little huffy and stuck her tits out a little more. "I would never advise a client to work without getting paid for his time!"

"You're not paying me for mine. In reality, you're getting a freebie on somebody else's nickel, and you know it. I don't mind helping Tony out, but just like everybody else involved in this, it's a spec deal, or its no deal. You choose." And I walked away. Within three steps, Tony was right beside me, heading for the shower.

"That was great! What do you want me to do?"

"Go take a shower, and expect some company."

"Then what do you want me to do?"

"Nothing! Let them do all the work."

Tony worked his way through the crowd to the shower, turned it on, and stepped in. The Grand Dame was still standing over by the bar, so she wouldn't be able to intervene until the damage was done, or at least well under way. I maneuvered myself into position, made sure Jack was ready, then signaled the girls. Tony's chiseled physique took on an Adonis glow when wet, and proved to be the perfect prop for my two paid assassins. Cyndi and Beverly appeared out of nowhere and began rubbing their hands all over his sleek body. As soon as the girls got totally wet, off came their suits, and they continued his full body massage with their breasts, buns, and various other body parts. The crowd was starting to really get into what was happening, and unfortunately so was Tony, so Cyndi slid her hand down inside the front of his Speedos and released the monster. Like Pumba through the hyenas, the Grand Dame plowed her way through the crowd and threw herself, mega-buck designer bikini, cover-up and all, over her precious puppie to protect him from those nasty little sluts. I immediately started clapping, hollering, and whistling just like at the pool bar, and so did the rest of the crowd, giving Cyndi and Bev an avenue of escape. Tony lifted Jennifer up and laid her across his left shoulder, then started waving and blowing kisses to his fans. I took a few more pictures, then just had to stop and laugh.

"Like I said before, you're a cruel dude." Jack was laughing his ass off, but when I conveyed Tony's story, especially about Jennifer's impaction, he dropped straight to his knees. "No more, please!"

"You guys are awful!" Suzan had a scolding look reminiscent of every old elementary school teacher God ever created. "Jennifer is as close to a regular here as can be expected. This is her fourth trip this year, and the tab she signs tomorrow will easily be in excess of twenty five thousand dollars."

"And how many different boys has she brought along with her on these trips?"

"Four." Suzan looked at both of us, then had to bite her lip to keep from laughing, too.

The party continued on with lots of drinking, laughing, and dirty dancing in the ankle-deep sand. I wandered the perimeter, being the voyeur, and getting more candid shots of singles, couples, and intimate little groupings of revelers. Terri and Janinne were inseparable throughout it all, which made me glad. It's really hard to entertain your girlfriend and photograph all these other people at the same time, especially when she's already the center of attention. I got some great shots of the two of them partying and dancing together, but what intrigued me the most was the fire and intensity in their eye contact with each other. Whatever had started in Janinne's office yesterday was certainly spilling over into all the events of today.

"Hey everybody, let's limbo!" Kimberly was jumping up and down with a long bamboo pole above her head, then started shaking her butt to the beat of the limbo music. She drafted two studly looking volunteers to hold the bar at her desired level, then made the first pass underneath. I had the perfect camera angle to get some awesome shots of her and the rest of the participants as they danced, jiggled, and hopped their way under the limbo bar. Of course, Cyndi just had to do it topless, which set a precedent for all that followed. I was enjoying the grand hallucination through my viewfinder, when I became aware of Roberta standing next to me.

"I'm heading for some refreshments," she said. "Can I bring you something to drink?"

"Sure, but aren't you going to make a pass under the bamboo?"

"Fuck no! With tits like these, I don't jog and I don't limbo. Center of gravity, you know, makes both activities a little too risky." She captivated me with a big Cheshire cat grin, then leaned closer, "I have a hard enough time just keeping my balance in a pair of those six inch 'fuck me' pumps Jack loves for me to wear around the bedroom."

"Whew, now that's a vision I'd love to see!"

"Anytime, Jeffrey," she replied. "Anytime at all."

Maria was walking around the crowd with a magnum bottle of champagne in one hand and a jug of white wine in the other refilling every empty glass someone was holding, when she purposely got my attention and pointed out to sea. At the opening of the bay, two cigarette boats were heading our way and closing fast. Even over the blaring of the dance music, I could hear the deep rumbling of the high powered, customized V8's as they approached at near top speed.. Jack must have heard them too, because when I turned to get his attention, he was already zoomed in on the ultra expensive performance boats aimed right towards us. It was easy to recognize Christian driving the first boat as he made a high speed turn dangerously close to the shoreline, then looped around to the pier to dock. The second boat made the same maneuver at a lesser speed, then pulled up along side Christian's boat and docked as well. I counted five men in the second boat, and three others beside Christian in the first. As soon as they disembarked and were all standing on the pier, two of Christian's boat boys hopped in the Scarabs and moved them into the sea cave. At this distance, it would be difficult to get a positive ID of who's who using my 80-200mm zoom at full power, but I snapped off some shots anyway.

With all the digital enhancement capabilities of the Image Center in San Diego, JJ might be able to make out a few of the faces in the small crowd of Christian's associates. From my vantage point, all I could tell from their dark hair and coloring was that they were either Arab or jungle Indian of some sort.

"Colombian pigs," Maria said, standing right next to me. "They are always the first to arrive for Christian's little get togethers, and he demands they be treated like royalty. The three men with Christian are the important ones, the other pendejos are only bodyguards, but all of them are pigs. When all the whores arrive for the party tonight, you will be able to see for yourself." Then she turned and walked away.

"Think those are the VIP's?" Terri got right up next to me and put her arms around my waist. It seemed like forever since I'd held her, so I put both arms around her and we embraced, camera and all.

"That's what Maria just told me. She says they're Colombians, and that I need to keep a close eye on you when they're around."

"You always do, lover. Before the light goes, I want to do my special trick for the camera, then sooner or later, you'll need to take me back to our cottage."

"Sure, Angel. What's up?"

"You," she whispered. "All this attention makes me horny!"

I kept a watchful eye on the elevated walkway leading to the boathouse waiting for the guests to arrive, but after 10 or 15 minutes, I came to the conclusion that they must be having some sort of meeting either there or in the sea cave. Wrong! I was totally surprised to see all of them coming down the trail from Christian's villa. No way could they have gotten past me, and since no VIP is going to climb the sheer rockface the boathouse is attached to, there had to be another secret conduit that connects the two. Without bringing the camera to my face, again I guesstimated distance and exposure, and fired off a few frames of the group. This time, Mahmood had joined them, and had obviously told Christian about our little encounter, because the petite Frenchman was strutting around like the leader of a L.A. street gang, with all his big brother's bully friends to protect him. It was easy to tell who the bodyguards were because they made no effort what-so-ever to conceal the firepower they were carrying. Gang and all, Christian walked straight up to me and dug his right index finger into my chest.

"I told you not to fuck with my friends, asshole!"

"No, you told me not to bother your special guests. This stupid mother-fucker was playing peeping tom, and just happened to get caught. In reality, I wasn't fucking with him, he was fucking with me. You should train your subordinates to be more professional, don't you agree, Senor," and nodded at the gold-laden Colombian standing beside Christian.

"My people are very well trained," was his stoic reply in near-perfect English. "Privacy is important to us all, Jeffrey Mason. We will respect yours, and you will respect ours. Agreed, my friend?"

"Absolutely!" I offered my right hand, and he shook it like the leader he was.

"Good! Now where are all these beautiful women I've heard so much about?" The Colombian leader put his arm around my shoulder, then led me and his entourage over to the bar, leaving Christian and Mahmood alone to swill in their own flatulence.

The party had definitely shifted into a higher gear of intoxicated frivolity as everyone was getting more involved in dancing and carrying on with each other. Jack and Roberta were in the limelight as she did her best to impress the crowd with her world-class dirty dancing techniques. He was having a great time with the video camera taking close-ups of her bountiful attributes, and those of Terri, Janinne, and all the other women in his surrounding vicinity, with the occasional swing of the lens across the crowd at the bar. I shared a glass of champagne with the Colombians, then excused myself to continue working, and to check out what the boat boys were doing. They showed up in a group, then began separately working their way through the crowd, doing their best to ferret out every female, available or not, and make some sort of contact. I was working my way to Terri and Janinne when I heard a scream and then the same kind of 'crack' only made when fist meets face. I turned to see one of the boat boys holding what was left of his nose with one hand and trying to fend off Roberta with the other. She landed another haymaker that took him off his feet, then proceeded to literally kick his ass until he managed to dig himself out of the sand and run for his life. The only thing that kept her from chasing him down and kicking his ass again was Jack holding on to her shoulders. When I reached them, she was still livid.

"That sorry little mother-fucker tried to stick his hand up my puss! First he dances up to me and offers me a vial, then when I turn my head to check it out, he grabs a hand full of clit and tries to finger fuck me!"

"Cool it, Rambo," Jack said, doing his best to maintain his composure while calming his wife down. "After the way you rearranged his face, he won't be getting any more pussy for a long time. I'm proud of you, Baby."

"Bert, Bert, what happened?" Terri was first of the others to reach the scene, followed closely by Janinne. "My God, are you hurt!"

"Only insulted, Honey." she replied, trying to regain herself. "We're attached to the greatest gift God ever created, and I reserve the right to share that gift with only those I choose." She got a glazed look to her normally warm brown eyes and raised a clinched fist face level, "But God pity the fool that tries to take it from me!"

I left Bert in the good hands of her friends, and went to inspect the impact point. I dropped down on a knee, raked my fingers through the sand, and came up with five amber vials with black plastic lids. On quick inspection, each appeared to be filled with well manicured cocaine. When I reached the others, I exposed the contents of my hand to everyone, then turned to Janinne, "What's going on?"

"Bait for Bimbos!" She had an expression that was half anger and half hopelessness. "Christian uses all means possible to lure people to his sick little sex parties. Free coke, free smoke, free whores, high stakes gambling, whatever you desire, he's got."

"And you can bet your sweet little ass he gets most of it from the people who just came in on those cigarette boats." I thought I had said that just to myself, but everybody's eye contact proved me wrong.

"Absolutely," was Janinne's reply. "Who do you think bought those expensive boats! I've made no authorization for their purchase, yet within the last six months, we now possess five of them. I'm no virgin to sex or drugs, and I've known all along that Christian supplies all the party favors for the entire club, but this is getting out of hand. I've warned all the staff, and we try to discourage all our guests from attending his drug-induced orgy, but he still lures quite a few hearty souls into his personal little hell."

"Is that why you close the club for his private parties?" Terri beat me to the punch.

"Oh, we're not really closed, Honey. They book and pay for maximum capacity, no matter how many people show up, which is fine by me. We cut down to an all volunteer skeleton crew, and everybody else gets a paid vacation. The problem is the going away party he throws for our normal guests that gets them involved in racketeering and rape with his Colombian buddies. How long is it going to take for the authorities to figure out what's going on! My God, they could seize this place and arrest us all."

"I doubt it, kiddo," was Bert's flat remark. "This is Mexico! Down here, a six figure 'donation' usually buys more than just a cup of coffee and a night in the Lincoln bedroom. In case of a problem, there's always the good old cash bonus to fix something or make something happen. Greed is a powerful motivator."

"So is death." This time I was positive that nobody heard me. Once these people have bought and paid for someone, that person either does what they're told to do, or disappears off the face of the earth. The amount of danger this club was in probably could be directly related to how deeply Christian was involved with the Colombians. Jack grabbed a vial, filled the lid with coke, then snorted the whole thing in one nostril. He grabbed his nose, fought off a serious gag, and turned red as a beet.

"Holy shit, this is the real thing!" Jack shook his head a few times, slammed his glass of champagne, then passed the vile to Roberta. She indulged herself with a small hit to each side, a slam of Taittinger, then passed the vile to Terri. Be it monkey see monkey do, or just 'what the fuck', Terri duplicated Bert's bilateral technique, and also the champagne slam. I'd never seen her do anything more than wine and a little smoke, so this was a unique situation in more ways than one. Not being my particular drug of choice at this point in my life, I passed on the invitation to partake, and quickly decided this party needed a change in direction.

"Hey Angel, what about that surprise? I think the timing and lighting are perfect."

"Ooh yeah, baby, I'm really ready now. Let's go over to the shower." She grabbed my hand and led me over to the scene of the crime. After waiting until everything was ready, including the entire crowd at the bar with front row seats, Terri winked at me and turned on the water. The music was blaring and the crowd was whooping and hollering as the yellow pigment of her swimsuit dissolved right before my lens, leaving her hot body wet and naked, with only sheer lace separating her from pure nudity. Everyone went ballistic as she danced and swayed to the music throughout the entire song, especially Janinne. I filled two complete rolls with classic shots well worthy of any publication, and living testimony to her God given magnificent charms that never cease to amaze me. Jack followed my lead and circled around during the performance to include the Colombians in the shots, but neither one of us strayed from the main attraction for more than a brief moment. Terri had the spotlight, and she knew exactly what to do with it. If she had any fear at all of the Colombians, that's not what she was showing them. When the music stopped, she bounced up

John McCraw

and down and waved a few times, then ran over and literally jumped into my arms, forcing me to grab her ass with my spare hand to keep from dropping her or the camera. She kissed me passionately, then nuzzled her face into mine and whispered,

"It's time for you to take me home, Jeffrey." No explanation was necessary, only a quick wave good-bye to our friends and a short walk to paradise.

A LITTLE SEXPARTY

Dinner proved to be almost as loud and rowdy as the beach party, but now everyone was cleaned, reamed, and dressed to scream into the night. Terri's green spaghetti strap silk sheath barely covered her ass, and left no doubt that she had nothing on underneath except a matching thong. And Bert! God have mercy on us all! She had on a short white racer-back tank dress made of ribbed stretch cotton that simply demanded that everyone take notice of her gorgeous body. Just like at the airport, she parted the crowd like Moses and the Red Sea everywhere she walked. While the girls were casually perusing the buffet, I reached over and clinked glasses with Jack.

"You're a lucky man, Jack Taylor."

"In more ways than one, brother-in-law, in more ways than one. I've got what's left of my health, enough money to be comfortable, and I'm married to the perfect woman." He drained his wine glass, refilled both of ours, then raised his glass to her. Either she noticed, or her radar was really working good, because she acknowledged his toast with a smile, a wink, and a cute little shake of her breasts. "See what I mean! And the very best part is that she fucks even better than she looks."

"Excuse me, but I'm gonna have to think about that for a while."

"You just go right ahead, Jeffrey. Even after all these years, I still think about it all the time. Once you and Terri have been married for a while, you'll see what I mean. If you think its good now, bro, just wait."

I certainly didn't have to wait long. Terri and Bert had made their selections and were heading back our way when they were joined by Janinne, wearing a very sheer lilac gauze peasant dress. I love breasts that move when a woman walks, and our ladies were absolute poetry in motion. Jack and I must have had real shit-eating expressions on our faces, because Terri stopped cold at the edge of the table and just stood there giving us both her sneaky little grin.

"What are you guys up to now?"

"Just watching everybody watch you, Honey," I replied. "Seems like you've got the whole crowd still buzzing over your performance."

"Thanks, baby, but I don't think it's me they're buzzing over." She put both hands on the table and leaned forward, exposing her cleavage to me and her tight little ass to the rest of the room. "Hey, I'm still a little buzzed myself from our performance in the privacy of our bedroom, not to mention all the little party favors."

"Amen to both, Honey." Roberta exclaimed, then nuzzled Jack with her majestic breasts. "Kind of like the good old days, right baby?"

"Better!" Jack sat Roberta down in his lap and gave her a loving kiss on the lips. "At least I'll be able to walk tomorrow without a handful of percodan and a bottle of tequila. Fuck, if I'd had shit this good while I was playing, we definitely would have gone to the Pro Bowl a few more times."

"Or still playing?" I knew better, but still had to ask.

"Fuck no!" Roberta slammed her fist down on the table, then cradled Jack's face in her hands. "It's not a game anymore, it's more like orchestrated manslaughter for big profit. Those sorry bastards in Detroit knew he had a career-ending neck injury in pre-season, but kept him shot up with steroids and Lydicaine just to keep him on the field until they got their money's worth, then lied about the whole damn thing when they tried to cut him."

"No shit, even the General Manager lied under oath that he was unaware of the extent of my injuries until we produced the doctor's report, the doctor, and two witnesses that were there at the meeting when he decided to fuck me."

"His perjury cost the team a cool two million cash, and every penny counted against the salary cap because they were forced to carry Jack on injured reserve for the entire following season. I'd like to think it also helped that stupid fuck to eventually lose his job!"

"Amen! All the talent in the world can't help if the GM doesn't know how to win."

"And has the backbone of a used condom," Roberta added. "Just thinking about that asshole pisses me off."

"Hey, cool it!" It was definitely time for me to change the conversation. "Speaking of assholes, don't you think we need to check out Christian's party tonight?"

"After everything I've said, you'd still subject Terri and Bert to all that decadence!" Janinne grabbed Terri's hand and gently held on to it.

"Not to participate necessarily, just to observe."

"Why you kinky little mother-fucker," Jack said, behind another shit-eating grin.

"I don't think anyone is going to mess with us as long as the guys are around," Terri said. "I have to agree with Jeffrey, I want to see what goes on."

"Me, too!" Bert replied. "As long as I'm with the right people, and can control the situation, I've been known to enjoy a good fuck party."

"What makes you think you can control the situation?" Janinne's voice was near panic.

"These two men right here," was her reply, then turned to Terri and spoke in her best deep Southern drawl, "After the incident at our previous encounter, I do think we should go change into something that prohibits easy accessibility, if you know what I mean."

"Absolutely! For some strange reason, I'm not very hungry for dinner, and the champagne tastes wonderful, so let's go take a walk and get safe and cutesy."

"Sounds good to me," Roberta replied. "We'll hit my place first, then yours if we can find it! I guess we'll meet y'all out at the beach bar in about twenty minutes."

And they were off into the night, leaving Janinne alone with Jack and me. She didn't say a word, just quietly ate her meal, sipped her Macon Villages, and watched the remaining crowd of guests thin out in a matter of minutes. She finally turned, made direct eye contact, and spoke to me.

"I want you to promise me that at least one of you is in the presence of those two girls at all times tonight. Do not, I repeat, do not leave them alone at any time while you're at Christian's villa. Women have been forcibly carried upstairs and gang raped at these little affairs! By the way, that's where the serious fucking goes on, upstairs. So when you've seen enough sex, drugs, and rock-n-roll, please leave, and consider yourself very fortunate to have survived. I understand your curiosity. I, too, was curious once, but never again. What started out as sexy playfulness got very ugly, very quickly, and I was damn lucky to escape unharmed. You'll know when it's time to leave, believe me."

"I appreciate your concern, and all the insights, but at this point in time, I seriously doubt Christian and his friends would risk an International incident and certain death over an attempted rape and subsequent murder."

"Don't kid yourself, Jeffrey. Something as simple as a boating accident could cover-up anything! No bodies, no evidence, no nothing, just a brief report filed with the local authorities and a copy sent to the State Department. Whatever the outcome of the following investigation, you'll still be just as dead, and Christian will still be here arranging his next party." She took a moment to sip some wine and regain her composure, then continued. "I'm sorry to unload on you about Christian, but Terri is so precious, and these parties just scare me to death."

"Sounds like you've been down this road before, but please, don't worry about Terri and Bert. There will be way too many witnesses around for them to try anything really stupid tonight."

"I hope you're right, for everyone's sake. Well, Suzan and I are hosting the lingerie party in the disco for the rest of our guests, so I'd better go make sure everything is ready and crank up the music so people will start showing up." Janinne stood and prepared herself to leave by fluffing her skirt and tossing her hair.

"Lingerie party?" Jack's eyes got as big as his smile. "And what will you be wearing?"

"As little as possible," she replied, then turned back to me and winked. "Roberta's not the only one who knows how to enjoy a good fuck party." And she sashayed across the floor and down the steps to The Cave.

When we could breathe again, Jack and I moved away from the table and headed over to the main bar for a drink. Our telepathy must have been working overtime, because neither one of us could speak, yet we both knew exactly what the other was thinking. After the word "champagne" rolled off my tongue to the bartender, I finally was able to make a sentence.

"Do you remember what you told me about Roberta?"

"Oh yeah. Do you really think Janinne could be the same way?"

"I doubt if we'll ever find out, but, God what a glorious hallucination."

"Amen!"

"Praying, gentlemen?" Jean Claude appeared out of nowhere and joined us at the bar. He was obviously in a great mood and just slightly toasted. "Did the girls run off, or are you guys out trolling."

"Both!" Jack replied.

"Actually, we're just killing time while the girls change for the party," I said.

"Wonderful! I can't wait to see them all dolled-up for the lingerie extravaganza!"

"I don't think so. They're getting all covered up for the party at Christian's instead."

"You're not stupid enough to let them go, are you?" JC was on the verge of ballistic.

"Not alone! With us, of course." Jack slammed his fist down into the bar. "Does everybody think we're just a couple of fucking morons incapable of protecting our mates! I seriously doubt some asshole from Colombia is willing to kill or be killed over some strange pussy. I'm with Jeffrey, all this bad mouthin' of Christian and his buddies only makes me want to get up there quicker and find out what's really going on. Since we have no intention of becoming fuck fodder for a bunch of South American weirdoes, can't you understand we're only going up there to look around and party a little before we choose to leave."

"Hey, if all you want to do is look, I can show you how to do that without getting involved with everybody else." JC made a quick look around, then huddled closer. "The villa is built on a man-made plateau, and part of it was physically carved out of the side of the mountain, making three sides of it rock and the other all glass. About half-way up, the main trail makes a dip through a ravine, then curves around to the villa. If you follow the ravine up about 70 meters, it starts getting real steep, then you come across a solitary, huge old tree at the top of the embankment to your left. Climb up to the base of the tree, and you'll be able to look down onto the patio area and main floor of the villa, and straight ahead into the upstairs loft bedroom. We refer to the loft as the 'flying fuck room' because its total design is for sex. Like I said, the front is all glass!"

Jack and I stared at each other, then back at JC. He noticed our curious expressions, then made another quick look around and smiled at us.

"Janinne and Suzan had to appear on demand of his Assholiness one afternoon, and I was worried, so I discovered that vantage-point out of need to know. About a week later, Christian was away with his girlfriend, so Janinne held a special staff meeting at the villa so we could all get acquainted with the numerous little perks Prince Wafik and Christian had installed in their fortress of solitude. I especially was fond of the AV room, with all its monitors, remote zoom lens cameras and recorders, lots of recorders, and a hot little AVID digital editing system. Whatever he's doing, he's bloody well equipped!"

"Since you're so well informed, how did Christian and his VIP's get from the boathouse to the villa without walking past us at the beach bar?"

"Simple, Jeffrey! There's a passageway that leads from the boathouse into the sea cave, and a stairwell direct from the cave up to the wine cellar in the basement of the villa. The Prince didn't want the extent of his drinking and whoring well known to his entourage and wives, so he had the 'escape route' created for security purposes."

"Looks like it's serving that same purpose tonight." I took my glass of champagne from the bar, walked to the edge of the steps, and looked out over the bay. Pulling up to dock at the pier was your basic 50 foot party yacht, complete with lights, loud music, and happy people. It tied-up only long enough to disembark about two dozen or more of its most rambunctious revelers, then chugged off back to sea to continue its quest for the perfect party.

"Local dignitaries and whores." Jack was simple and right to the point. He put his arm around my shoulder, then handed me a fresh bottle of Mumm. "Brother-in-law, it's time we found our women and made our move before all the good seats are gone."

"Amen, brother! All this talk makes me want to be the first one at the beach bar, if you know what I mean. I don't treasure the thought of them waiting for us all alone."

"No shit! I may not be able to run, but I can walk pretty damn fast and not spill a drop, so come on, we gotta go!"

Jean Claude bid us a fond adieu with a reminder that the lingerie party in the disco would be going on until the wee hours of the morning, so if we got finished early at Christian's, to please feel free to come on down and join in the festivities. We basically brushed him off with a nod and a wave, then headed down the blue trail towards my cabana and the beach bar. We were barely outside of the ring of illumination from the pavilion, when Jack stopped to take a double hit from another vial, then tried to pass it on to me.

"No thanks, man."

"What's wrong, Brother-in-law, you don't like this shit?"

"Let's just say, I've done way more than my share and lived to talk about it. Truthfully, it's not that I don't like it, I just don't want any!"

"Good for you, Jeffrey. I guess I tried everything legal or illegal to make me bigger-better-faster-stronger while I was playing, and I've smoked pot since high school, but this nasty little white powder has been my favorite party drug for a long time. The year I got traded to Cleveland, we wound up playing Houston for the Division Championship in a fucking blizzard, both on the field and off. A bunch of us pooled our money and bought a pound of outrageous blow for the game and celebration to follow. Of course, we kicked their ass, but by the time we finished all the toot, it was the next Saturday, and Houston came back up to Cleveland as a wildcard and kicked our sorry butts right out of the playoffs. Moon and Givens had a fucking field day against us."

"Exactly my point. In the long run, it's gonna get ya!"

"Yeah, but you know what they say, 'Life's a journey, so enjoy the ride!'"

"I do have to admit, some of the excursions have been pretty fun." I pulled out a joint and lit it before we continued our trek down to the bar. Even at our rapid pace, by the time we reached our destination, a second joint had been consumed and the champagne was open and flowing. The beach bar was deserted, so I was happy to see we had beaten the girls to our rendezvous point, but by the time they finally blessed us with their presence, all the champagne was gone, Jack's vial was empty, and the last joint was only a cloud.

"Hey guys, what's shakin'!" Terri and Bert looked way too happy as they casually strolled up to us like they were on time instead of 30 minutes late. My baby put her arms around my neck, pressed the full length of her luscious body into mine, and kissed me like she wanted to make love right here, right now. Considering the fact she had on the romper from hell with at least two hundred tiny little buttons, by the time her vital parts would have been exposed, her mood would have swung in another direction completely. I was very familiar with her happy-go-lucky playfulness from previous champagne induced sexual encounters, but the expressive nature of her eyes was unique to me. Oh, I'd seen that glazed-over look before, just never on her precious face.

"God, baby, you feel so good," I whispered.

"I know that's right! Ooh Jeffrey, I tingle all over! Whatever planet I'm on, I like it."

"I'll remind you of that in the morning, Honey." She held me tightly as I rubbed my hands all over her back and buns. I peered over the top of her head to see Jack and Roberta doing the same thing, enjoying a passionate embrace, when suddenly they both burst into outrageous laughter.

"She's definitely ready to go," he said, when he could control himself. "Damn, look at all this body armor! Bra, panties, bodysuit, shorts, and a shirt that ties and buttons. There ain't nobody gettin' in there, and I couldn't reach a fucking thing!"

"Bingo!" Roberta stood back, did her best imitation of a runway turn, then a Vanna White "Ta Da" for all to enjoy. "Like I said, nobody gets in without an invitation."

"I'm really kind of excited," Terri exclaimed. "I've never been to a real orgy before."

"It's just a party," Roberta replied, "only a lot friendlier. Just remember the golden rule, Honey. You've got all the gold, you make all the rules."

Arms intertwined with the girls in the middle, the four of us headed up the trail to Christian's villa. Jack got into a few tales of some of the NFL orgies he and Bert had attended, and she amazed me with a story about a certain well respected team owner that routinely supplies the opposition a free, all-night booze, drug, and fuck-for-all at one of his hotels the night before all important home games.

"That's one way to maintain the best home-field record in the league," I said flatly.

"He only did it when they played a team with a chance to beat them." Roberta laughed out loud, then continued her story in between giggles. "Poor Jack, when he played for Atlanta, he had to pay for his own whores!"

"Aw, baby, don't go there, not again."

"OK, OK, this we have to hear," Terri squealed.

"After a rare win in Candlestick Park, we wound up in a penthouse suite at The Mark with about 35 football players and their ladies and friends. Jack immediately proceeded to get totally fucked up because he had intercepted the mighty Steve Young twice and recovered a fumble. Once the dancing started, so did the fun part of the party. Very shortly thereafter, Jack got a bit carried away with this hot little redhead on the dancefloor and proceeded to impale her tiny body upon his mighty cock for over three straight songs while still standing up. Well, kind of standing up. Anyhow, the way she moved, manipulated, and teased him while he did his best to fuck her brains out was absolutely humbling. When all was said and done, she thanked him for the ride, then charged him $500 for the public fuck. I was so impressed with her style and technique, I paid her myself! The best part of the story is that Jack was so fucked up on booze, pills, and coke that he doesn't remember a damn thing."

"Go ahead, kill me, tell them the rest."

"I have every second of the most awesome fuck I've ever seen in my life on video tape. I sent Heather a copy, with a letter of appreciation for all the things she had taught me and how well they worked in our bedroom, and she was nice enough to send me back another video full of more of her special moves, techniques, and guaranteed secret weapons."

"Nothing wrong with a good education!" Terri nuzzled her face in my shoulder, then nipped me with her teeth.

The trail became only couple size after we crossed the ravine and headed uphill into the jungle. The actual pathway was rimmed with low intensity garden lights, but the trail itself was dark to the point of being uncomfortable. As Terri and I were leading the way through the eerie illumination, I couldn't help but think that this trail could not be the primary route to the pavilion and food. The volume and intensity of the rains in this part of the world could easily make the villa inaccessible for days. I doubt even a well loved 300 lb. Saudi Prince could survive three or four days without room service, much less navigate a muddy trail and traverse a flooded ravine in a downpour to attend a buffet. There had to be another way.

As the trail crossed a small clearing, I noticed the red glow of a cigarette next to a tree just inside the edge of the jungle. After a quick scan revealed no other movement or glows, I moved Terri to the opposite side of the unknown, and released her hand, freeing mine.

"Hey amigos, you goin' to the party? I don't think so!" The Mexican boat boy was drunker than shit, and fried to the gills on coke. He could barely talk, and his eyes were blood red slits, but he certainly got his point across. The sorry mother fucker put a straight-arm in my chest, then held a cigarette lighter up in his left hand and lit it right in Terri's face. "We got plenty 'nuf swinging dick up there, but the cunt can go ahead."

Macho Man left himself totally defenseless to the quick right cross that damn near snapped his neck and spun him to his right, then Jack grabbed him by the hair on the back of his head to keep him from falling, and smashed him face first into the biggest tree he could find. The tough Mexican thug collapsed like a marionette at the base of the tree and never moved another muscle. Jack and I stared at each other for a few seconds, then we broke into laughter and exchanged high fives.

"That's what I call teamwork, guys," Bert exclaimed. "Now I'm really ready to crash and trash this fuck party. Come on everybody, I need a drink!"

We heard the music long before we saw the luminescence radiating from the villa. The trail and jungle ended right at the edge of the patio, which was rimmed by a three foot rock wall. I took a quick look to my right, and sure enough, there was the huge tree at the top of the embankment JC had mentioned. Its base was about twelve feet higher than the floor of the patio, and total distance from the tree to the back of the house was no more than 35 yards. Even in the dark, the villa looked like something out of a James Bond movie, the way it seemed to just grow out of the side of the mountain. Everything was either built, or covered with hand cut native rock, including every exterior wall, the wishing well in the middle of the patio, and the huge Jacuzzi nestled in the far corner. However, just as described, the entire face of the villa was all glass.

The wishing well was filled with champagne and wine on ice, so we grabbed a bottle of Moet and four glasses for a toast and a slam before we threw ourselves to the wolves inside. Even as Jack was still pouring, we were approached by a dynamic young Mexican woman wearing only a pair of red spandex hot pants, matching red pumps, and carrying a small round silver tray.

"Good evening, and welcome to the villa," she said, with only a hint of an accent. "My name is Sage, and I'm one of the designated coke whores for this evening. If there is any way I can serve you, please don't hesitate to ask." She lowered the silver tray, opened the silver sugar bowl, and passed Terri a silver spoon.

We took a moment to catch our breath after Sage left us, then took a stroll over to the hot tub. This custom made pleasure pool was at least twelve by twelve, with numerous cozy little buckets and benches on the inside, and there were barstools around a smooth rock ledge on three sides of the exterior wall, with corner stools and steps on the fourth. The water was fresh and clean, with only a small amount of chlorination, and the perfect temperature for a warm tropical night of fun and frivolity.

"Hey guys, guess who's about to get the lead in a new flick!" Tony did everything but float as he bounded over to the tub, then proceeded to hug each and every one of us. "Jennifer is cutting the deal as we speak. She's got some fat Colombian to guarantee 25 million dollars up front for the production of my debut film. Now all we have to do is look through a few scripts, find a director, and away we go!"

"Terrific!" Terri kicked her charm into gear and mesmerized the poor boy. "If you need a special lady or two in your new movie, I know where you can lay your hands on quite a pair."

"Or a pair of pairs," Roberta exclaimed.

Tony stood there mentally debating the issue, when out came the Grande Dame herself with a butt-ugly Colombian I remembered from the first boat. She acknowledged my presence with her eyes, but purposely chose not to speak to me.

"If you will excuse us, we have a business deal to conclude in the Jacuzzi, so Tony, if you'll get us a fresh bottle of champagne, please."

We took the hint, and made our way over to the well for a refill before we headed inside. Tony was still in hyper-space over the movie deal, but Roberta brought him down to earth real quick with her straight shooting business savvy.

"Nothing involving that much money is ever this easy to pull off, especially dealing with 'foreign investors' like these guys. You're way out of your league on this one, kiddo, so watch your ass."

"You sound like a lawyer, or an agent."

"Try both."

"Damn, if this deal falls through, maybe you can represent me on the next one."

"Cool it, hotshot. I'm semi-retired, and I only deal in athletes, not actors." She gave him a quick undressing with her eyes, then made a discreet nod of her head in the direction of the hot tub. "She'll do everything within her power to not blow the deal, so just be supportive and go along with the gag. Besides, you wouldn't really want me to be your agent because when it comes to the way I 'handle' my clients, I'm strictly a hands off kind of girl."

"That's too bad. Be that the case, may I ask why you're here?"

"Let's just say we're not here to talk business." Roberta raised her left hand, and Sage was there in a matter of moments to serve and satisfy.

We entered the villa through the sliding glass door and were immediately inundated by fans, well-wishers, and other people who had attended the beach party. Jack and I both stuck close to the girls, but it was damn near impossible for either of us to maintain any type of concentration on their fluffy conversation due to the erotic costuming of all the hired help. I counted three more designated coke whores in hot pants and heels, a half dozen waitresses in open-cupped lace corsets with stockings and pumps, and at least fifteen or more blatant sex toys walking around in outfits that ranged from sweet little baby-dolls to leather-bound savage sluts. The legitimate female guests may have had on their party dresses, but the whores were dressed to party.

The interior of the villa had the same spectacular effects of a Hollywood designed ultimate bachelor pad and fuck palace. The entire wall to my left was more of the same rough cut native rock from floor to raised ceiling, with a sunken pit group surrounding a hand carved fireplace closest to me, then a much larger group encompassing a monster sized TV in the far corner of the room. Separating the two comfort zones was an immaculate garden area, complete with waterfalls and fish ponds. The center of the main floor was two steps above the sunken group, and two steps below the TV zone. This wide open area was furnished in a more classic antique style geared more for elegance and conversation rather than football games or fucking, and had plenty of room to dance around on the Italian marble floor. Against the wall to my far right was an exposed stairway that led both upstairs and down. Lots of people were coming and going from the downstairs, but an armed guard at the top landing was very particular as to who was allowed upstairs. Considering the fully automatic designer machine-pistol he was brandishing about, very few people even attempted to pass his way, much less argue his decision. On the far side of the stairway were doors marked with the universal symbols for segregated rest rooms, and closer to us was an arched doorway leading into a full kitchen. With no exceptions, every wall was filled with magnificently framed original paintings, and an occasional print from one of the Grand Masters, but the most unique ornament was the open balcony and double French doors in the upper middle of the opposing wall. My guess was that the doors led from Christian's bedroom, so the Deacon of Decadence could watch over his flock as they tried to fuck themselves to death.

I grabbed Terri's hand and led her down three steps to the main floor, with Bert and Jack right behind. We walked through the seating area and straight up to an original Knox Martin that had caught my eye from way across the room. Terri and I had attended an exclusive gallery opening of Knox's traveling collection in Houston a year before the real money started finding its way to our mailbox. We were forced to come home empty handed, but the next time will be a different story. For such an arrogant little asshole, Christian sure had a damn fine eye for art.

"Hey Brother-in-law, turn around and look up!"

We all spun around and looked up into the open loft that made up the second floor of the great glass wall in time to see one of the sex toys giving a little oral gratification to one of the real guests from the club. Our view of the glorious event was only slightly hindered by the glass railing, but the angle made it impossible to see who else might have been involved in the tryst, like maybe his wife. Whatever else was going on up there, the look on his face made it clear beyond a shadow of a doubt that he was enjoying himself.

"Damn Jack, people aren't even dancing yet!"

"What do you call that, butthead. Let's go find our favorite waitress, then check it out."

We maneuvered our way to the stairs, but I purposely led us down to check out the lower level instead of up past the gatekeeper into the unknown. Downstairs consisted of an adult gameroom, complete with two full sized pool tables, numerous pin-ball machines and electronic games, and a little mini-casino area for blackjack and poker. Up against the far wall was a bar area, and behind it was my target, the wine cellar.

"Hey, Honey, considering how long it's going to take me to get out of all this protection, I think I need to head to the ladies room before the situation becomes desperate. Care to join me?"

"Absolutely," Terri replied. "All this champagne needs to go somewhere!"

"OK, let's all head back upstairs," Jack responded.

"Cool it, Rambo. Nobody's going to fuck with us in the bathroom, so just stay here and indulge yourselves in a waitress or two until we get back."

"Bert's right, Jeffrey. I think we'll be OK, just don't get too involved until we get back." Terri winked at me, then kissed me on the cheek and whispered, "I'd hate to miss anything important!"

They moved with great haste to the stairs and disappeared up into the main flow of things. Jack made a very nervous 360 of the gameroom, then said,

"Fuck it, man. I'd better take a leak, too. We'll all be back in a few minutes."

Almost in the blink of an eye, Jack was up the stairs and standing guard outside the ladies rest room. I praised myself for the turn of outrageous luck, then made a direct line to the bar and wine cellar. The pool tables were both busy with coed activity as I passed between them, but the hot spot of the gameroom was the bar area where Cyndi and Bev were entertaining the gold-laden leader of the Colombian entourage. Cyndi's silk blouse was unbuttoned and tied under her exposed breasts, and Bev had untied her wrap around chemise to both tantalize and tease the South American goombah into whatever game they were playing. When Cyndi saw me walking over, she disengaged for just long enough to shake her tits at me and smile.

"Where's the camera, Jeffrey? I'm in the mood to perform!"

"Sorry, Darling, but I'm off duty. My sole purpose is to check out the wine."

"So we meet again, Jeffrey Mason." The Colombian put forth his right hand and best effort, but he was way too blitzed to carry on an intelligent conversation for very long. "I am Don Fernando Munoz and these are my women for this evening. They are trying to persuade me to follow them to Spain after my business has been completed here, but I say to them, what does Spain have to offer that this private little oasis does not. Ambiance is only a tool used by those of inadequate sexual means my friend, if you understand."

Beverly rolled her eyes, then removed her hand from his crotch so she could light a cigarette. She took a long draw, then slid off the bar stool and grabbed me by the arm.

"I'm in the mood for something red. C'mon, let's both go check out the wine cellar."

I opened the climate-control door for her, then followed her into wino heaven. There were easily two hundred cases of wine racked and stored in this cellar fit for a King, or Crown Prince. I pulled a bottle of Bordeaux from the rack, dusted off the hand written label, and read aloud,

"Gruaud-Henri, St. Julian, 1970. Oh my God, this is private label wine bottled specifically for the owners and family. This should be fucking awesome!"

"Check this one out, Jeffrey. Lafite-Henri, Pauillac, 1962. Damn, all this shit is older than me! Do you think it's still any fucking good?"

"Let's find a fucking cork-screw and see for ourselves! It's a lousy job, Bev, but somebody's got to do it."

"May I help you?" We both turned to see a stunning blonde in coke whore attire standing in the doorway. She was smiling and friendly, so I didn't get the feeling of being caught with my hands in the cookie jar. All real, all woman, and all wow with the wicked combination of big soft eyes and a sultry smile, she was nasty Barbie with perfect breasts and a tight ass.

"Just admiring the collection," I answered, returning her smile, "and wishing I had a corkscrew and a few glasses."

"No problem, Jeffrey Mason. My name is Kathy, and I'll be glad to open and serve for you. This is one of Christian's cellars that is open to his friends and associates, so please, choose whatever you like. If you will excuse me, while you make your selection, I need a refill myself." She turned and showed the true perfection of her gorgeous ass to both of us, opened a cabinet, and exposed an industrial strength cocaine grinder and packager. She scooped numerous heaping coffee cups of coke from an opened kilo into the top of the unit, switched it on, and filled her sugar bowl with the finely processed powder from the funnel below. After the bowl was full, she filled at least a dozen individual vials that screwed into the base of the same funnel. After all was said and done, she brought over a rectangular piece of polished black marble with two long lines of cocaine ready and waiting. Bev scarfed hers down instantly, but I startled our curvaceous hostess when I took the slab away from her and said,

"None for me right now, but please let me hold this for you." She tossed her long blonde hair to one side, flashed her big brown eyes at me, then smiled and inhaled the whole line in two quick hits. After waiting a moment to enjoy the initial rush, Kathy spooned out four tiny little piles on the marble I was still holding, then looked at Beverly and winked.

"This is for us," she purred, "and for you." then used her index fingers and thumbs to pick up two of the mounds and began rubbing her nipples with the cocaine. Bev opened her chemise to fully expose her bountiful breasts, then proceeded to duplicate Kathy's titillating trick. Judging the degree of erotic pleasure by the expressions on both their faces, I made myself a mental note to try this out on Terri at a later point in time. Like tonight!

"Now it's your turn," Bev said to me, then reached up and kissed Kathy on the cheek. "Go ahead and tell the lady what you would like, then we can both watch her perform."

Before I could answer, the door in the back of the cellar burst open, and six more people joined the party. The four guys looked like they felt awkward in their tourist attire, but the two ladies were right at home in their tied silk blouses and denim miniskirts.

"Hello, and welcome to the wine cellar. I'm Kathy, one of the special hostesses for this evening, so if there is anything I can help you with, please don't hesitate to ask. The villa is straight through that door, so, enjoy yourself."

The ladies led the way like they knew the routine, but the last two guys out the door were too overwhelmed by the sight of Kathy and Beverly to have ever been here before.

I had found what I came to see, and was holding on to two bottles of Pavie-Henri, St. Emilion, 1966, so it was time to get out before Terri were to come along and catch me in the wine cellar with two topless women rubbing cocaine on each other's nipples. I kissed them both good-bye, picked up two vials for later, then left the girls alone to finish what they'd started in a little privacy.

Finding a corkscrew and the proper glasses was no big deal in Christian's fully stocked bar, but when the real bartender finally showed up and saw me foraging around in his little area, he was less than pleased. I immediately vacated his comfort zone, but refused to allow him to pour the wine for fear his shitty attitude would contaminate the vintage, which pleased him even more. Not being a confrontation junkie, rather than sitting at the bar and asking for trouble, I chose a tall drink table with barstools closer to the pool tables to set up shop and enjoy the incredible wine. And incredible view! One pool table was now involved in an all female game of strip eight ball, and the other was occupied in a whore vs. bodyguard grudge match. The taunting and teasing going on between the latter group of combatants was hot and heavy, with the whores having the distinct advantage of being underdressed. One of my favorite ploys was when this hot Oriental babe put a knee up on the table and leaned way over to try a corner shot, fully exposing her bare vagina to me, her opposition, and everyone else who cared to have a look. She knew exactly what she was doing, because by the time she finally took the shot, we were all getting weak in the knees.

"Leaping labia, Batman," Roberta exclaimed. "I never knew pool was so viewer friendly!" She and Terri sat down on the stools while Jack remained standing with me. "I don't see any wet spots on the table, so I guess these are still just the preliminary rounds." She took note of the deep red velvet liquid sitting in the stemmed crystal goblet in front of her, swirled, sniffed, then swirled again, and finally brought the glass to her lips and tasted the wine. "Jeffrey, where did you find this delicious Bordeaux?"

"I found it alongside five or six dozen other cases of classic vintages all labeled just like this one," I replied, passing her the bottle. Roberta's eyes really lit up when she read the label, sniffed the wine in the bottle, then read the label again.

"Six dozen cases!" Roberta was so excited she almost shook herself right off the barstool. "Jeffrey, this is private label perfection. An entire collection of bottles like this would be worth a fortune. The old family of growers have been trading wine back and forth with each other for centuries, and the French government has always wanted its share of taxes for the privilege. To break the burden of heavy taxation in the early 30's, bottles labeled like this, with the duel names, began to be exchanged as 'gifts of love' between the families, thus exempt from all taxes. Not only did it hold up in court, the practice still goes on today among a few of the old crowd."

"So that's how Henri Morea bypasses all the import/export laws concerning the ample supply of French wines available here at the resort. Christian is family, therefore all the wine is merely a gift to him, and he simply hands it out to his friends for free." I could have added lots more to the conversation, but Roberta had the ball and she was on a roll.

"Exactly! The wine is never sold, therefore no taxes are due." She was very pleased with both the wine and herself, even though I was the only one listening. Jack and Terri were glued to the exhibitionists on the pool table, watching and waiting for who would be the first bodyguard to slam-dunk which whore on the green velvet, and neither one really cared for the very expensive, very exclusive private label Bordeaux.

"Too dry!" Terri remarked. "Maybe with a leg of lamb, but not tonight."

"I'm with you, Honey." Jack smiled real big, "Champagne is the perfect accompaniment for what's on my menu this evening." He picked Kathy out of the crowd at the bar, hailed her with a polite gesture, and stared at her breasts as she strutted over to us. As Jack helped himself to the sugar bowl, the background music made a distinct change from soft, light jazz to loud, shake your ass disco, and the ambiance of the party heated up right along with it. Kathy danced at the table with me first, then Jack, as the ladies took their turns with the antique silver spoon. When they finished, again I held the tray while Kathy enjoyed herself with more of Christian's finest. Right before she left to go work over the rest of the crowd, Kathy passed me two elongated three gram vials during a quick embrace, and whispered,

"This is the best of the best for you and your lady. Thanks, Jeffrey, you're a real sweetheart. By the way, does Terri like girls?"

"I don't know," was my only honest answer. "Ask her and we'll both find out."

"She's gorgeous," Kathy replied, with a smile and a wink. "I just might have to!"

Curiosity forced us to vacate our downstairs table and follow the stream of people back to the main floor. Although not overly crowded, considering the total number of guests still at the resort and all the new faces walking around, well over half of the patronage here at Christian's had to come from outside of the club. Instead of the four of us going straight out into the middle of the dancefloor and doing our thing, I led us on another lap around the main floor for the mere simple pleasure of just looking around. My first observation was that all the dancing was not limited to the dancefloor. I counted two couch dances going on in the TV zone, at least three in the formal area of the main floor, and one lucky guy getting into double trouble down in the submerged pit group. Unlike a strip club with rules against touching, both dancer and victim had free reigns to do as they wished with each other, and they did. The hottest dancer of them all was a red-headed Mexican girl who had some headless suit pinned in the corner of an antique couch, and looked like she was trying to slowly brush his teeth with her thin patch of pubic hair.

"Damn, she's good!" Jack exclaimed. "This is just like some of the parties we used to have in Miami. Great coke, good music, and hot Latin ladies that know how to dance!"

"Speaking of hot," Terri said while tugging on my arm, "check out what's on the stairs!"

Moving up past the armed guard was a Tyra Banks look-alike in only her bra and panties with two suits in hot pursuit. They seemed to be the leaders of a small procession of couples, singles, and groups heading up to the loft. To my surprise, Christian was now standing at the bottom of the stairs orchestrating the parade, and being his over-animated, under-classed self. The whores may not have minded him copping a cheap feel, but some of the amateurs got pretty indignant when he tried to slip his hands up their dress or inside their blouse.

"If that's a prerequisite, I'm not going!" Terri crossed her arms and glared fire at him.

"Like I said before, Honey, you've got the gold, you make the rules." Bert got a real mischievous look in her eyes, whispered something to Jack, then took off all by herself to the stairway. All smiles, she tried to walk around Christian and go straight up the stairs, but he stopped her, and they got into a conversation. A very brief conversation that ended with her strutting back over to us with a shit-eating grin on her face, and Christian looking like a stroke ready to occur.

"What happened!" Terri was bounding with curiosity.

"I told him I just wanted to go upstairs to talk to that black chick, and he replied that upstairs was for fucking, not talking, then he says, 'Come with me and I will fuck you till you scream."

"Then what did you say?" Jack was not a happy boy, and Bert knew it!

"I politely told him that he was mistaken, to get inside these hot pants, you have to have a big prick, not just be a big prick."

"Holy shit, Bert, no wonder he's pissed!" Terri kept looking back and forth between Roberta and the commotion surrounding Christian at the bottom of the stairs.

"No, he's pissed because the last thing I said was that if he ever got his little dick that close to me, he'd be the one screaming."

"Amen!" Jack was beaming. "That's my girl."

A hot Taylor Dayne song came blaring from the speakers, and the girls decided it was time to dance. We made our way to the dancefloor, and the girls really began to cut loose and play. Cyndi, Bev, and Fernando joined us for one quick dance, then they headed upstairs after extending us a personal invitation to come along. The whole time, I continued to scan the crowd for unusual behavior or impending danger. So far, the only thing out of the ordinary was the growing number of males, and an ever decreasing number of females.

"Hey, can we play?" Kathy and Sage had danced their way through the crowd, and were more than willing to accept an invitation into our little group. They were all smiles, of course, but I could tell Kathy had something to say. When Sage turned around to serve some other dancers, I took the tray from Kathy and held it for all of us. Just as I suspected, she danced real close, then spoke softly only to me.

"I'm not trying to be rude, but I think it's time for you to leave. Christian is really angry, and is working up some kind of scheme that involves all of you. No matter what anyone says or does, please don't go upstairs, OK!"

"No problem. I'd never subject Terri to gang rape, no matter what politically correct term is applied to it. Of course we're curious as to what really goes on up there, but if the situation is uncontrollable, count us out. I just wish there was a place where we could observe safely. Terri was pretty excited about attending her first real orgy."

"That's easy!" Kathy stepped up to the big screen TV, flipped it to the right channel, and wham, there we were in the middle of the orgy via Christian's closed circuit network. Someone was obviously controlling the multiple camera set-up by remote, because scenes would fade in and out from different angles and would zoom in and out on specific people and groups. The occasional wide angle pan showed an even mix of men and women, so far, but most of the spectators were male. Cyndi and Beverly were giving Don Fernando a serious work over, and Tyra's twin was taking care of two white execs, sans suits, but the rest of the participants seemed more to be couples and simple one-on-one confrontations.

"Nothing out of the ordinary happening up there," Bert remarked. "Just your basic fucking. Check it out, even the whores look bored."

"I don't really know what I was expecting, but this isn't it." Terri just stood there, arms crossed, with a blank expression on her face. "That doesn't even look like fun."

"Amen, Honey." Roberta put her arms around Jack and rested her head against his. "Since we have no intentions of going up there and showing them how it's done, let's go find someplace private and have our own party."

"That sounds good to me!" Terri got a little glimmer of excitement back in her eyes. "I'm ready for some privacy. I don't mind being looked at, but I hate the way some of these creeps are staring at us."

Sure enough, the majority of unattached men in the room were gawking at Terri like she was the last beer at a fraternity party. There seemed to be four or five little clusters of guys, each working on a gameplan to get their hands on something delicious that didn't belong to them, and none of these men were guests of the resort.

"Fuck it, let's go!" Once again, Jack got straight to the point.

Kathy led us to the patio door, but stopped cold before she opened it, and turned back towards us. The look on her beautiful face made the hair on the back of my neck bristle.

"Now's not the time to go out there," she said. "I have a better way to get you away from here without having to deal with what those assholes are doing. Come with me to the wine cellar and I'll show you."

As we made our way back across the main floor, the adventure on the TV had switched from the loft to an overhead view of the patio and hot-tub where the Grand Dame and two other women were servicing at least seven or eight Colombians from every angle imaginable. The perfectly framed picture on the screen that showed the illustrious Jennifer St. John with a dick in each hand, one in her mouth, and another pounding away from behind only meant one thing to me. Blackmail! Whatever is on that screen is most certainly being recorded.

"Damn! When I told that Bozo she wouldn't blow the deal, that's not exactly what I had in mind!" Bert had made a complete stop to look at the TV, but moved quickly when Jack nearly lifted her off the floor with a single forearm snatch.

Kathy led us downstairs, past the whore and bodyguard fuck-for-all on the pool tables, and into the private sanctuary of the wine cellar. She made sure the door was locked behind us, then made a direct line to the grinder. In a matter of moments, she returned with five monster lines on a very familiar piece of black marble, but this time, she helped herself first, leaving me the final line after everyone else was done. Using the foil-cutter on the end of Kathy's corkscrew, I divided my line into four smaller ones, and two little piles, then held the stone for all to enjoy. After the lines were gone, I requested Kathy to demonstrate her cocaine nipple rub for Terri and Bert, which she did without hesitation.

I couldn't help but enjoy the look in Terri's eyes as she thoroughly got off to watching Kathy thoroughly get off to rubbing coke into her hard nipples. The suggestion was now implanted, later tonight was going to be an adventure!

"I hate to break the mood," Bert said, "but I gotta pee real bad! Can you get us the fuck out of here soon."

"No problem," Kathy said, with a smile and a wink. "Walk through that back door, and you'll be in the boat house in about 90 seconds, if you can move that fast. C'mon, I'll show you." And away she went out the back door, tray and all.

We followed Kathy down a long, but well lit spiral staircase until it ended on a landing that smelled like sea water and faced a water-tight steel door. Our voluptuous guide entered a six digit code into the keypad, and the door opened onto another landing at the top of a curved stairway that led down to the boat dock. She led us past the five cigarette boats all secured for the night, and up a ramp into the back of the boathouse. Sure enough, the restrooms were just where Kathy had said they would be, so Jack, Bert, and Terri made immediate use of both of them, leaving us alone.

"You seem to know your way around pretty well," I said. "I take it you've been here a number of times?"

"This is my third gig as a hostess, but I'd love to come back as a real guest someday. I adore nudity, so this cute little outfit doesn't bother me in the least, but I sure would like to have the ability and privilege to tell some of those Colombians to go fuck themselves, and leave me alone." She meandered over to the front door and stared out at the moonlight bouncing off the ripples of the bay. "I may be a little wild and crazy, Jeffrey, but I'm not a prostitute. If I choose to have sex with someone, it won't be because they bought me; it will be because I want to. When I can make a thousand dollars by just flashing my breasts and passing out free cocaine in a tropical paradise, who needs to be a hooker!"

"Amen! I just hope your help in our escape doesn't put you in too much trouble with Christian and his associates." I could tell by the expression on her face that she appreciated my concern for her well being.

"Thank you, but I don't see any problems. You asked to see the wine cellar and boat house, so all I did was my duty as hostess to show you what you wanted to see." She smiled and winked, then said softly, "After all, my whole purpose is to please, is it not?"

"Absolutely!" I chose not to pursue that topic without ample back-up, so I just returned her smile and changed the subject, for now. "How long will you be here at the club?"

"Unfortunately, I have to leave first thing in the morning. Why do you ask?"

"I'd like to see you in front of a lens sometimes. Ever been to Houston?"

"Ever been to Oregon?" Her flirtatious body movement gave the question mystery.

"Actually, yes. I have an old friend that used to live in Portland, and she, well, anyhow . . . yes I've been to Oregon. What's up?"

"I recently inherited my Grandparents home on the Mackenzie River and now live there full time. Parties like this have their place, but when you and Terri are ready to sit in a hot-tub, drink some killer local wine, and just watch the river run, I'll be more than ready to let you grab a camera and have your way with me." She smiled, but was looking over my shoulder. "Actually, both of you would be even better."

"Hi, there!" Terri walked straight up to us wearing nothing but her thong panties. "It's too damn hot to put all this back on. Before we can go anywhere else, Jeffrey, I need a bath, or a shower, or something!"

"How about a swim?" Kathy stepped out of her heels then peeled off the red spandex hot-pants. "There's a diving board with over thirty feet of crystal clear water under it just waiting for us at the end of that pier. If I can find the switch, there's even underwater lights!"

"Sounds like heaven, so what are we waiting for!"

"One for the road," Kathy replied, then passed Terri the spoon.

Bert emerged dressed just like Terri, and Jack, well he just emerged, but both were game for a swim and another spoonful. The switch was an easy find, but towels were another matter altogether. With the exception of the paper kind in the toilets, there wasn't a towel in the house. Kathy got a brain thrust that almost illuminated the entire room, then walked straight to the telephone and lifted the receiver.

"Hi, I need towels and champagne for five at the end of the pier, please," she said, with just enough sensuality to convey a message of need. "Yes, of course, that will be fine. Thank you very much. Good night." She burst into a huge grin that forced her to hide her face for a moment, then spurt it out, "See, I told you I always wanted to be a guest here. They just asked if we wanted embossed robes to go with our Taittinger and towels."

The cool water was a welcome relief from the heat and humidity, and, OK, I admit it, swimming and horsing around with three naked beauties wasn't all that bad either. Terri has the reckless abandon of a child sometimes, and tonight she released all her fears and tensions into the majesty that is the Pacific Ocean. She had a blast, no pun intended, flying off the end of the pier at full speed for that exhilarating eight foot freefall into the on waiting wet cushion of water. As a matter of fact, every single one of us did. I did my share of stupid human tricks, then enjoyed just floating around watching the ladies airborne antics from water level. Our goodies were soon delivered by two young men in an electric cart that they simply backed all the way out to the end of the pier and unloaded. When given a choice between spitting sea water or sipping champagne, I'll choose door number two almost every time, as did everyone else in the water, so we all took turns going up the ladder to the towels and treats. Being the perfect gentleman I am, I waited in the water at the bottom of the ladder until each and every one of the ladies were safely up and on the pier. We wound up sitting on our robes around the brass tub that held the iced down champagne like it was a campfire, and very quickly began to enjoy the tranquility that comes from being around the ocean. Shortly into the second bottle, Jack and Roberta made good use of the spoon, then left to pursue some "quality Jack time" in the privacy of their room, leaving the three of us alone. Kathy and Terri talked about Oregon vs. Houston for visiting and photographs, and their decision was that the only fair solution was to do both, then judge for ourselves. The girls seemed to hit it off pretty well, and were very relaxed with each other.

"Well, I hate to break this up," Kathy said, with her usual smile, "but I know where there's another party going on tonight. Since I have no intentions of going back to Christian's, I think I'll get cleaned up and check out the lingerie party in the disco. It's still early, and I've got to do something with all this cocaine, so why don't you join me?"

"We'll see how I feel after my shower," Terri replied. "I may not be in the mood for another loud and rowdy kind of party."

"I understand completely!" Kathy winked at me, then passed Terri the silver tray. "One more for the road, then it's off to see the wizard."

We walked Kathy back to the boathouse, exchanged polite kisses, then continued on to our quiet little cabana. After losing sight of us, Kathy went back to the telephone, and dialed a three digit extension.

"Hi, it's me . . . . Yes, they're safe and heading back to their cabana . . . . I agree, she's gorgeous! . . . . No, I doubt it . . . . Sounds wonderful! I'll just head upstairs, grab a quick shower, and be waiting for you . . . . Me, too! It has been a long time . . . . Of course I remember the code, silly. It's the day we met."

After a quick rinse in the shower to separate myself from the sea water, I threw on a pair of silk boxers and sequestered myself to the front porch to evaluate the day's activities and smoke a joint. Not being much on notoriety, the one glaring reoccurrence from today's events was that everybody already knew my name. Even the Colombian warlord called me by my full name before we'd been introduced! Oh well, JJ did say to make a spectacle of myself and the girls, so I guess everything is proceeding according to plan.

The speakers in the ceiling began to spew out some soft jazz, a hand on the rheostat brought the lights to dimly decadent, and out stepped Terri in a white lace demi with matching g-string, white stockings and white heels. In one hand was a new bottle of Taittinger, and in the other was the hand mirror from the bathroom with an ample pile of white powder on it. She set the party favors down on the coffee table, fetched two new flutes, then sat across me and brought my hands to her breasts.

"This is the kind of party I had in mind," she whispered. "I feel way too good to waste this on the dancefloor."

"I have to agree," I replied, and forced myself to continue the massage. "You feel way too good to waste this on any floor. Let's go."

"Cool it, buddy!" She reached around and placed the ice cold bottle of Taittinger on my bare abdomen and started to open it. "I've got a few things planned for you, so just relax and enjoy yourself. I'll let you know when it's time to go."

After she served me my champagne, and allowed me to hold the mirror while she helped herself via a rolled up $500 travelers check, she began the entertainment with a toast and a slam, then dribbled the remains on my chest and began to kiss them off. Her bra was off with the flick of the wrist, for once, and she started slowly brushing her nipples from side to side against my skin all up and down my stomach and chest. Sensing her need to be touched, I fondled and appeased every part of her within reach, taking her further up the ladder of ecstasy and making her quiver. After an inspiring round of passionate kissing, she sat straight up, arched her back, and begged for me to satisfy her insatiable appetite to have her luscious breasts caressed. Seizing the opportunity, I reached to where I had placed the mirror, pinched a small portion of the powder, and proceeded to drive her up the wall with Kathy's trick. At the apex of pleasure, Terri fell forward, rubbed her breasts all over my face, and whispered,

"Let's go!"

ROOM WITH A VIEW

I awoke to the gentle rumblings of a morning thundershower and the sound of an electric cart coming up the pebble drive. Terri was sleeping soundly, and deserved all the rest and recuperation necessary from her magical performance that only started on the porch. Her insatiable desire met its match in a unique sexual marathon that was just too damn good to stop, and no way were either of us in the mood to quit. If she wanted to sleep until noon, so be it, she earned that right. I slid out of bed, picked up the silk boxers from the wicker chair, then headed to unlatch the front door. Tired, but nowhere near the hung-over state I was in yesterday morning, I was still totally unprepared for the perky redhead waiting for me when I opened the door.

"Good morning, Jeffrey," Suzan beamed, then blew right by me to set the breakfast tray down on the table. "Not only am I your designated breakfast bunny, I'm also your secured courier for film to the airport this morning."

"Sssh. Please, Terri is still asleep." I poured two cups of coffee, passed one to Suzan, then headed to the locked safe to retrieve my camera bags. Terri remained peaceful and content, so the arrival of Hurricane Suzan hadn't disturbed her, at least not yet. I slipped back onto the porch, then started unloading all of the exposed film on the table. When the pile reached a dozen rolls, Suzan couldn't contain herself any longer.

"How much of that is me?" she asked.

"Oh, let's see, there was the private beach, two swimsuit sessions, and some candids at the beach party, so probably at least twenty-five or thirty shots should be you. Why?"

"I'm just so excited about all of this, and I want to do more." She was tap-dancing around something, but I knew she'd get to the point in short order. "What I really want is to do some real sexy stuff like you did with Roberta and Maria. As long as Terri doesn't mind, I want you to make me into the next Pet of the Year."

"Terri won't mind at all, but what about Jean Claude? You certainly have the face and figure necessary to uphold your end of this arrangement, but considering the sexual playfulness and allurement required for the poses, neither one of us needs any problems with your new husband. As long as he says it's OK with him, it's OK with me."

"Terrific! I know he won't mind, but do you think we could do the pictures in private? I think both my courage and stress levels would be much more manageable if I didn't have to perform in front of a crowd."

"I agree 100%! For me to be able to get what I want from you, I don't want an audience, either. I'll need to control your attitude without any distractions." The doubt in her eyes forced me to back off a little and try a different approach. "It's just a game, Suzan, and nothing you can't handle. There's a lot more to being sexy than just laying there with your clothes off, but it's also fun and exciting. Just ask Bert!"

"I don't have to," Suzan replied, "I could see it in her eyes. I really want to feel that way about me, too!"

"What's going on, kiddo? I never would have thought that confidence would be your short suit."

"Let's just say there's a hell of a lot more I need to learn about being a married woman than merely having sex with a man."

"Spend some time with Terri and Roberta. They're experts!"

"I intend to," she said with a smile, then grabbed the film envelope and was gone.

After croissants, fruit, coffee, and another long shower, I settled in on the couch to enjoy the tranquility of the soft, tropical rain. Terri was still asleep, but I did check to make sure she was also still breathing. Today's calendar was unplanned and unscheduled, so whatever happens will be either spontaneous or pre-determined destiny. I was off in the ozone mentally drifting when I heard a gentle rapping on the door.

"Good morning, Jeffrey!" Maria was all smiles standing under a large golf umbrella in a peach French cut T-shirt and tight white denim shorts. She beckoned me to join her, passed me the umbrella, then threw her arms around me in a very passionate embrace.

"We're being watched," she whispered. "Act like you're happy to see me, then take me inside so we can talk."

"No problem," I replied softly, then maneuvered my hand to the back of her neck, tilted her head backwards, and then kissed her like I've wanted to do since I first saw her. She responded with such erotic enthusiasm I was tempted to throw her down in the wet grass and make love to her, no matter who was watching. Maria opened her eyes and looked at me for a split second, then closed her eyes and offered herself to me again, which I gladly accepted. After our second impassioned kiss, she buried her face in my chest for a moment, then allowed me to escort her inside.

"I'm glad you're OK," she began, "I was worried when you didn't show up for our party, but what I've heard this morning is even worse. Christian is super-pissed about last night, and has vowed revenge against you and your friends. It is for that reason I bring you this," and she opened her purse and handed me an older model Colt snubbed-nose .38 Special, fully loaded with silver-tipped hollow points. "My father gave it to me when I moved to California, but I think you need it more, now."

"Thanks, but no thanks." I certainly didn't need to get caught with a gun in my possession! "What the hell is he so pissed off about? We checked out the party, thought it was boring, and left."

"He says you humiliated him in front of his associates, then stole one of his women from the party for yourself." Maria eyes darted around the room, then looked warmly back to me. "I know the second part is not exactly true, but what did you say to him?"

"Actually, Roberta made reference to his inadequate genitalia after she was refused entry to the fuck room upstairs without him being first in line to have sex with her. After that, Kathy took us from the wine cellar down to the boathouse and pier, we all took a swim, then everyone went their separate ways. I have no idea where she went, but Kathy did not come back here with us."

"Oh, I know where she went," Maria said, with a mischievous little smile and wink, "and so does Christian, but he still wants to blame you for the insult. I really feel like you're in danger, so why don't you want my little 'equalizer'?"

"Considering all the firepower the Colombians are walking around with, if they knew I was armed, they'd have every excuse to shoot first and not think twice about it. This may sound rather stupid, but in my situation, being unarmed is probably safer for everyone."

"Speaking of safer, I guess I should leave before she wakes up."

"That's not a problem, but maybe we should step outside before we say good-bye."

I grabbed one of my cards from the camera bag still on the table, jotted my cell number down on the back, then passed it to her before stepping outside. She smiled at me, then put my card in her purse along with the revolver. At the bottom of the steps, she pressed her body into mine, and kissed me like she really wanted to be ravaged. After a second elongated kiss, I put my cheek next to hers and whispered,

"By the way, who do you think is watching?"

"Oh, you know, the birds, the trees, the flowers . . . ."

I locked eyes with Maria, held her face with one hand, then smiled and kissed her one last time.

By the time Terri finally woke up and got her act together, the morning and the thundershowers were almost over. Not saying much, she stumbled through her morning routine in a lethargic stupor, barely acknowledging my existence with the exception of a warm, wet hug when I wrapped a towel around her following her shower. Standing in the doorway in an exquisite two piece gold foil thong and floral parea, Terri looked like she just stepped off the cover of Cosmopolitan, but hiding behind her Armani sunglasses, something was askew.

"How do you feel this morning, Angel?"

"I don't," was her reply. "I don't hurt, I don't feel bad, I just don't feel! Between all the champagne and cocaine, my brain is still numb. If this is what being a dumb blonde is like, I'm not interested! My God, Jeffrey, I'm wrecked! How do people do this?"

"In moderation, Honey. You just got a little carried away, but that's the nature of the beast." I put my arms around her in a loving embrace, then continued, "Think about it, you really didn't eat anything for dinner, yet you drank champagne all night long, and we didn't even attempt to try to get to sleep until around four this morning. I wouldn't exactly describe what we did last night as making love, but Honey, you were awesome."

"See, I knew all this was your fault!" She leaned away from me, then raised her sunglasses and tried to smile. "You fucked my brains out, and I want them back!"

The heat and humidity following the rains didn't exactly help Terri's delicate condition as we navigated the blue trail up to the pavilion. She by-passed the refreshing water of both pools and went straight to where the buffet was suppose to be, but wasn't. A jovial young black man in chef's attire came bouncing up to us with a huge grin on his face.

"Oh, good morning, my fine friends, good morning! I can see that you are hungry and in search of food, so please, sit here and tell Andre what you would like. Breakfast, lunch, or whatever, I am here to stop the rumbly in your tumbly."

"Just feed me," Terri exclaimed softly. "Nothing real spicy, please. Think delicate."

"Me, too," I added, "with lots of fresh juice over ice."

"I will prepare for you one of my specialties, pretty lady. Eggs Benedict a la Andre for two, with all the trimmings for a nice brunch." He waved at a lovely Caribbean Queen, who returned his smile and nodded, then he turned back to us. "My associates will be here straight forth with the first course, so simply relax and enjoy."

Andre strutted across the empty pavilion floor and disappeared into the kitchen. Before the doors had even stopped swinging, our waitress had brought a pitcher of fresh orange juice, a pot of coffee, and some wonderful breakfast pastries. Terri started out slowly, but once she realized she could swallow normally, her attitude and appetite got much better.

"Well, good morning, you two." Janinne looked stunning in a short baby blue stretch knit halter dress that accented every wondrous curve of her delicious body. "I was beginning to get concerned. Everyone else left for the airport over an hour ago, and Jack and Roberta have already eaten and gone back to their room, but I still needed to see for myself that everything was OK with the both of you."

"She'll be fine after some food," I said.

"And an infusion of new brain cells!" Terri added from behind her sunglasses.

"I understand completely," Janinne replied. "Too many party favors, I assume. Well, don't you worry, Honey, I have the perfect cure upstairs in my penthouse. After you've eaten a hearty meal, come on up and I'll fix everything."

"God bless you," Terri said with another attempted smile. "Anything you can do will be greatly appreciated."

"You'd be surprised what I can do." This time it was Janinne's turn to smile and wink.

Andre himself brought out our culinary masterpieces only moments after Janinne excused herself and headed upstairs to prepare for our arrival. He stood and waited until we had tasted and approved every item on every plate, then sat down and joined us.

"As you are aware, the club has only a handful of guests to feed over the next few days, so all meals will be prepared on a one-to-one basis, with the exception of the evening buffet. The grill and kitchen will remain open 24 hours, of course, and your morning breakfast tray will be delivered to your cabana as usual, but if there is something special I may create for you and your lovely lady, please do not hesitate to ask."

"As a matter of fact Andre, I came across some outrageous Bordeaux during a cellar tour last night, so do you think you could find a leg of lamb or prime rib laying around to complement something red and wonderful?"

"But of course, my friend." His smile grew to such grand proportions, I could have easily counted all his teeth. "I personally guarantee you will enjoy the freshest lamb you have ever tasted, even if I have to go chase the little fellow down myself."

"That's a charming thought," Terri said, peering over the top of her sunglasses at me.

After we had eaten everything but the silverware, Terri and I meandered our way to the lobby and the bank of elevators. On the end was an elevator marked Penthouse Only, so we pushed the button.

"Hello!" Janinne's voice sounded different coming from the intercom speaker above the security keypad.

"It's Jeffrey and Terri," replied my mate.

"The elevator's on it's way!"

In moments, the doors opened and we stepped into the antique designed car with only two buttons to push, L and P. When we reached the top floor and the doors reopened, Terri and I stepped into another architectural marvel designed for the rich and famous. The entry foyer was all marble, and steps led us down into the sunken living room where Janinne stood waiting in a long ultra-sheer gauze gown. Just like with the rest of the building, the wall facing the ocean was entirely glass, so the back-lighting effect silhouetting her perfect shape through the transparent cloth was dazzling.

"Welcome to my humble abode," she sighed. "Mi casa es su casa."

As with her body, there was nothing humble about her abode. The open concept design allowed us to stand where we were and see everything but into the bathrooms. To our left was a small kitchen in an alcove on the same level as the foyer, then an arched doorway that led into the raised bedroom, where there stood the largest four poster canopy bed I'd ever seen in my life. Each hand-carved post had to be at least a foot in diameter, and the massive sleeping area looked like it could easily accommodate five or six adults in complete comfort. To our far right, what could have been a second bedroom was designed as an open wardrobe and library, complete with a multi-media computer system and enough books to open a store. But the crème de la crème, with the exception of Janinne of course, was outside the glass wall and green covered awning on her patio. This penthouse had it's own private swimming pool built into the roof of the building, a semi-circular free standing shower made of glass bricks, and a large oval redwood hot-tub under a floral arbor; all of which were surrounded by classy color-coordinated patio furniture and tons of plants.

"Holy shit," Terri exclaimed, "this is absolute paradise!"

"I think so, too, Honey." Janinne laid her arm around Terri's shoulders and moved her to the sliding glass doors. "Just wait till you see my view."

From where I was standing, the view was already pretty damn good as they walked across the patio towards the railing. After a moment to calm myself, I joined them for a look-see of Janinne's private domain. Straight down from the railing was the roof to the pavilion about five floors below, the pools to its left, then the row of bungalows that disappeared into the jungle. With the exception of an occasional glimpse of a red tile roof, the entire estate was camouflaged in the over abundant tropical foliage and landscaping. The area around the beach bar was visible, as was the end of the pier, but most of the beach itself was hidden by the tops of the palms and trees. The water and mountains were awesome, so all in all, it was the perfect view for any royal figure, no matter how that statement is defined. For the entire property, the only signs of life on display from Janinne's balcony were two people in the main pool and the unmistakable Count Von Spengler pulling a solo at the pool bar.

"I really worry about him," Janinne said. "He told me he's the heir-apparent to a multi-million dollar European publishing house with massive private estates in Germany, Belgium, and The Netherlands, but says in all his life has never done anything significant to deserve the position. I'm afraid we've adopted him until he decides to start doing business in any fashion other than the internet."

"Or he's adopted you," I replied. "If a man can afford a thousand dollars a day, what better place to conduct business and live the perfect life. With the right contacts, even I could live here and sell pictures of you, Roberta, Suzan, and Terri to whoever has the most money at the right time. Now that I think about it, do you have any time shares or long term lease deals available?"

"At a thousand dollars a day, we could stay here about two weeks max, dear, then we'd have to sell your house, so you'd better start taking some serious pictures real soon. Your studio in Houston only costs you about fifteen hundred dollars a month, so I suggest you make a few phone calls before you close up shop and move operations south."

"Wait a minute, Honey," Janinne intervened, "as General Manager, I can swing any deal I damn well please, so if you want to set up shop here for a while, I'm willing to negotiate a deal." She walked over to the hot tub, pulled the gown off over her head, and stepped into the gurgling water. Terri followed in an instant, leaving a trail of designer swimwear on the cobblestone walkway, with me right behind. We were all getting comfortable in the chest deep, luke warm water when Janinne reached behind her and passed me a chilled bottle of white wine. When I read Puligny-Montrachet on another Uncle Henri private label, I knew we were in for a real treat.

"You aren't expecting me to drink anything, are you?"

"Absolutely, Honey, that's part of the plan." Janinne held up two heavy crystal stemmed bowls for me to fill, then passed one to Terri. "This is my favorite cure for a 'party-over.' Start with a good meal, then mix lots of warm jets with some of the most expensive white wine in the world, and just kick back and relax. I promise, we'll all feel better when the wine is gone."

"Amen." I poured myself a hearty portion, clinked glasses with the ladies, then jumped face first into the glorious golden nectar. "Why feel numb when you can feel slightly intoxicated and wet all over."

"What the fuck," Terri exclaimed, then took a long sip of the magnificent Burgundy. "Oh my goodness, this is wonderful! Just don't let me drown, OK?"

"Of all the things I'd let you do, drowning is not even on the list." Janinne clinked glasses with Terri, then drained her crystal bowl. Holding her empty glass for a refill, she locked eyes with me, then gave me her best Cheshire cat imitation, "So, how was Christian's little fuck party?"

"Boring!" I replied.

"Yeah, no kidding," Terri added, then held her empty glass up for more. "There was nothing new going on up there! We would have been the main attraction."

"Or main course!" Janinne's eyes were like ice. "You do realize that they were waiting outside on the patio for your attempted escape, don't you! What Jennifer St. John did for money would have been done to Terri and Roberta for the sheer fun of it. I have no doubt that you and Jack would have kicked some serious ass, but while you're pounding your way through the pawns, the kingpins would have been pounding away on the girls while the big boys held them down and waited their turn."

"Is that what happened to you?" I caught Janinne off guard, but only for a moment.

"Almost." She clinked glasses with Terri, forcing her into another glass draining toast.

"Jeffrey, would you mind getting us another bottle of wine. My personal vinocave is the entire right side of the refrigerator, so go find something fabulous for me and Terri, please. There's plenty more of what we just enjoyed, or various other vintages and vineyards, so choose what you like, but please make the selection white." She smiled and blew me a kiss. "Remember, my recipe only works with the most expensive white wine."

"Yes, Ma'am." I slid my wet butt out of the tub, grabbed a towel, and moved inside to attend to the chore at hand. The tinted glass made me virtually invisible to the girls, so I moved up to the bedroom to get a quick look around, and a better view of the tub as well. Whatever they were talking about, the girls were so locked into each other I could have been wearing a feather boa with flashing lights and still not be noticed. An inspection of the bed proved it to be 100% hand carved, with an extra-firm motionless waterbed mattress, and pieces so big that the only way they could have been brought up to the penthouse was by helicopter or crane. A quick browse and usage of the master facilities verified them to be even more opulent than those in our cabana, yet similar in size and design due to the same black marble and polished brass motif.

Janinne's personal vinocave was of the 400 bottle variety, and was damn near full to capacity. Designed for easy access, it still took a few minutes to peruse all the white Burgundies before selecting a bottle of Uncle Henri's Chassange Montrachet for us to try. I made quick and skillful use of a corkscrew, then just had to pour myself a glass for the privilege of having the first taste. Rich and elegant, this vintage was crisper than the previous bottle and more in tune with my palate.

To keep from having to chug down the magnificent vintage, I strolled into the living room to kill a little time and check on the ladies. They seemed to be sitting a little closer together, and were still visually engrossed with each other, when Janinne simply leaned forward and kissed Terri full on the lips. I watched in amazement as the kiss grew into a passionate expression between two hungry individuals. I couldn't see Janinne's hands, but knowing how Terri responds to touch, I had no choice but to assume that they were embracing under the water. Being typically male, I found the visual experience to be erotic and stimulating, but unlike the sortie with Kimberly at the pool bar, this was no game. These girls were really responding to each other in no uncertain terms. Not wanting to disturb the situation or create an embarrassing scenario with a rude interruption, I returned to the vinocave to refill my glass and grab a second bottle of Montrachet. After checking to make sure they weren't involved, the wine and I returned to the tub.

"Sorry that took so long, ladies," I began, while filling their glasses, "but, I had to have a taste to make sure everything was wonderful, and you know how I get carried away."

"A bottle to fill and a bottle to chill, I like this man's logic," Janinne purred. 'It's not like we didn't miss you or anything, but I completely forgot how thirsty I was until you showed up with the wine. So, what do you think of my little collection?"

"Awesome seems to fit everything about you," I replied.

"I agree," added Terri. "This is delicious Jeffrey, you did good. Now if you will excuse me, it's time to check out the facilities or burst."

"I find bursting so inappropriate in a hot-tub, don't you, Jeffrey? Yes, Honey, you're excused. If you like the bathroom in your cabana, you're going to love mine."

Terri stepped out of the tub, barely blotted herself with a towel, and said,

"Right now that poor little bush is starting to look pretty damn good, so any bathroom at all will do just fine." Without further adieu, she dashed her nakedness into the penthouse and disappeared behind the tinted glass.

"Are you angry with me?" Janinne seemed to be hiding behind her wine glass, but something told me it was a ploy, not a defense. "I just made a blatant pass at your girlfriend, and I know you saw us kissing. Are you the jealous type?"

"Not now. I'm very protective of her, but what the hell, I enjoy kissing her too! If Terri doesn't mind, why should I?"

"Good answer! Terri's right, you're a wonderful man. So, you wouldn't mind us getting a little closer, as long as you're involved?"

"Terri and I are also best friends, so she gets to decide how close to you she wants to be. If I get to vote, of course I want to be involved!"

"Even if I don't do men?"

"Whatever. The common denominator in this equation is Terri."

Janinne raised her glass to mine and took in a relaxing deep breath of fresh air. All the nervous tension she had built up floated away in the mist from the bubbles and jets, and the calming effects were highly visible in her body language as she again became at ease with me. On the other hand, the wine and my mind were racing through the imagery of sharing a bed with two bi-sexual women that just happen to be living Goddesses. Shit like this never happens to me, so all I could do was imagine the storyline, but my, oh my, what an action adventure. I could see Terri walking around inside, so now was the time for any last minute questions, but before I could say a word, a friendly foot began rubbing my leg.

"Thanks, Jeffrey," she said with a warm smile. "You really are a true gentleman."

Terri hit the patio running, laughing, and holding on to her breasts. She nearly jumped into the tub, and immediately begged for more wine.

"This is wonderful, I'm starting to feel real good again," she exclaimed. "I couldn't help myself, so I just had to take a roll in that bed of yours. My God, it's huge! A person could get lost in there!"

"Not you," Janinne replied. "Prince Wafik had that bed made for the loft in his villa, but never got a chance to even have it assembled before he left. I found it in storage and designed the penthouse to accommodate it. Do you realize it took a helicopter to get the headboard, footboard, and all the other pieces up here! On days when I don't want to go downstairs, it's big enough to spread my whole office around on."

"It's big enough to have a board meeting on!" I had to put in my two cents.

"Well, since there are only three of us, you are correct. However, Christian is not allowed in my penthouse, much less my bedroom, so I think Unkle Henri and I will stick to using my office for dealing with Christian and his band of fools."

"So Unkle Henri knows all about Christian and his Colombian connections and friends?"

"Unkle Henri is a very well informed man, Jeffrey. He's very pleased with the high profitability of the resort during my tenure as GM, but is overly concerned with the personal wealth Christian is accumulating as a direct result. With money comes power, and Christian has shown he can't handle either one, much less both. Between the Colombians and his rich bitch little girlfriend, Christian is trying to run with an elitist group that allows him to occasionally participate for no other reason than his status at this resort. If they only knew the truth."

"Well, hey, fuck Christian," Terri exclaimed. "Actually, no thank you, let's don't. We've got to have something better to talk about, so let's talk about today. I want to go for a ride on a boat, how about you?"

"I'd like to take some pictures of you riding on a boat, and doing a few other things. What would the two of you feel about an afternoon session together?"

"I can arrange for one of our snorkeling boats to pick us up at the pier and take us to the other side of the bay for a snorkel and swim, then we could land at another private beach for a little picnic and photographs. It would be a shame not to include Roberta and Jack, and Suzan and Jean Claude, so all I need is a time from you, then I'll make all the arrangements and make sure everyone is notified."

"I can't promise close-ups, but I'll do my part to be gorgeous," Terri added.

"Like you could be any other way, dear. Everything sounds good to me, but we do need a little time to take care of some business today, in the form of about a dozen new batik outfits with accessories, and two or three specific swimsuits for covershots. My plan was to use the archery range around three this afternoon for my location, so I guess we could be back by four or so, change gear, and be at the boat by four thirty."

"My ass! How many times do you expect me to change clothes in an hour, get glamorous, and take pictures, dear? I'm good, Jeffrey, but even Wonder Woman would have a hard time meeting that schedule."

"How about some help?" Janinne said with a big grin. "Suzan and I would love to help change you, and keep you at your glamorous best. How about it?"

"Sounds good to me! The contract states that Jeffrey is the photographer and I'm the model, but it doesn't say we can't use other people for doubles and group shots, so come prepared to work both sides of the camera."

"You drive a hard bargain, Honey, but I think I can handle it. Tell you what, Suzan and I will pick you up at your villa in a couple of carts at around two forty five to help with all the clothes and gear, then we can spend more time taking pictures and less time getting back and forth. We'll do our best to stay out of the way and help, then whenever you're ready, we'll jump on in and give it our best shot."

"Terrific!" I reached over and emptied what was our third bottle of Montrachet into our glasses, and offered the girls yet another toast. "Rumor has it that the people behind these batik fashions are putting together an international campaign, so here's to seeing your boobs in their dresses in every magazine and billboard around the world."

"I beg your pardon," Janinne stood up with her hands on her hips. "These are not a pair of imbeciles impaled on our chests. They are neither morons nor fools. They are living tissue, they are called breasts, and they deserve to be kissed for the insult."

They were, they are, and I did. Each and every one of them.

Back in our cabana, Terri and I were curled up in our bed on the verge of drifting off for a well deserved nap. She had been very quiet during our walk from the penthouse, and had made no mention of her private encounter with Janinne, so I didn't either. She snuggled her nude body against mine, laid her head on my chest, and said softly,

"This place is very special. Everyone really seems to love me. Thanks for bringing me here, Jeffrey."

16

SHOOT ME, PLEASE

Janinne's magical cure worked like a charm on Terri, because she awoke from her induced slumber refreshed, rejuvenated, and back to her stylish perky self. I pampered her with one of my personal touch baths from head to toe, including her hair, then a gentle massage using her favorite perfumed moisturizing lotion after drying her with the softest towels I could find. She was both receptive and responsive to my touch, and showed her appreciation with numerous hugs and kisses. Best of all, her eyes were alive with emotion again, so she was ready to mesmerize the camera and photographer one more time.

While Terri put the finishing touches on her hair and make-up, I laid out the batik outfits and accessories to get a better idea of what we were up against. The three swimsuit shots should be quick and easy, especially with Terri in the right frame of mind, then my plan was to introduce the batik fashions as solos first, then let the girls cut loose in some playful groupings as a finale. For a little added inspiration, I placed Jack's boom-box and some hot dance tapes in the to-go pile. If nothing else, maybe the music will help keep everybody loose and in step with each other.

My beautiful lady stepped out of the bedroom wearing only her baby blue silk make-up robe and walked straight up to me. She tilted her head to the direction of the ambient light, gave me one of her for-camera-only pout and smile combinations, then a coy little grin and wink.

135

"So, what do you think?" She asked.

"Gorgeous!" I reached inside her robe and pulled her closer to me.

"Jeffrey! Don't you dare kiss me!" She pulled away and pretended to get angry for a moment, then relaxed, pointed her finger at me, and almost smiled. "I know what you think of me, but what I was asking you about is my new lipstick. Janinne gave it to me and I wanted your opinion."

"If it tastes as good as it looks, I'm all for it."

"If you're a good boy, you'll be able to find out soon enough," she replied, then walked back towards the bedroom, stopping at the door. "I promise you, it's worth the wait."

Janinne and Suzan arrived on schedule and in the mood. They blew past me like I was only the doorman on their way back to Terri and all her make-up magic in the bathroom. Since all my gear was ready, and there was no telling how long the girls were going to indulge themselves behind closed doors, I opened the stash drawer in the armoire and retrieved a small joint. I had to smile at myself for being only fingertips away from at least nine grams of some of the world's finest cocaine, and having no desire whatsoever to pop open a vial and enjoying a face full. I guess in my case, it's just a simple matter of time and place. I had my time with cocaine, but now there's no place in my life for it.

After a peaceful smoke in the pleasant confines of a shaded hammock, I reentered reality when I opened the front door and caught all three of them in the semi-nude process of trying on the outfits. Suddenly, I became the Answer Man in the 'What do you think of . . . ?' contest. After voicing my opinion on each and every one of their queries, they went back to debating amongst themselves, and eventually did what they wanted to do in the first place, which I fully expected. And women think guys are predictable!

All packed up and loaded for bear, I put my life in the hands of fate by allowing Suzan to be my chauffeur for our journey to the location. Janinne and Terri were following at a leisurely pace, but Suzan had her pit-bull mentality focused on getting there first. All my gear was securely fastened down in the back, but more than once I wished there were seat belts in the front. We zoomed down the main path that paralleled the beachfront, then made a sharp left at the white trail and shot straight uphill to the archery range, beating Janinne and Terri by an easy five minutes.

"Hot damn, that was fun!" she bellowed, then stood, raised both hands above her head, and did a slow serpentine stretch all up and down her spine. Channeling all that enthusiasm into a creative posture might be a challenge, but well worth the effort if her vibrancy can be converted to sexuality, then transposed onto film. She's got all the right tools, now it's time to show her how to use them.

"So, what did Jean Claude say about you being Pet of the Year?"

"Go for it!" Suzan replied. "He says we can do whatever it takes to make me feel provocative and sexy. Forgive me if this sounds silly, but I want my pictures to be so hot his dick gets hard every time he sees them!"

"Doesn't sound silly to me," I answered with a grin. "Sounds more like a newlywed with a craving to please her husband. Don't ever lose that zeal, kiddo."

"Never!" Suzan squirmed a little inside her cotton romper, then broke out in a huge smile. "This is all so new to me, I never thought I could feel this way about a man."

"Love is its own peculiar entity, kiddo. One day you're perfectly content with your life, then wham, in walks a blue-eyed, wild Irish redhead that blows your doors off and makes you act like a puppy."

"Wait a minute! Terri's a natural blonde of German descent."

"Just a figure of speech, Suzan." Yeah, right! Even after all these years, if I let myself, I could still smell Mary Margaret's perfume on my skin, taste her lipstick on my lips, and feel her tall sumptuous body intertwined with mine. In a world where the reality of today and the fantasy of tomorrow are so overwhelming, it's nice to open the vault and enjoy a brief glimpse of the pleasures of yesterday. If and when I let myself, that is.

Speaking of reality and fantasy, Terri and Janinne came driving up on the path that led from the pavilion, and were accompanied by royalty. Count Von Spengler had taken up residence in the back of the cart and was holding on to what looked like a tub full of champagne on ice. As long as he doesn't interfere with what we're trying to accomplish, I really don't have a problem with him enjoying the view. After all, without people like him who appreciate my work, I'd be just another self-unemployed camera jockey. When the cart stopped, I walked up to him and extended my right hand.

"Welcome to the Wide World of Sportswear."

"Thank you, my boy," he replied, and shook my hand vigorously. "The ladies were kind enough to extend the invitation after I helped them with the champagne, but I don't want to be a distraction. Business is business, my boy, so I promise to be a silent observer in this endeavor and let you do your job."

"No problem, Count," I said with an honest smile. "If it's OK with the girls, it's A-OK with me. Besides, somebody has to open the champagne."

"Certainly," he roared, then got wide-eyed and pointed over to where the girls were standing. Terri was being undressed by Janinne as Suzan held the mirror for her to make a final check of her hair and make-up. I could tell she was enjoying all the attention and pampering, because she never even bothered to look my way until she was thoroughly pleased with every aspect of the way she looked. Glamorous beyond belief, and totally nude, she finally turned to me and asked,

"What's first?"

"Let's do the green floral first, then the turquoise crochet, and finish up with the black string." I gave her as warm a hug as possible without mussing her hair, then whispered, "You're gorgeous, Angel. Let's show these people how it's done."

Terri gave me a wink, then strutted over to the cart to pick out the first suit. The green floral 2 piece was special because it had a cleavage enhancing top and hot pants style bottoms that looked like they had been spray-painted on. I could tell both Janinne and the Count approved because she couldn't keep her hands off Terri's ass, and he wished he could. The Hasselblad was loaded with chrome, and the lighting and model were perfect, so I offered her my arm and escorted her to the point of attack.

Working from a tripod gave Terri a focal point to fixate on, and she slipped into character as soon as I gave her the que. Oblivious to the people around me, Terri began her slow sensuous movements and heart-melting expressions focused only for the camera. Using only hand signals, she followed my directions to perfection, and drove me and the audience into a burning rage of desire with her overwhelming combination of sensuality, sexuality, and visual delights.

"Oh my God, she's delicious," Janinne exclaimed softly. "Look at the way she glows!"

"Now that's what I call cover material," answered Count Von Spengler. "Her face alone would sell a million copies."

The twelve shot series, and a quick playful pass with the Nikon took less than five minutes. When Terri gets in her performance mode, she seems to be able to anticipate my requests and wastes little motion as she passes from pose to pose with a smooth and comfortable ease. In the brilliance of the overcast tropical sky, Terri's eyes were almost the same color as the turquoise crochet suit, so during our second five minute fling,

I concentrated more on face shots after doing the fashion routine. Now that she was all warmed up, I was ready to do something special with the black string bikini. By request, Janinne had brought one of her huge sheets for me to use as a prop, so the Count assisted me to lay out and secure the sheet flat on the ground, then came the ladder, and finally it was time for the best part, Terri. She knew what was coming because she didn't even bother to put anything on but her best pearls, then with bikini and matching black stilettos in hand, Terri walked out to the middle of the sheet, turned perpendicular to the direction of the light, and sat down. After putting on her heels, Terri raised both arms above her head in a full stretch, then gracefully reclined into a relaxed horizontal position. I had the ladder in place in a matter of moments, then joined her down on the soft Egyptian cotton.

"Am I in the right spot?" Her eyes were warm and playful as I knelt next to her in a moment of peace. No matter her number of years, the child in this woman was still very much alive and doing quite well. She handed me the suit, then cupped her succulent breasts with her hands, and whispered deeply, "OK, big boy, lay it on me."

Which is exactly what I did. Instead of wearing the suit, I simply laid it across her. Covering the vital areas took some very skillful hand placement of material, but alas, an artist's work is never done.

"You love this, don't you!" Terri asked, with a hint of sarcasm.

"Of course, I love this, Honey. I love this, and I love that, and I really love those, and these keep me coming back again and again."

"Jeffrey!" She escaped the facade of Supermodel, and spoke to me as the woman I love. "Have I ever told you that these poses make me incredibly horny?"

"Every single time, Angel," I replied. "I can see it in the film."

From the top of the ladder, I shot straight down on my gorgeous companion as she decreased the motion in her poses, but enhanced her level of expression. After she'd had enough of the straight stuff, Terri tossed the bikini aside and began a game of peek-a-boo with the camera that evolved into Penthouse style erotica that got everybody's attention.

"Either stop that or make room for all of us!" Janinne yelled. "The human body can only withstand so much torture!"

"Me next!" Suzan exclaimed wildly. "That's exactly what I want to do!"

I hopped down off the ladder, helped Terri to her feet, then personally destroyed her lipstick with no opposition whatsoever. She opened her eyes only long enough to make direct contact with my soul, then returned my kiss with her own soft-lipped interpretation of oral aphrodisia.

"I love this, too," she whispered while holding on to me. "You've created a monster."

Before I could answer, Janinne and Suzan were all over us, shoving glasses of Moet in our faces and forcing us to disengage or drown in the golden bubbly. I held up my hands in surrender, then followed the procession back to the carts and more champagne. The girls were getting excited about being in the shoot, so with a glass or two of sparkling fortitude and a little music, they should both feed off Terri's energy and cut loose for the camera.

I walked over to the Count for a refill of champagne and a reload of new film for both cameras. After waiting until all the ladies were naked, I suggested he take a fresh bottle over and refill all their glasses, which he agreed to immediately. With the dance music cranked up, he bopped over and played the role of dancing sommelier as the ladies swayed to and fro while doing the hair and make-up routine, all of which I captured both on film and with the video camera for JJ. I didn't think Count Von Spengler was a player in Christian's little games, but I figured JJ and company would enjoy seeing the true difficulties of my assignment.

As I expected, Suzan was the first to be ready and chomping at the bit to be turned loose in front of the camera. She literally dragged me over to the wooden park bench, then sat down and started posing for her pictures. With the exception of me having to ask her to slow down her motions, she flowed through our first series like a seasoned veteran. I took the lead on our second set and worked her through a series of still poses that forced her to take direction and use more of her personality to achieve the finished product I wanted. Again, her vibrant aura poured through her eyes and smile as she out-performed my every expectation. Janinne and Terri joined us when they were ready, and we did the first series of group shots, then more singles of each one before sending them to change. All in all, the shoot was going even smoother then I had expected, but the best was yet to come.

Terri ran through six or seven outfits in rapid succession with the other girls providing off camera assistance, then it was time for the grand finale with each of the ladies in their favorite and most alluring costume. I couldn't help but notice all the whispering and giggling going on while they put the finishing touches on their appearance and outfits, but discounted any pre-meditated madness and just filed it under a 'girl thing'.

Count Von Spengler had found himself a shady spot under a huge crape myrtle and had plopped himself down in the cool grass. As the girls were still primping and priming, I joined him for a glass of Moet and a little R&R. I have to admit, it really felt good to sit down for a moment and let my heart rate decline.

"Jeffrey, my boy, you have a flair with women that brings out an honest playfulness that can only be attributed to trust. For too many years I've watched the way the Italians and French manhandle their models for hours trying to achieve what you've just accomplished in a matter of minutes." He took the time to fire up one of his Cuban stogies, then turned to me and smiled. "When I left Germany, I was a tired old man in dire need of an attitude adjustment and a change of scenery. Now that I am refreshed and rejuvenated, I feel I can return to Europe with a new perspective on my life, but the scenery I want to take home with me comes from your camera. With your permission, I want to introduce your work to my associates in the European market. My boy, with my endorsement and contacts, all you'll need to do is tell me is where to send the money!"

"I appreciate your enthusiasm, Count, but in reality, all this talk about being a Supermodel is just a joke. Sure, we've done some ads and catalogs, and we stand a good chance of being published in Playboy in the near future, but to put her in direct competition with a six foot, surgically enhanced Superstar would only be leading Terri into a fall, and I'd never allow anyone to hurt her like that."

"I agree, Jeffrey," he replied, "and neither would I. My group controls the publishing of somewhere around thirty-five different magazines and publications. I intend to write articles about Chateau Pacific for each and every one of them, and will need illustrations and cover shots for each one. I can not promise anything else, but I can guarantee your photographs will be in every article and her face will be on every cover."

"I have to admit, it sounds pretty good, but what is this endorsement going to cost me? I don't mean to be a skeptic, but in this day and age, everything seems to have a price tag attached to it."

"You've already paid your tab with kindness and friendship, my boy. I've got more money than I could ever possibly spend, and at my age, when I want a woman, it's easier to just go rent one and be done with it." He roared with laughter, then put his arm on my shoulder. "It's easy to see that the two of you have something very special, and my only desire is to promote it to its highest level of profitability for the both of you. Now, if I'm not mistaken, the ladies are ready to perform again, so get off your ass and go back to work. I intend to sit right here, finish off this champagne, and enjoy the view."

"Yes, sir."

Sure enough, all three were the essence of batik-clad sexual fantasy, and ready to fulfill the dream. Even in her stacked heels, Terri was still significantly shorter than Suzan and Janinne, but since I wanted to catch them in playful motion, I had no choice but to put her in the middle and just let things happen. With the boom-box pumping out some hot Toni Braxton, I lined my ladies up parallel to the focal plane and turned them loose to sway and dance to the music without regard to the camera. They had adorned themselves with sunglasses, beads, and funky hats so eye contact wasn't a necessity, so they were free to turn, spin or whatever they pleased to get into the music and mood, which they certainly did. The motor drive pulled the 36 exposure roll through the camera in very short order, so when it came time to change film, I was surprised that Terri left her two buddies and came over to join me.

"I hate being so fucking short," she said in a helpless tone. "I feel like they just tower over me. My God, Jeffrey, I can't compete with them."

"You don't have to compete with them, Honey," I replied, then gently held her face to get her full attention. "You're one of the most beautiful women on this planet, with all the right pieces and all the right moves, so make them compete with you!"

I could see the wheels spinning inside her head by the look in her eyes, then she smiled, kissed me on the cheek, and whispered,

"I love you, Jeffrey. You're right, it's time for me to throw down the gauntlet."

Terri slammed down a glass of Moet, changed the music to the more up-tempo style of Taylor Dayne, then strutted back over to her unsuspecting accomplices and danced around a little waiting for me to get ready. I didn't have a clue as to what she had in mind, but once I gave them the signal to begin, it didn't take long to figure out her game plan. Terri began her slow strip-tease by bending over and sliding out of her panties then throwing them at the camera. As Janinne and Suzan looked on, she raised her skirt up to her hips and continued to dance, playing a game of peek-a-boo with her ass and slick vagina. Well, monkey see, monkey do! Suzan had her panties off in a split second, with Janinne following right along after only a brief moment of hesitation, and the games began.

As the music rocked on, Terri dropped her top, then slowly helped Suzan out of hers, then they both proceeded to not only remove Janinne's blouse, but totally strip her without losing a beat. By the time all was said and done, all three were completely nude and doing their best imitation of three drunk sorority sisters lip-synching their favorite hot disco tune, and I had shot three full rolls of the gala event. The Count and I gave them a standing ovation at the end of their number, and they waved, bowed, and blew us kisses before all the hugging, kissing, and laughing took over. The five of us shared a joyful embrace and another fresh bottle of Moet together, then Suzan had the audacity to notice the time on her watch.

"Oh my fucking God," she shrieked, "we're supposed to be at the boat in five minutes!"

"Here ladies, throw on the three suits I used in the shoot, take the rest of the champagne, then dash on down to the pier. The Count and I will load up my gear, drop off everything I won't need at the cabana, then we'll meet you there as soon as we can."

Terri must have been reading my mind, because she passed the green floral hot pants set to Suzan, the black string to Janinne, and kept the crochet thong for herself. They were dressed in a flash, then took the not-so champagne laden cart and went flying down the white trail with Suzan at the wheel. The Count and I picked up our mess, folded the huge sheet, strapped down all my gear, then took a moment to enjoy the last bottle of Moet in a little peace and quiet.

"My boy, I want you to know how serious I am about my offer," he started. "You have a marketable talent that deserves to be enjoyed everywhere."

"Including Italy and France?"

"Especially Italy and France! The only thing you stand to lose is your ambiguity. You don't mind being famous, do you, Jeffrey?"

"I won't know till I've tried it, Count."

SKINNY SNORKELING

After dropping Count Von Spengler off at the pool bar, at his request, I drove the cart back to my cabana to leave the Hasselblad, all exposed film, and the majority of my Nikon gear in the safety net of dry land. In case of some moronic accident, like we sink the damn boat, or something equally catastrophic, I didn't want all my camera equipment consolidated in one disaster zone. On the other hand, if the boat blows up and the cabana burns to the ground, I'd have to take that as a subtle hint that God wants me to find a new profession. Knowing that everyone was waiting for me at the pier, I hit the front door running with a pre-determined game plan as to what goes where and why, but everything changed when I opened the safe. Nothing was missing, but certain items, like the video camera bag and my film canisters, had been moved around. Not rearranged necessarily, just not as I had left them. A quick inventory of Terri's jewelry box again proved nothing to be missing, but my things had definitely been looked through.

The drawers in the dresser that held my clothes in them had also been rifled through, confirming my suspicions that the perpetrator was after information, not inventory. Nothing was missing! A thief would have taken our watches and jewelry, or our wallets, cash, credit cards, or traveler's checks, but this guy was definitely after something else. If his target was my exposed film from the beach party, it was in JJ's hands by now and probably souped and edited for conspirators. Since I was already late, I went ahead and locked my camera bags in the safe, slid into my swimsuit, then grabbed my Nikon and some film and headed towards the door.

I left the cart parked in my front yard, but before I made the short walk to the pier, curiosity forced me to check out Christian's private trail. Sure enough, the soft and soggy jungle trail had maintained evidence of two sets of footprints made well after the morning rains had ceased. Now that I knew who, the real question was why. Considering his massive ego and equally sick mind, maybe he just wanted to play with Terri's underwear so he could tell all his buddies he had his hands in her panties. For that matter, he probably took a pair out of the dirty clothes pile for proof! Oh well, since that's as close as he will ever get, might as well let the sick little bastard enjoy himself rather than make a scene and have to kill him. I caught myself smiling at the thought, but I couldn't tell which one amused me the most.

The twenty-four foot covered dive boat looked dwarfed next to the mighty Hatteras, but considering its complement of passengers, the little wooden boat was just as charming and much more festive. I stopped at the shoreline by the beach bar just long enough to get their attention and take a few shots of our rowdy crew, then made a mad dash past the boathouse to join in on the fun.

Roberta looked stunning in a bright orange 2 piece thong, and Jack's shit eating grin was evidence of both his approval and state of mind. No sooner than I was aboard, JC pulled away from the pier and headed the slow moving putt-putt boat out into the bay, and Suzan passed out the champagne for the first of many toasts.

"What did you do with the Count?" Terri asked during our first embrace.

"He wanted to hang out at the pool bar," I replied. "He said something about not wanting to be a sub-species on the food chain, then just laughed."

"He doesn't know how to swim, Jeffrey." Janinne slid her arms around Terri's waist and gave her a little squeeze. "The Count said he grew up in Bavaria, where the only water warm enough to get in was associated with a bath tub, so swimming was never a priority. Growing up in Miami, hell I could swim before I was five years old!"

"Me, too! My mother and I used to hang out at the pool in our apartments nearly every day, and Dad had a pool in his backyard, so I had the best of both worlds," Terri said. "No matter where I stayed, I had a pool and lots of other children to play with. Dad and my step-mother had six kids, and the apartments were always full of youngsters."

What Terri neglected to say was that her mother was always full of vodka, and manipulated her daughter with guilt and pity until she passed away. Not a good example of the perfect childhood, but I can't complain about the results. Terri is as strong and beautiful on the inside as she is on the outside, and she loves me without reservation, as I do her. Eternity would just be too short of a time to be in love with my little blonde haired, blue eyed Goddess.

"Brother-in-law, you've got to try some of this shit," Jack exclaimed, then shoved one of his monster joints in my face. "This gourmet-designer weed will make you see God!"

"Just what I need, buddy, another religious experience. Somewhere between last night and early this morning, Terri had me talking to God on a one to one basis."

"Jeffrey!" Terri did her best to blush, but we could all see through her facade. "OK, OK guys, me too, but haven't you ever wondered who atheists talk to when they're on the verge of orgasm?"

"Their lawyer," Bert exclaimed! "No one else has absolute power."

JC skippered us out towards the mouth of the bay, then hung a slow left which took us towards the cliffs that line the southern edge. The water was a beautiful shade of deep blue and clear enough to see the bottom the entire way, especially when we reached what appeared to be a ledge close to the rim. We anchored about twenty yards away from the cliffs, then JC joined us in a toast and a toke.

"It's amazing how the quality of the smoke improves when Christian has one of his little sorties with the Colombians," he said after exhaling. "I'd almost bet their presence was more than circumstantial in the arrival of this super-duper dope."

"I doubt anyone would take that bet." We locked eyes and reached an immediate agreement. Whether he was the inside informant or just astute of the situation, JC was absolutely correct in his assumption. Christian was using Chateau Pacific to the advantage of the Colombians for the distribution of cocaine and marijuana, for a fee, of course. Via land, sea, or air, the resort was one step closer to the United States for the illegal contraband of the cartel.

"Hey, let's get naked and go snorkeling!" Roberta had stepped out of her suit and was only wearing a mask and a smile. "Last one in has to watch!"

Well, I purposely let everyone else strip and jump in while I fiddled around with my Nikon, only to climb up onto the roof of the dive boat and get some great shots of four of the most beautiful female buns in the world, floating at water level while watching the fish below. No where in any hemisphere could there ever possibly be a greater tribute to the female derriere than right here, right now. Suzan, Janinne, Roberta, and my beautiful Terri, all face down in the blue Pacific, were the combined reason why God created women and zoom lenses. I easily polished off a full roll of chrome, then laid my Nikon on the towel next to me, stripped off my swimsuit, and did a perfect one and a half in the pike position into the cool water.

After thirty minutes of sheer pleasure, we beached the wooden boat in the soft sand and waded ashore for the ultimate topless gourmet picnic. Andre had prepared an array of tasteful delights that included an assortment of cheeses, fresh fruit, cold Teriyaki chicken strips, and pasta salads, to complement the chilled bottles of Macon Villages and Soliel Blanc that went down way too easily. During the process, I took some unique candids of JC and Suzan, and Bert and Jack enjoying themselves in a moment of true romantic interlude. I couldn't help but wish I could put the camera down and enjoy the same with Terri, but without the camera, we wouldn't be here at all. The man with the eye combined with the woman with the perfect look makes for the ultimate example of Catch-22. Who says God doesn't have a sense of humor!

After doing some serious posing with the two couples, and doing a few silhouettes of Terri and Janinne holding hands while walking on the beach in the early twilight, we all settled down to finishing off the wine and enjoying the end of the day by watching the sun set over the Pacific. Suddenly, the solitude was broken by the sound of an approaching jet aircraft spiraling down from above. The pilot made a high speed, low level fly-by in the custom designed Gulfstream V, then began a suicidal, water-level approach at a speed that had stall written all over it.

"Oh my fucking God," Bert exclaimed, "is he going to try and land that plane on this little fucking runway!"

"He'll do more than try," JC replied. "He's going to do it. I've watched him do it three times before, expecting the worst, and he's pulled it off every time."

"We don't call him Rambo for nothing," Suzan added.

"Who the fuck is he?" Bert asked.

"He's not the problem," Suzan stated coldly. "That plane belongs to Christian's girlfriend. We're about to be blessed with her Assholiness and personal bodyguards."

Janinne pulled the last bottle of champagne out of the tub, ripped the cork out, then took a long draw straight from the bottle. Before passing it on to Suzan, she took one more hit of the smooth bubbly, then held the bottle up in a salute.

"The Dragon Lady cometh," was all she said.

ENTER THE DRAGONLADY

By no coincidence, it was obvious that each of our ladies had taken a little extra time to be dazzling for dinner. Terri had dried her hair perfectly straight with just a slight undercurl on the ends, and redone her make-up to photographic quality. She then slid into a short little silky blue Oriental print strapless sheath that over-emphasized her bountiful bustline and classic hour-glass shape, completing the total package. Although my favorite view of her is when she's fresh out of the shower, I do love the way she can transform herself into a super-sexy covergirl. Roberta had her magnificent breasts tied up in a very sheer gauze top with a matching wrap-around long gauze skirt, Suzan was wearing a floral sarong over a white one piece Danskin, and Janinne was into leather and lace with a black leather mini-skirt and a white lace bustier. All in all, they were more than ready to combat anything the dragon lady might have to offer.

"Damn, ladies, all of you are lookin' fine tonight," Jack bellowed. "Is there going to be another hot party at the master's house or something?"

"Oh, no!" Suzan glanced around the room, then continued. "She hates competition."

"I'll bet Christian is catching hell for his little fuck party as we speak," added JC.

"Isn't that a lovely thought!" Janinne sipped her Montrachet then smiled at Terri. "Like I told you, she refuses to stay in his villa because it smells like whores."

"She should know!" chimed Suzan.

"Tacky, tacky, ladies," I said, jumping into the fray. "Just who the hell is she?"

"Her name is Amanda Tu," answered JC. "She is the ultimate rich bitch, queen of the decadent jet-set, and spoiled beyond repair. Her father is a Hong Kong shipping magnate worth billions, with ties to almost every money making enterprise in Asia, be it legal or illegal. That new Gulf Stream V was her Christmas present from Daddy this year."

"Rumor has it that her allowance from the family business is a cool one hundred million dollars a year," Suzan said with a sneer. "Can you imagine!"

"Worst of all, not only is she rich and totally decadent, she's fucking gorgeous, too!"

Suzan slapped JC on the shoulder and gave him her stare of death. "She is not! Just because she has the most beautiful body money can buy doesn't make her fucking gorgeous. Beauty comes from the soul, not the scalpel! Hell, her attitude alone makes her one of the ugliest women in the world."

"Amen," added Janinne. "If you think Christian is an asshole, just wait! In her mind's eye, there is no one in the world more important or beautiful than she is. Just ask her, I'm sure she'll tell you the same thing!"

"And be prepared to be treated like the hired help," Suzan added. "I'd like to deck her if it weren't for Conan and Rambo."

"Who?" Terri's eyes got even bigger than normal.

"Her two bodyguards," Janinne replied. "Another gift from father to protect his precious little princess and make sure she always gets her way."

"Don't leave home without them," Suzan said with a surly grin.

"In a way, I kind of feel sorry for Christian," said JC. "No, really! Think about it. He's been a totally worthless, spoiled little rich boy all his life whose sole purpose is to grow into an arrogant asshole who always gets his way, then he falls in love with a woman who is ten times worse! His family is rich enough to pay cash for this place, then sink another 15 or 20 million in it just so he will always have a job, but she could write a check for the whole damn thing out of her allowance. They got into a huge shouting match the last time she was here, and she slapped the shit out of him in front of a whole lot of people. Before Christian could even think about retaliating, Conan had his ass pinned against the wall, adding insult to injury."

"Now that's the PC way to win an argument," Roberta said with a smile.

"Why in the world would he put up with that?" I asked. "No offense, ladies, but no amount of sex, no matter how good it is, is worth all that."

"None taken, you chauvinist pig," answered Janinne. "Money and power is my guess. Like JC said, her family is worth billions, and she runs with an elite group of decadent youth that comes and goes as it pleases, without restraints or remorse."

"My question is what the fuck does she see in him?" Terri's eyes were cold blooded.

"Birds of a feather, I assume," she replied. "Christian's family has been influential in the French viniculture since the early 1800's, and is very well respected in the international banking and import-export markets. Uncle Henri told me that this resort was acquired to help Christian try and make something out of his life."

"Excuse me," Terri said, "but the three of you actually run this place, don't you?"

"Bingo," Suzan replied.

"And it's also on the other side of the world from the rest of his family," added JC.

"OK, people! Look, we don't care what Christian does or who he does it with, as long as he leaves us alone," Janinne said. "Or just leaves! Luckily, she takes him along on some of her jaunts around the world, and life here at the club becomes normal again."

"No kidding," Suzan smiled and took a sip of her Meursault. "The best part is that when Christian leaves, so do all his bizarre special guests and their little kinky-fuck toys. And speaking of little kinky-fuck toys, looks like we're about to be blessed by the presence of her majesty, the queen of them all."

I had noticed the average looking man in the Hawaiian shirt make a detailed sweep of the room, but now I knew why. He was frontman for the entourage coming into the dining area from the marble entry way. On Christian's arm was a stunning Oriental woman with long straight black hair wearing a floor length, yellow-on-yellow silk sleeveless chi-pao, perfectly fitted to emphasize her slender torso, and slit up to her hips on both sides. Her huge breasts danced freely inside the glimmering fabric as she walked in her six inch heels, disproving Suzan's theory of implants and making everyone in the room sit up and take notice. Trailing the elegant princess and her toad was the biggest Chinese man I'd ever seen, standing at least 6'3" and carrying a solid 300 lbs. on a very stout frame. He followed them to their table, held her chair for her, then stood quietly behind her, scanning the room with his cold, dark eyes.

"Oh my fucking God!" Jack's eyes came close to popping out of his head. Had he been wearing glasses, he certainly would have suffered corneal abrasions from the impact. "JC, you're right. She is fucking gorgeous!"

"If she could just find a surgeon who could make her taller!" Suzan burst into laughter, then tried to subdue herself with more wine.

"Now that really was ugly," Terri replied. "Not everyone needs to be 5'7" to be beautiful, do they?"

"Amen, Honey," Janinne answered. "You're living proof."

"And so is she! That's one of my favorite things about doing still photography," I said to them all, "With body parts like those, even a total cunt can be transformed into a raving beauty, with the correct lighting, of course."

"Gee, now that really makes me feel good about myself!" Roberta crossed her arms over her mountainous breasts and glared at me.

"Don't be silly, Bert," Terri said, trying not to laugh. "Just because you happen to be a lawyer doesn't mean you're a total cunt!"

Our laughter was interrupted by Andre, but only after he joined us in our group guffaw. His jolly demeanor seemed to fit right in with our boisterous behavior.

"Are we having fun tonight or what?" he said between laughs. "As you requested, I have prepared both a leg of lamb and a generous prime rib for your Epicurean delight this evening, and have robbed the master's cellar to procure a selection of the finest Bordeaux's from both the 1966 and 1970 vintage, as well as an elegant '76 Gevrey-Chambertin from one of Mr. Henri Morea's personal vineyards. The seafood buffet is available for those of you who desire a more tropical bill of fare, and since we are not overwhelmed with people, I will gladly serve you in either formal courses, or informally, as you choose."

"Hell, Andre, just bring it on," Jack replied. "We're in the mood for food, so if you bring it, we'll eat it. We did enough damage with the white wine this afternoon, so pop some corks and bring on the reds."

"Amen," added Roberta. "After what I tasted last night, I'm ready for more!"

"So be it," he answered, then turned towards the kitchen and made a circular motion with his raised hand. Within moments, a young woman was pushing a cart towards us loaded with various pates and meaty appetizers, as well as six bottles of Bordeaux and two distinctly shaped bottles of red burgundy. The selection of wine consisted of three bottles of 1970 Leoville-Henri, St. Julien and three bottles of 1966 Lynch-Henri, Pauillac, all of which had the same hand-written labels as the ones I had found in Christian's cellar. Needless to say, each and every one of them was rich, elegant, and had a velvet-like texture on the palate. Terri and I chose to start with the burgundy, saving the heavier Bordeaux for the leg of lamb and prime rib, as did Janinne, but everyone else dove head first into the opulent west bank big boys.

I couldn't help but to keep glancing over to the table with Amanda, Christian, and Conan the Barbarian standing guard. Christian was trying his best to be entertaining, but she had that typically rich "bored shitless" look on her face. She dismissed her servers with a backhand flick of her wrist, and tasted two bottles of white burgundy before acknowledging her approval with the slightest nod of her head on the third selection.

Considering what magnificent treasures dwell in the wine cellar, I couldn't help but wonder how much of her attitude was for show, and how much was taste. Or lack there of! No matter what she was like on the inside, she was an array of visual delights on the outside.

"Get me some photographs of her for publication, and I'll make you a millionaire!"

I turned to see Count Von Spengler standing behind me with his glass of port in his left hand and extending his right for me to shake. I stood up to accept his hearty welcome, then offered him a seat at our table, which to my surprise, he declined.

"No thanks, my boy," he said, then smiled. "Tonight's going to be my last night here in paradise, for a while at least, so I've made arrangements for a dynamic duo to join me in my cabana for a close encounter of the personal kind. With your permission, I'll retrieve all your personal data from Janinne and put it on my laptop for future use and correspondence. It's my intention to spend some quality time in New York with some of my friends and associates discussing the promising future of a certain model and photographer before I board my flight for Paris, where I intend to do the same with my European counterparts. Enjoy a little rest and relaxation while you're here, Jeffrey, because you will be a very busy boy afterwards. Here are some of my cards with all my numbers and addresses, but if you need me, the quickest way to reach me is via my international pager." The Count noticed Amanda's interest in our conversation, so he turned his back to her and continued. "Amanda Tu is a hot property on the international marketplace of publicity. Her family is tremendously wealthy and very secretive, so a good shot of her would be worth thousands of dollars, but your kind of pictures, especially nudes, would be worth an easy million. I refuse to buy anything from the paparazzi, but a legitimate photograph from your camera would put both your names on the front cover of every periodical in the world."

"Don't hold your breath, Count. I seriously doubt her bodyguards would let me get that close." I looked over his shoulder and made instant eye contact with Amanda. To my surprise, she neither snarled at me nor looked away. She actually almost smiled, then turned her attention back to her conversation with Christian. "I would love the opportunity to have her in front of my camera; but only up close and personal, not at a thousand yards with a long telephoto lens."

"I agree," he replied, "but now's not the time for a debate on the finer points of decorum. I've got to retrieve some champagne and get back to my cabana. I don't mind if they start without me, but I would hate to miss anything important."

"Amen!" Again we shook hands, and he was gone.

To Jack's specifications, Andre served our huge meal family style, with heaping platters of roasted lamb, prime rib, and an assortment of fresh vegetables, each with its own gourmet sauce. Both the quality and quantity of food instantly ended all conversation as we all proceeded to stuff ourselves royally with the bountiful feast. By contrast to our decadent oral orgy that only required our servers to maintain a safe distance, Amanda and Christian were being lavishly waited upon with each course beginning with a fresh setting of the table, then the presentation of the wine, and followed by the food. By the time our waiters finally cleared away the debris and brought the coffee and port, Amanda was only on her third course. Andre rejoined us, bringing along a dessert tray that almost made me nauseated. I was so stuffed, I was miserable.

"My, we were hungry tonight, weren't we," he said. "Would anyone care for dessert?"

"I know what I'd like," replied Jack, staring across the room at Amanda.

"Put your dick back in your pants, big boy," Roberta said with a grin. "You're not having any of that, ever!"

"Then why is she walking over here, Baby?"

Sure enough, Amanda Tu was walking over to our table, followed by Conan, of course, but she wasn't coming to see Jack. She locked eyes with me halfway across the room and walked straight up to me with a peculiar expression I couldn't decipher.

"You're Jeffrey Mason?" she asked.

"Yes." Good boy, kill her with your charm.

"It's my understanding that you're here on assignment. I would like to extend an invitation for you to join me on my boat tomorrow so you can take photographs of me. I admire the work you've done with Miss Clark, and would love the opportunity to be your willing subject."

"It would be my pleasure, Amanda," was my immediate response. "Tomorrow afternoon sounds fine to me. What time would you like me at the boat?"

"If 2:30 would be convenient, we'll shove off for open water soon thereafter."

"I don't see any problems with that; have camera, will travel."

"Excellent!" She actually let down her facade and smiled, showing the exuberance of her youthful age, but only for a moment. She turned to leave, then stopped and looked back over her shoulder at Jack. "Bring your friend along, Mr. Mason. I'm sure he can be useful." Then she walked away.

"Why that fucking little bitch!" It took both Jack and I to restrain Roberta and keep her in her chair. "Let me go! I'll kick her skinny little ass from one end of this place to the other, and that fucking Chinaman, too!"

"Cool it, Rambo," Jack said, trying desperately not to laugh. "Gee, Baby, I didn't know you were the jealous type."

"I'm not, and you damn well know it, but that was a direct challenge," she replied.

"Consider the source, Bert," Janinne said. "She was only looking for a response. What the fuck, let them go! That will give us girls the perfect opportunity to drive into town and do some serious shopping."

"Absolutely!" Terri winked at me over her snifter of cognac. "What better revenge than to go spend all their money on ourselves! Besides, it's my understanding that this time of year, Manzanillo is full of rich guys with big boats."

"And speaking of drive, I almost forgot we've got an 8:30 tee time at Boca del Rio tomorrow morning," JC stated. "We've made arrangements with the pro shop to fit each of you with a set of clubs and some comfortable shoes, so all you need to do is be dressed and ready to leave by around 7:30."

"Aw, do we have to be dressed?" Terri said with a cute little giggle.

"I'm sure they'll make an exception for you, Angel," I replied. "Actually, we don't play golf, but we'd love to come along."

"Yeah, somebody has to open the beer," Terri exclaimed.

"Exactly! But do you really think the course director would allow seven people to play together in one group?"

"No problem, Jeffrey," Janinne replied. "In all honesty, there will be eight of us playing together tomorrow. The club manager is a personal friend of mine, and she always joins us when we come to play." Janinne took a moment to swirl and sip her cognac, then continued. "Besides, we own it."

The emergence of a large group of loud and rowdy Colombians and their local associates helped all of us decide it was time to vacate the pavilion and move on to bigger and better things. Nobody was remotely interested in the disco, so we grabbed a few bottles of Mumm and all headed down to the beach to walk off dinner. We left a pile of shoes at the beach bar, and headed south to the far end of the beach through the warm sand. Upon reaching the far end, we made a toast to our near perfect day, the moon and stars, and tomorrow. Jack pulled out one of his famous monster joints, and to my surprise, even Janinne and Suzan joined in the celebration and enjoyed a toke or two of the dynamite Colombian smoke.

As we strolled back towards the beach bar in near silence, twice I caught a glimpse of the two figures observing us from the treeline while following a parallel course. They must have thought we were too drunk to notice, because they were less than discrete in their movements, or whoever they were either had no training in stealth surveillance, or just didn't give a shit if we saw them or not. Whatever the case, if anyone else noticed them, they didn't say a thing, so I didn't either.

As we hung out at the beach bar finishing the champagne and another joint, the lights on the pier came on, as did the lights on the Hattaras. We all watched Amanda and her two bodyguards walk down to her yacht and board, but Christian was nowhere to be seen.

"I guess she's not in the mood to be entertained," said Suzan in a very pointed tone.

"They are engaged," Janinne replied, "so maybe she's saving herself for the honeymoon!"

"Oh, please!" Roberta plopped down on a barstool and held her stomach. "Maybe she's as stuffed as we are and just wants to die alone. I don't know about the rest of you, but I'm too full to fuck!"

"I agree," echoed Terri. "I've got to get out of this tight dress before I explode! No sexy nighties for me tonight, Jeffrey, just a big T-shirt and a soft bed."

"Thank you, God," I answered to myself.

BOCA DEL RIO

Breakfast at the pavilion proved to be a blur of coffee, croissants, and fresh fruit before we all piled into Janinne's white Suburban and headed to the golf course. I brought one Nikon and a few rolls of film, but left the majority of my gear in the cabana to lighten my load. Terri and Roberta were back to their jovial selves, and both looked rather tame in their casual golfing attire, but Bert's main concern was with her foundation garment.

"This is a vacation, dammit, I only brought bras for effect!" she bellowed, then showed everyone her sheer lacy underwire demi, designed for cuddling and cradling, not competition. I couldn't help but admire the awesome view, and nod my head in agreement. Cuddling and cradling would be a wonderful place to start.

JC had taken off earlier to make my film run to the airport, but we were still standing by the truck when he pulled the other white Suburban into the parking lot of the golf club. Anxious to get out on the links, he herded us towards the pro-shop and our hostess. Inside, we were greeted by Carmen de Vasquez, manager and teaching pro of Boca del Rio. Although not as glamorous as the fab four, she was still a very attractive woman in her early thirties, around 5'6", with shoulder length black hair, big golden-brown eyes, and a well toned athletic body on full display via her tight Polo shirt and golf shorts. She kissed and embraced both Janinne and Suzan, then smiled graciously throughout the rest of the introductions.

She had obviously done her homework, because she had already picked out our clubs by height, and offered us an assortment of shoes in the right size range. The only thing she didn't have readily available was a 36-DD sportsbra for Roberta.

The course at Boca del Rio is laid out between a high set of mountains and the shoreline. The front nine goes from the beach up to the foot of some majestic cliffs then makes a dogleg to the right, paralleling a winding lagoon fed by the small river that drops down from the mountains in a series of waterfalls. With jungle to the left and water on the right, staying in the fairway was mandatory to keep up with a favorite golf ball, which made Terri and I very happy we weren't playing. Everyone else, including Roberta, was very competitive and played a strong front nine. More than once, however, she had to replace an escapee after a power shot or a long drive, which kept all of us laughing, and all eyes focused on her during every shot, including the camera.

The back nine opened with a long tee shot across the river, then continued with a number of holes that required placement rather than power to be successful as the course traversed jungle, sand dunes, and lots of moguls before opening out onto the beach itself for the long par five 17th hole. The 18th hole was a short par three that only required an easy 8 iron, but the green was on an island in the mouth of the river, i.e., Boca del Rio.

With the exception of Carmen's 76, she literally kicked ass on the back 9, everyone else shot in the mid 80's and was very pleased with themselves as we sat around the clubhouse enjoying some well deserved Margaritas and a light lunch. Carmen agreed to join the ladies on their afternoon shopping spree into beautiful downtown Manzanillo, and also accepted an invitation to return with them to Chateau Pacific for dinner afterwards.

The ride back to the resort proved beyond a shadow of a doubt that Terri and I had consumed a few too many Margaritas, because neither of us could keep our eyes open. We bid Janinne a fond adieu with hugs and kisses, grabbed a couple of cans of Coca-Cola from the main bar, and made our way back to our cabana in almost complete silence. After a quick rinse in the shower, Terri and I dried each other off, then headed for the bed. We just laid there for a few minutes enjoying the intoxication of pure relaxation, then she snuggled up against me, kissed my cheek, and whispered,

"I love you, Jeffrey!"

Our lips met, and when I rolled towards her, she maneuvered our hug into a full body embrace, and our kiss became much, much more.

Pinned up against the cold tile wall of his shower stall, Jack Taylor had his hands full in more ways than one. Roberta was on a quest to not only fulfill all forms of personal satisfaction, but also to render Jack totally useless on his sea trek with Amanda. She forcefully rubbed her breasts and lips all over him, used her hands to complement her actions, while all the while begging him to do the same to her. Once she had his complete attention, she squatted down and captured his fully erect penis between her mountainous breasts for his favorite kind of personal massage. Knowing full well the limit of her victim's resolve, Roberta waited until the last minute, then led Jack "pull-toy style" out of the shower and pushed him down on the bed, where she continued her assault.

"Time to feed the beast," she whispered, then climbed aboard and went ballistic.

"Oh my God," he said when he could talk, "you're a fucking wild woman!"

"You mean I'm a wild woman when I fuck, don't you?" She had him right where she wanted him, and knew it! After reaching her first screaming orgasm, she rolled over on her back, pulled him close, and begged for more. "Give it to me, big guy," she said between gasps. "I want everything you've got." And she did! Three more times!

Laying on sweat soaked sheets and enjoying a moment of tranquillity after their multi-orgasmic performance, Jack was thoroughly convinced he had the world's most perfect woman curled up all over him. Tall, slender, gorgeous, mammoth breasts, and an insatiable sexual appetite all added up to the soulmate of anyone's lifetime, especially his! Glancing at his watch to make sure he still had time to grab a shower before heading to the boat, Jack embraced Bert one last time before slipping out of bed. Or so he thought!

"Going somewhere, big fella?"

"Time for a shower, baby," he whispered. "Then, you know, I've got to meet Jeffrey."

"Oh, I remember," she replied, "I'm just not through yet." She drew a line with her fingernail from his chest to his genitalia, gave him a squeeze or two, then pounced on him with her mouth.

"Oh, my God! What are you doing?"

"Silly boy, have you forgotten already?" She made sure she had eye contact, and his full attention in hand, then continued with a sly grin. "I'm not taking any chances with you, so I'm not leaving her a drop!" Then she vigorously proceeded with the job at hand.

"Oh mercy, mercy me!" Jack filled both fists with sheet and held on for life.

20

PSYCHO-BITCH ON THE BOAT

When I met Jack at the beach bar, he was drinking a cold bottle of Carta Blanca with his left hand, and holding another wedged in his crotch with his right. Considering the extreme degree of passion that abounds at Chateau Pacific, and Roberta's level of expertise, I kind of guessed his dilemma, but still had to ask.

"What's up with the two beers, my brother?"

"I think she's trying to kill me, Jeffrey," he answered in a pitiful tone. "It feels like she sucked off at least two layers of skin!"

"Oh, poor baby. Maybe you should ask Amanda to kiss it and make it better!"

"It'd be the kiss of death, brother-in-law," he replied, then took a moment to stand up with the least amount of discomfort possible. "God forbid I fall in the salt water!"

We walked up the boardwalk to the boathouse, then made a left down the pier to the Hatteras, where Rambo greeted us with a smile and handshake. He escorted us into the air-conditioned main salon off the back deck, then politely asked me to open my camera bags for inspection.

"Just routine, Mr. Mason. I hope you don't mind."

"Not at all. No guns, no weapons, and no illegal substances!"

"We've got plenty of that aboard, so all you'll need is a few cameras and some film."

"That's all you'll find, except for a few joints in Jack's shirt pocket," I said with a smile. "And please, just call me Jeffrey. Amanda and Count Von Spengler are the only royalty around here, and he left today."

"That's too bad, I like that old fart," he replied, then extended his right hand to me again. "I'm David Weston, Jeffrey. The Count and I have spent many an hour sitting at the pool bar getting drunk, swapping stories, and watching Kimberly do her thing."

"He financed a performance between Kimberly and Terri that stopped the free sex show going on in the pool and brought on a standing ovation."

"No offense, but I'd pay to see that myself." David opened a glass enclosed bookshelf and tossed a few Private Edition catalogs on the coffee table. "Your girlfriend is a knock-out, but I hope she isn't the jealous type. When Amanda found out you were going to be here, she changed her schedule for the entire month just to make sure the two of you got together. Just between us, I think she's decided she wants to do a layout for one of the major magazines, you know, like either Penthouse or Playboy. She met some hard dick with a business card from Penthouse at an après-ski bar in St. Moritz a month or so ago, and he offered her a cool million bucks for the right kind of pictures. She blew him off, but the idea has stuck with her. Hey, it's not like she needs the money, but she'd love to be able to say she's done it."

"And have proof sitting on the coffee table!"

"Exactly!" David uncorked a bottle of Dom, and poured glasses for all three of us. "Amanda's not a shy person, so don't be surprised when she not only tells you what she wants, but tells you how to do it, too. People say she's a plastic surgeon's masterpiece, but don't believe it. She works out damn hard everyday to maintain her figure, as I'm sure you're going to find out very soon. Like I said, she's not exactly what you would call shy, especially when it comes to her sexuality and her body."

It was easy to see David enjoyed his job as easily as it was to see the Glock in the shoulder holster underneath his opened Hawaiian shirt. I fiddled around with my Hasselblad for a moment, then asked,

"Do you always carry?"

"Always!" he replied, then pulled the Glock to show it off. "There's no telling where Psycho-Bitch is going to take us, or who's going to be there when we arrive, so we have to be prepared. I mean, fuck, her family is worth billions, so we're part of the package that allows her the personal freedom to live her life as she pleases. Which she does very well! These

Glock .40 cals were her Christmas presents to Chang and I this year, along with a few other goodies." He walked over to another enclosed bookshelf above a credenza, but this time, the whole thing opened away from the wall exposing an arsenal of automatic weapons and other toys for big boys. He bypassed the two M-16s and picked up what looked like an Ingram MAC-10. "This bad boy has been refitted to handle .40 cal, too. I haven't had a chance to use it on anything but inanimate objects so far, but it seems to work quite well. The next time we visit a certain area of South America, I know a former business associate of hers I intend to try it out on."

"Sounds like you like your job," Jack said with a shit-eating grin.

"This is the best job in the world," David answered. "Think about it, buddy. Travel, money, women, all the goodies I can handle, and I get to play with some of the most expensive toys in the world. Boats, jets, cars, guns, whatever; I get to play with them all! I just wish I had a little more time to enjoy them."

"Isn't she a bit difficult at times, though?" I had to ask.

"Sure, but hell, who isn't! Rule number one to this job is the simple understanding that she's a very spoiled little rich girl who gets to have whatever she wants, whenever she wants it, period. I'm just the hired help that keeps her safe, takes her wherever she says go, and brings her home alive and well."

"What's rule number two?" Jack took the words right out of my mouth.

"Never forget rule number one!" David laughed out loud, then added. "And don't fuck around with Chang! He's the forth generation of his family to work for the Tu's, and is a total psychopath when it comes to Amanda. He'll do anything she asks, without question or remorse. Don't let his appearance fool you either, he's not slow or stupid. Chang is quick as a cat, strong as an ox, and has a passion for cruelty. In my five year tenure, we've only clashed twice, and I lost both times, badly."

"So, just don't piss him off," Jack replied.

"Or her!" David refilled our glasses, then added, "Just be cool, and she'll respond."

"Looks like we're about to find out," I said to all. Amanda was heading our way on the pier, followed by Christian carrying her shoulder bag, then Chang, empty-handed. She was wearing a white fishnet cover-up over a white one piece maillot, white heels, and a broad rimmed straw hat with a white cloth band. Needless to say, she was stunning in both dress and mannerism. David moved quickly to the back of the boat to help her step aboard, took the shoulder bag from Christian, then put his hand in the middle of Christian's chest, denying him entry to the boat.

"What the fuck is this?" Christian screamed. "You can't keep me off my boat, I'm going with you! Get out of my way, you fucking asshole!"

Chang grabbed Christian by the back of his shirt, jerked him straight up off the pier, and set him down about three feet behind where he stood before. Chang quickly stepped aboard, then started waving bye-bye to Christian as David pulled the Hatteras away from the pier.

"Come back here, you fucking cunt!" Christian was livid as he literally jumped up and down on the pier as he continued to scream at us. "I'll get your sorry little ass for this, Bitch! You fucking cunt!"

Chang walked over to the outside stereo controls and cranked up the volume to drown out Christian's tirade, then opened the ice chest and returned with a fresh bottle of Dom and a chilled flute for Amanda.

"Thank you, Chang," she said, then sipped her toxic bubbly. "I wish Christian would stop acting like such a child in front of my friends. He treats me as if I'm his personal toy that no one else is allowed to play with! Seriously, Jeffrey, you're involved with a beautiful woman, but you don't try to dominate and possess every moment of her time, do you?"

"I don't have to," I began. "Terri enjoys being the toy. As a matter of fact, we both do! Besides, as you well understand, possessiveness and jealousy are too easily turned around and used against you by a good manipulator."

"Bingo!" Amanda cracked a smile and clinked glasses with me. "I need to go inside and put on something a bit more comfortable, so enjoy yourself for a few minutes, then we can get down to business."

Without waiting for an answer, Amanda walked straight through the salon and disappeared down the stairway, with Chang following close behind. Jack and I climbed the ladder up to the bridge to join David at the controls, and, to our surprise, the first thing he did was pass us a party joint he had just lit. One taste proved the smoke to be deliciously different from the Colombian being circulated at the chateau.

"I picked this up from an old Marine buddy of mine on the Big Island yesterday morning," he said. "I like to bring something different to the party, and Gunny always shares the cream of the crop when I drop by for a visit. The whole time we were in Saudi Arabia, all he talked about was retiring to his home on Hawaii, and keeping my ass alive. He lived through Nam, Grenada, and Panama, so I figured he knew what he was doing, and stuck real close. Friends like that, money can't buy, so I bring him seeds from the best of the best I can find in my worldly travels, and he shares the results he cultivates."

"I agree." I thought of JJ and our peculiar relationship, and couldn't help but smile. "Friends like that, money can't buy."

"Amen," Jack added. "A friend with weed is a friend indeed!"

We cruised out of the bay and into the open waters of the Pacific, heading north along the majestic coastline. After the smoke was gone, Jack and I returned to the salon to prepare ourselves for the Princess, but neither of us was ready for the precious little China doll that came up from the master stateroom. Dressed in only a short white silk robe, Amanda had transformed herself from the harsh facade of Psycho-Bitch into a soft and cuddly covergirl for Seventeen magazine. A very well developed covergirl, I might add, but still quite passable for a high school junior with a flair for natural make-up and the sweet glow of youth. She flopped down in the overstuffed chair directly across from Jack and I, then accepted a fresh glass of Dom from Chang, and dismissed him with a polite nod of her head.

"I'm so glad Christian isn't here," she stated flatly. "He would only get in the way."

"I have to agree with you," I replied. "If this is the real you, I much prefer what I'm seeing now, rather than . . ."

"Psycho-Bitch or the Dragon Lady?" She smiled into her glass, then looked back up at me. "The real me is in each and every one of those people, Jeffrey. My father expects me to be a hard businesswoman, Christian wants me to be a slut, and you, well, for you I'll be sweet and seductive, on the outside."

"And on the inside?"

"You'll just have to wait and find out, Jeffrey."

Holy shit! Let the games begin. She had thrown down the gauntlet and I picked it up. She was a tiger in sheep's clothing, and I was the shepherd with a net. Whatever the outcome, this was not going to be anywhere near an ordinary photo session with Amanda. She had turned the A/C down in the cabin to increase the chill factor and make her hard brown nipples nearly jump through the soft silk fabric for a magnificent, but planned effect. Amanda was an extremely sexy and well educated woman who knew perfectly well what drives men wild, and was starting to play with the both of us. I didn't have to look at Jack to know his abused member was coming back to life again, and neither did she. Our hostess climbed out of her chair, exposing a partial breast from her opened robe, and walked over to the bar, where she put her right knee on a barstool, then deliberately reached across for another bottle of champagne, fully revealing her bare ass and perfectly slick "special package" to Jack and I.

"Oh my God!" Jack whispered to himself; but if I heard it, so did Amanda.

She had a huge smile on her face when she turned around and handed me a fresh bottle of Dom to open. After I refilled her glass, she offered me her hand and said,

"Come with me, please."

She escorted me to the glass doors leading to the back deck, and when I opened them for her, she stepped outside and walked straight to the ladder leading to the bridge. She climbed the ladder until her ass was about face level, then just stopped.

"I'd like some photos taken here, and up by the instruments," she said, then continued up to the bridge. Needless to say, the view from the bottom of the ladder was awesome! "Next, I want to lay down on the chaise and you can shoot down on me from here. I'd like to finish up on the bow, and then move inside to my cabin for the grand finale. Will there be a problem with lighting?"

"Not at all, Amanda. I've come fully prepared." I noticed David's shit-eating grin, then stirred the pot a little myself. "I hope you don't mind if I make a few suggestions."

"Of course not, Jeffrey," she laughed. "I want my photographs to be your very best work, because we're going for nothing less than international publication. My father may shit a cow, but I want to be a celebrity, not some infamous debutante locked away for safe keeping until some blueblood asshole like Christian consummates a merger with my family's fortune. No, fuck all that, I want to be a star."

"That's all I need to know," I answered. "Now that you've given me a target and a goal, everything else is just going to fall right into place. Shall we get started in the salon?"

"Sounds wonderful, I'll go change."

"Not on your life."

Jack was still sitting on the couch when we returned to the salon, but the Dom was history. I reached into my bag and retrieved my trusty Nikon D200. After rechecking all the settings, I said a quick "Dear Lord, please don't let me fuck this up!", and moved over to Amanda at the bar. She had brushed out her wind-blown hair and was ready to go.

"Let me work you through some classic poses first," I said, while taking a light reading from her face, "then we can improvise. Always try to make your movements in slow motion, even when following my directions, and try to keep eye contact with the camera. Terri says she lets her mind and her emotions control her expression, which seems to work very well for her, so, for whatever it's worth, good luck and let's go."

There was plenty of light to work with, so I simply leaned her against the bar, dropped the robe down off her shoulders, handed her a crystal flute of champagne, and got started. Considering the perfectly round symmetry of her magnificent full breasts, it was easy to see why people would think she was the recipient of augmentation, but the way they moved proved otherwise. It didn't take Amanda but two quick frames to get right into the mood of the posing and sensual playfulness. She was a natural exhibitionist who loved teasing the camera by touching herself and allowing her expressions to pass from innocence to orgasmic and back again. I moved her on and off the barstools in a series of seductive poses that she enhanced by continuing to touch and fondle herself, as well as talk to herself. I couldn't understand what she was saying, but whatever it was, she was responding, and I was starting to sweat.

"Why, you're perspiring Mr. Mason," she teased. "Is it uncomfortable in here, or do you always sweat in the presence of a naked woman?"

"Only those who look like you, Princess."

She smiled and gave her breasts a big squeeze, then disappeared down the steps to her cabin. In less time than it would have taken me to change film, she reappeared wearing an ultra-sheer soft gauze mini-dress and carrying something small and red, which she tossed to Jack.

"Slip into these trunks and I'll let you be in some of my pictures," she said with a sneaky little grin, then turned to the ever-present Chinaman. "Please escort Mr. Taylor to the bridge, Chang, and stay there with him. Jeffrey and I will be joining you there shortly, but we need a few moments of privacy, please." She strutted over to the glass doors which silhouetted her outrageous body through the sheer fabric, raised her hands above her head in a full body stretch so we all could enjoy the view, then blatantly waited for them to leave the room. As soon as we were alone, she walked right up to me and began,

"Please don't be afraid to touch me, Jeffrey. I really need your help and inspiration, so talk to me, touch me, do what ever it takes to get me to do what you want. The art of seduction is merely an illusion of forbidden fantasies when dealing with a smitten fool, but not when it comes to the camera. I realize this is strictly business, and admire your professionalism, but this non-model model needs a more hands-on approach that requires your personal touch to be more realistic; so seduce me, tease me, come play with me. Do to me what you do to Terri to get her to respond."

"You're doing everything I could ask for, Amanda. That Nikon is just a tool in the hands of another smitten fool, so don't think your seductive illusions are being wasted on an inanimate object. What makes Terri so responsive is that she understands the facade of film, and has the ability to look straight through the camera and right into my psyche. I don't expect you to become clairvoyant, so all you really need to understand is that behind that camera is just a man who may be cool on the outside, but barely holding it together on the inside."

"Just like me!"

"Well, I wouldn't exactly call you a man."

"Thank God!" Amanda threw her arms around me and gave me a big hug. I responded in kind, and held her in my arms for a few more seconds, then kissed her lightly on the forehead. "No way," she replied, and laid a major lip-lock on me for what seemed to be forever, then rested her head on my chest. "Thanks Jeffrey, I'm much better now."

"Me, too!" Much better than what, I didn't know, but after a kiss like that, I had to be better than I was before. Amanda slipped downstairs to repair her lipstick and I went straight to the champagne to refill my courage.

Her confidence was soaring when she returned from her stateroom, and whisked me away to the back deck to begin our next series. Amanda had spiced up her make-up for a hotter, less innocent look, and her attitude changed right along with it. Like a stripper, she teased me with her body language as she swayed and posed herself on the ladder, switching back and forth between sensual and seductive to wild and crazy, and always communicating with me through her eyes and lips. She was definitely in the zone, and enjoying the hell out of it, especially when she purposely exposed her vagina to the camera and stroked her labia with her fingertips.

"Mr. Taylor, we need you now," she yelled up to the bridge, then hopped down from the ladder to the deck. Amanda threw the remains of her gauze dress in the salon and returned with a bottle of Ban de Soliel suntan oil, which she handed over to Jack, and said with a smile, "Rub this all over me please."

I positioned them to where she was standing with her back to his chest, and backed off enough to get the majority of her body without revealing his identity. After all, my only goal was to get him involved, not killed. She poured the oil on her radiant breasts, and he did his best to slowly rub it in, which she acted like she thoroughly enjoyed. I wore out my zoom getting a tight shots of her face, breasts, or whatever, then bouncing back outside to capture the whole package. In contrast to Christian, she looked almost tiny, except her breasts, of course, against Jack's massive muscular frame. Amanda had been blessed with a magnificent body, but the muscle tone of her abs, ass, and legs proved David to be absolutely correct in his assessment of her personal work ethic.

Jack got a little too close on one of his oily passes of her inner thighs, so she politely disengaged and moved over to the chaise. To get the sun at the proper angle, I got David to change headings, then had a quick conference with Jack before we started taking more pictures. With Amanda lying on her stomach, I positioned Jack to where he was standing down by her feet, but well out of the frame and lighting, and the games began.

"Come on, Princess," he taunted, "show me your perfect little ass."

As soon as she heard the first frame being fired off, she started to respond physically, and willingly joined in the adult-rated verbal stimulus. I just stood on the ladder and fired off frame after frame while he taunted and she teased.

"You want some of this, big boy," she crooned, then brought her knees up under her hips, arched her back, and pointed her ass and special package right at his face. "It's hot, and it's wet, but you can't have any."

"Oh baby, you couldn't handle all this," he replied. "Once you've taken a ride on the King Cobra, you'd never want Christian's little worm again."

"Silly boy," she responded with her unique sly grin, "he doesn't get any either!"

Luckily, I ran out of disc space and had to call a truce before they turned show and tell into screw and scream. Amanda made a dash down to her cabin while I changed flash chips in the salon and took a moment to compose myself. She was phenomenal through the lens, and had a flair for expression that complemented the pose and enhanced the sexual fervor. A lot of these shots may be a bit too erotic for Playboy, but her contact at Penthouse will be more than impressed.

Amanda emerged from her cabin in white thong bottoms, high stacked white heels, and wearing a white captain's hat. She danced over to the cooler and retrieved yet another bottle of Dom for me to open, then stood and waited for me to serve.

"God, I feel so good," she squealed. "I never dreamed getting naked in front of a camera would make me feel so hot and nasty. Damn, Jeffrey, do you make everybody feel this way?"

"Oh sure," I laughed. "People can hardly wait to get naked in front of me!"

"No, I'm serious. I've never experienced such a strong cerebral stimulation of my sexuality. Now I understand what you meant when you said Terri lets her mind and emotions control her expression. My God, it's wonderful!"

"I'm glad you're having a good time," I answered with a straight face. "As a matter of fact, me too! Shall we continue?"

"Oh yeah, but you'd better watch your ass," she said, then strutted over to the glass doors. Amanda looked back over her shoulder and smiled, "Jack's not exactly my type."

Our next series proved to be playful to the point of being silly as she pranced and posed by the controls of the vessel. The short working distance of the bridge prohibited anything longer than head to butt shots without distorting her petite figure, so we worked the entire series in less than five minutes, then moved on to the bow. After another of her quick trips to her cabin, Amanda returned in a pair of Versace sunglasses, and nothing else. Her dark hair and tanned body proved to be an excellent contrast to the stark white deck of the yacht as I worked her through a series of floor poses shooting down from the bridge, then from the point of the bow. She was really getting off to what was happening and to being the center of attention as she continued to entertain us with her passionate playfulness. On my suggestion, she worked a bottle of Dom into the poses first as a prop, then as a sex toy by capturing the neck of the bottle between her breasts in a tittalizing embrace. Amanda then took matters a few steps further by pouring half a bottle of Dom all over her breasts and rubbing it around. After rolling over on her stomach, she got to me again by first spreading her legs and pouring champagne down the crack of her ass, then she raised up to her knees, stuck her special package right in the camera, and finished pouring the bottle across her labia. I zoomed in on the tiny bubbles dripping from her lips, and stayed right with it for a few more shots through another of her personal massages. When she rolled over on her side to finish up with some classic horizontal poses, I zoomed in on her face and had to smile. Amanda was sweating, too!

"It's time to go inside, Jeffrey," she said with a smile. "It's too damn hot out here!"

We stopped in the salon only long enough for me to pick up my camera bags and another bottle of Dom, and then headed downstairs into the master stateroom. I was floored by the opulent majesty of living quarters that looked more like the honeymoon suite of a floating Ritz Carlton rather than a mere fishing vessel. The entire motif was a unique combination of teak, brass, glass, and mirrors, complete with thick pile carpeting, antique brass wall sconces, and a queen sized pedestal bed with oversized pillows. Even the head followed the same theme, including an all glass and brass shower. All in all, it was nothing short of fucking awesome!

I fired up my three remote strobes and attached them to the sconces while Amanda took a moment to brush out her hair and cool off. She opened the top drawer of her dresser and retrieved a mirror containing a single edged blade in a gold holder and a very familiar looking pile of white powder. She cut herself out two thick lines of cocaine, sucked them down with a custom made glass straw, then completed the ritual by following the drug with a slam of Dom Perignon. Hell, no wonder she felt so damn good! I watched in amazement as she repeated the entire procedure, then turned to me and asked,

"Are we ready?"

"I am if you are," was my only response.

She just nodded, then headed to the shower for another round of touchy-feely playful poses in the palatial confines of her glass enclosed play land. The type or amount of intoxicants she used were totally irrelevant when compared to the quality product we were achieving for her portfolio of photographs. Even if she wasn't a Princess, Amanda would have no problem getting published in either magazine just on her looks alone. Even Mr. Hefner himself would have to bypass his affinity for tall, leggy blondes when presented with the presence of Amanda Tu.

"I need a real bath now," she said after stepping out of the shower and wrapping herself with a monogrammed towel. "Please send Chang down, Jeffrey. We'll call you when I'm ready." Amanda passed me a crystal flute of champagne for a toast, then made a bee-line to the mirror still sitting on top of her dresser.

ROUND TWO

The mighty Hatteras quietly plowed a steady course northward through the tranquil swell of the deep blue Pacific waters as Jack, David, and I sat on the bridge enjoying a rolled combination of the Hawaiian and Colombian herb. Once the smoke was gone, David continued with his tales of Amanda and her lifelong bodyguard, Chang.

"Oh yeah, he bathes her, washes her hair, the whole routine! He always has. Hell, he even used to change her diapers. Chang was twelve years old when she was born, and he's been her personal guardian ever since. Like I said, he's totally devoted to her, and will do anything she asks, without question."

"What does he think of her extravagant lifestyle," I asked.

"Do you mean lifestyle or sex life? Whatever she wants is A-OK with him, as long as the guy doesn't piss her off or fuck her around afterwards. After a three day fuck-for-all at an Italian ski resort, a certain little snot-nosed rich boy learned that lesson the hard way after he got caught at the bar with his hands in the wrong panties. She kept her cool in public, but went ballistic later and told Chang to kill the bastard, which he did. He beat that arrogant little asshole to death with a tree trunk, then just left him there for someone else to find. Some skiing accident, don't you think!"

"Sounds vaguely familiar," Jack said, then winked at me and gave me a high five.

"What I can't understand is what a gorgeous young woman like Amanda sees in a slob like Christian," I stated coldly. "After all, she's the one with all the money and toys, so what the fuck does she need him for? I have to agree with Terri on this one, there's no way it's a sex thing."

"You've got that right," David replied with a cruel smile. "You should hear that sorry little mother fucker beg for it. No, whatever her game is, romance ain't it."

"But aren't they engaged?"

"Yeah, sorta," he answered. "She uses their engagement as a leverage tool in her game of manipulate and control. Look guys, I don't really know what she's after, but she's playing that stupid fuck like a cheap guitar, and has been for almost a year. If he's dumb enough to think she'd really marry his sorry ass, then he deserves what's coming. And I can promise you, it won't be her!"

David tossed his head back and roared with laughter. Jack fired up another joint to keep the spirit moving, and I did my best not to stymie the onrush of information flowing from David by asking too many specific questions about Amanda, so I tried to focus on Christian, but to little avail.

"I understand she takes him along on some of her excursions," I said in a careless monotone. "How does he react to her control pattern on their little jaunts abroad?"

"Same as he does right here," David answered with a grin. "He acts like an idiot! One minute he's trying to impress the world by playing macho man business stud, then the next he's kissing her ass in the hopes of getting some pussy, which he never does. The majority of the people that come to these little parties he throws here at the club, like Munoz and his fellow Colombians, are people he's met through Amanda."

"My God, is Amanda involved in their line of business?" I had to ask!

"Fuck no! The princess gets invited to their fiestas because of her party-hearty attitude and her social status, not her business dealings. She's only a consumer, not a distributor. Whatever Christian has going with the Colombians is totally separate from each of their love affairs with Amanda. Like I said, the princess loves to party, as do most of her friends, so that's why she gets invited to their very private gatherings. Quite frankly, if it weren't for this club, nobody would give Christian the time of day."

Bingo! Another piece of evidence linking Chateau Pacific with Christian's dealings with the Colombians and their bag of goodies, but who are the others? If the information is correct so far, my job is almost over and I can get on with taking pictures, as soon as I find out who the players are. The Colombians were only the first to arrive, so all I need to do is wait for the next set of businessmen to show up, and JJ and his friends will know what's going on down here. Colombians are pretty two dimensional; they sell cocaine and marijuana, and buy or support both legitimate and illegitimate businesses to launder all the cash. If all the evidence proves true, then the DEA will take over the investigation, and Christian and his buddies will be their problem! The phone on the dashboard rang, and David grinned the entire time he received the message. He hung up the receiver, then just winked at me and pointed downstairs.

The air in the salon was cool and sweet with the essence of fresh perfume, but once I got into Amanda's stateroom, the atmosphere was heavily laden with her rich and very private French collection. She was standing in front of the mirrored wall wearing a floor length, ultra sheer, white lace robe over white stockings and heels while Chang finished brushing her long, silky, straight black hair. She smiled at me through the mirror, and watched me as I quickly turned on all the strobes, grabbed my cameras, and got down to business.

Chang gladly departed after two quick candids of him playing beautician, then it was time to turn it on, and Amanda was ready. She was stunning right where she was standing, so I asked her to stay facing the mirror, open her feet about twenty four inches apart, and talk to me through the glass. She swayed a bit from one hip to the other, and continued to touch and play with herself while making seductive suggestions to the camera as I zoomed in and out, and fired at will. Amanda turned and leaned against the mirror, arching her back to where her magnificent breasts jutted straight out, then, locking in on the camera with sexual eyes that were both clear and focused, she brought both hands up and began to slowly caress her breasts. Just like working with Terri, this was way too easy! I simply moved in a semi-circle around her, framed, focused, and shot at least 50 frames of a very sexy woman in the pleasure pit of her own private yacht. Even if they only wind up hanging in my personal gallery, these awesome photographs will be the ones my friends drool over for a long time to come. Hell, me too!

As I stopped to change film in the Hasselblad, Amanda glided past me to get to her champagne on the dresser, and returned with some tissue.

"You're perspiring again, Jeffrey," she teased.

All I could do was smile and wink at her, then hide my face with the Hasselblad and concentrate on hers. Amanda curled up on the bed in a soft, sensuous pose, then proceeded to melt the lens with eyes and expressions accentuating the innocence of youth. She rolled over onto her stomach and continued the visual onslaught of my senses with her eyes and lips at first, then switched gears, rose up on her knees, and started taunting me with her ass and special package. I could hear her talking to herself, but she was still talking to me with her eyes.

At the next film change, she went back to the dresser, but this time, Amanda also went back to the pile on the mirror. After serving herself, she offered the mirror to me.

"No thanks."

"That surprises me, Jeffrey," she said. "A man of your talent should be able to appreciate one of the finer things of life."

"Oh, I know all about appreciation," I replied. "Let's just say I've lost my taste for it."

"That's a shame, this is some of Fernando's finest." She walked over to the bed, served herself again, then set the mirror down on the headboard. Returning for more champagne, she stopped and whispered, "Get ready. This is going to be hot!"

I refilled both our glasses for a toast and a slam, then again for sipping, and led Amanda back over to the bed. Whatever she had in mind, now was the time for show and tell! The princess responded in the time it took for me to pick up a camera, because when I focused the Nikon in on her gorgeous face, she was already out of the lace robe and well into her performance mode. She started out on her side for a few soft innuendoes, then shifted back to her knees and elbows for another round of taunting and teasing without the obstruction of sheer white lace. Amanda seemed to be playing a game with me, because now that I could actually hear and understand what she was saying, her taunts were getting more specific and straight to the point.

"Oh, I'm so wet," I heard her say. "I want to feel you inside of me. Oh yeah, come on!"

I was staying objective, but my task was becoming more and more difficult with each wet wag of her pussy at me. The sly grin on her face was living proof that she knew she was getting to me, and loved every minute of it. I got her to roll over on her back for a few shots from the side, then I literally stood on the wooden frame of her pedestal bed so I could shoot straight down on her, and all hell broke loose. Amanda brought both hands to her breasts and started squeezing and massaging them again, without losing eye contact with me, and also continued her verbal onslaught. The heat and intensity of our endeavor increased with every frame, and the look of sexual desire in her eyes passed straight through the camera and played havoc with my mind.

She brought both hands down to her inner thighs for more sensuous touching, squeezed her breasts together with her arms, then opened her legs for easier access and a better look for the camera. I zoomed in on her face for a few quick shots, and noticed she was playing with her tongue on her lips and teeth, but the gaze of her eyes was becoming less focused. Zooming out, it was easy to see what was going on. Amanda had returned her right hand to her right breast, but her left hand was still between her legs, and both hands were busy.

"Oh yeah, touch me . . . . , kiss me . . . . , taste me," she whispered out loud. "I'm so wet . . . . , I want you inside me."

She began to quiver, and beads of perspiration started to form on her upper lip as the one-way train to ecstasy picked up its rapid pace. She had passed the point of no return and was well on her way.

"Oh God, yeah baby . . . . , oh yeah, yeah . . . . , now, oh yeah baby, now, now, now!"

And wham! Right before my very eyes, and the camera's, Amanda exploded in a massive orgasmic tremor that shook her from head to foot, and literally lifted her off the bed. She collapsed into the soft, damp comforter, took a moment to catch her breath, then raised her hand to me and smiled,

"Champagne, please."

"Absolutely, darling," I replied. "You've earned it."

When I returned with the bottle of Dom, Amanda had rolled over on her side and was serving herself again off the mirror. I refilled our glasses, then hers again after her traditional slam, then sat down on the edge of the bed to relax for a moment. Our work was over, at least for now.

"Amanda, you are an explosion of visual delights."

"As you just witnessed, all my explosions aren't entirely visual, Jeffrey!"

"Amen, Darling." I said with a smile. "Amen indeed!"

She bladed herself another serving of cocaine, then laid back down on the bed to continue our conversation. I could tell she was very pleased with herself, but missed the mischievous look in her eyes.

"Are you sure you wouldn't like a little taste," she asked.

"Positive. Like I said, I've lost my taste for it."

"I bet I can change your mind."

"Oh, really! Are you going to make me an offer I can't refuse?"

"Something like that," she replied, and then rolled over on her back, and dropped a small pile of cocaine on each of her nipples. "Care for an Oriental snow peak, Jeffrey?"

Oh, what the fuck! I cupped her magnificent breasts with my hands, brought my nose down to inhale the white powder, then followed each with a swirl of my tongue and a kiss. If nothing else, I proved to myself beyond all doubt that her breasts were absolutely, positively real, and that my will power could be compromised under the right circumstances. Amanda put both arms around my neck, and pulled me down for a friendly, but passionate kiss.

"See there," she smiled, "that wasn't so bad, now, was it?"

"Not at all, but next time, let's try it without the coke."

"Next time, Jeffrey? Why wait for a next time!"

The ringing of the telephone on her nightstand shattered the mood of what she had just said like a brick through a plate glass window. She rolled over to answer it, and immediately shifted gears.

"Yes," she said in a harsh tone. "Oh, very well. Thank you, David."

Amanda rolled back over to me, but was obviously in a different frame of mind.

"I'm sorry, Jeffrey, but we're going to have to put this on hold for a while. Christian is on his way at high speed, and will be here in a few, very short minutes. Since what I have in mind for you requires much more time, we're just going to have to reschedule."

"No problem, Princess. No sense making waves."

"Making waves is exactly what I had in mind," she answered with her devious little grin. "I bet we could scare the hell out of the fish."

"Without a doubt, Amanda. Without a doubt!"

When Christian pulled up in his 38' Scarab and tied on to the Hatteras, I was amazed at how small it looked next to Amanda's power cruiser. David, Jack and I were sitting in the salon enjoying another round of pure Hawaiian, and Chang had returned to Amanda's side to help prepare her for Christian's arrival, when he hopped over the railing and burst through the back doors. It was easy to see at first glance that Christian was not a happy camper.

"You see that I have found you," he screamed. "No one can escape me, so pack up your gear and get the fuck off my boat!"

"My boat, dear," Amanda replied as she emerged from her cabin. "And as you can see, we've already finished, with everything." She was barefoot, and wearing a white terri-cloth romper which she had purposely left unbuttoned, exposing the majority of her breasts. "Next time, buy yourself a faster boat."

"You fucking slut! Well then, since you'll never see him again, how was he?"

"The best, my darling. Absolutely, the best."

Christian took three steps towards me, then was stopped cold by a stiff-arm in the chest by Chang. He then grabbed a fistful of Christian's shirt and lifted him to face level.

"Calm down, little man, or I'll feed you to the fish!" Chang's voice was deep, clear, and to the point. He lowered Christian to where his feet could almost touch the floor, then just let go.

"David, please take Jeffrey and Mr. Taylor back to the club in the Scarab. Christian and I obviously need a little time and privacy to settle our differences, so return my guests to their ladies, then you may take the rest of the evening off. I doubt if we'll be back until way after dinner, so indulge yourself in a bartender or two."

"Absolutely, and thank you, ma'am." David lost no time in grabbing up our gear and shuffling Jack and I out the door to the speed boat. Amanda followed, with Christian in hot pursuit, followed by Chang, and she walked straight up to Jack.

"Thank you for all your help," she said in an almost child-like manner. "You've got the strongest hands I've ever felt." Amanda gave him a warm little hug, then stood on her tip-toes as he bent forward so she could kiss him on the cheek. Expecting the same, I was shocked when she threw her arms around my neck, pressed the full length of her body into mine, and filled my mouth with her tongue.

"What more can I say, Jeffrey," she said softly. "You're wonderful."

This time, Christian was ready to explode, and I don't mean via orgasm. Jack jumped into the scarab, received my camera bags, then stepped aside to give me room to come aboard, but turned his back for the split second I needed a second pair of eyes. As soon as I put my foot on the side rail to step over into the Scarab, Christian dashed forward and shoved me off the back of the Hatteras and into the water. Had the props of either boat been turning, I would have been cut to ribbons. When I reached the top of the water, I was ready to kill the little bastard.

"Cool off, lover boy," he screamed at me. "Just wait till I tell your fat ass little bitch how much fun you had with my fiancé! She's my whore, not yours!"

Before I could move, Amanda swung him around and decked him with a fist to the face and a foot to the groin. I made my way to the Scarab, and as soon as I was aboard, David kicked it into gear and we sped off. I watched with great pleasure as Amanda slapped the shit out of Christian one more time for good measure while Chang held him down.

"She's got him right where she wants him now," David shouted over the roar of the twin V8s. "He'll be begging for mercy, then begging for pussy before it's all over. The best part is that he won't be getting either! Fire up another joint, Jeffrey, and let's make this puppy scream!"

22

PENTHOUSE PARTY

After a spirited romp across the surface of the Pacific at near warp speed, David guided the Scarab up to one of the ladders on the pier, shut down the massive power plants, and we all climbed out. As per his radio request, the lovely and talented Kimberly was sitting on the pier in her usual one piece maillot, eagerly awaiting our arrival.

"Hi, guys," she exclaimed, then gave David a big hug. "I'm glad she's going to give us this much time together. Boy, do I have plans for you!"

"If you don't, I have a few suggestions." He moved his hands down from her waist and squeezed her sculpted ass. Even barefooted, Kimberly was easily two inches taller than he was, but it didn't seem to matter to either of them. My interpretation was of two hungry people eagerly awaiting the fulfillment of their desires.

"I have a message for you two guys from Janinne," she said, without letting go of David. "Boss Momma's throwing a very private party for all of you up in her penthouse to keep everyone away from the other special guests that will be arriving soon. The girls are already up there, so whenever you're ready, head on up. By the way, she told me to make sure you bring your cameras."

"Sounds interesting," I replied, then turned to Jack. "I need a shower and some clean clothes, so do you want to meet me up there, or say, meet me at the pool bar in about thirty minutes, or whatever?"

"If we're going to a party, I need to do some serious rolling, so I'll meet you at the pool bar. Hey David, are the two of you coming?"

"Oh no," he stated with a smile. "The party I have in mind only requires two people. Besides, I have a reputation as a bad ass to protect."

"Amen!" Kimberly blew us a kiss and waved bye-bye as they walked away arm in arm.

Even though I was early, I didn't have to wait for Jack because he was already sitting at the pool bar with this awesome redhead hanging all over him. Tall, slender, and well blessed, I watched in total amazement as she not only rubbed her body all over his to the beat of the music, but literally forced his hands down the front of her bikini for a free sample. I hated to break up the party, but for his own sake, he had to be warned.

"Hey, brother-in-law, did you know that the penthouse has a great view of the pool bar?"

"Oh fuck! I was just minding my own business when Red showed up and invited me to play with her tits. Damn Jeffrey, she doesn't even speak English, but she got her point across in no uncertain terms. I'm a dead man!"

"Maybe not, but we gotta go, now."

I grabbed Jack by the arm and led him towards the pavilion, and away from potential disaster. The redhead just stood there with her mouth open in total disbelief, then flipped us the universal one-fingered salute and shouted,

"Jutos!"

"What the fuck did she just say," Jack asked as we ran up the steps.

"I'm not sure. She either thinks we're Jewish, or that you're my girlfriend."

The moment the elevator opened in Janinne's penthouse, we knew we were in for a bizarre evening. Standing to greet us was Janinne herself, wearing only red Spandex hot pants with matching spike heels, and holding an all too familiar silver tray that was fully equipped, just like the lady holding it.

"Hi, I'm Janinne, you're special hostess for this evening. I wanted you to feel right at home, so I dressed accordingly."

"Yes, you certainly did," Jack replied, then helped himself to the contents of the silver sugar bowl while I just stood and stared.

We followed our hostess through the sunken den, past a wonderful little buffet of finger food and appetizers, then out onto the patio where the rest of our women were hanging out by the pool. Terri and Bert were laid out on a pair of double chaises enhancing their all-over tans, while Carmen and Suzan sat on the edge of the pool with their feet in the water, smoking a joint. Under the shade of a covered table halfway between the pool and the hot tub was a brass trough filled with wine and champagne in an icy bath. Janinne took the time to step out of her heels and hot pants, revealing the pastel pink thong she was wearing underneath, then grabbed the tray and led us over to the girls.

"Hey, guys," Suzan hollered, then held up the joint for one of us to take. "We don't mind sharing our smoke with a couple of real men."

"Fair is fair," Jack said, then knelt down between the two bare breasted ladies and used the roach to fire up one of the party joints hiding in his shirt pocket. "We like sharing with real women, too."

Carmen seemed totally at ease with being topless in front of Jack and I, as did Suzan, but I couldn't help but wonder how much the glazed-over expression in both of their eyes had to do with their give-a-shit attitude. Janinne took the time to serve Terri and Bert first, then joined us at the edge of the pool to share another round of party dust. Jack and the ladies all helped themselves, but I still abstained. Then again, no one offered, nor did I explain Amanda's technique to get me to participate.

I felt two familiar arms wrap themselves around me from behind, and the sound of my favorite voice,

"Hi baby," she said with love. "Did everything go OK on the boat?"

"Perfect," I replied, then turned around and held her in my arms. "How's my angel?"

"Right now, I'm feeling pretty good."

"I couldn't agree with you more," then held her a little tighter, and whispered, "I love you very much."

Terri leaned away from me to make eye contact that reached all the way down to my heart, then gave me her sweetest smile, and said, "Yes, you do."

We strolled over to the beverages for some champagne, then continued over to the not-so-hot tub and she jumped right in. In a matter of seconds, I slid out of my tropical attire and joined her for a private soak.

"So, did you spend all our money? Looks like everybody had a pretty good time!"

"Yes and no," she replied after a kiss. "We had a great time, especially Roberta and I, and I think we have enough money left to get home on. Bert brought a vile of goodies, so we'd sneak off to the bathroom, or double up in a dressing room and partake. We sat outside at the Marina Cantina and drank shots of Hornitos, teased the natives, and laughed our asses off after we finished shopping, then Suzan brought out the smoke on the way home, so we're all toasted."

"We cruised around in the Hatteras, smoked pot, and drank Dom Perignon most of the afternoon, so Jack and I are in the same shape." I chose not to mention the snowpeaks.

"So tell me, Jeffrey, what's she really like?"

"Actually, when she's not around Christian, she's very charming. I found her to be intelligent, witty, and much younger than I expected. My guess is that Amanda's probably 23, or 24 at the max."

"She's only 22," Janinne said from behind me. "I want to know all about the Dragon Lady, too." She refilled our flutes, then stepped out of her thong and joined us. "What I can't understand is why does she waste her time with Christian? There must be something else going on in her sick little mind besides romance. I mean, yuk, not only is he a jerk, he's more than twice her age, too!"

"According to David, sex isn't a part of their relationship."

"David?" Janinne asked with a puzzled look.

"Rambo. His real name is David Weston. In his own words, he says Amanda's been playing Christian like a cheap guitar for over a year, but he doesn't know why. She refuses to have sex with him, but acknowledges the fact that they really are engaged. Let me tell you, she keeps Christian on a short leash, too!"

"Sounds to me like they're both after something, other than marriage."

"You just hit the nail on the head, Honey," Janinne replied. "The question still remains, what are they after!"

"And what does the club have to do with it? David also said that no one, especially Amanda, would give Christian the time of day if it weren't for this place."

"That's the fucking truth," said Janinne, then slammed down the rest of her Moet.

"Without Chateau Pacific, he'd be just another worthless piece of shit!"

"But he is a worthless piece of shit," Terri said with a grin. "Without Chateau Pacific, he'd be a homeless, worthless piece of shit."

We laughed so hard, it drew the attention of the others, so they joined us in the tub. Jack passed around the tray one more time, and fired up another joint before stripping down to his trunks and getting wet. Suzan and Carmen left their bottoms on, too, but once they were in the bubbling water, all three of them quickly converted to the pleasure of pure nudity.

Even with seven adults, Janinne's hot tub still had plenty of room for everyone to be comfortable without feeling crowded. We all laughed and carried on at a relentless pace, until Terri decided she needed to make use of the facilities, then led a mass exodus of bare femininity to the inside plumbing, leaving Jack and I alone to fend for ourselves. The late afternoon sun had dipped below the mountain tops, so we were on the verge of another glorious tropical sunset in our own little bit of paradise. We took a quick moment to move the liquid refreshments within reach of the tub, then just kicked back with another joint to ease into the ambiance of our warm, wet surroundings.

"What do you think they have in mind for us this evening?"

"Fuck if I know," Jack replied in between puffs, then exhaled and a huge grin spread over his entire face. "Whatever it is, I hope it includes some serious tittie fuckin' and pussy lickin'!"

"Amen, brother-in-law, Amen indeed. After looking at Amanda's special package all afternoon, I could use a close encounter of the wild and crazy kind, be it one-on-one, or in a pile of drunk, horny women."

"Drunk, horny, beautiful women, Jeffrey. Don't forget beautiful. God does have a sense of humor, so you have to be specific what you ask for!" Jack looked around for a moment, then continued, "Damn, they must have taken the party favors with them!"

"No problem," I answered, then reached over and retrieved another joint from my shirt pocket, and handed him one of the three-gram vials Kathy had given me at Christian's party. His eyes got great big, then just looked at me and smiled. "I was hoping Terri would be in a playful mood, so I brought her a little incentive. Not that she needs any, but, oh my God, the other night was nothing short of phenomenal!"

"Amen, brother-in-law. Roberta had me feeding the beast until the crack of dawn!"

Jack helped himself to some of Christian's finest, then, to his surprise, so did I. Not a lot, but just enough of a taste to counter-act some of the alcohol, and also to fuel the hallucinations of another sexual extravaganza with Terri. I was lost in the mental images running rampant through my little gray cells when Jack kicked me to get my attention and pointed to the penthouse doors. Still totally nude, Suzan was strolling back over to the hot tub with a lit joint in one hand and an open bottle of Mumm in the other that she was drinking out of. With a slight stagger in her step and a real air-head expression on her face, she stopped at the edge of the tub only long enough to kiss Jack on the top of his head and pass him the smoke, then jumped in and seated herself right between us. Jack reciprocated by passing her the vile, and she jumped right into that, too!

"Ooooh yeah, I feel real good now," she said, then grabbed Jack's hand and put it on her breast. "Don't you think so?"

"Absolutely!" He smiled at me, but didn't remove his hand. "I don't mean to be rude, but where is your husband?"

"Who cares! That sorry bastard got all pissed off because I wanted to go party with the girls this afternoon, then screamed at me because I was drunk when we got back. He said he worked out some deal with Christian to be the concierge while Christian hob-knobs with his special guests tonight at dinner and later at the disco party. When I asked why, he just yelled and told me to go fuck myself!" She took a moment to have another hit off the joint and bottle, then winked at me and continued. "I told him that wouldn't be necessary."

"So, he won't be here at all this evening?" I asked.

"Fuck no! And I won't be going back to our place either." I felt a hand on my leg under the water, and by the expression on Jack's face, so did he. "Tonight, I'm going to stay right here and party with my friends. To hell with that asshole, I'm in the mood to get fucked up and fucked!"

I was glad to see Terri and the girls coming out to our rescue, even if they were all wearing Chateau Pacific monogrammed white terrycloth robes. Nudity is not as important as safety, and being naked in the hot tub with Suzan was getting to be unsafe for all of us. Drunk, stoned, and hell-bent on revenge is not exactly the proper attitude for a beautiful woman to have sex. No matter how wonderful it might be at the time, sobriety would probably cast an entirely different light on the activities of the previous evening to a married woman. Then again, maybe not!

The reason for the robes was because Andre had arrived with a luscious array of fresh seafood and other tasty dishes for us to enjoy while dining al fresco. The jovial Jamaican took only a few minutes to set up the new buffet, then joined us in a champagne toast to his culinary expertise and the beauty of the evening. If only on the inside, he blushed when Janinne and Bert simultaneously kissed his cheeks, then he quickly departed to attend to his duties downstairs. All in all, he left the penthouse a very happy man.

We had little problem forcing ourselves to overcome the appetite suppression of the cocaine and doing as much damage as possible to the delicious meal he had prepared for us. I opened two fabulous bottles of Meursalt to complement the grilled snapper, stuffed flounder, and piles of cold boiled shrimp and crab, then settled down with Terri on one of the double chaises to consume my fair share.

"Tonight's going to be much more fun than the other night at Christian's," she said, then leaned over and kissed my face. "This time I'm going to eat more, drink less, and concentrate on making you happy, just like you did for me. We've planned a little show for the camera, then it's time to party. Be prepared, we spent all afternoon deciding what to do for you in front of the camera, and afterwards, too!

"Sounds interesting, but what's the deal with Suzan and JC? She's really loaded!"

"She's really hurt, too, Jeffrey. Whatever he said to her after we got back from our shopping expedition must have been pretty brutal to cause her this much pain and anguish. I don't see him as the overbearing, jealous type, so whatever happened must have come as quite a shock to her."

"I agree, Honey. You can tell how much he loves her by just watching the way he looks at her, so something else is going on here." I couldn't help but wonder how much Christian was involved in this plot to undermine their relationship, and why. Whatever "deal" he made with JC to be his concierge must have had some serious strings attached to make a man intolerable to his wife's wants and needs. Divide and conquer has been an efficient tactic ever since Eve and the snake, but what could be his goal and purpose of causing a rift between JC and Suzan. For whatever reason, it was working very well.

Terri and I took our wine glasses over to the railing to watch the sunset over the bay, and were immediately joined by Roberta and Jack. We stood in silent observation, letting the beauty soak into our own personal aura and permanent memory banks, then Bert leaned over and kissed Terri on the cheek.

"So, did you tell him what to expect?" she asked, looking back and forth between us.

"Oh no," Terri replied with a sly grin. "I want Jeffrey to be completely surprised."

"He'll be surprised all right," Roberta exclaimed, "And so will Jack! C'mon Honey, let's go powder our noses and get ready to party."

Before she walked away, Terri opened both of our robes and pressed her nude body into mine for a full frontal hug. We kissed, then she whispered,

"If I were you, I'd make sure I had some film in my camera."

At Janinne's request, Jack and I moved the ice trough back over between the pool and the shower, then set up two chairs for ourselves. When I asked why, her reply was that they wanted to show off what they had bought today, then they had something planned to break the ice and start the real party. Left to our imagination, anything was possible, so we just did what we were told. I had brought the camera bag with all my strobes and stands, so I set up a lighting system using one strobe on the Nikon and two more with slaves on stands to fill out the pattern, then double-checked to make sure there really was film in the camera. To help compensate for the ever decreasing natural lighting, Jack and I redirected some of the decorative spotlights to concentrate on the area around the shower, then all that was left to do was fire up another joint, open some more champagne, and wait for the show to begin. Both of us wanted to go inside and check on the girls, but neither of us wanted to spoil their surprise, so we just sat back and waited.

Janinne stepped out for a moment to check on our status, and to explain the reasoning behind tonight's performance. She was still all covered up in her terrycloth robe, but I could see Terri's handiwork in her glamorous make-up, and easily recognized her Oscar de la Renta perfume, which Terri knows is one of my very favorites. Janinne accepted the flute of Taittinger, but instead of the chair I offered, she chose to sit on my lap.

"You've been wonderful to all of us," she began, "so we've decided to do something wonderful for you. We had so much fun planning this, we almost got thrown out of the Marina Cantina for disturbing the boat snobs. Once Bert made the initial suggestion, everything and everybody, including Carmen, sort of fell right into place." She gave me a warm hug and a quick little peck on the lips, then stood up to leave and said, "We're really jazzed about what we've got planned, but don't forget, guys, the real party doesn't start until after the show."

Our first hint of what was about to be came in the form of the music that flowed from the outdoor speakers strategically placed all around the patio. The first tune came from a bump and grind Diva of rhythm and blues, singing about how much she's got to give, and what she's going to do with it, then the mood continued with some serious jazz designed for the sole purpose of caressing specific body parts. Jack made use of the vial while I switched on the strobes, then it was time for the show to start.

The entertainment began with a parade of five gorgeous ladies all decked out in various different pieces of very naughty lingerie they must have found at Fredrick's of Manzanillo, because none of the outfits they were wearing came out of the Private Edition's collection we had brought with us to photograph. Roberta led the way in a crop-top lace cami that barely covered her over-abundant breasts, and a matching G-string; followed closely by Terri in a lilac colored stretch lace chemise, and Janinne in a killer pair of ultra-sheer, baby blue, baby dolls. Suzan was next in line in a black stretch lace teddie, and Carmen ended the parade in a pale lemon satin and lace cami and tap pants set that screamed "Look at my hard brown nipples!" Roberta handed me the silver tray she was carrying as she passed by, then led her entourage over to the open area next to the shower where they continued to prance and dance to the beat of the sexy music. I took the initiative to spoon out an Amanda sized line on the rectangular piece of polished marble next to the sugar bowl, then motioned for Bert to step out of the chorus line and come join me. She did a cutesy little "Who, me?", then strutted over, bent forward at the waist so I would get the full effect of her magnificent cleavage, and sucked down the party dust with one of the custom made glass straws. Before returning to her partners in crime, she lifted the front of her cami, grabbed the back of my head, and playfully flogged my face with her bountiful breasts, then did the same thing to her husband. Terri was next to dance over and indulge herself, but her follow-up surprise was to step across my chair, fully exposing fantasyland, and giving herself a quick little rub. Janinne, then Carmen were next in line, and both were a little more subdued in their post-indulgence performance by simply backing off and squeezing their breasts for both of us, but Suzan made up for their conservative manner with a more hands on approach. After sucking down a double shot of coke, she turned to Jack Taylor, guided a nipple into his mouth, then reached inside his robe and started massaging his cock! Satisfied with the results of her exploration, Suzan rejoined her companions as they continued their seductive innuendo. Now that the ground rules had been established, it was time to get to work, so I passed Jack the silver tray, and picked up my Nikon.

No matter what song was playing, the scenario remained the same, but now the girls were grouping themselves much closer together for what appeared to be Act 2. Slowly but surely, they began undressing each other, with Carmen being the ringleader of who did what to whom. By no coincidence, Janinne and Terri coupled up, and Roberta and Suzan did the same while Carmen bounced back and forth adding her assistance, and being assisted herself. Through my 80-200 zoom, it seemed like Bert was having the most fun of all, while Terri and Janinne were getting much more involved in each other rather than the game at hand. I took a moment to check on my fellow voyeur, and found Jack just as I expected him to be, totally mesmerized. The flashing of the strobes only heightened the intensity level of their performance as the girls stripped down to nothing but their next surprise of the evening. They had all bought themselves matching belly chains!

When the first roll of film ended, Jack used that as an excuse to join in on the fun while I made the quick change. He danced over to our beauties and served each and every one of them another helping of party dust while they all huddled around and continued to bounce and sway, but in the close confines, it was very obvious that they were also getting more involved with each other, too. Breasts were being rubbed against breasts, buns were being rubbed against buns, and hands were being used to explore and caress all over. Zooming in for effect, it was easy to see that their arousal levels were getting over saturated, and so were mine! Wherever all this was leading, they were most certainly enjoying the ride.

After serving himself, Jack returned to his seat and the girls went for the champagne. They each grabbed a bottle of whatever, then opened them and began drinking and pouring the bubbly all over each other. Suzan was the first one to start licking the champagne off of Roberta's breasts, then they all got into the act. Being the tallest, and by far the biggest, Bert was the easiest target, but each and every one of the ladies got the chance to be on both sides of the sensuous give and take of their erotic party game. At high mag, watching Terri caress Janinne's breasts with her hands and face, then flick those hard nipples with the tip of her tongue did as much for me as it did for each of them! Judging by the expression of sheer pleasure on Terri's beautiful face when Janinne returned the favor and indulged herself in Terri's magnificent breasts, this was no act.

Once the champagne was gone, the ladies moved their show over to the shower for the next chapter of their stimulating performance. At first they laughed and giggled as they rinsed the champagne off of each other, then their playfulness took an erotic turn as they got more specific as to the body parts they were concentrating on. Carmen stepped out of the frame for a moment, and when she returned, I had a better understanding of what Janinne meant when she mentioned breaking the ice before the real party started. She returned with a silver ice bucket filled with small cubes from the brass trough, and immediately they began using the ice in their little scenario, but this time, only Suzan played the victim while the other four supplied the erotic stimulation. After filling their mouths with ice, Roberta started kissing the back of Suzan's neck, Terri and Janinne each attacked a breast, and Carmen dropped to her knees to assault Suzan's special package. Add eight hands to the stimulus pattern, and within what seemed to be a few very short minutes, Suzan started to quiver and quake, then imploded in a screaming orgasm so intense she would have fallen had the others not held her up. Proud of their accomplishments, the ladies playfully laughed and rubbed ice all over each other, then made a mad dash over to Jack and doused him with the remains of the bucket before shoving him into the pool. They allowed me only enough of a grace period to set my camera down, then gang tackled me, stripped the robe from my body, and threw me into the pool as well. The girls jumped up and down at the pool's edge, taunting and teasing us, then ran inside, leaving Jack and I cold, wet, and all alone. If for no other reason, the shock of the cold water provided an instantaneous and welcome shift towards sobriety, so after a few more moments, I hopped out of the pool, quickly dried off, then slipped back into my shorts and shirt.

"Damn, Jeffrey, do you think that's the end of the party?"

"I hope not, but I need to secure my gear just in case things get too rowdy. Nikons don't know how to swim, and when it comes to strobes vs. concrete, concrete wins every time."

"I understand completely, sorta like Astroturf and knees."

By the time I had the lights back in the bag, Jack had dried off, redressed, and fired up another party joint for us to enjoy while we waited for the next chapter of our erotic evening to unfold. Relatively speaking, the night was still young, but with the schedule we'd been keeping, and the amount of intoxicants that had been consumed, the sinking spell I was experiencing seemed well deserved. With my addictive personality, cocaine wasn't an option, so I took a stroll over to the railing to let my body absorb the energy and beauty of the moonlight over the bay. Jack joined me with the smoke and more champagne, then to our surprise, out walked Terri and Roberta in long lacy gowns. They strolled over to us like Goddesses on a fashion runway, then without hesitation, started to undress us.

"Sorry, guys, but the evening's not over yet," Bert exclaimed softly. "If you want to come to our slumber party, you've got to be dressed accordingly."

"Or undressed accordingly," Terri added. "When Janinne said it would be safer if we all stayed here tonight, Roberta suggested we throw an old fashioned girl's slumber party, and invite you guys to crash it." Her eyes were full of mischief as she undid my shorts and dropped them to my feet, then began her sweet seduction by rubbing her lace-enclosed breasts all over me. I responded in the physical manner she fully expected me to, and she focused her efforts on the part of me she had well in hand. Terri maneuvered me "pull-toy style" over to one of the double chaises, shoved me down, then added her many oral talents to her continuing onslaught of my manhood until she had reduced me to a quivering, shivering mess, with a huge smile on it's face. Totally pleased with herself, she kissed me passionately, then curled up in my arms and whispered, "Before I take you into a room full of seductive women in slinky nightgowns, I had to make sure you wouldn't forget me."

"That's totally impossible," I replied, still gasping. "You're unforgettable."

"I was hoping you'd say that. Now it's my turn, Jeffrey. Let's go inside."

After a quick stop to retrieve my robe, and another at the brass trough to pick up four more bottles of ice cold champagne, Terri led me through the glass doors into the sunken den, then directly up into Janinne's bedroom where everyone else was waiting. Carmen took Terri by the hand, kissed her on the cheek, and guided her into the center of the huge bed with all the other girls, then offered me a seat at the foot of the bed against one of the massive bedposts, as she had already done for Jack on the opposite side.

"Relax and enjoy," she said, then helped me set the champagne down in a much smaller brass trough placed in the middle of the short table that ran the length of the footboard. On each end of the table, the girls had placed a slumber party survival kit for Jack and I, consisting of a crystal champagne flute, a matching Waterford ashtray that contained four perfectly rolled joints, a lighter, and a three-gram vial of cocaine. Terri was correct in her assessment of the situation, because each of the girls was wearing a long, slinky nightgown, complete with lace and slits in all of the appropriate places, and the combination of their hair, make-up, and perfumes had completely bypassed suggestion and jumped face-first into seduction.

I pulled a bottle of Mumm out of its icy bath, wrapped it in a towel to prevent any cold drips, then filled all the ladies flutes while Jack took the time to fire up two joints and pass one to Roberta. The girls were lounging in a semi-circle around Suzan, who was laying on her side and transforming a mound of cocaine from the sugar bowl into five monster lines on the black marble slab. They whispered and giggled amongst themselves as they sipped their champagne and passed around the joint, but Jack and I were relegated to being only silent observers, at least for now. Suzan served herself first, then held the slab for Roberta, who then held it for the rest of the ladies as they indulged themselves in the party dust. After a toast and a slam, and then another hearty second round, it was time for the real party to begin. The girls were primed, the champagne was flowing, and the drug-induced eroticism had reached a fevered pitch.

As if in unison, the ladies started cuddling, then nuzzling each other in a very soft manner that evolved itself into gentle kissing and caressing. Jack and I just sat back and watched as the ladies became reacquainted with each other, then again split into two groups, with Suzan and Roberta teaming up, and Janinne and Terri becoming more involved with only each other while Carmen remained a free agent invited into both duos. The kissing became more passionate, but the touching and caressing remained very soft and sensuous. Unlike any adult video I'd ever seen, much less any personal experience, these ladies were extremely delicate and gentle with each other, yet very effective. In direct contrast to my experiences with Bull Dike Betty and her girlfriends, no one was screaming "Fuck me, you bitch!" or "Where's my dildo!" Our ladies truly remained ladies as they pampered each other with soft sexual stimulation. Terri and Janinne were completely at ease with each other, and it was Terri who first slid the straps down off of her shoulders and invited Janinne to enjoy unobstructed access to her magnificent breasts. I couldn't help but wish I had my camera, but then again, I wouldn't want anything to spoil or disturb the beautiful intimacy being experienced right before my very eyes. Roberta, Suzan, and Carmen were being much more physical and playful in their approach to each other, but Janinne and Terri remained focused on the sensitive and loving nature of each other's needs. They were portraying a perfect example of the difference between having sex, and making love.

I took a moment to check on Jack after lighting myself a joint, and he was totally engrossed in watching his wife participate in an all girl menages-a-tois. The expression on his face was one of passive enjoyment of Roberta's pleasure, but his body language was more like that of a leopard watching three sheep grazing right beneath his tree. Sooner or later, he was going to pounce, but for now, figuring out which one to do first while not losing the other two would suffice. There wasn't a doubt in either of our minds that he would and could get all three.

Watching Terri help Janinne out of her gown ended my temporary distraction with the others. Now that both of them were nude, they began rubbing their breasts together as well as kiss and fondle each other. Again, Terri was the first one to reach down into fantasyland and caress Janinne's special package, but once contact was initiated, Janinne reciprocated in less than the proverbial New York second, then laid Terri down on her back for ease and comfort. With every passing moment, the intensity of their passion elevated closer and closer to the state of inferno that I know exists within Terri when she makes love. I've seen it, and I've felt it, but never as only an observer.

With Janinne laying on her side, kissing and nuzzling Terri's neck while continuing her sensual touching, Terri turned her head towards me, opened her eyes and smiled, then reached her hand out and motioned for me to join her. I crawled over and kissed her gently on the lips, then to my surprise, Janinne leaned over and joined us, making it a three-way kiss.

"She's wonderful," Janinne said softly. "Thank you for sharing."

"My pleasure."

"Mine too!" Terri exclaimed. "You both make me feel so good."

"Shall we continue?" I asked Janinne. "I think I know something we'll all enjoy."

I opened the vial in my hand and poured a pile of cocaine on each of Terri's erect nipples, then proceeded to show Janinne the fine art of snowpeaking. By the time we repeated the maneuver, then took a few moments to further enjoy her luscious breasts, Terri was about to go berserk.

"You've got to try that," she whispered to Janinne. "It feels so decadent!"

"In a minute," she replied, then slid down past Terri's waist. "Honey, if you thought that felt decadent . . . . ,"

She began by kissing Terri's labia, then gently introduced her tongue to Terri's precious toy. My baby just closed her eyes, let all her muscles relax, and started breathing through her mouth. Yet another pattern of behavior I'm very familiar with, just not from this angle. Not wanting her delicious breasts to feel ignored, I concentrated my efforts on making sure that they felt both appreciated and well loved. Terri's body started a slow ebb and flow as she allowed herself to ease into the rhythm of the seduction, and fall ever deeper into the joyful abyss of her personal pleasure. She began to whimper and gasp, then quiver until she was consumed by a slight tremor that seemed to last about five seconds. I could feel her whole body relax as she settled back down onto the soft cotton sheets, and I immediately moved to place my lips on hers. Terri's response to me was powerful and passionate, and we engaged in a swallowing match to see who wanted to consume who the most. I pulled her towards me and rolled over on my back, which placed her laying on my chest. She rubbed her breasts in my face while I played with her sculptured ass, then she slid down my abdomen until she encountered and consumed me. Terri leaned over and kissed me again and again as she moved her ass in small circles while forcing me deeper inside her with every motion. We made solid eye contact, then she kissed me again and whispered,

"Are you watching what's happening around us?"

I turned my head to see Carmen and Janinne fully engrossed with each other, while Roberta and Suzan were perfectly content at this point to let Jack have his way with both of them. Without losing her rhythm, Terri squeezed her body into mine, and after a moment or two, looked straight into my soul and whispered,

"Everything you've got belongs to me, and I want it all. Sorry Baby, but I'm not in the mood to share this with anybody."

DAY FIVE

I awoke to the aromatic marvel of fresh coffee, as well as the momentary confusion of not knowing where I was, or how I got there. Luckily, I recognized the little blonde sleeping next to me, and through the mental fog, pieces of my surroundings helped me to remember we were still in Janinne's penthouse. How we wound up in the middle of the floor in her sunken den, I didn't have a clue, but at least we were safe, sound, and still together. I looked around to see Roberta all stretched out next to Terri, Jack sprawled out all over the sofa, and Janinne and Suzan still sound asleep in the comfort of her huge bed. Carmen was standing in the kitchen enjoying the first of the coffee, so I decided to get up and join her. I was clueless as to the whereabouts of my robe, much less my clothes, but since she was stark naked, and I didn't want to deprive Terri and Bert of our only sheet, my only choice was to hope that my nudity wouldn't matter. I mean, after all . . . .

"Did we have a good time last night, or what!" she said with a perky smile, then passed me a mug full of the strong Mexican blend.

"As far as I can remember, a good time was had by all."

"Then you remember correctly, because we most certainly did." She refilled her mug, then winked at me. "I'm heading for the hot-tub, care to join me?"

"Absolutely. Maybe I can find my clothes out there, somewhere."

We stepped over and around the bodies on the floor, and managed to slip outside without disturbing any of the sleeping beauties. The pool looked too cool and refreshing to pass up, so I set down the coffee and dove face first into the brisk water. Rinsing away the cobwebs only took a few moments, then it was off to the hot-tub and Carmen.

"So, what did you think of our little surprise last night?"

"I have to admit that I certainly had a good time," I replied, "and so did Terri. What I don't recall is how we wound up in the middle of the floor. The last thing I remember is holding on to Terri after we made love in the bed."

"Which time, Jeffrey? I thought you were finished, and was ready to make my move on Terri, when you just rolled her over and did her again."

"By request, as I remember." I looked at her and smiled. "I also recall your encounter with Janinne, and something about screaming."

"Yeah, Janinne and I are special pals. We hit it off the first day we met. Actually, the three of us hit it off, and had a great relationship going until Jean Claude showed up and took Suzan away from us. By the way, it was Suzan that did most of the screaming you heard. That's only the second dick she's had since she was a sophomore in high school, and, well, let's just say Jack took care of business last night."

"You said most of the screaming?"

"OK, so now I've had my dick for the year, too. Hell, if Janinne hadn't gotten up and moved to where you were, he probably would have fucked her too, or at least tried. He may be a throwback to the Neanderthal days, but that man certainly knows how to fuck!"

"What's Jean Claude going to say about last night? Don't you think he's going to be a little pissed off that his wife got her brains fucked out while he wasn't around."

"Who cares! That jerk-off doesn't deserve her in the first place." She took the time to light a cigarette, then continued. "Like I said, we had a sweet little relationship going until he showed up with his big dick attitude about six or seven months ago. He went straight after Janinne at first, then when she put him in his place, he turned his attention to Suzan. They escaped to Acapulco with a group of people the last time Christian threw one of his special parties, where Jean Claude proceeded to get her good and fucked up, then take advantage of her. Suzan was sicker than shit and in tears when she called Janinne the next morning to tell her that not only did JC get her drunk and fuck her, but when she woke up, she was wearing a brand new wedding ring! Oh, he says he loves her, and she's putting forth her best effort to adapt, but I wouldn't trust that sneaky Jew bastard any farther than I could throw him."

"Wait a minute, I thought he was French Canadian?"

"French Canadian Jew, and don't ever forget it," she replied. "He's one of the most self-centered, self-serving people I've ever met. Just because he's fucking the assistant manager, he thinks he's in charge of the whole damn place. We've tried to be nice to him, and even invited him to our bedroom for a little get together, but he insisted on being a jerk. Janinne and I were very up-front with the fact that we don't do men; well, at least not most men, and that we did not want him to touch us. After please don't, please stop that, and take your fucking hands off of me failed to get my point across, I damn near drove my fist through his face when he tried to stick his hand up my ass. For Suzan's sake, I'll be nice to him in public, but he knows not to fuck with me ever again."

"How does Janinne feel about him?"

"How do you think she feels! Suzan's been her best friend and lover since their freshman year at Coral Gables. More than anything else, Janinne loves Suzan and wants her to be happy, and if Jean Claude is the one that makes her happy, so be it. End of story. I'd like to say I feel the same way, but I can't even force myself to trust that sorry mother fucker. One of the greatest pleasures in my life is kicking his ass all over my golf course twice a week." She looked to my right and a big smile spread across her face, then she made eye contact with me again. "Did you ever notice how similar Janinne and Terri are shaped? In the light of day, it's almost scary how much they look alike."

I turned to see the two girls walking towards us with coffee mugs in their hands, and wearing nothing but sunglasses. Even though there was at least five inches difference in their height, they certainly could have gotten their body parts out of the same mold.

"Can you believe they're at it again!" Janinne said with a huge grin. "When we came out of the bathroom, Jack had Suzan bent over the edge of the bed and was pounding away while Roberta kept giving her tips on what to do next. I'm surprised you couldn't hear her screaming all the way out here."

"Nothing like a little personalized hands-on instruction," I replied.

"No shit!" Terri kissed me on the cheek and continued. "The next time JC gets a hold of her, she's going to blow his fucking doors off."

Carmen just winked at me and smiled as the ladies joined us in the bubbling water. It didn't take long before the tropical heat and humidity started to crank up, and the hot coffee and luke warm water weren't helping the situation either as the girls became less comfortable and were starting to perspire, just like me.

"I don't want to spoil the party, but I'm in the mood for a bath and some breakfast," Terri exclaimed. "If we're still scheduled to shoot lingerie this afternoon, I'm going to need some rest and relaxation time."

"No problem, Angel. I need to spend some time coordinating tomorrow's big swimsuit shoot, so today's a good day to kick back, relax, and spend a quiet day." Janinne was so focused on Terri, I had to call her by name to get her attention. "Janinne, I would like to incorporate some of Unkle Henri's finest wines into our lingerie shoot, so would you mind sending an assortment of the ones he favors the most to our cabana? I think it would be a good idea to send him a special photograph of someone wonderful holding something wonderful to put on his wall. What do you think?"

"Sounds great to me," she answered, without diverting her eyes from Terri, "as long as I get one for my wall, too."

"Absolutely," Terri replied for me.

We made an uneventful trek back to our cabana and headed straight to the shower. After washing both of us, I left Terri standing in the cool water for an extended rinse cycle, dried off, then headed to the fresh fruit and croissants. I was halfway finished with my first concocted delicacy of apricots and strawberries when I heard footsteps on the pebbles and a knock at the front door.

"Good morning," David said when I opened the door. "I'm sorry if it's still a bit early, but the princess wanted me to get this to you first thing this morning."

He stepped inside and passed me a thick envelope, which curiosity forced me to open immediately. The first thing that caught my eye was the band that surrounded the wad of new 100 dollar bills. It said $10,000. There was also a hand written note that read;

"Dear Jeffrey,

Thank you for a magnificent and quite inspiring afternoon. I'm sorry Christian had to spoil the ending, but certain attitudes are indigenous to his character, or lack thereof. Please accept this token of my gratitude as a retainer for your time and services, and also a deposit on first rights to the marvelous photographs you created of me. It is very important to me that no one here at the club see these photographs before I do, especially Christian.

I have a business proposition to discuss with you, and would like to invite both you and Miss Clark to join me for dinner aboard my boat this evening. If all is agreeable, David will call for you around 7:30. Best wishes to you and yours, ...AMANDA"

I looked up to see David watching my every move and expression. He was smiling, and waiting for me to make the next statement.

"Please tell Amanda thank you, and that we will gladly join her for dinner. Damn, is she always this generous?"

"Only to people she likes," he replied. "She worked out extra hard this morning so she'll look even better the next time you take her pictures. Just between you and me, I haven't seen her this happy since the first time she set eyes on this place. I think . . . . Oh, mercy . . . . Good morning, Terri. I know we haven't been formally introduced, but I'd know you anywhere."

I turned to see my beautiful lady leaning against the doorway into the bedroom, wearing only a bright yellow thong, her new belly chain, and a sneaky little grin. She had her arms crossed over her bare breasts, but not for long.

"Good morning," she responded, then walked over and offered her hand. "You must be David. So, what are you getting us into now, Jeffrey?" Terri casually poured herself a cup of coffee and plopped down in one of the overstuffed chairs.

"We've been invited to have dinner with Amanda on her boat tonight. Any problems with that, Angel?"

"None at all. As a matter of fact, after all the nice things you said about her, I really want to meet Amanda, as long as Christian isn't around. She sounds like a wonderful person, but quite honestly, he makes me sick."

"Me, too," David replied, "but you didn't hear me say that. Like the note says, I'll be here to pick you up around 7:30. For you, Jeffrey, the dress is casual, but for you, gorgeous lady, I suggest you consider something hot and fabulous, because that's what the hostess will be wearing." He took a moment to fire up a joint, and let the drama of his last statement have a moment to sink in. "By the way, I'm going to take my own personal Scarab out for a run and an errand for the princess later this morning. Kimberly's the only one coming with me, so if you would like to join us, there will be plenty of room."

"Absolutely," Terri replied without hesitation. "I know we've got work to do today, but I'd love to take a ride on a fast boat."

"Terrific! Do you know how to ski?"

"Absolutely!"

"Great! Kimberly loves to ski, so that would be an excellent excuse to get some shots of the two of you without catching too much flack from her. I'll send Kimbo to find you when we're ready, so until then, adios. Oh yeah, if you happen to have a video camera, bring it along!"

Andre was thrilled to see us when we walked into the pavilion for Terri's well deserved breakfast, but it was the other diners who came unglued when she made her entrance. She had upgraded her outfit to include the triangle patch top to her swimsuit, floral parea, and stacked-heeled sandals, but the way they were staring at her, she may as well have been butt naked. The crowd was well dispersed, and consisted of seven distinctive and separate groups; one Korean, two Mid Eastern, two South American, one from Eastern Europe, and the last easily recognizable as Vietnamese, but every eye in the room was on her. There were a few other women in the dining area, but they were just left-overs from the previous night, and looked like it. Terri grabbed my arm with both hands and held tight as we followed Andre to our private table.

"I hate the way everyone is gawking at me," she said quietly. "I'm used to being looked at, but not with such hungry stares. I don't like this at all, Jeffrey."

"We won't be here long, Angel," I said, then turned to Andre. "My friend, we're on a tight schedule, so is there something wonderful you can create fairly quickly?"

"But of course!" He held Terri's chair for her, then sat down next to her. "I understand the way you feel about these uncouth foreigners and their penetrating eyes. My darling Karin is hiding in the kitchen because of their unwanted advances, and she wears a wedding ring from me! I shall create for you a special omelet that takes only a few short minutes to prepare, and if you would be more comfortable, I will gladly serve it to you out by the pool."

"Yes, please," Terri replied, then put her hand on his. "Your darling Karin is a very fortunate woman, because you are truly a wonderful man. Thank you, Andre."

"It is my pleasure, pretty lady. For you, anything."

Breakfast took on a much more leisurely atmosphere in the friendly surroundings of the main pool gardens. Terri was calm and relaxed here, and the '85 Dom Perignon didn't hurt her feelings, either. Andre's treat was just that, as the shrimp, pico de gallo, and pork were folded into an egg extravaganza that was covered in a light chili and cheese sauce. Add a few hash browns and some fresh slices of tomato, and the delicious meal did its best to cure any residuals from the previous evening's festivities. There was some activity around the small pool and bar, but we were all alone, and very content to be that way.

After everything had been consumed, we strolled over to the pool bar and ran into Jack and Roberta, who were crashed on a pair of floats. We told them about our upcoming boat ride and asked if they would like to join us.

"Fuck no!" he exclaimed without opening his eyes. "I'm drained, man."

"I wonder why," teased Bert. "That poor girl was starving and didn't even know it."

As we continued our stroll down to the beach, I had a great deal of difficulty keeping my hands off Terri. The mental pictures of last night's pleasures, and the reality of her delicious body in that yellow thong made me want to lay her across the first hammock we could find and continue my life long ambition of loving her every second of every day for the rest of eternity. My insatiable desire for her must have been obvious, because when we passed the swing in the floral arbor, Terri led me straight to it, put her arms around my neck, and kissed me with every square inch of her body.

"I love the way you want me," she whispered as we embraced. "Do you realize you made love to me four times yesterday? I want you too, baby, but you know how to show it much more than I do. Does that ever bother you?"

"When I've got you in my arms, nothing bothers me, Angel."

"You asked me to marry you again last night while we were making love on the floor. Promise me that after we're married, you'll still want me just as much."

"Promise you'll still make love to me on the floor, and it's a deal."

Terri unbuttoned my Hawaiian shirt and laid it down on the soft grass, then quietly slid out of her swimsuit and pulled me to her. As we made love among the flower pedals, she opened her eyes and whispered,

"No one could ever love me as much as you do. Yes, I want to be your wife."

BIG BAD BOAT

Terri was well over an hour into her nap by the time Kimberly finally showed up at our door. I had spent my time taking a leisurely browse through all my mental notes on locations and lighting while doing a thorough check-up on all my camera gear. I know they're just inanimate objects, but I think my Nikons actually feel better after a delicate cleaning and a good blow-brushing. I know I do! Kimberly was wearing a very sexy French cut one piece maillot that was the same ice blue color as her eyes, and she seemed to have a genuine glow about her this morning.

"David really wants me to let you take some pictures," she said, then locked eyes with me. "Let me be honest with you, I've got some nasty scars from an emergency hysterectomy, and a few more from a nigger bitch with a knife over a three line part on Baywatch, but he says you can fix all that and make me look beautiful. Do you really think there's hope?"

"Beyond a doubt!" My curiosity got the better of me, and I had to ask. "So, who finally got the part on Baywatch?"

"I did," she replied with a sly grin, "and I hope that bitch is still having reconstructive surgery on her mouth and face, because I crushed both cheekbones and kicked her fucking teeth out. My dad's a Navy SEAL, and so is my older brother, so I wasn't exactly raised to be what you would call delicate."

"I'll bet that did wonders for your early social life!"

"Oh yeah, that and the fact I was 5'10" at fifteen really helped get me lots of dates."

"I wish I'd known you at fifteen, because you would have been working for me. I still have clientele on my referral list that refuse to use any talent over the age of eighteen."

"You wouldn't have liked me at fifteen," she said, then a huge smile spread across her beautiful face, "but by the time I turned seventeen, I was pouring out of a C cup, and driving my daddy insane."

"I can only imagine." The noises coming from the bedroom could only mean that Sleeping Beauty was awake and stumbling around looking for something. I smiled at Kimberly and said, "If you'll excuse me, I'll go check on Terri and see how long she's going to need to get ready."

"I'm ready right now!" I turned to see Terri with her hair pulled back in a pony-tail under an Astros cap, and wearing the same yellow one piece suit she wore for the shower scene at the beach party. She walked straight up to Kimberly and gave her a big hug.

"You missed a great party last night."

"Oh no I didn't!" Kimberly smiled, then leaned over and gave Terri a kiss. "I had David all to my self until around 10 last night with no distractions. Our quality time together is extremely limited, so we have to take full advantage of every opportunity that presents itself. However, if David hadn't been around, Honey, I guarantee you I would have been up at Janinne's last night getting my share. Speaking of David, grab your shit and let's go."

I picked up the canvas bag with the video camera, as well as my small Nikon bag with only two lenses, one camera, and lots of film, and we headed out the door. One of the things I love about Terri is the fact that she has the ability to shed her feminine instincts to take everything imaginable along with her, and just bring the basics. Lipstick, hairbrush, and suntan oil were the only items she asked me to stash in one of my bags, which left her empty-handed and ready to play.

The scarab moored at the bottom of the ladder was certainly different from the ones I'd seen before. This bad boy was painted various shades of Naval gray in a distinctive camouflage pattern, and even though the high performance engines produced a deep and heavy rumble, they were muffled so as not to sound like a race car with open headers. The three of us stood on the pier while David and one of the boat boys gave the craft a final check, then he motioned for us to come aboard. I thought the young Mexican was going to split his Speedos as he watched Terri climb down the ladder in her T-back suit, then he graciously helped her aboard. After stashing my camera gear in the forward cabin, he returned with a very familiar catalog.

"This is my good buddy Ramon," David said to the both of us. "Ramon, this is Terri Clark and Jeffrey Mason. If you ever need anything around here, this is the man to call, because I trust him like a brother. Terri, would you be so kind as to autograph this catalog for him?"

"Of course I will." She signed the cover, then flipped to the inside back cover which consisted of a full page shot of her in a very sheer white lace chemise that silhouetted every curve of her delicious body. She signed her favorite shot, he sighed, then made a mad dash up the ladder to show his buddies. "I love doing that for nice people," she said.

"Yeah, he's a good kid," David replied. "He was born and raised in a little village about eight miles up the coast, and does his part to support his whole family with what he makes here at the club. I pay him $100 a day to take care of us while we're here, and he earns it. His family has fished this coast for generations, so he knows all the little secret places to take Amanda on her excursions to catch dinner. She lets him drive the Hatteras, and since we give all the fish we aren't going to eat to his family, they don't mind sharing their number one son and favorite fishing spots with us."

"That's very generous of her," Terri said with a curious smile. "Amanda likes to fish?"

"No, Honey," he replied, "Amanda loves to fish. She calls it mindless therapy that brings her back to the reality of life."

"The reality of life with a 2 million dollar fishing yacht," I added.

"Exactly!" David smiled and we exchanged high fives. "In all honesty, with the top of the line power-plant, custom designed interior goodies, and state of the art Naval electronics and communications equipment, she fitted out closer to 4 million and change."

Terri and I just stared at each other with mouths open as David pulled the Scarab away from the pier and headed for the mouth of the bay, and open water. All four of us were standing behind the controls at first, then David cranked it up and it was time to sit or be thrown down as the twin turbos thrust the sleek craft to over 40 knots in a matter of seconds. Terri and I shared the co-pilot's seat, and by the gleam in her eyes, it was easy to see that she was thrilled with the experience of flying across the water at super-sonic speed. David steered us south along the mountainous coastline for about five minutes after we were in deep water and well clear of any sea-stacks or barrier reefs, then made a hard right, and took us due west at full throttle. Our level of exhilaration soared as the beastly engines rumbled and roared, the tachs passed 4000 RPM, and the speedometer reached 60 plus. Be it knots or MPH, we were hauling ass!

David eased back on the throttle after the coastline had completely disappeared behind us, then turned the helm over to Kimberly and made his way into the forward cabin. He returned with a bottle of 85 Krug, four plastic flutes, and a lit joint of something that smelled wonderful. One taste proved it to be something as exotic as the Hawaiian he shared with Jack and me on the Hatteras.

"It's Thai," he said in between tokes. "This comes from the Royal Family's private collection, and makes Don Fernando's shit taste like stinkweed. Amanda has a cousin that gets it for her by the kilo."

"Sounds like a marvelous free trade agreement to me," Terri exclaimed after exhaling the remnants of a good hit. "Holy shit, guys, if you expect me to ski, I can't have any more of this!"

"Speaking of skiing," I asked, "where do you plan on doing it, and what kind of errand are we on?"

David just smiled and passed me a pair of high powered Zeiss binoculars, then pointed towards the northwest. On the horizon, I located what appeared to be four or five ships sharing a common anchorage in the calm Pacific waters. He served the champagne, then pointed the Scarab in their direction.

"We're going to pay a quick little visit to one of those vessels," David said. "Then I thought we'd create a little chaos by letting our ladies ski around the boats while we take a few pictures before we head back to the club."

"And a little video tape, I assume?"

"Exactly!"

As soon as we finished the joint, David pointed our hot rod towards the ships and cranked it up one more time. As we got close, he slowed down and asked the ladies to sit on the back deck for show, then took off his Hawaiian shirt to expose the shoulder holster he was wearing for the same reason. In my gut, I knew what he was doing, but at this point, I could only assume why.

There were only four cargo ships in the anchorage, and David zigzagged between them so everyone could get a look at us before he docked our craft at the gangway of an Ecuadorian freighter named the Yolanda Bonita. We all knew we weren't invited aboard even before he asked us to stay, then spirited himself up the stairs and disappeared. I expected the girls to get a lot of attention from the gawking sailors, and so did they, but it was the guys with the AK-47's that made us all a little on the nervous side. To break the tension, I asked the ladies to take a quick dip in the ocean, which they were glad to do. Luckily, David returned in very short order with a small nylon gym bag that he immediately stashed in the cabin, then motioned for Terri and Kimberly to come back aboard.

"Sorry, but we need to get the hell out of here right fucking now," he said to all of us after helping the girls out of the water. The sight of Terri in her transparent swimsuit made him pause for a brief moment of appreciation, then he got right back to business. "I know we still need a reason to take a few pictures before we get away from those crazy assholes up there, but letting you ski right now is just too fucking risky. I hope you understand."

"Absolutely," Terri replied without hesitation. "If they're anything like the assholes we encountered at breakfast, I'm ready to leave right now. Start this fucking boat and go get your camera, because if all you need is a distraction, we can take care of that."

Terri whispered something to Kimberly as they walked to the back deck and sat down, then they helped each other out of their wet suits, and started posing and waving to all the guys while David pulled us away from the gangway. I didn't waste any time retrieving the cameras, and shot stills and videos of not only our luscious ladies, but all the ships and their markings as David drove around smiling and waving while making sure he did his part to give me the right angles. As we broke away and began our journey back to the club, he turned to check on the girls, then looked at me and said,

"Look, Jeffrey, I know who you are, and I know why you're here, because I'm the one that sent for you."

TERRI IN THE AFTERNOON

Thanks to less than half of a joint of Thai that David gave us to share before lunch, our quick stop at our cabana to rinse off the salt water and let Terri change into something more conservative than a transparent swimsuit turned into a love feast that lasted well past any desire for food. After yet another run through the shower, while Terri prepared herself for our upcoming lingerie shoot, I was relaxing outside in the hammock with a cold can of Coca-Cola when Suzan and JC drove up to our doorstep. They were all smiles and lovey-dovey with each other as they held hands and walked over to me.

"I see you're into the hard stuff," he said, then offered his right hand.

"Oh yeah, enough is enough." I shook his hand, but didn't get up from my position of comfort. "I need to get down to business and give Terri my best effort this afternoon, so I'm trying to calm my act down and lay off the alcohol for now."

"Too bad," Suzan exclaimed, "We've just brought you an assortment of Unkle Henri's favorite wines for props in Terri's pictures, and we were sure you'd want to sample a few of them before, during, and after the shoot."

"I did say for now, didn't I?"

"Yes, you did," she replied grinning, "So, where is your partner in crime?"

"She's inside making herself beautiful."

"That shouldn't take long," JC said with a smile.

"Oh, you'd be surprised," I answered. "I think she wakes up that way, but then again, who am I? What the fuck dude, when she's happy, I'm happy."

"Did you hear what he just said?" Suzan turned JC's face with her hand to make sure eye contact had been established, then kissed him. "I'm going inside to help while you strong, manly men unload the wine and talk about us."

We both watched in earnest as she danced her ass all the way to the cabana. I had no idea what was going on between them, nor did I really care, but I also knew I had no intention of discussing anything that happened last night with her husband.

"I want to thank you for baby-sitting last night while I did some very important work," he began. "With Christian tied up with Amanda, and Suzan out of the way, I got a chance to get up close and personal with Don Fernando and a few of the other special guests, so now I've got a better idea of what's really going on around here. In all honesty, you've been just the diversion I've needed."

"No extra charge, my friend." Now it was my turn! I hopped out of the hammock and walked him over to the edge of the jungle. "Since you seem to be the answer man around here, come show me how this trail leads to Christian's villa."

"Easy enough," he said flatly, then took off up the trail. "It's really closer than you think. I guess the Prince used to keep his favorite mistress in your cabana, because it's the first right turn off of the Royal Pathway and is pretty easy to navigate, even in the dark."

"Is that what you call the main trail, the Royal Pathway?"

"Christian named it, as well as making it off limits to everyone but himself. He's added quite a few more side trails, and lots of electronic surveillance to maintain privacy and satisfy his sick little need to watch the sexual habits of his guests. The whole 'security system' is networked into the A/V room at his house, and into his office. Hell, he even put cameras in Janinne's penthouse while she was away on personal business."

"I know you're not kidding, but if it's common knowledge that Christian has invaded her private domain, doesn't she care?"

"Oh yeah! She wanted to kill the little bastard, but chose to install a kill switch instead. So now, Christian only gets to see what she wants him to. Sounds pretty kinky to me."

As we made our way up the well manicured jungle trail, the mental pictures of last night's sexual extravaganza appearing live on Christian's big screen TV for all his buddies made me cringe. Certainly, Janinne must have had the cameras turned off, or is that why Terri was so popular at breakfast this morning! On the other hand, I seriously doubt if JC would be so jovial had he watched his wife screaming with pleasure while Jack pounded away with his tower of power.

Jean Claude held his hand up for me to stop, then squatted down and slowly moved forward. I imitated his motion and followed for a short distance until we came to an intersection with another, slightly wider trail. He placed his index finger vertically across his lips, then pointed to a surveillance camera mounted on a large branch of a tree that was in perfect position to monitor the main trail, and anyone coming up from the trail we were on. He nodded for us to retreat a few yards, then spoke quietly,

"If those were mine, they'd be set on motion detectors to pick up any activity at any time of day. With the caliber of specialists walking around guarding the envoys for tonight's big meeting, you can count on all the cameras being active. Let's get the fuck out of here before we get spotted."

"So where's the villa from here?"

"Damn, you're curious! Turn left and the Royal Pathway dead ends behind the hot-tub in about a hundred meters. The only bend in the trail is when it goes around the ravine, but like I said, you'd never make it without getting seen, especially now."

"I'm not that curious. I only want to know how to get there and what to expect in case I need to pay him a visit."

JC gave me a peculiar look that bordered indignant and disgust, then headed back towards the cabana at a rapid pace without saying another word. I followed as best I could, but his long loping strides and knowledge of the proper footing along the trail gave him a distinct advantage. Although it took us only a few short minutes to reach the clearing, I had already developed both a dislike and a distrust for my companion. Something about his mannerism was in direct contrast to the happy-go-lucky newlywed that he would lead all to believe was his total existence. I was starting to agree with Carmen, this jerk was working an agenda all his own, and I was in no position to trust him, especially not with something as precious as Terri's life.

We entered the cabana to find our ladies relaxing on the sofa with a fresh bottle of Taittinger sitting on the coffee table, and a pile of cocaine on the mirror next to it. JC stood there and glared at them for a moment, then stormed out the door, set the box of wine in the yard, and drove off in the cart. The expression on Suzan's face showed no surprise what-so-ever to his actions, and her only response was to pick up the mirror, serve herself, then hold it for Terri.

"Isn't he an asshole?" she said in a very matter-of-fact tone. "His `Holier than thou', `God's gift to women' attitude is starting to wear pretty thin, if you know what I mean." She took the time to serve herself another hardy portion of cocaine, then continued, "He actually had the gall to tell me that if I'd stay sober and stop fucking Janinne and her girlfriends, Christian would make him the next General Manager after she was gone!"

"I didn't know she was planning on leaving?" I said.

"She's not! And even if she were, Unkle Henri would select the next GM, not Christian." Suzan sipped her champagne, then broke into a huge grin. "Looks like I've been dumped on your doorstep again. Oh well, is there anything I can do to help in your shoot this afternoon?"

"Absolutely," Terri said. "Take that fucking cocaine away from me, and come help me finish my make-up. We've got some serious work to do for our favorite client, and I won't accept anything less than looking my best for both them and Jeffrey."

I walked over to the sofa, helped Terri up to a standing position, and embraced her. Of all the things she could have said, those were the perfect words for the situation at hand. I held her tightly and whispered,

"I love you, Angel. Thanks for keeping things in perspective."

"You're welcome," she replied, without letting go. "There'll be plenty of time to party after we get finished, but for now, I need to be gorgeous."

"You always are."

We spent the next 2 1/2 hours doing what we do best, working together to create beautiful images of one of the world's most stunning women in and out of exotic lingerie. With the doors, windows, and skylights providing all the natural lighting necessary, I moved Terri from one location in the cabana to another, utilizing the ambiance as a prop to enhance the sensuality of our photographic endeavor. Terri was magnificent, as usual, as she swayed her delicious body to and fro, and used her eyes and face to toy with me and the camera. Suzan oooh'd and aahh'd in the background, and made sure we incorporated at least two separate bottles of Unkle Henri's wine with each outfit we shot. My favorite sequence was done in front of the standing mirror, where Terri stood in white pumps and worked through a series of outfits that ranged from a long, flowing lace gown all the way down to Private Editions' new line of sheer stretch lace bra and thong panty sets. I loved being able to show off both sides of her luscious body in one photograph, and so will our client. Or should I say clients! We took the time to include something wonderful for Playboy at each of the locations, and again Suzan was very helpful by keeping me focused on the assignment and not throwing the camera down and indulging myself in Terri's overwhelming sexual charms. When all was said and done, the three of us plopped down on the sofa to enjoy something to drink, something to smoke, and some good old fashioned camaraderie.

"You two are incredible together," Suzan exclaimed. "I can't imagine a more perfect fit between two people. If there really is such a thing as soulmates, you're it."

"I think so, too," Terri replied. "I never expected anyone to ever love me as much as he does. When we get back to Houston, I get to start planning our wedding."

"How wonderful, but why wait until then?" Suzan raised her flute for a toast, and smiled. "Why don't you get married right here? Of all the parties we've had, I think your wedding would be the ultimate celebration of life."

"As much as we've grown to love this place," I answered, "that sounds terrific, but I doubt if what few friends we have could afford the accommodations."

"I do believe you have some trade-outs coming for all the pictures you've taken for the club, so I wouldn't worry about that. I may only be the assistant GM, but I don't see there being any problems, if you catch my drift."

"See there," Terri said to me with a smile, "I always knew you'd come in handy for something sooner or later."

After another bottle of champagne, and all the cocaine had disappeared in the midst of conversation, Suzan embraced both of us and left to go visit Jack and Roberta. She was warm and toasty, and well on her way to another night of partying as she danced her way down the driveway and disappeared from sight. We held each other for a few moments of peace, then it was time for Terri to begin her preparations for our evening on the boat with Amanda. She wouldn't tell me what she was going to wear, but promised it would be unforgettable.

I had taken the time to go through the entire shower and shave routine, dressed myself accordingly, and was relaxing on the porch with a magnificent glass of Unkle Henri's 1990 Volnay when Terri stepped out in her silk make-up robe in need of a little support. Her hair was curled and pulled around to one side, her exotic make-up was both lightly done and very effective in bringing out her sensuous eyes, yet she still had an air of uncertainty about her. She tasted my Volnay, made a sour face, then sat delicately on the arm of the sofa.

"I can't believe I'm so apprehensive about tonight," she said in her shyest voice. "Would you mind opening another bottle of champagne for me? Maybe I just got ready too early and now I've got all this nervous energy to contend with."

"I'll be glad to open you some champagne, Angel," I replied, then broke out in a sneaky grin of my own. "But if we really have the time, I think I know the perfect cure for all that energy you've got contained."

"Thanks a lot, Jeffrey!" She tried to act offended, but her radiant smile shown through like the morning sun. "No offense lover, but we're not exactly the quickie type. By the time you finished with me, I'd have knots in my hair, my make-up would be smeared all over my face, and we'd both need another shower. It's not that I don't love you, but let's save all that for later. For right now, I just need something to drink that's cold and bubbly, and maybe a little more of that wonderful smoke David gave us."

I opened my darling another bottle of Taittinger, fired up the Thai, and got her to snuggle up with me on the sofa with the promise of only a friendly fondle or two. After the smoke was gone, I followed her into the bedroom with the bottle of champagne, but was immediately ousted as soon as she was ready to shed her robe. I accepted my dismissal with dignity, kissed her hand in a knightly manner, and retreated to the couch to finish up the Volnay and dream about what we're saving for later.

DINNER CRUISE

I was wandering aimlessly around the grounds of our cabana, soaking up the beauty of its floral gardens in the golden hues of another spectacular tropical sunset, and thinking about a wedding. Suddenly, David just seemed to appear on our driveway, holding a small bouquet of flowers. He smiled as I approached him, then stuck out his right hand.

"Good evening, Jeffrey. I hope you don't mind me being a little early, but I wanted to talk to you before Amanda takes charge and dominates your entire evening."

"No problem, my friend. Terri's still getting ready, and I know better than to get in the way, or try to rush her, so I'm just out here enjoying a little tranquility and some outrageous red Burgundy. Care for a glass of Volnay?"

"Hell yes," he answered, then shifted to a more serious expression, "but first I need to clear the air and apologize. I took you on our little excursion because I thought it was important for you to see the freighters anchored out there, and get a better idea of what's at hand here. Those ships are loaded to the fucking gills with drugs, weapons, and other contraband for sale or trade at tonight's meeting of the social elite of the international black market. All I was doing was picking up a kilo of Don Fernando's private reserve for Amanda's nose, just like I've done before, but what I didn't expect was the hostile reception I got from the captain and his exec for bringing you and the girls along. Fuck man, not only were they pissed off, both of them were so fucking loaded, they wanted to kill us, steal the boat, and keep the girls for their personal entertainment." He stopped for a moment to catch his breath, then continued, "I'm sorry Jeffrey, I'm supposed to be a professional bodyguard, but I damn near got us all killed."

"Don't worry about it," I replied. "My only request is that we keep this strictly between ourselves. I'm only here to take pictures of Terri and the club, and be an observer. Terri knows nothing about any of the ulterior motives for my being here, and for her own safety, I insist it stays that way. You say you know why I'm here, and who sent me, so I need to know who else is privileged to that information."

"Nobody," he stated. "Not Amanda, not Kimberly, not anybody. I flew Apaches for the Marines during Desert Storm, and got to be friends with some great people in the intelligence community. After I mustered out and got my job with Amanda, I was approached by a former Marine Captain I had met that told me if I ever came across anything interesting during my travels with the princess, I had an outlet for the information that would guarantee complete anonymity. About six months ago, he contacted me again and started asking questions about Christian and his association with Don Fernando. After he confirmed the fact that his people had no interest in Amanda, I agreed to help, and reported back to him right after the last little meeting they held here about three or four months ago. When I learned about the big meeting being held tonight, I contacted him again."

"And his friends contacted my friends . . . . and I got sent down here to take pictures and observe. So, let's get down to the bottom line. What do you know about the meeting, and who are the participants?"

"Like I said, it's a gathering of the social elite from the international black market. They whore it up for a few days, have an all night business meeting, then whore it up for a few more before going home. The only other thing I know is that Don Fernando picks up the tab, and Christian gets a cut of the action for being the host."

"My friend wants me to find out who the other participants are. Do you think Amanda might know them, too?"

"Ask her! Look Jeffrey, the princess likes you a lot, and is really looking forward to partying with you tonight. She's got a case of Dom on ice, and is already into the cocaine and Thai sticks, so be prepared. All you'll have to do is let her get a little more wasted, bring it up in casual conversation, and I'm sure she'll respond to anything you ask her. If Amanda likes you, and believe me, she really does, she can be a terrific ally with a heart as big as her bust line, so just relax and be yourself. She's not into girls, but I know for a fact that the princess would love for Terri to be her friend, because not only is she gorgeous, she's Amanda's size and shape."

"This sounds too easy, but what the hell, it's better than having to trust JC."

"Amen!" David made a quick look around, then continued, "I wouldn't trust him as far as I could throw him. Kimberly told me about how he drugged and seduced Suzan, and has tried to take over since their so-called marriage, but just between you and me, he smells too much like an agent for my personal taste. There's something going on behind that Cheshire cat smile, and I think you feel the same way."

"Absolutely! Hey buddy, we need to go check on Terri and pour a little more vino before we have to go. I certainly don't want our charming hostess to have to wait for us!"

We strolled inside and were halfway through the last of the Volnay when we were blessed by Terri's magnificent presence. She walked out in a royal blue embossed silk halter dress that was cut to fit her every curve and forced every eye in the room to zoom in on the way it emphasized her dynamic breasts. It wasn't the shortest dress I'd ever seen her in, but it was damn close. We were both speechless, so she made the first audible move.

"Are those flowers for me, or have you boys been spending too much time together?"

"Of course they're for you," David answered blushing, then handed her the bouquet. "Forgive me for staring, but beauty such as yours deserves to be fully appreciated."

"Thank you," she said, then blew him away with her eyes, "but have you already forgotten that you've seen me naked, twice?"

"No way," I replied for my again speechless friend. "Those images are probably permanently engraved in his mind."

"Absolutely," he said when words would finally come out of his mouth. "My God, lady, do you have this effect on everyone?"

"No, not really," she replied with her best coy little grin, "but it's nice to know that I still can when I want to. Remember, you're the one who asked me to dress this way."

She took two steps backward and did a fashion turn so we could enjoy both the low cut back and the way it almost fully exposed the profile of her breasts from each side. I stepped over to the vinocave and retrieved a bottle of Mumm and three fresh flutes.

"That deserves a toast," I said, then popped the cork and poured. After we enjoyed the first slam, David reached into his pocket and pulled out a round, hand tooled silver container that was about two inches in diameter and three quarters of an inch thick. He twisted off the top to show it was completely filled with finely manicured cocaine and handed Terri a short glass straw.

"A gift from the princess," he said then held it while she served herself. Terri damn near choked from the first hit, but composed herself, sipped her champagne, then hit the other side and slammed the rest of the Mumm.

"Holy shit," she said when she could speak, "That's what I call a body rush! Oh my God, Jeffrey, I'm tingling all over." I refilled her glass and she took another long draw before stepping back into the bedroom for a final check before we left for the boat. David closed the container and placed it on top of her dainty cocktail purse, then fired up a small joint for us.

"I mixed a little Thai with my Hawaiian to get things rolling," he said. We each had a toke, then he passed it to Terri when she rejoined us. "Here you are, pretty lady. This should help take the edge off, then my friends, it's time for us to go."

Terri couldn't navigate the pathway or the pier in her heels, so she was still barefoot when she stepped aboard the Hatteras for the first time. David escorted us straight to the bar in the main salon, seated Terri on a barstool, then opened the first bottle of Dom Perignon for the evening. He joined us for a toast, then excused himself to go tell Amanda we had arrived. Terri was awestruck by the elegance of the custom designed interior as her eyes darted all around the room, trying to absorb everything, then focused back on me. Her mischievous look should have prepared me for what she was about to say, but didn't even come close.

"Do you remember when I said that I was going to wear something unforgettable?"

"Absolutely, lover, and you did. Your body in that dress is nothing short of awesome."

"Thank you, Jeffrey," she said with a sly grin, then grabbed my hand and put it on her thigh. "Amanda may be young, beautiful, and exotic, but don't you ever forget that I'm the one who's not wearing any panties." She gently guided my hand up her leg, and sure enough, the doorway to Fantasyland was unobstructed.

"Oh my God, Angel! Now that you have my brain racing, how could I ever forget?"

"That's exactly what I had in mind, Darling! So don't forget that no matter what Amanda serves for dinner, desert will be served in our bedroom."

I leaned over and kissed her lightly on the lips, then she winked at me when we clinked glasses to seal the deal. No doubt about it, this woman was my soulmate for life.

"Good evening." Amanda emerged from the stairway down to her cabin with bright clear eyes, a radiant smile, and her huge Chinese companion. She looked flawless in a tight and fitted, strapless black floral silk sheath that cradled her breasts and just barely covered her nipples. It was only slightly longer than Terri's dress, but was slit up one side all the way past the top of her thigh. Terri stepped down from her barstool, making them exactly the same height in heels, and the girls exchanged the traditional European greeting of kissing both cheeks, then Amanda offered me her hand, which I kissed. Chang nodded his acceptance to me, then stepped behind the bar and poured Amanda a crystal flute of Dom. The last one up from below was David, but he only stopped long enough to hold the barstool for Amanda to be seated, then he said,

"With your permission . . . ."

Amanda only nodded, then he walked straight to the glass doors, and was gone. In moments we felt the mighty diesels come to life, and our voyage began. As soon as we pulled away from the dock, Chang set out a large rounded piece of polished black marble on the bar, placed a heaping tablespoon of manicured cocaine in the middle of it, then laid out an assortment of glass straws and a solid gold single edged blade. Amanda cut out two hefty lines, then handed Terri a long straw.

"Please, help yourself," she said smiling. "I understand Jeffrey doesn't care for this brand of party favors, so all this is for you and me. The road to friendship begins with the first step, so shall we get started?"

"Absolutely," Terri replied, then inhaled her line in two short hits. Amanda just smiled, then sucked the other line down all at once. She cut out two more lines of cocaine, sucked one of them down with her other nostril, then passed the slab back to Terri, who duplicated her initial technique. The ladies clinked glasses, slammed down their champagne, and the friendship was off and running.

"Your boat is exquisite," Terri began, "and Jeffrey's been ranting and raving about your master stateroom. Would you be offended if I asked to see it?"

"Not at all. As a matter of fact, I'd love for you to see it." Amanda extended her hand for me to assist her off the barstool, which I did with pleasure, then they retrieved their refilled flutes and headed for the stairwell. Amanda hesitated at the top of the stairs only long enough to address her constant companion. "I think we'll be fine, Chang, so please join David on the bridge and enjoy the ride. I'm sure Jeffrey can handle the champagne, and any other chores that may arise on our guided tour."

I took the hint and accepted the fresh bottle of Dom handed to me by the huge Chinaman, and followed the ladies down to the lower foyer. Amanda opened the door to her suite, but paused for a moment and spoke to Terri.

"Chang and David each have suites on opposite sides of the craft, and the galley, communications center, and guest bath are located in-between. Now, if you'll follow me, I'll show you my room."

Terri was completely blown away by the opulence of Amanda's private domain. She wandered around smiling like a five year old in Toys-R-Us for the first time, and made all the right comments to our gracious hostess. When she saw the brass and glass shower, Terri put her arm around Amanda's waist, tilted her head towards her, and said,

"Gee, I'm sorry I already took a bath. That shower looks totally decadent."

"It is," Amanda replied with a sly grin. "The hand-held shower head has three pulsating speeds; relaxation, stimulation, and masturbation!"

After showing off all the closet space, Amanda led Terri to the tall dresser where she pulled out the same antique mirror I'd seen before, then they both walked over to the bed and sat down across from each other. The princess carved out four lines from the pile of cocaine, laid down on her side, and offered Terri first shot at the goodies by setting the mirror down on the bed between them. From my angle of view, Amanda was all but falling out of the top of her dress with both nipples fully exposed, and Terri was doing just about the same thing as she leaned forward, and then reclined. As both girls laid on the bed and enjoyed the coke, the idea of a menage-a-tois made a brief, but graphic romp through my testosterone-induced sub-conscious, and it must have put a shit-eating grin on my face, because Terri whispered something to Amanda and they both looked at me and started giggling. Rather than just stand there and look stupid, I chose to walk over and serve them more champagne, and look stupid.

"It's nice to know I amuse you, ladies," I said, while trying not to slosh the very expensive champagne all over them.

"Play your cards right, Jeffrey, and you might be the one being amused." Terri's eyes flashed me the mischievous look I've grown to love, then she and Amanda burst out laughing and served themselves one more time before rolling out of bed. After adjusting their breasts and mussing with their hair, the ladies slammed another glass of champagne, then it was time to move on to bigger and better things.

Amanda led us through the main salon and out through the glass doors onto the rear deck. The mighty Hatteras was running smooth and easy in the golden array of sunset as we headed north along the coastline about a mile offshore. I could still see the lighted buoys marking the entrance to the bay at Chateau Pacific, but those were the only lights visible along the entire majestic coastline. We stood there in silence, admiring the view until we ran out of wine, then Amanda made a head motion, and we followed her up the ladder to the bridge. Ladies first, of course!

"We're having fresh red snapper for dinner, but we have to catch it first," Amanda said to us once we were all on the bridge. She waited for Chang to open and serve a fresh bottle of Dom from the ice chest, then continued, "There's a splendid snapper reef about five miles from here that must have a population of more than a hundred thousand fish. Ramon, David, and I caught over fifty of them in less than an hour our last time down here, so I don't think we're going to go hungry tonight. At least not for dinner!"

"We're going fishing?" Terri asked, then burst out laughing. "Dressed like this, we're going fishing! Girlfriend, I like your style!"

"Being rich is not a crime, Terri, but it does have its advantages." She clinked flutes with both of us then slammed down the bubbly. "So if we want to drink Dom Perignon, snort the world's finest cocaine, and go fishing in our Versace party dresses, so be it!"

"Amen, sister . . . . Amen."

I gently grabbed Terri by the arm to get her attention, then whispered,

"Versace, darling?"

She batted her big baby blues and flashed her pearly whites, then said to me in her sweetest voice, "Don't worry, baby. It was on sale."

By the time we reached the reef, Chang had produced two very expensive looking snapper rigs, a bucket of bait, and an ice chest ready for our potential dinner to chill out in. As the girls were climbing down the ladder, I accepted David's invitation to stay on the bridge and smoke a joint while Chang did all the dirty work below. We kept the speed down to a slow crawl while Terri and Amanda worked each side of the boat, dropping their baited hooks down to the hungry fish below, and reeling them in as fast as they could. Chang worked a steady pace of unhooking and rebaiting until the count reached an even dozen fish, and all of them looked at least six pounds or more. Without breaking a nail, or much less touching a fish, the girls had caught more than enough for our dinner in less than fifteen minutes. They embraced like they'd just won the Superbowl, then dashed inside the cabin to fix their windblown hair and powder their noses. David fired up another joint, and started a slow turn to port.

"Time to head on back," he said. "The princess made arrangements with Andre to cater all the side dishes to surround the entrée they just caught, and by the time we get back, Chang will have all of them cleaned, filleted, and ready for our chef to throw on the portable grill. Andre said he's going to create an Oriental style dining pagoda on the end of the pier to enhance your culinary experience, so all we have to do is pull up to the dock, turn on a little light jazz, and dinner will be served." He sucked down another hit of the awesome Thai-Hawaiian combo, then passed it to me, smiled, and handed me another party-sized joint from his shirt pocket. "No offense, amigo, but if I were you, I'd be spending the next twenty minutes downstairs with those two hot rods instead of hanging around up here with me. Amanda should be in the mood to start some serious smoking, and drinking, and carrying on before dinner, so get on down there and ask her whatever the hell you really want to know about this place. Like I said, she likes you a lot, so just stay cool and she'll probably give up more than you bargained for."

I took his advice after one more toke, and climbed down from the covered bridge to check on the ladies. I found them sitting on the sofa together enjoying yet another bottle of champagne, and to my surprise, smoking a joint. I seated myself across from them on the love seat so as not to interfere with their conversation, and also to enjoy the view. Their hair was brushed, their lips glossed, but their shoes were still off as they both sat facing each other with their feet curled up underneath them. I just sat there in silent observation of both their bonding and beauty until they ran out of champagne and needed something from me.

"I'm sorry, Jeffrey, have we been ignoring you?" Amanda held up her empty flute and smiled. "Would you be so kind?"

"My pleasure." I refilled all of our glasses, then made my way over to the bar for a new bottle. On the bar was a crystal cigarette holder shaped like a book, and inside was about a dozen rolled joints. I grabbed two, fired one up with the matching crystal lighter, and returned with a gameplan to switch gears on their conversation.

"So how did you arrange for us to have a private dinner without your fiancé throwing his normal shit fit or crashing the party?"

"Very simple, Jeffrey," she replied. "He already had plans with Don Fernando and the other dignitaries for dinner and a business meeting."

"Dignitaries?" The screwed up look on Terri's face emphasized her question.

"Dignitaries . . . . businessmen . . . . assholes, whatever you want to call them is fine with me." Amanda took a long draw off the joint, held it as long as she could, then exhaled and continued, "I've known Don Fernando since I was 10 years old, and it's because of his business relationship with my father that I get invited to parties all over the world. He's a good man with a kind heart, but the other brokers are nothing short of egotistical vermin."

"Like Christian?" Terri pulled no punches and hit Amanda right between the eyes with her version of the truth. "Forgive me for being blunt, but what does a beautiful young woman like you want with an arrogant old asshole like him. My God, Amanda, with your brains, beauty, and bucks, you could have any man you wanted! Why him?"

"Thank you for the compliments, but I think you give me too much credit. Men like Christian are attracted to me because of one thing, and one thing only, my money. Being that one dimensional immediately puts them at a disadvantage, which I exploit at every opportunity. With Christian, however, the game has taken on a whole new level of intrigue because of the grand prize."

"And that prize would be Chateau Pacific?"

"Correct." Amanda smiled at me and tipped her glass my way. "I fell in love with the resort the very first time I saw it, which is exactly how Christian says he feels about me. I know that's a lie, because I had his background investigated and found a pattern of lies. He says he's the owner, which he's not. He says he runs the resort, which he doesn't. He even told me he owns vineyards in France, which he certainly doesn't. The only truth about Christian is that he's lived off his family's wealth all his life, and now he wants to live off mine."

"But Amanda, if all you want is the club, why not just buy it and fire his sorry ass!"

"That's exactly what I have in mind, Terri, but there are a few legal problems that would rear their ugly heads if the resort were to leave the hands of the Morea family."

"So you're willing to marry him just to get your hands on this club?" Terri asked.

"Oh no! Fuck no! Never! Our engagement is only a vicious tease on my part to keep Christian on an even shorter leash. Legally, Christian has no claim on this club, or anything else owned by the Morea family, especially their vast fortune in vineyards and the wine industry. Henri Morea has a modest trust fund set up in his will to take care of Christian, but it also states in no uncertain terms that he is to receive no part of any of the family's holdings, properties, or businesses for fear of ruining the family name, or destroying generations of hard work."

"Smart man," I said to them both. "Does Christian know about the will?"

"Not a clue," she replied with a cruel grin. "He still thinks he's the sole heir to the entire estate, when in reality, everything goes to Unkle Henri's niece."

"Be that the case," I began, "if you can't own the club outright because it has to stay in the family to maintain the supply-line to all the free wine from France, and marrying Christian gets you absolutely nothing, your only option is to buy into a partnership with Unkle Henri."

"Or the niece." Amanda smiled at herself and slammed her champagne. "Henri Morea is not easily impressed with money. My father offered him ten million dollars in cash for a two acre vineyard in Montrachet, and he refused because those vines created the wine for his dead brother's wedding. The niece, however, was not raised in France, and has lived a very modest lifestyle with comfortable, but limited funds, so that same ten million dollars might be worth a lot more to her for simply letting me be a silent partner. The only thing I would want to change about Chateau Pacific is to get Christian and his business dealings with those whore mongers away from here before they destroy the integrity of the club."

"So where does Don Fernando fit in with these whore mongers?" I had to ask the baited question to lead her into what was coming next.

"He's just a broker," she responded in a flat tone. "He sets up deals for his clients, then helps both parties with specific arrangements like payment, shipping and handling, or anything else he can do to get a bigger cut. Now that he's moved his money-making machine out of Colombia and into Ecuador, he doesn't attract as much scrutiny as before, so business is booming. I'm sorry to say he's the one who showed Christian how to generate some significant cash by hosting three or four of these little parties a year, so now Don Fernando can have these gatherings at five or six different locations around the world."

"These gatherings seem to be for the kind of people that don't exactly have what you would call a legitimate storefront with normal business hours, so who are they?" I watched her eyes for any adverse reactions to the question, but she didn't even flinch.

"Brokers . . . . lawyers . . . . Wheeler-dealers, whatever. They represent factions that control different commodities on the international black market. Don Fernando's clients have tons of cocaine to sell, and massive amounts of cash to buy anything that might generate a profit, so that's why he's the host, but don't jump to the conclusion that this is only about drugs. The third world has a mad craving for technology, be it military or industrial, so this is the perfect outlet for the big boys and their spin doctors to dump last year's secrets or any surplus material without breaking any embargoes or trade agreements."

"So what you're saying is that Don Fernando and his clients from the various Colombian cartels are using their drugs and money to become an exclusive international fence for anything they feel will turn a good profit, or make them more powerful on the world market."

"Exactly," Amanda replied. "And for a percentage of the take, as well as an influx of cash, Christian allows them to use and abuse this beautiful resort as a meeting place."

Amanda excused herself for a few minutes and made her way down to her cabin, leaving Terri and I alone in the salon. She winked at me, then shifted her position on the sofa to where she fully exposed her bare assets to me and began a slow massage of her private entrance.

"I wish we were back in our cabana right now," she purred. "I love the way this combination of ingredients makes me feel so hot and nasty. Would you please come over here and lick me 'til I scream!"

"Certainly, my love," I replied, and moved slowly over to the couch, "but don't you think our hostess would have a cow if she caught us fucking on her expensive sofa."

"Who gives a shit, Jeffrey!" She threw her arms around my neck and tried to devour me with her hungry mouth. Instinctively, my left hand grabbed a handful of her soft curly hair, and my right hand went straight up between her legs. Terri lit up like a sparkler, and was both ready and willing to shift into the next gear, when the glass doors opened and David entered the salon. He smiled all the way over to the bar, where he picked out one of the joints and fired it up.

"See, I told you you'd have more fun down here with them instead of up there with me," he said with a shit-eating grin. "Tell the princess we'll be ready to dock in less than five minutes."

Amanda rejoined us only moments after David went back to the bridge, and to our surprise, had changed into a short black silk robe and matching silk boxers. Her unencumbered breasts danced freely under the soft fabric as she walked over to us and extended both hands.

"You two are wonderful," she said with a warm and genuine smile. "That dress was just too tight, and too hard to get out of, so I decided to get comfortable for dinner. I hope I didn't take too long."

"No, not at all," Terri replied. "As a matter of fact, we were on the verge of joining you when David came to tell us the boat was ready to dock."

"Poor Jeffrey," Amanda said, still holding our hands. "Just as things start to get interesting, we always seem to run out of time, don't we? I hope the three of us can resolve that problem before we have to leave the resort and get on with our lives."

"Me, too," Terri purred. "With all we've put him through over the last few days, I think Jeffrey deserves a little warm and personal attention from the two of us."

Before I could figure out what or how to respond, the large Chinese man-servant of the princess entered the salon via the glass doors, held them open, and said in all the proper tones of the Queen's English,

"It is time."

PAGODA TIME

Andre had outdone himself in creating the perfect atmosphere for our gourmet meal, even if the pagoda did look more like the top half of a gazebo nailed to the end of the pier. It was furnished with Oriental rugs covering the wooden slats of the pier, color coordinated pillows to sit on, and a beautiful hand carved pedestal table the perfect height for dining on the floor. Brass lanterns were suspended from the roof of the pagoda to provide both ambiance and illumination for our dining experience, and the jovial Jamaican had even come up with an awesome display of crystal and china, as well as a floral arrangement to complete the table setting. All in all, he had done a terrific job for the three of us in less than an hour's time.

David and I helped the ladies off the Hatteras, and after a cheerful greeting by Andre and Karin, we sat down and were immediately presented our first course of cold boiled shrimp and crab cocktails served with the first of many bottles of a magnificent Batard Montrachet. At first sip, I knew everything I'd read about the spectacular vintage was only a vain attempt to describe the sheer pleasure of enjoying it on one's own palate.

"The wine is excellent," I said to our hostess. "It's young and vibrant . . . ."

"Just the way you like things," injected my darling companion, and then slid my free hand up under her dress as a subtle reminder.

"I agree," Amanda stated, while swirling her wine in the oversized crystal goblet. "With the noted exception of Dom Perignon, vintage Port, and certain classic reds, I prefer my wines to be young and alive, especially the whites. I don't care what the critics and wine snobs say, when it comes down to my taste buds, they tell me the younger the better."

"That's all that matters," Terri replied. "Jeffrey taught me that the only opinion that counts is your own, and it applies to more things than just wine."

"Absolutely!" I raised my glass to the ladies and had a personal toast.

As we finished with our appetizers, then worked our way through our salads, I was amazed at how well our evening was going. The ladies were getting along splendidly, with no signs of competition or petty jealousy, and there was nothing fake or false about their attitude towards each other, or me. The only thing I found to be peculiar was their ferocious appetites. Had I consumed even a third of the volume of cocaine they've indulged in tonight, I wouldn't have been able to eat for days, yet they seemed to be enjoying every single bite. Once we got into the grilled snapper, I had to ask why.

"Purity," Amanda responded. "Don Fernando always makes sure I get the best of the best before anyone else gets their hands on it. It's the cut that gets added every time the coke changes hands that tears up your stomach. I learned that lesson the hard way, as I'm sure you did too."

"Oh, yeah! That's one of the main reasons I stopped enjoying it."

Amanda discreetly rubbed her nipples with her thumbs, then looked straight through my eyes and into my testosterone production facilities.

"I still think Terri and I can, and will, change your mind about that."

"For some strange reason, I don't doubt that in the least." We smiled at each other and let sleeping dogs lie. For now, at least.

Once the main course had been cleared from the table, Andre presented us with a small assortment of bite-sized deserts and a pot of Jamaican Blue Mountain coffee to finish our meal. After making a point about saving my desert for later, I poured myself another glass of the delicious Montrachet and watched as the ladies oooh'd and aaah'd while working their way through the decadent little delicacies. In all honesty, they were pretty damn cute together in a friendly, heterosexual way.

"Amanda, what are you doing tomorrow morning around nine?"

"Excellent idea, Jeffrey," Terri exclaimed.

"Tomorrow morning around nine sounds a little early for me," she answered, "but I guess that depends on what you have in mind?"

"We're shooting the final round of swimsuits for Sunset Limited tomorrow. Our plan is to shoot around the pool in the morning, then shoot down at Janinne's private beach in the late afternoon." I hesitated for effect, then popped the question. "Janinne, Suzan, and Roberta have already agreed to participate, but there's always room for one more. Would you care to join us?"

"Oh God, Jeffrey, I'm too ugly in the morning to even consider it! I'd love to come watch, but there's no way I'd dare step in front of a camera before noon." She took a moment to calm down, then the twenty-two year old little girl on the inside overwhelmed her mature sophisticate facade. "Can I still be in the afternoon session?"

"Absolutely," Terri barked. "This is going to be great! Finally there's going to be somebody my size to pose and play around with. It's so damn hard to compete with other models when they make you feel like a shrimp."

"I understand completely," Amanda said with an honest smile. "My dear Terri, there's no way they can compete with you because they aren't even in your league. Thank you for the invitation. I'll watch and learn from you in the morning, then be ready for later."

"Sounds like a plan to me. All you'll need to do is sign a release form, and we'll be able to publish your shots in the catalog. Do you have a problem with that?"

"Not at all, Jeffrey," Amanda replied, then smiled at me over her coffee cup. "And speaking of publication, when do I get to see the shots we did yesterday. If they're as good as I think they're going to be, and I have full confidence in you that they will be, I want to get them in the hands of Playboy and Penthouse as soon as possible."

"I agree. The film is already in San Diego being processed, as are the CF chips, so I expect everything will be sitting on my desk when we get back to Houston in three days. It will take a day or two to edit through all the shots, so I could probably have your portfolio ready for viewing in about five days."

"That's wonderful, Jeffrey, but unfortunately, I'll be in France pursuing a new business venture. My plans are to stay at Chateau Pacific only as long as you're here, then fly directly to the south of France for at least four or five days, if not longer."

I could almost feel the wheels turning inside her head as she mulled over various possible solutions, but it was Terri that came up with the first, and best suggestion.

"Why not let us bring them to you," she said with a glowing radiance. "Once we get the Sunset Limited and Private Editions presentations finished and shipped, we're going to need a vacation, a real vacation, and the south of France sounds wonderful."

"That's an excellent idea, darling! Not only will it give us a good excuse to see France, it will also give me the chance to put a stock portfolio in the hands of Count Von Spengler to see if he's legitimate about publishing my work." I looked over at Amanda to watch her reaction, then asked, "What do you know about the Count?"

"In all honesty, very little," she stated, "but I can certainly do some checking for you. David seems to like him, but since his family owns one of the largest publishing houses in Europe, my father has demanded that I avoid him like the plague to make sure I don't wind up in the press."

"Excuse me, but what do you think your father is going to say about the press you're going to get in Playboy and Penthouse!" Terri took a deep breath to calm herself, then continued. "If you're going to play the game, Amanda, play to win. Considering your infamous status and massive fortune, you can fully expect both publications to put you in every single international edition they produce, as well as their larger domestic issues, so why not go for a full media blitz by allowing the Count to put you on the cover of his most prestigious publications, too! I know you don't need the money, but a girl can't have too many magazine covers, or good publicity."

"Terri's got a good point, Amanda. If achieving star status is your absolute goal, why not let Count Von Spengler help all of us. Besides, something a little less sexually oriented might help your father get over the shock of seeing his little girl up close and personal in a gentleman's magazine." This time it was my turn to catch my breath before I tossed the room-service fast ball down the middle of the plate. "For your information, the Count already asked me to get some good shots of you, and offered a million dollars cash for the best one."

"Consider it done, Jeffrey," she replied without hesitation. "But like Terri said, if you're going to play, play to win. If he offered you a million dollars for one photograph, think what we could negotiate for an awesome twenty shot series! Business deals are my forte, so why settle for a million when I can arrange for you to get five or ten."

Terri and I just looked at each other and gulped. We've had people toss numbers at us before, but never in multiples of seven figures! I've dealt with lawyers and agents long enough to know the difference between reality and bullshit, but the number of zeros behind the initial figure was still mind blowing. A million dollars may only be pocket change to the princess, but not to me or Terri.

"I've got an idea that might allow us to take care of all our needs in one fell swoop," Amanda stated. "I've got a cute little villa in St. Tropez that would be perfect for both some relaxation and more photographs, as well as provide an excellent home-court advantage for our negotiations with the Count. Can you even imagine him trying to say no to Terri and I while we're sipping champagne and lounging around the pool totally nude? I don't think so! I'll send David to pick you up in Houston, then when we're ready, we can contact the Count and ask him to come join us. After we've cut the deal and made both of you millionaires, we'll hop on a yacht and cruise to Monte Carlo so we can celebrate in style."

"Now that's my idea of a plan," Terri exclaimed. "Even if he blows off the deal, just being in St. Tropez sounds wonderful."

"Believe me, there's no way Count Von Spengler's going to blow off this deal, because my plan is to offer all three of us together in a package that would let him dominate the European market with Jeffrey's photographs. Anyone else who wants us will have to deal directly with him, so he's in a no lose situation." Amanda reached out and held hands with both of us, then smiled warmly. "I may only be a flash in the periodical pan, but you two will be around for a long, long time. The combination of your charm and beauty with his talent has already proven to be a marketable commodity, so why not ask for a percentage of your fair share of the profits up front. Everyone else does!"

"I'm going to be diplomatic and agree with both of you," was my answer. "If the Count wants to be our European representative and hand us a chunk of change up front, why not! If he declines the offer, well, that's OK too. We'll still have a great time together, and I've always wanted to experience the true hedonism that is St. Tropez."

"After the tranquil beauty of Chateau Pacific, I'm afraid you'll be disappointed," she answered. "The south of France may be many things to many people, but I find it to be overcrowded and over-rated."

"Considering the fact that we've never been there before, I'm sure we'll be too excited to care," Terri exclaimed.

"Again, I'm going to have to agree with both of you. The thought of being alone with the two of you at a private villa in St. Tropez sounds more like a wet dream come true rather than a business trip, no matter how over-rated the area may be, so me and my cameras will be ready, set, go!" I turned my attention fully on Amanda, and tried to be as discreet as possible. "Would your business venture in France have anything to do with Henri Morea and your desire to acquire Chateau Pacific?"

"You're very perceptive, Jeffrey Mason," she replied with that same cruel smile. "I feel it's time for me to make my move before Christian discovers he already has enough money and power to not only control his situation, but to also lead the little rat pack he's running with now."

"I assume you're referring to the 'dignitaries' that have arrived to conduct business for their infamous employers from all over the world?" Terri asked.

"All over the third world." Amanda replied. "Like I said, Christian's turning this beautiful resort into an open air market for all the most loathsome filth on this planet. Those assholes will be up all night screaming at each other about who's shit is more valuable, and who's boss is more powerful. Combine Colombians, Koreans, and Arabs, God, I hate fucking Arabs, in one room, and the only thing worse than the way they act is the way they smell! Henri Morea would have a massive coronary if he knew what was really going on here."

"Let me guess," I said with a straight face, "while in France, you just might drop a few hints to Unkle Henri about Christian's marketing endeavors during negotiations to help him make up his mind about price, or simply just sway his decision in your direction."

"As I've said before, I always get my way."

"Ooh, the Dragon Lady surfaces!"

"Actually, Jeffrey, I've always preferred Psycho Bitch," she said with her best smile. "Now, enough about my soon to be ex-partner and his band of thieves. Let's talk about photographs . . . Our photographs . . . And our next session at my villa in France."

And we did.

From their point of observation, the three people seated under the pagoda looked small and insignificant. With one click of the mag wheel on the night scope mounted above the high powered rifle, individual features could easily be made out. One click more, and Christian could place the crosshairs at the top of Amanda's massive cleavage.

"Bang! I've just blown the tits off that frigid Nazi cunt!"

"Soon, my brother, soon. The wrath of Allah will descend upon her and she will become no more than a grain of sand in a windstorm. For now, feel the balance of the weapon in your hands. I'm told each round is hand tooled to guarantee accuracy at up to 1300 meters. The electronic sighting, silencer, and full magazine only adds to the stability of this fine weapon."

"You're not selling me an automobile, Mahmood, so cut the crap. The rifle is excellent, but I just wish it could be me who pulls the trigger and blows her away."

"The hand of Allah works in mysterious ways, my brother. Maybe it will be you, or me, who is blessed with the ability to carry out his will. Within forty-eight hours, all the pieces will be in place, and then . . . ."

"Yes, yes, I know. The slut will be dead, and we will posses the majority of her vast fortune to do His will."

"Ha'am dul Allah!"

"Yes, Mahmood. Praise be to God. Now, let's get back to our guests and make some money for our own pockets."

NIGHT MOVES

Our barefoot stroll back to our cabana was very light-hearted, and filled with joyous predictions of our upcoming encounter with Amanda, the Count, and a private villa in the hills above St. Tropez. Add the euphoric stimulation from all the intoxicants we had consumed over the course of the evening, and needless to say, the electricity flowing between us had a definite sexual overtone. The evening was still fairly young, but the kind of party we had in mind had nothing to do with a disco!

We had been back in the air-conditioned salon of the Hatteras barely long enough to taste the '62 Noval vintage Port when Amanda received a call from her father that brought our evening to an immediate halt. David made the announcement only minutes after she left the room that he was to escort us back to our cabana, and that Amanda regretted having to end such a wonderful evening so abruptly. He walked us to the beach bar, then left us alone to enjoy a moment of privacy on a wooden bench under the tropical moonlit sky. Before leaving, David embraced us both, and passed me two more joints and a three-gram vial of Amanda's favorite uncut delicacy. Terri choked down a capful, and I fired up a joint, but then it was time to immediately deal with our thirst, so we gave up on the heat, humidity, and moonlight, and headed back to our cabana for some air-conditioning, ice-cold champagne, and clean sheets.

We'd been in our not-so humble abode only long enough to take care of a little oral hygiene and change into something comfortable, when there came a friendly rapping on our door. I tossed my cotton robe over my silk boxers and swung open the door to find Janinne standing there with two bottles of Taittinger Comtes de Champagne and a big smile.

"Room Service," she said, then stood there waiting for an invitation.

"Come in, please," I responded, and held the door for her. She was attired in a sexy little gauze short set that was cropped and tied to accent her bustline, and sheer enough to be totally provocative even in the subdued lighting of the porch. I took the two bottles of champagne from her as she passed by, then just stared at her perfect ass while she strolled over to the sofa and sat down. I quickly stashed one bottle in the vinocave, then put the other in an ice bucket and worked my way over to the sofa by way of the china hutch to retrieve three new crystal flutes.

"I'm sorry to disturb you," she stated as I poured the first of the magnificent bubbly, "but I just didn't want to sit up there in my penthouse all alone tonight. Can we do something like go over our schedule for tomorrow, or just sit around and drink some champagne for a while?"

"Of course," I replied. "Why not both?"

"Both what, Darling?" Terri stepped out from the bedroom in her baby blue silk make-up robe, winked at me, then kissed Janinne on the cheek.

"Drink champagne and talk business, dear," I answered, and handed her a flute.

"Oh well, that's a nice start," she replied, then plopped down on the sofa next to Janinne. Terri had brushed most of the curl out of her hair and was definitely in her comfort mode, but I could also tell she had freshened up her make-up and re-applied her lipstick for the tactical purpose of wanting to be kissed. She produced her new silver container from the pocket of her robe, showed it off, then opened it and shared the contents with Janinne. After a slam and a second hit for each of them, I refilled our glasses, lit a joint, and initiated our conversation with a question.

"So, what is our gameplan for tomorrow, Janinne?"

"I told everyone to meet us here around nine to get dressed and do make-up, then I guess it's off to the pool for our shoot," she answered. "I can't find Jean Claude anywhere, so I asked Andre to be prepared to help in case we need any food or wine for props. He said he would do something special with carved fresh fruit, and asked if you would mind doing a few shots around the breakfast buffet to show off his work."

"I don't mind at all, but with the two of you standing there, no one in their right mind is going to be looking at the fruit."

"I hope you're right," Janinne replied with a distinct sneer. "I would hate to be upstaged by a pile of melon balls."

"Impossible!" I took a moment to get a good read on Janinne, then hit her with a baited question. "What would you say if I told you I wanted Amanda to join us for our photo shoot tomorrow?"

Cool, calm, and unfazed, she looked me right in the eyes and replied,

"I'd say that dinner must have turned out very well. This is your shoot, Jeffrey, and if you feel she would be a worthwhile addition, then so be it. My only problem with Amanda is her attitude, not the way she looks."

"Dinner did turn out to be unforgettable," Terri said, grinning. "Amanda's actually a very nice person, with a unique personality and a bizarre sense of humor. If you and I had been raised at her level of financial affluence, I imagine most people would think we were somewhat eccentric, too."

"Somewhat eccentric! Honey, that would be the understatement of the millennium. Oh well, I'm glad you like her, because she's invited me to have lunch with her on the boat tomorrow, and now I'm asking you to come along for support. What do you think she wants with me?"

"That depends," Terri answered. "Do you mean before or after lunch?"

"You are so bad! No, really Honey, did she say anything about me, or the club, that I need to know about?" Janinne took a second to drain her flute, then held it out to me for more. "I'm sorry, but people with that much power scare the shit out of me sometimes."

"I don't think you have anything to worry about," I said with as much reassurance as I could muster. "Amanda has only respect and admiration for you and the job you do here at Chateau Pacific. She said the only thing she'd change about this place is Christian."

"Fuck, who wouldn't? You have no idea how much his parties and special guests worry me. Sure, they reserve the entire club, and they pay cash. But its dirty money, and it could cause us to be closed down by the authorities."

"Renting a room is not a crime," I said calmly, "especially when you run a hotel. But if your hotel is being used as a distribution point, and sharing the profits as well, then I think the authorities would be eager to check out your operation."

"Unless they were getting a cut, of course." Terri was all smiles and eyes.

"Of course, darling."

"Oh, my God! Is that what you think Christian is doing? With all the artwork and speedboats he's been buying over the last six or seven months, I have wondered where the money's been coming from, but I never dreamed he'd be greedy enough to jeopardize everything for a little personal gain. I feel so stupid!"

"Calm down, Janinne. I'm not saying that's what he's doing, because I don't know what he's doing. All I'm saying is that Amanda loves this place as much as you do, and if nothing else, now you have at least two common denominators going for you in case the conversation starts to drag tomorrow over lunch."

"Absolutely," Terri exclaimed. "You both love the club, and you both want to dump Christian before he destroys it."

"Excellent, darling! Look, Amanda only wants to observe the morning shoot, and will participate in the afternoon session, so tell everyone to be open and friendly to her so she won't feel uninvited or out of place. When you see her tomorrow, try and remember she's just a 22 year old little girl out to do something new and exciting, just like you."

"I wish I was only 22 again," Janinne replied.

"Not me," Terri said, then raised her glass to me. "I love the way my life has progressed, especially over the last two years. I'd never want to go back to the time before I knew you. Our future is filled with far too many wonderful things for me to ever want to regress. We're going to celebrate our life together every day, because good or bad, it will only be a memory tomorrow."

Terri stood and walked over to the hutch to pick up David's three-gram vial and her mirror, then made a stop at the vinocave. She handed me the fresh bottle of Comtes, and while I opened and poured, she did the same thing on the mirror. Terri served herself first, then bent over and held the mirror for Janinne, showing the entire world that her robe was definitely untied and that she was totally naked underneath. She slammed her glass of champagne, refilled it herself, then walked over to the bedroom door and stopped.

"I hope you're through talking business," she said, then leaned up against the wall. "Because, if I have to work tomorrow, it's time for me to go to bed." With a bottle of champagne in one hand and a mirror full of cocaine in the other, she ignited a fire with her eyes and smile, "And I'd like some company."

The only light was coming from the bathroom, so I took the time to walk over and turn on a small table lamp for ambiance, and also to get a better idea as to what was going on. Terri pulled back the covers on the bed, then sat down and served herself another round of inspiration before holding the mirror for Janinne. After returning the favor, then placing the mirror on the nightstand, Janinne turned back to Terri and allowed her to untie and open her gauze shirt, then raised both hands to her hair while Terri fully indulged herself in the majesty of those perfect breasts. The voyeur in me was perfectly content to just stand there and watch, so that's exactly what I did. I just stood there and watched in total amazement as the ladies cranked up the heat of passion. Unlike any adult film I'd ever seen, these girls were gentle with each other, and very soft and loving with their touches. They were both responding well, and neither one seemed to have any complaints, when Janinne opened her eyes, reached out with her right hand towards me, turned her palm up, then motioned with her fingers for me to join them. This kind of shit just doesn't happen to me, but now wasn't the time to think about it. Now was the time to respond and react.

From behind her, I slid my index fingers under the collar of Janinne's shirt, and she lowered her arms to let it fall to the ground. With my hands now down by her waist, it was easy to fill them both with her glorious ass and softly rub and squeeze it. The feel of soft gauze over firm bare skin easily dispels the suspicion of panties, so I was momentarily thrown back to the images of her sitting open legged on my sofa just minutes before as I tried not to stare and wonder at Fantasyland. Janinne reached around and grabbed my hands, moved them to the front with the exclusive purpose of untying her shorts, then helped me as we wriggled them down off her hips and onto the floor. Holding her hair again, Janinne allowed me to kiss her neck and shoulders, and when I felt Terri's hands enjoying her ass, I was blessed with the pleasure of becoming acquainted with Janinne's magnificent breasts. As I continued to kiss her neck, Janinne arched her back and started rubbing her ass up against me in response to her pleasure, then pulled the first surprise of the night. She turned towards me, ripped off my robe, and then threw her arms around my neck and kissed me with the full length of her body. She ground herself into me and held on tight like she was trying to squeeze herself right through me, while at the same time smothering my mouth with her soft lips. After a second, more passionate kiss, she turned back to Terri, stood her up, and kissed her the exact same way.

I took a moment to fetch the champagne bucket and refill our glasses, and also to catch my breath before becoming totally mesmerized by these gorgeous ladies. Even more erotic than their exquisite physical charms was the beauty of the passion they shared for each other. Not only were they beautiful, they were beautiful together! The visual monster that lives inside me wanted to go get the video camera for hard copy, but I figured I'd probably remember this night for the rest of my life, so why take the chance to disturb them and fuck things up! It was just as easy to observe and enjoy as the girls sat down on the edge of the bed and made use of the mirror one more time. Terri was the first to pinch a small amount of cocaine and rub Janinne's nipples, but only the first. They both got extremely playful in very short order as they rubbed, snorted, and licked the party dust off each others nipples, and became more sensuous with their hands. When they paused to giggle about something, I interrupted only long enough to pass them their champagne for a slam and a refill, then another slam before they returned to the mirror, and then each other. I took their empty glasses from them, and they began a slow sultry kiss that turned out to be more than I could endure. I was just standing there getting into the tenderness of the moment, and the next thing I knew my hands were gently caressing their breasts. To my surprise, they seemed to enjoy it, so I continued my endeavor, foul as it may seem. As if on que, the ladies reached up and removed my silk boxers in a flash, and suddenly I was the one being fondled.

The ladies stood up and we had a tender, loving embrace, then I got to hold the mirror as they helped themselves first with a straw, and next with their fingers as they started their playfulness again. Well, enough was enough. I got them to sit on the bed at first, then maneuvered them down on their backs to where their inside breasts were right up against each other. I laid a pile of cocaine on each of their nipples and had a bilateral snowpeak off two of the most beautiful women in the world, and followed up with a tongue lashing of their hard nipples. If I live long enough to tell my grandsons about it, I wonder if they'll think their grandmother was one of the vixens! I was thoroughly enjoying the fact that I had both of their nipples in my mouth at the same time when I heard Terri say,

"Two can play that game, Jeffrey."

Terri brought my face up to hers and kissed me softly for a moment before turning those duties over to Janinne, then she worked her way down my abdomen and began her favorite lip maneuver. Being assaulted by two mouths at the same time on separate ends was joyous enough, but when Janinne crawled down to join Terri, the intensity level increased by at least four. From the way they were positioned on the bed, I could reach both of them, so I kept my sanity by drawing a response from them by stroking their labia and playing with man's favorite toy.

Janinne made her next surprising move when she straddled my chest on her knees and backed herself down on my face for a mustache ride. Life was getting better by the second, and just about the time Janinne started reacting to the pleasure of our endeavor, Terri assumed a straddling position facing her, worked me inside with her patented slow downward spiral technique, then reached out and started playing with Janinne's breasts. My view of the proceedings might have been partially obstructed, but I wouldn't trade this seat for anything else in the world. Just as things were starting to get really intense, the ladies hit me with their ultimate surprise, they traded places! Terri assumed the position to receive my oral stimulation while Janinne wasted no time sliding me inside for a personal guided tour of No-Man's land. Again, I found myself trapped in a non-visual position, but the physical sensations made up for it in spades. The ladies seemed to be enjoying themselves, too, because not only were their gyrations getting stronger, things were getting much noisier and more rowdy. I couldn't understand everything they were saying to each other, but moaning and groaning, and speaking to God has a universal translation. Janinne started to quiver and shake, and just about when I was ready to lose control, the girls traded places again. This time, however, Janinne stayed facing me and simply slid herself up my chest and planted Fantasyland across my face for the grand finale. At last I could finally see her, and both hands went directly to her fabulous breasts to help both of us fully enjoy the experience. Terri had me right where she wanted me, and knowing my reactions like a well scripted playbook, she was doing her best to give us both the greatest pleasure she possibly could. Janinne started to quiver again, but this time I could hear her gasping and whimpering until she became totally engulfed in a full body tremor. Well, feeling her orgasm on top of me did wonders for my self esteem, but shot the hell out of my self control. Terri could tell what was going on, and immediately began escalating the intensity of her maneuver until I no longer had any ability whatsoever to stop the runaway train. She tossed her head back and squealed with delight as I made my final thrust and erupted deep inside her.

POLITICS OF CONTRABAND

The main room of Christian's villa was afire with activity as each of the trade factions had their final, last-minute jam and cram sessions before the hosts finally arrived and the real party began. Tropical chic seemed to be the dress code for those who had previously participated in these events, with silk and linen being the front-runners in shirts and slacks, leaving the suits to be labeled as either rookies or second lieutenants in the organization. The bad boys carrying all the heavy hardware were just as easy to spot because they may have been wearing jackets, but they were in no way trying to hide all the sophisticated weaponry they had attached to their very expensive bodies. If the players were really the top dealers in the International black market, then their protection would also be the best that money could buy. In a cash business that deals in millions of dollars at the shake of a hand, only a fool would go to a meeting with a smile on his face, and a mere cellular phone on his belt.

The Korean delegation seemed to be the most hyper of the units, with each and every one of its members doing his best to wipe away a huge shit-eating grin off of his face. For a poor country with millions of people near starvation, these boys were far too happy, and way too overdressed for a tropical business dinner. Whatever they had up their designer sleeves must have been a biggie, or all of their combined intoxicants had induced delusions of grandeur that were contagious. All of the other factions were more laid back, with a wait and see attitude, and could have cared less that it was almost midnight and no negotiations had begun because Christian and Don Fernando had not officially called the meeting to order. The whores were nowhere to be seen, so it was only men walking around talking, picking at the late night buffet, and enjoying all the free booze and drugs they could hold. With all the hardware on display, one error in judgment could and would lead to an immediate blood-bath, so it's a good thing everyone was more low-key than the Koreans.

Don Fernando stepped out onto the stairwell from the second floor, took a moment to survey the crowd below him, then proceeded down the stairs in response to the applause generated initially from his entourage, and then from the other brokers to show solidarity. After shaking a limited few hands of only the most important guests, he moved directly to the head chair at the long banquet table in the dining area and raised his hand for quiet.

"My friends, I apologize for the late start, but now it is time to get down to business and make a few worthwhile investments that will benefit each and every person in this room." He paused for a second round of forced applause, then again motioned for silence. "Our host will be here momentarily, so if the leaders from each delegation will please join me here at the negotiating table, we will be able to conclude our business in the least amount of time, and then return our attentions to the assortment of ladies that Christian has acquired to take our minds off all the money we're going to make for both our benefactors and ourselves."

In very short order, every seat at the table was taken, with the noted exception of the head seat on the opposite end from Don Fernando. Once everyone was in position, Christian and Mahmood made their grand entrance from the downstairs game room, followed by four voluptuous vixens in standard coke whore attire of spandex hot-pants and matching stilettos, and each of the ladies was carrying something special. Poor Christian looked dwarfed by the Tyra Banks look-alike with obvious implants as she followed the two men to the table, then set down her silver tray containing two unopened kilos of cocaine, and took up her position standing behind Christian's chair. The other three waitresses pealed off in different directions and began passing out samples from their sugar bowls to all the other men in the room who were not sitting at the table.

"Gentlemen, I apologize for the delay," Christian sneered, "but I had a discipline problem with a certain employee that had to be resolved before I could devote my entire attention to the business at hand." He took a planned moment to acknowledge Tyra with his eyes, but looked away too soon to see her roll hers at the ceiling. He may have missed her personal slam, but no one else at the table did. "Now, let me go over the rules of play, and then we shall begin. First, and of utmost importance, all transactions are conducted in U. S. dollars, and all fees to the host will be paid up front and in cash. Second, any and all notes, memos, or records taken about this meeting or of any transactions derived from this meeting will be destroyed before you leave this room, or you will not leave this room alive. We are all honest businessmen, are we not, therefore no records are necessary other than a gentlemen's agreement and a handshake. Third, all deliveries between buyer and seller are to be made in International waters, therefore any import problems are strictly the sole responsibility of the buyer. Last, but not least, we follow the standard rule of half down, and half on delivery of the product. Now, if there are no questions, I will turn the floor over to Don Fernando while you inspect his newest batch of powdered currency."

"Thank you, Christian, for laying down the law." Don Fernando took a moment to pause for effect and let a big grin take over his entire face. "But as we all know, laws are made to be broken. Everyone here has wants and needs from our market, and my job is to do everything in my power to help make those arrangements possible. As you know, I represent a consortium of investors whose main purpose is global distribution of the world's finest cocaine. Whether bought directly or used as trade, the wholesale price for a kilo of our cocaine for this meeting is only $7,500. Once it is in your possession, we could care less how many times you step on it to increase your profits, thus the advantage of dealing with us rather than an independent distributor that may have already made that first step. Sitting offshore in safe international waters, there are vessels carrying over 15,000 kilos of uncut product, and we have the capability to duplicate that amount every two weeks. In conjunction with my two fellow South Americans that are present this evening, we also have somewhere around 8,000 kilos of marijuana onboard for immediate delivery as well."

Don Fernando sat back in his chair, sipped his champagne, and studied the participants sitting around the table. As usual, the two Arab contingencies were definite buyers with nothing to trade, and the Vietnamese were here to unload their newest vintage of heroin on the world market, but it was the Koreans and eastern Europeans that presented him the greatest mystery as to their attendance. As tightly as they were playing their agenda, the natural assumption would be that they were sellers, but not necessarily. With Obama still in office, and the former Soviet Union undergoing social and economic upheaval on a daily basis, anything was possible.

"Before we begin," he said coolly and calmly, "I wish to expand on something that was alluded to earlier. Cocaine is the ultimate currency on the world market, and will be for quite some time to come." He reached into his shirt pocket and retrieved a wad of new one hundred dollar bills folded neatly in a gold money clip, then casually tossed it on the table for all to see. "Here is the cost of one kilo of my uncut cocaine. Cross any border with this in your pocket, and it's still only worth around $7,500; whereas with my currency, successfully cross that same border, and you've increased its value by at least 50%. For those of you who have something to sell, I recommend using my currency as a way to increase both the value of your product and the profit margin for you and your organization. Now, without further adieu, I open the floor for discussions and proposals."

In less than a heartbeat, the leader of one of the Arab factions stood up and began his address to the table.

"My name is Haleel Abdul Aziz, and I represent the Islamic Brotherhood. Our goal is to flood the Israeli market with high quality drugs to destroy the will of their decadent youth, and . . . ."

"Please, sir," Christian interrupted, "we don't give a shit who you are, who you're with, or what you intend to do with our product! I could care less if you personally cram a fistful of dope up the ass of every Israeli man, woman, and child you can reach, as long as I get my money. So, what do you want, and how much can you afford?"

"Considering the fact that Osama Bin Laden personally contributes to our cause, and has provided a Jordanian freighter for transportation of your product, I can afford anything I want." He turned away from Christian in disgust, and addressed Don Fernando instead. "At current market price, I place my order with you, sir, for 4,000 kilos."

"Excellent!" Don Fernando smiled at the Egyptian businessman/terrorist, and purposely ignored Christian's greed-induced joy. At 5% commission, Christian just made a million and a half in cold cash for doing nothing but being the host. "Since you have your own transportation, I assume you have brought the 30 million dollars necessary to complete the transaction?"

"Of course." Haleel replied, and then accepted a suitcase from his associate, unlocked it, and passed it down to Don Fernando. "15 million dollars in new currency, as requested."

"Perfect. As long as your brothers in Iran didn't print these bills last week, I gladly accept your deposit and look forward to concluding our transaction tomorrow." Don Fernando stood as the Arab walked up and shook his hand, then returned his attention to the rest of the participants at the table. "As you see, doing business here is very simple. Now, it's time to find out what our European friends have to offer us tonight."

The smallish man with coal black hair and blue eyes as cold as steel stood and raised his glass to his fellow participants.

"Good evening, Gentlemen. My name is Sydney Dvoretsky, and as this is my first visit to one of your sessions, I wish to thank you for both the invitation and opportunity to participate in this worthwhile endeavor." He took a long draw from his glass of champagne, then turned to one of his associates and motioned him to bring a trunk over to the table. "I represent a group of businessmen from the former Eastern Bloc who have purchased and reopened three manufacturing plants that specialize in small arms. For your inspection, I have brought samples of our three current product lines. Rather than try to re-invent the wheel, we 'borrowed' the best designs from Kalashnikov, Heckler & Koch, and SIG to create weapons that are reliable, durable, and deadly accurate. Our first sample is a hybrid cross between an AK-47 and a SIG 551 fully automatic assault weapon, which we call our AR2. It utilizes a standard 5.56 NATO round, and with our custom designed alloy bolt, has a faster rate of fire than the M16A2. Our second item looks and feels like a Heckler & Koch MP5SD submachine gun for a reason, and it's a good one. Our lead design engineer worked at H & K for over ten years! We chose to manufacture this weapon in both 9mm and the new.40 caliber for maximum performance in close quarter battle conditions. The third item is my personal favorite, and has the potential to be a standard in the industry for many years to come. We took the best characteristics from the H & K PSG1 and the SIG SG500 classic sniper rifles and created a new, semi-automatic long boy that has electronic sighting for total accuracy up to 1800 meters, is perfectly balanced for ease of operation, and fires a.50 caliber Magnum round for absolute stopping power. The suppression system allows zero flash or flare, and keeps it from sounding like a sonic boom when fired, but due to the magnum load, it still sounds like an elephant fart."

"A large elephant, or a small one?" Don Fernando smiled at his guest, then motioned for a bodyguard to bring over the submachine gun. After giving the weapon a quick once over, the lean, paid assassin passed the efficient little killing machine over to his boss. "I can tell by the gleam in your eyes that you like this new little toy, Roberto, so you may keep it. And now, my new friend, what is your production capacity and how large of an inventory did you bring?"

The European remained calm and collected, but it was easy to see he was pleased with the reception his products had received. He took the time to sip his champagne before answering Don Fernando.

"Unlike your associates in Colombia, we are incapable of producing 15,000 units every two weeks," he replied with a smile. "However, I did bring 400 units of the SMG940 that you are so fond of, 700 assault rifles, and three of our new sniper rifles. As Christian Morea has already claimed one of these rifles as part of his commission, there are now only two left for sale at this time. On a weekly basis, we can produce fifty AR2's, thirty SMG's, but only one sniper rifle. We also design and manufacture our own ammunition for optimal performance with all of these weapons."

"The craftsmanship is excellent," remarked the leader of the Vietnamese faction, holding one of the AR2 assault rifles. "Compared to the first and second generation surplus garbage we are receiving from our former allies, I must insist that you sell the entire allotment to me for my personal cadre."

"On the contrary, General Huang," interjected the spokesman for the second Arab contingency. "Our Royal Guard always carries the finest weapons in the world, therefore we must have these masterpieces to protect the shrines of Mohammed. It is the will of Allah."

"Is it the will of Allah that your Royal family is one of my best customers?" The young General composed himself in an instant, then simply smiled at his Arab antagonist. "Hypocrisy is indeed its own evil, don't you agree, Ahmed?"

Don Fernando stood and raised both hands as a symbol of peace. "Gentleman, please. I feel I have a solution that will appease all parties for now, and will allow for an increased production of these magnificent weapons in very short order."

"That is a wonderful thought," replied Dvoretsky, "but we are still a small company with limited resources."

"Exactly my point, sir. Rather than just buying your weapons, my offer is to buy your company and expand it. My plan is to build new, larger facilities in Ecuador with the capability of increasing current production rates by at least four times, and modernizing your existing facilities to maximize its capabilities as well. As long as your design group doesn't mind an occasional junket to South America, and your investors don't mind getting bought out, I feel we have a very workable proposition."

"I agree! Getting our investors off our backs is one of the main reasons I'm here, Don Fernando. We have been craftsmen all our lives, but capitalists only recently, so I'm afraid we didn't exactly negotiate the best deal with our financiers when we approached them with our request for funding. As president of the company, I have full authority to strike any deal I find to be good for our future, but I certainly don't look forward to asking our Bolshevik investors to take an early cash payoff."

"You won't have to," Don Fernando replied with a shark-like smile. "As I am chief counsel for your new investors, I insist upon being the one to handle the negotiations for the transferal of ownership." Don Fernando opened the suitcase he received from the Egyptian, removed three tall stacks of strapped bills, and handed them to Dvoretsky. "As a showing of my good faith, please take this and pay your people well."

"But what about my guns!" demanded the General.

"Ask the new owner," Dvoretsky replied with a smile.

"Thank you, sir, but as you are still my president, what do you recommend?"

"Divide the shipment into thirds," he replied without hesitation. "The General would get his share, as would the Saudi's, and the final piece of the pie would go to our new investors as a showing of our good faith."

"And payment, Mr. President?"

"I only understand one form of currency, so for now, again I must defer that question back to you, Don Fernando."

"Excellent! I can see that this relationship is going to work out just fine. And now, since General Huang, Mr. Ahmed, and I have already agreed to our standard contracts, the only business left for us to address comes from our friends from North Korea. Gentlemen, it is time to let us all know what you have been smiling about all evening."

A slender young man in his early thirties stood, nodded to his elders, then turned and did the same to both ends of the table. From his briefcase, he retrieved two discs and set them on the table.

"Gentlemen, we have been given the honor of offering the newest technology in American missile guidance systems for sale to the highest bidder. It has been tested and proven to be accurate, therefore we ask the bidding to start at 10 million dollars."

"Ah yes, the Loral papers," Don Fernando said, then continued. "We knew these papers would surface, the only question was when. I assume the Chinese rocket that crashed in Manchuria last month was a test of the new system, so tell me, sir, was it a success or a failure?"

"A great success," was the young man's reply. "The missile traveled over a thousand kilometers and impacted within ten meters of its target. Attached to our new generation of long and short range missiles, we now have over 40 targets pinpointed around the world for nuclear annihilation if we so choose."

"American politics can be very profitable, don't you agree," whined the General. "Our seven figure contribution led to a new trade agreement that also reopened a conduit for my finest and most profitable export. Due to my increased cash flow, I am now expecting my first shipment of your new missiles in 60 days, as are your brothers in Iran, Mr. Aziz."

"For defensive purposes only," smiled the Arab.

"In more ways than you think, my friend. Let me put an end to this before we all start telling Obama jokes," Don Fernando exclaimed. "I will start and end the bidding at 2 million dollars. According to my sources, the information is accurate, but incomplete, meaning that President Clinton screwed his country, Loral screwed the Chinese, and now the Chinese are trying to screw the world with a white elephant that doesn't exactly do everything it was supposed to."

"How can you say that!" The young Korean was near panic. "I personally witnessed the test, and I am the one who downloaded all the information onto these very discs."

"I have no doubt about the information," Don Fernando stated calmly, "but for every offensive measure, there is a defensive counter-measure. American satellites have the capability to redirect the course of an incoming ICBM by either altering or confusing the on-board guidance system, and since Loral designed both systems, your new high tech missiles are now defenseless once they leave the ground."

"If that is true, then why waste our money on something that doesn't work!"

"Our money?" Don Fernando stared Christian down, then redirected his efforts to the Koreans. "Because the guidance system does everything it's designed to do, it does have some value, therefore my offer to you still stands. I'm sure your associates in the Yakuza can turn two million dollars worth of product into a figure closer to your asking price, so please take the time necessary to consider my offer. As we will be here another few days enjoying the hospitality of my associate and finalizing our negotiations, there is no hurry to force a decision tonight." Don Fernando gestured for a hostess to refill his champagne glass, whispered something to her that made her grin, then took two huge hits from her sugar bowl while she poured. He stood, raised his glass in the air, and allowed a massive smile to completely take over his face. "Gentlemen, our work is done, the champagne is cold, and the cocaine is magnificent. It is time for us to enjoy ourselves. Release the dancing girls and whores!"

I pushed the eject button on the Panasonic Blu-ray recorder, and out popped all the evidence JJ could ever hope for on one disc. Working the remote surveillance system from the AV room was child's play, now all that's left for me to do is get back to my cabana without being caught. Getting in was easy, I just followed a stoned-out guard down the Royal Pathway and in through a camouflaged doorway on the side of the villa, then did away with him. He never saw me . . . . he never heard me . . . . and he never knew what hit him. I borrowed his blue jean jacket, Oakland Raiders cap, and 9mm Uzi, then stashed his body in an old utility closet for safe keeping. The AV room was exactly where JC and Janinne had said it was, so I didn't have to waste any time or motions looking for it, and luckily it was unoccupied. I watched the monitors as the main room filled with loud and rowdy whores looking to hook up with someone special to party with, so now was the perfect time to leave before someone decided to make use of this room. I stashed the disc inside my shirt, pulled the cap down over my face to avoid recognition, and cocked the Uzi just in case. With all the two-legged distractions walking around, getting out of here should be easier than getting in. I had left Terri and Janinne sleeping peacefully in each others arms, so as long as they were still asleep when I returned, the only evidence of my little sortie was lying dead in a closet.

My plan was to go past the trail to my cabana, then disappear off the security monitor and work my way back home, but you know what they say about plans. I could sense my companion long before I located him behind me and to my left. He followed me past the trail to my cabana, then started closing the gap between us as I continued my nonchalant stroll down the pathway. I varied my stride with an emulated drunken stagger and stumble to prevent my assailant from matching me step for step, and just as I suspected, baited him into a false sense of confidence that made him careless. I was fully prepared when I heard the two quick closing steps behind me, and dropped to my knees a split-second before the collision that was suppose to take my head off, but only knocked off my cap. In full camouflage gear, my assailant landed face-first on the trail, bounced right back up to his feet, and glared at me through his nylon mesh hood.

"You!" he growled, then pulled a K-Bar from an ankle sheath and moved in for the kill. I guess he expected me to just stand there and let him gut me, because even the Uzi in my hands didn't deter his straight frontal assault. Having neither the time nor temperament to fuck around with this dude, I cut him down with a three-round burst that blew his heart right out of his chest cavity, and shattered the peaceful tranquility of the tropical night. With great haste, I ripped the black face-mask off the dead man to confirm his identity, then grabbed his ankles and dragged Jean Claude's body into the jungle.

DAY SIX

The amber tones of the pending sunrise were just starting to peer over the crest of the coastal range as a solitary figure paced the enclosed confines of Janinne's private beach, keeping a close eye on the horizon. The sight of two Zodiac boats moving at maximum speed towards him brought a smile of satisfaction to the face of Mahmood, and a sense of relief. His cellular phone call to the offshore vessel had been well over two hours ago, and since the arrival of his associates needed to be in total secrecy, he was starting to get a bit apprehensive. The shallow draft of the two boats allowed them to make their way over the protective reef with ease, then zipped on up to the shoreline where eight heavily armed commandos and one young woman disembarked.

"Welcome, my sister," Mahmood said after their brief embrace. "The time is getting short and I was concerned about you."

"I apologize, my brother, but our infidel Captain was hesitant to obey my orders and bring his ship into Mexican waters, so now he sleeps with the fish. The new Captain prays to Allah that our mission will be successful."

"As do I, my sister. Come, we must get to the rooms I have chosen before we are detected, and someone else has to die."

I awoke to the sounds of laughter coming from the running shower, and the unmistakable aroma of Janinne's Oscar de la Renta perfume on my pillow. Considering all the events of the last twenty-four hours, I was content to just lay there and be thankful for all the blessings life had bestowed upon me, especially my beautiful companion. I was on the verge of dozing off again when I felt a familiar hand on my face.

"Good morning, lover," Terri said softly.

I raised my lids to gaze into the face of an angel with the eyes of a woman. Totally nude, except for the towel wrapped around her wet hair, she pulled the sheet back and laid her soft, round breasts on my bare chest, and I embraced her with all my heart. She cuddled with me for a few moments, silently returning my affection, then whispered,

"We decided to let you sleep as long as possible, but I'm afraid it's now or never if you expect to be ready when our guests arrive."

"Thanks, Angel," I replied, without letting go. "How do you feel this morning?"

"Happy, healthy, and well loved," she answered. "You're a wonderful man, Jeffrey."

"I'm glad you think so, because you're everything in the world to me."

We took another minute or two for our raw emotions to flow between us, then it really was time to get my act together. I eased my hold around my darling angel, and after we sat up, I was startled to see tears running down her precious face.

"What's wrong, Angel?"

"Nothing is wrong, silly boy," she replied, trying to smile. "I just never expected anyone to ever love me as much as you do."

"My pleasure, pretty lady."

"Mine, too!"

I kissed her tears away, then made my way to the coffee and the shower. Janinne was standing naked in the bathroom brushing out her wet hair, and as I passed by, she winked at me in the mirror.

"Good morning, Jeffrey."

"Yes it is," I replied with a smile. "Did you sleep well?"

"Better than I have in a long, long time," she answered, then stopped brushing her hair and turned towards me. "Last night was incredible! The two of you completely exhausted me, yet I feel totally relaxed and refreshed. And waking up with Terri in my arms was, well, I guess you understand."

"Absolutely. She's living proof why God created love."

The shower felt wonderful all over my body, but even the warm water couldn't wash away the image of Suzan's husband laying dead on the Royal Pathway with a grapefruit-sized hole blown out of his chest where his heart used to be. There's no way I could try to explain to her what happened, especially not right now, so my only choice is to stay cool and hope someone doesn't find his body before we leave. Why he was there, what he was doing, and why he wanted to kill me, I'll never know unless JJ can pull a rabbit out of his hat with a good explanation. So today, I get to take erotic photographs of a beautiful woman I just made into a widow, and she doesn't have a clue.

By the time I was finished with all my personal preparations, the bedroom of our cabana was filled with a flurry of commotion as all four girls were flying around trying to figure out which three swimsuits flattered their figures the most, even though they had already made their choices days ago. Poor Jack had been exiled to the porch for interference, and lewd behavior, of course, but seemed content to just stand in the doorway and observe the scene while smoking a joint. Suzan and I exchanged pleasant smiles as I passed through, but Roberta made a point to bounce over and give me a big, bare chested hug.

"I know what you did last night," she whispered. "Terri told me everything, and I'm jealous. The next time you decide to have a party, I expect to receive an invitation! Suzan spent the night with us again last night, and I'm starting to feel neglected."

"How does Jack feel?"

"Jack feels with his dick, so I imagine he's feeling pretty good after the last few days."

We giggled a little, then she grabbed my ass with both hands and mashed her overwhelming breasts into my chest one last time before returning to the task of finding another pair of tops to accentuate her majestic pair. As she walked away, I couldn't help but smile at the thought of her unleashing those monsters on top of me in a rage of passion. Roberta Taylor was a unique combination of beauty, brains, and breasts that would scare the shit out of most normal men. Thank God I've never considered myself anywhere near normal!

Jack was in rare form this morning as I watched him plop a small amount of strawberry preserves into the bottom of a champagne flute, then fill it with Dom Perignon.

"Toast and jelly," he said, then passed it to me, and made another. "I'm feeling fine this morning, Jeffrey, after some serious fuckin' all last night. Damn man, there's nothing shy or timid about Suzan anymore. Her husband must be a dickless loser, because she goes totally ballistic, like a starving animal, when I stick mine inside her. Hell, if I was a Mormon, and she wasn't already married, I'd take her home with me."

"I doubt if you have to worry about her being married," was my only reply.

In the short time it took me to get my camera gear all set for this morning's activities, I was surprised to find that the girls were ready, too. Not ready to shoot, of course, but at least ready to head on to the pool. Jack grabbed the boom-box and video camera, I threw on my two camera bags, and each girl carried a tote bag with their two extra swimsuits, make up, and other essential items, and away we went.

We were all both pleased and relieved to find that both pools, the pool bar, and the majority of the pavilion were completely deserted upon our arrival. There were a few stragglers trying to force down a late breakfast, but for the most part, what few people we saw were staff members. Since my first location was going to be the waterfall at the shallow end of the main pool, the ladies set up shop in the cool shade of the pavilion by the main bar to finish their hair and make up routine. Andre must have ESP, because within moments of our arrival, he came bounding out of the kitchen followed by two young women carrying pitchers of ice water and a stack of large plastic tumblers. His huge smile seemed to encompass his entire face as he came straight up to me and shook my hand.

"Good morning, my fine friend, good morning! It gives me much joy and happiness to see your collection of glamorous subjects is still intact, because, as you can see, my two cute little bartenders have failed to show up for work this morning. These charming young ladies from my kitchen staff have volunteered to be at your service until Kimberly and her brunch shift are on duty. I think you will find what they lack in experience, they make up for in enthusiasm."

"No problem, man," I answered in my best Jamaican imitation. "As long as they can find the champagne, I know how to open it. Besides, with the exception of a quick toast to get things rolling, I doubt if we'll be doing any serious drinking before we're finished with the morning shoot."

"Good! That means Andre has done the right thing." He dashed behind the bar and returned with a large fish bowl containing a magnum bottle of champagne immersed in an icy bath. "While perusing Christian's private cellars, I came across this magnum of Veuve Clicquot that begged to be set free, so I took the initiative to have it properly chilled for just such a toast. Shall I serve?"

"Absolutely, my friend. When it comes to great champagne, there's no time like the present."

Andre and his little friends had a great time making a big deal about opening the bottle and filling the flutes for each of us; then at our insistence, three more for themselves. We raised our glasses to a good shoot with great results for all of us, then downed the magnificent bubbly and went back to work.

As I fully expected, Suzan was the first to be ready, but instead of dragging me down the stairs in a fit of hyper-anxiety, she was calm and cool. Her suit selection was an electric lime one piece thong with a deep plunging scoop in the front, and an almost non-existing back. Needless to say, with her long curly red hair and sleek physique accentuated by the cut and cling of the suit, she looked fabulous. While working her through a series of standing poses before getting her wet, I kept getting locked in on her expressions coming from her eyes. All the fire and pizzazz was still there, and possibly even more than before, but something was definitely different about this incendiary red-head. And then it hit me. Like a brick between the eyes, it hit me. What I was seeing in her for the very first time was confidence. True, uninhibited, confidence that only comes from inner peace, and it showed. She let me pose her, and shape her like a living doll, then she would just focus in on the camera and blow me away. Whatever Jack and Roberta have been teaching her certainly was working this morning!

The way the clouds were breaking up, it was going to get real bright, real quick around the waterfall, so I had no choice but to get all the girls together for a little rapid fire photography. Still working in singles, but with the others now prodding each other on, I told each one to give me her best six shots in rapid sequence, then change places. Once we moved into the shade of the pool bar, things could slow down, but for right now, it was move it or lose it. The girls responded with an All-Star performance that seemed to help them unwind and get into the fun part of being a model from the get-go. They teased each other into being competitive, and provided lots of verbal support for the subject, while me and the Nikons did our best to take care of our end of the deal.

Roberta was last, and had something special in mind after she finished her six shots. She waded under the arched bridge, untied the back of her suit, then slowly backed out towards me, playing peek-a-boo with her arm-covered breasts, and teasing the camera unmercifully with her mischievous eyes peering over her shoulder. Once she stepped out of the shade and into the brilliance of the direct tropical sunshine, Bert had no choice but to close her eyes, so I told her to turn towards me, lift her face to the sun, and just walk to me. Like a Goddess emerging from the sea, I framed in on the majesty of her form and face as the angle of the light sculpted her every delicious curve, and the water line got lower with every step. When the water hit about mini-skirt level, I had to stop and change film, and also let my breathing return to normal.

Before moving over to the pool bar area, Andre wheeled out his "pile of melon balls" which actually turned out to be a clever, multi-level display of watermelons carved into various sized baskets filled with fruit cut in all different forms. The ladies were delighted to stand around the display, sip champagne, and look stunning in their sexy swimwear, so we nailed lots of birds with this one stone. Andre got his shot, the club got some good P/R shots, and the swimsuit people get the best of both. Consider a back cover with four fabulous females in four of their hottest designs, making fruit look dull and tasteless.

We made a quick stop on the garden side of the arched bridge for another round of standing poses, then the girls decided it was break time so they could fix themselves back to a level of perfection and change suits. I had no choice but to agree, so Jack and I moved all our gear to the bar area, and sat back in the cool shade with a Coca-Cola and a smoke. Well, at least I did. Jack hopped behind the bar and mixed himself about half a gallon's worth of the boldest gold Margarita known to mankind, then poured it into a pitcher of ice and started sipping. It was time for me to get creative, but not that kind.

Terri came walking up to me from the garden path that leads to the bathrooms wearing a soft pink floral two piece thong that caused Jack to gasp, and best of all, she was alone. She wiped my sweaty face with a napkin, then kissed me on the cheek and whispered,

"Just you and me, big guy. Right here . . . . right now . . . . let's do it."

No answer was necessary. My only choice was do I rub my face in her awesome cleavage, or do I reach for my Nikon? Although I have been wrong before, and given that sometimes she's been known to change her mind, I still voted for door number two and reached for my D200 instead of one of her tasty body parts. She led me down to the end of the thatched roof for maximum lighting while still in the shade, and proceeded to pose herself in a series of shots that started out for the swimsuit people, but ended up with Playboy in mind. Terri was aglow with energy, yet clear and focused on her assignment of being seductive and alluring for both the camera and myself as she used everything within reach as a prop to help her in her seduction. She caught me by surprise when she leaned over the barstools and fully exposed her precious package for a picture. Usually she's not that bold, but I took it in stride and did everything within my power to help her succeed. Terri was in the mood to be sexy, and it showed. The lighting made her look almost golden with radiant aqua eyes, so I couldn't help but take lots of face shots for no one's pleasure but my own. For her next trick, Terri curled up on the bar facing my direction, then began to taunt me with her body. She pouted and rubbed, and rubbed and pouted until she knew that I was sweating profusely, then she rolled over on her back, opened her legs for the full effect, and turned up the heat. With her left hand on her left breast and her right hand near Fantasyland, she had me right where she wanted me, and poor Jack near a stroke, and she loved every minute of it. When I finally did have to stop and change cards, she hopped down from the bar without any help and walked straight up to me, grabbed my crotch, and smiled.

"If I can do that to you from twelve feet away, think of what I can do closer, OK?"

She left me standing there in my delicate condition, and walked down the steps into the pool. Jack passed her a glass of champagne, by her request, and she settled in on one of the underwater barstools in the shade for a temperature adjustment and some well deserved R&R. I took the time to empty my pockets and slip out of my sandals, then found myself sitting on the stool right next to her, kissing her passionately.

God allowed us a wonderful amount of time to celebrate our love and affection for one another before the other three girls finally showed up for work. They were "lost" without Terri, so they fiddled around with each other long enough for the heat to spoil their makeup, then they had to start all over again. Terri rolled her eyes at me, then waded to their rescue for her final blessing of how wonderful they looked before it was time for me to do my trick. I had no choice but to continue my work in wet shorts, but I guarantee it was well worth it. If the perfect woman isn't worth soggy underwear, who is?

The girls were all in a mood to be smooth and easy, so working them through a series of poses seemed almost too easy to produce the quality product rolling by, frame by frame. Their bodies were beautiful, beyond any doubt, but it was their expressions that kept blowing my doors off. Janinne's eyes were electric, Suzan was mesmerizing with her soft lips, and Roberta was playing a hallucinating game of show and tell with her wants and desires by baiting me with a little wiggle here and there, and a come play with me stare.

The last sequence turned out to be the most fun for everyone because I got all the girls to hang out with Terri on the underwater barstools while Jack stripped down to his Speedo's and played the role of bartender-sex object. To get the right angle for the shot, it was either stand in chest-deep water or use a telephoto lens and shoot from the bridge, so I chose to spare the pending disaster and sweat my ass off on dry ground. Terri agreed to put her bottoms back on, but liked my idea of leaving her topless so she could be the tease. Although I thought I had given them ample directions as to what to do, once I gave them the cue to start, all hell broke loose. Tranquility lasted only long enough for Jack to pour and serve champagne for each of the ladies, then I guess somebody farted, because they all started cracking up and laughter took over the entire situation. I kept on shooting, but the more they tried to stop, the worse things got, especially when Kimberly showed up and no one could tell her what happened without everyone bursting into laughter.

"Is this how you discipline your troops, Jeffrey?" I turned to see Amanda standing at the foot of the bridge with Chang right behind her. "If I'd known this assignment was going to be a party, I'd have gotten here sooner."

"I do seem to have lost control of the situation for a moment, don't you think?"

"So it would seem," she replied with a smile. Amanda was wearing a pale yellow gauze romper with nothing on underneath and a pair of gold rimmed aviators under a big straw hat. She walked up and hugged me around the waist as a showing of support, then just stood back and observed. David stepped into the frame only long enough to say hello, and shake Jack's hand, before retiring to a chair out by the pool for an unobstructed view. For a moment, everyone stopped what they were doing and just stared at me, waiting for orders or something.

"Let's try something easy! Everyone watch Jack mix a batch of something, and by the time he's finished, we will be too. Start out by standing up so I can see the suits, then just take it wherever you want to!" I zoomed in on Jack and Kimberly as they joked around about something, then to my complete surprise, they moved back to where they were in front of the ladies, and dropped into position for an arm wrestling match. His idea worked brilliantly because the ladies automatically locked onto the competition and started prodding and cheering the combatants. With Roberta and Janinne on the left, and Terri and Suzan on the right, I framed the competition with four designer bodies in four designer suits. Actually, three and a half, but who's counting! I kept firing away, just as Jack kept toying with Kimberly until he finally got tired of the game and slowly but surely powered her arm down into submission. He jumped up and started his Hulk Hogan posing routine, but she climbed right in his face and started voicing her disapproval of his behavior in no uncertain terms. Playing or not, it did spark a different type of reaction from the ladies that led to an additional round of photographs. The next thing I knew, Kimberly was into a WWF posing routine, then Jack joined her, and suddenly everybody was flexing their muscles and gritting their teeth. Terri again found a way to make her tiny presence known as she stood on her barstool, stuck her butt out towards the camera, and then started doing her own version of show me your muscles. She was so captivating, everyone else just seemed to stop and watch her. I shot until the emotion was gone, then offered my arm to Amanda and we walked over to join the party.

I thought the girls were tired and ready to quit for the morning, but three out of four were dying to change and do more pictures, so Terri stayed on her barstool while the others scurried off to the bathroom. Before I even had time to change lenses, Amanda had stepped out of her gauze romper and taken up residence on the stool next to my tired, but precious angel. The girls immediately slipped into an easy conversation, so I excused myself to tend to my cameras and talk to David and Jack.

I had finished readying all my cameras, and the three of us were finishing a rolled taste of the islands, when up walked a solitary female from the upper rim of residences wearing only a tank top, a pair of bikini panties, and some cheap sunglasses. About 5'4", 115 lb., with long black curly hair, and an adequate C cup, this woman was no beauty, but would definitely be a sought out target in any bar, on any night. She pranced over to the bar to pick up a towel and a glass of champagne, then made her way to the same chaise where Terri met the Count, got naked, and went through a short stretching program before lying down. I didn't have to bother with the Nikons because the Sony Digital captured every freeze-framing second and sent it straight to San Diego.

"Who the hell is that?" I asked David.

"I don't know who, but I sure know what she is," he replied in a strange mono-tone. "She's a soldier, Jeffrey. Look at the strength in her back, and the power in her legs. She's a killer, in every sense of the word."

"OK, but for who? She looks Lebanese to me, but that doesn't mean a whole lot considering all the factions working out of there. Do you think we could be just over-reacting to a whore with a fetish for kick boxing?"

"Maybe, but I don't think so." David took a huge hit off the joint, held it as long as he could, then exhaled and continued. "Considering the way she carried herself, she's nobody's bodyguard. Whatever organization she belongs to, you can bet she's one of the leaders. I didn't see her carrying anything, so she's either got a derringer stuck up her ass, or somebody's watching through a scope. Either way, I'm not fucking with her at all."

"Me either," Jack remarked. "That woman has ugly tits."

David and Jack went back to where they could serve Amanda and Terri, leaving me alone to go over my gear and collect my thoughts for the next session. My eyes danced around behind my Ray-Ban's as I watched the young woman stand, put only her tank top back on, and walk straight over to me. I didn't have to bother fumbling around with the video camera, because it was already on.

"Good morning," she exclaimed, "I take it you are the photographer I've heard so much about?"

"That depends on what you've heard," I replied with my best smile. "My name is Jeffrey Mason, and I'm here on assignment shooting swim suits and leisure fashions for the next few days. Since I haven't seen you around before, I take it you're new here, too?"

"Oh, I've been around," she answered with a chill in her voice, "but this will be my first full day as a guest of the resort. Tell me, why here and why now, Jeffrey Mason?"

"One of my agents worked out the details, I just show up where and when they say show up, and shoot what they pay me to shoot. Does that sound familiar?"

"What do you mean?" She ruffled for a split-second, then calmed right down.

"Well, if you're into fashion photography, you know the routine. Are you interested in photography, Miss . . . . ?"

"I have no interest in photography, Jeffrey Mason, only photographers." She turned to walk away, then stopped only long enough to say, "My name is Sidiki. In Arabic slang, that means good friend."

259

I watched her walk back over to the chaise, disrobe, and lay down one more time, still wondering who she really is. Her interrogation of me was quick and clean, just like my answers, so now the way she choreographs her next move will let me know if she considers me a threat, or a target. None of the above would be my preferred choice of answers, but if David is concerned enough to intensify his defensive alert status, I would have to be a fool not to do the same. And my momma didn't raise no fool!

Suzan, Janinne, and Bert all showed up together again, but this time they were ready to shoot without Terri's blessing, so I kept them in a group and we went from setting to setting around the pool and bar, and I let the ladies show off. Each of them had graduated to the next level, where they were confident with themselves, comfortable with me, and liked playing the game, so I just turned them loose and let them play. Terri was obviously tired and needed to recharge her energy levels, so for the rest of this morning, I let the other three carry the ball. As disinterested as she acted, even Sidiki watched and smiled a few times as the ladies performed their magic for the camera.

I had moved all the girls back in the pool around Terri and Amanda for a topless grand finale that even Kimberly joined in on, thanks to David, when down from the pavilion poured about thirty people with Christian in the lead. They were all totally wasted, especially Christian, and looked like they'd been that way for a few days. He led his party of whores, businessmen, and bodyguards right up to where we were trying to work, and started showing off for his friends.

"Ah, there she is," he began, "my fuckless bride hanging out with her fuckless friends. Stand up sweetie, and show everybody your plastic tits. I don't get to touch them either, but she sure likes to show them off to everyone else."

""You shouldn't talk when you've been drinking, dear," Amanda replied. "It lets everyone know what a dickless brain fart you really are. Enjoy your whores darling, the party's almost over."

"For you, maybe, but not for me. I made over five million dollars in only one night, so who needs you anymore! I don't need your fucking money, I don't need your fucking family, and I don't need your fucking shit. If I want a little pussy, hell, I'll just go buy me some. A man of wealth doesn't need a wife, so you should be grateful that I'm still willing to take you off your parents' hands. Go ahead, save your precious pussy for our honeymoon, but I intend to make full use of my manhood!"

"That shouldn't take long," Terri responded, "so do us all a favor and go get started somewhere else!"

"Bravo!" David replied, and started applauding. "I have to agree, it's time for you to leave before you find out how expensive reconstructive surgery can really be."

"Call off your dog, bitch, or I'll have him neutered," Christian replied, then turned to his entourage. "This is my club that I built with my own two hands, so if I want to have a fucking orgy in the disco, so be it. Come, my friends, let's go fuck our brains out and leave these egotistical cunts alone so they can finger themselves!"

"What a fucking jerk," Suzan exclaimed, then turned to Amanda. "I'm sorry, but I don't understand how you could ever let that man touch you."

"That's easy," she answered. "I don't!"

"Oh my God," Janinne squealed, "then you really are a virgin?"

"Heavens, no! Not since I was thirteen, but he doesn't know that. I don't expect you to fully understand, but jerks like Christian were born to be manipulated, ladies. This is my game, and I get to make all the rules."

"And I thought I wasn't going to like you," Janinne said, then put her arm around Amanda's shoulders. "Jeffrey was right, we do have some nice things in common."

AFTERNOON DELIGHT

Everyone followed Terri and I back to our cabana to drop off their suits, relax a little bit, and get squared away on our afternoon session when Suzan dropped reality right in my lap. I'd done a good job of keeping Jean Claude off my mind, but she fixed that with her first complete sentence.

"Since nobody has seen my fucking husband since he dumped me here yesterday afternoon, I guess it's up to me to make the film run to the airport before we miss the early afternoon flight, too. With Janinne and Terri tied up with Amanda for the next hour or so, why don't the rest of us pile into the Suburban and make a party out of it? I'd really hate to make that trip all alone."

"I hadn't thought about what I was going to do with myself while Terri was gone, but if you really want some company, I wouldn't mind going along. I mean, after all, it is my film." The last thing I wanted was to be alone in a car with Suzan for the fifty minute drive, but Jack and Roberta were both non-committal. "Hey, brother-in-law, why don't you roll a few, I'll bring my cameras, and we can stop somewhere along the way and do some real intimate photographs."

"No way," Roberta replied. "If Terri and Janinne are going for a boat ride, and you're going to help occupy Suzan's time, I've got a few plans of my own for this man, so don't count on seeing us again until we meet back here at five."

"That's a great idea, Jeffrey," Suzan exclaimed. "I do know a great spot that's really isolated, so we could take the kind of pictures I've been wanting. They certainly won't be for Jean Claude, but that's OK, they'll be for me. Let me go make a quick change, and I'll meet you in the driveway in about fifteen minutes."

And like a shot out of a gun, she was gone. After thanking me two or three dozen times, Roberta herded Jack out the door and they went back to their room to feed the beast. Terri and Janinne didn't appear to be in any hurry at all, and seemed to be content to sit back and sip champagne while I went about my business of preparing a camera bag for Suzan's surprise, and rolling a few joints for my personal state of mind. I also made damn sure the video I recorded last night was included with all the film I put into the padded courier envelope, then sealed it with some tamper proof tape to insure its unmolested safety. When it was finally time to go, both girls kissed and embraced me, but it didn't seem like either of them was sorry I was leaving them alone in the privacy of our secluded cabana.

Suzan was more than just a few minutes late by the time she finally walked through the lobby and found me at the main bar sipping on a Coke. She had redone her hair and makeup, and was wearing a baby blue cotton romper that was loose enough to mask her figure and leave no marks on its contents. She was bright eyed and eager to begin, but hopped up on the barstool next to me for a quick moment to lay out her plan.

"Look, Jeffrey," she began, "I know we have a long drive ahead of us, and I really want it to be fun, so let's not talk about Jean Claude once we leave this bar. I know in my heart that he used me to get in good with Christian, and he was extremely jealous of my relationship with Janinne, but now he's gone and it's time for me to get on with my life. I don't know if I'll ever see him again, but I'm OK with that. He made his choices, and I've made mine, so now it's time to move on. To be honest, I really enjoyed learning how to satisfy a man, especially with Jack and Roberta's help, and I look forward to meeting more men in the future, but I doubt if I'll ever get married again. I hated the way he was so totally possessive of me and my body, mind, and spirit. I'm not some horse that needs to be broken, I'm a woman that needs to be loved by a real man who understands kindness."

"I agree, Suzan. You're a beautiful woman with a unique personality that deserves to find the right kind of man who will nurture and enjoy a loving relationship with you, not dominate and suppress you. Nobody enjoys living in a cage, pretty lady. Not you or me."

Suzan leaned over and kissed me on the cheek, then stood up and let me hug her. I had no doubts about her sincerity or her ability to move forward, but I still didn't want to be the one to tell her I killed her husband, be it in self defense or not. I threw my camera bag on my shoulder, patted her on the butt, and moved her towards the door.

The two joint drive from the resort to the airport in Manzanillo was filled with laughter, and seemed to fly by. After a quick stop at Boca del Rio on the return trip for a bite of lunch with Carmen, I found myself parked on top of a cliff overlooking the deep blue Pacific waters. Suzan sat in complete silence for a few moments, taking in the grandeur of the view, then turned to me and smiled.

"I like to stop here on the way back for a little peace of mind and tranquility," she said, and pulled a joint out of her purse. "I hope you're not in a hurry."

"Not at all," I replied. "Is this the place you had in mind for pictures?"

"Oh no," she answered. "The place I have in mind for us is much more private."

Once back on the road, Suzan was fairly quiet for at least the next twenty minutes, then she made a right turn onto a dirt road that took us up into the mountains. We followed the narrow road uphill through the dense vegetation for another fifteen minutes or so until she came to a small clearing on the left, where she pulled in and parked the truck. She reached behind the front seat and passed me a bottle of Mumm out of the ice chest to open, and again went back to her purse, but this time she pulled out a three-gram vial of white powder and sucked down two big capfuls. I poured her a glass for the traditional slam, then she repeated the entire process, as I've grown to expect. We sat for a moment, finishing our glass of champagne, then she looked at me and grinned.

"We've got a short walk ahead of us, so we might as well get started. I brought two more bottles of bubbly and a few extra goodies, so if you'll bring the ice chest, I'll take you to one of the coolest places on the face of the earth."

Suzan grabbed her tote bag and led me up a well established trail that had been cut through the overwhelming vegetation and rugged terrain generations ago. As soon as we were totally enclosed in the jungle canopy, I could hear the roar of falling water and feel the cool change in climate. The trail started to parallel a flowing creek carved out of the slope of the mountain, and within minutes we were staring up at an eighteen foot waterfall that cascaded into three stair step pools before forming the creek. The areas surrounding the pools were lush and green, with lots of ferns and mosses blended into the soft carpet grass that was fed by the ever present mist, further enhancing the natural beauty of Suzan's secluded paradise. She helped me set everything down, then filled my arms with her slender body.

"Don't you just love this place?" she asked. "Carmen brought Janinne and I here right after we started hanging out together, but I think I'm the only one who comes back on a semi-regular basis. Janinne has her beach, and Carmen has her golf course, but when I need my space, I come here."

"It's beautiful, Suzan. I know a place in the Oregon Cascades with lots of similarities, both mental and physical, but unless you're a Great Pyrenees with a big dog attitude, the water's way too fucking cold to even think about getting wet."

"Not here," she replied, then stepped out of her romper and into the large pool. She held her hair up with both hands to keep it from getting wet, and by the time she was waist-deep in the cool, clear water, the Nikon and I were framed, focused, and firing away. She waded in until the water was almost up to her shoulders, then made a U-turn and slowly walked back towards me. Using the waterfall as a soft focus background, I stopped her two or three times to let the water level work as a prop for an enticing series of shots, then handed her a towel and her glass of champagne when the time came to change film.

"You're incredible, Red," I said, as she wrapped the towel around her waist and sat down in the soft grass. "Five days ago, you wouldn't have even considered doing this, and now look at you."

"Five days ago, there were lots of things I wouldn't have considered doing, but not anymore!" She looked up and dazzled me with her serpentine charms. "Now that I really know what to do with a man, being a bi-sexual female means that I get to enjoy the best of both worlds, so watch your ass, Jeffrey, you could be next!"

"Only in my wildest dreams, pretty lady."

"Mine, too, Jeffrey."

The second roll of film started out with Suzan doing floor poses on the soft, moist grass, then I moved her to the edge of the pool and continued the horizontal format. She was alive with energy flowing from her eyes, but her body movements were cool, calm, and calculated. We both enjoyed the playful responses we were receiving from each other, and it was easy to see that she was thoroughly pleased with herself and her new found sexuality. The more seductive the pose, the more she got into it, and the more she teased the camera. The third roll was more of the same Penthouse style of posing, but by now her serious mood was over and she was ready to play. We played peek-a-boo with her breasts, ass, and special package, then the film ran out and it was time to stop. I set the camera down, slid out of my shirt and shorts, and joined her in the cool water with a fresh bottle of champagne for a well deserved attitude adjustment.

By the time I finally got back to my cabana, it was almost three o'clock and I was ready for a nap. Suzan and I consumed all three bottles of champagne before we left her magic waterfalls, and both of us were having an extremely difficult time keeping our hands off each other when we finally made the decision to get up and go. After making one last stop on the side of the road for a final round of passionate kissing, we agreed to hold that thought until later when Terri could join us and it wouldn't feel so much like adultery.

I was surprised to find the front door locked, but when I used my key and quietly made my way inside to find Terri asleep on the bed, I was glad she had been concerned enough with her own personal safety to lock the door. I tried my best not to disturb my sleeping beauty, but when I came out of the bathroom and lay down beside her, she opened her eyes and smiled at me.

"Hi, lover," she whispered. "I was just exhausted, so after lunch, I decided to lock myself in and get some beauty sleep."

"It must have worked," I replied, "because you certainly are beautiful."

Terri looked at me with hunger in her big blue eyes, then buried her face in my chest and curled up all around me. I immediately put my arms around her and held her with all the love and compassion I could muster. For a tough little tomboy with the heart of a lion, she was also well versed in the art of cuddling.

"I really missed you today," she said softly. "Janinne wanted to play as soon as you left with Suzan, but it just wasn't the same without you."

"I'm glad," I replied. "I would hate to be replaced, no matter how beautiful she is."

Terri rolled herself on top of me for a full length, horizontal kiss, then rose up on her arms to where she could rub her nipples against my chest.

"That would be impossible, Jeffrey," she said with the slyest of grins. "Without you, it's only foreplay, and you know how I hate limitations."

UNKLE HENRI

The golden amber of sunset still filled the skies over the small 17 acre vineyard of pinot noir vines that were now 73 years old. Henri Morea had stood on this particular hillside, at this particular time, nearly every day of his life. Francois Pavie planted those vines for his grandson on the day he was born, and every evening after supper, Henri Morea and his grandmother would take a stroll out of the chateau and check on his vines. On his tenth birthday, he was taught the art of winemaking with the grapes from his own vines by his grandfather, uncle, and father. Now, he alone controls the family vineyards, domain, and network of distribution, yet here he stands, night after night, enjoying himself with a glass of wine and a breath of fresh air. As the oldest of three brothers and two cousins, all male, he was primed from the start to be the keeper of the family business. Cousin Francois, next in line, was trained to handle the money. He now lives in Geneva and is quite busy with his brokerage house. Younger brother Andre has lived in Israel, or Palestine, since he and their beloved grandmother were smuggled there in 1939 to escape the insanity of the Nazi occupation. He is now an Import/Export magnate in Tel Aviv and only comes to France as a diversion from an occasional holiday abroad.

The family amassed several fortunes following the war as the boys took their acquired knowledge into the business world, and made a killing. Literally! In 1962, middle brother Isaac was slaughtered by Yassir Arafat's henchmen for brokering a massive arms deal for Israel, and only days after arranging a new distribution plan of all the family wines for North America that made instant millionaires out of the remaining four boys, Cousin Pierre was the victim of a senseless murder-suicide at the hands of his estranged wife. Throughout it all, Henri Morea has been right here, growing grapes, making wine, and making money. Lots of money. Just last week, a stupid Japanese paid over thirty million dollars for a small piece of an insignificant lower vineyard near Montrachet that totaled less then 7/10 of an acre. Idiots! At three hundred dollars a bottle, it will take them over 20 years just to break even. In 1941, a French vintner with questionable Jewish heritage traded the entire 35 acres for passage to Lebanon for his small family along Henri's personal smuggling conduit. Real Estate and vineyards were the two favorite items of trade for safe passage out of France. After the war, the family had holdings all over the country, and thousands of acres of vineyards throughout the pristine growing areas of Bordeaux, Champagne, Burgundy, and the Cote du Rhone. For the very few vintners who returned, Henri offered them the opportunity to regain their old properties for merely a modest rent to be paid in wines from the vineyards. He was now twice the hero, once for saving their lives, and now twice for restoring them to their former life.

Becoming the patriarch of the domain in 1943, Henri promised he would always surround himself with family at the chateau. Now, only a very small staff occupy the stately mansion with him. No children, no family, no heirs. He and Francois were always too busy with the business to marry, and Andre and his family are too engrossed with being Jews to even care about France, much less the family estate. As long as the wine keeps flowing and the profits keep rolling in, Francois and Andre have always been content to let Henri take charge of the domain. Now, the question is who will take Henri's place. It certainly won't be Isaac's son, Christian. At the time of his father's murder, Christian was already a headstrong pompous ass with delusions of grandeur, and he was only 12 years old. Thirty plus years later, Christian is still a detriment to every thing the family stands for. Tradition means nothing to a man whose sole purpose is to live a decadent lifestyle and line his pockets with gold.

There is one alternative to just passing the reins to an ungrateful, and undeserving nephew. As with Chateau Pacific, Janinne Pavie has proven herself to be intelligent, honest, and trustworthy with the portion of the family business she controls. Uncle Henri couldn't help but smile as he continued to think about her while navigating the vineyards surrounding his castle. Cousin Mimi had done an excellent job of raising her all alone in Miami after Janinne's mother passed away from pneumonia following a difficult childbirth. As far as Janinne knew, Pavie was only an adopted name.

His latest conversation with Janinne had only fanned the flames of distrust that surround Christian. She had mentioned how wonderful the three new Scarabs were, and what a generous gesture it was to provide the guests of the club such luxuries, if only

Christian would allow them the opportunity to use the high performance speed boats. No authorization for such a massive expenditure had come from Henri's office, so it was time to visit Mexico unannounced and check on his nephew's new business dealings. The trip would also allow him the pleasures of seeing Janinne, and spending some quality time with the not-so-little girl who has always referred to him as her guardian angel. After a flight to Miami for a quick visit with his cousin, it would finally be time to set the record straight.

THE IMAGE CENTER

SAN DIEGO, CALIFORNIA—Seated around the large rectangular wooden table in the bright and airy West Coast designed conference room, the five gentlemen perusing the folders of information laying open in front of them could be bankers, or real estate agents, or simple businessmen, but not here, and not now. Today, this innocent-looking room contained two key members of the DEA, the Assistant Secretary of Commerce, the West Coast Director of the CIA, and Special Agent Jonathon Jamison Walker. Although amused at some of the images placed in their folders, each man knew the serious nature of the meeting. Without standing, or even raising his voice, Deputy Director Anthony McCurdy was first to speak.

"Gentlemen, while we're waiting for the final two members of our panel to join us, I wish to congratulate Special Agent Walker on both his operation and choice of operative to provide us with such detailed information in such a short amount of time. Although edited for content, I also want to thank him for sharing a few extra photographs and video footage of our man's cover while on assignment for us."

"Absolutely," replied Assistant Secretary Matthew Lawrence. "This is one file I can guarantee the White House would love to get it's hands on."

JJ took the Glock 17 out of his shoulder holster and laid it on top of the unopened file in front of him. Only when he was sure he had the undivided attention of everyone in the room, then, and only then, did he open his mouth.

"Be it known that no file, nor any part of this file, leaves this room as long as I'm alive. You've all seen the tape we received today, so you know the serious nature of the situation I put my man in, and the deadly repercussions that would exist if anyone leaked his association with the intelligence community. I used his professional reputation to get him into a position to help us, and God knows he certainly has, but in our line of work, he's only an amateur."

"A very talented amateur," interjected the Deputy Director. "Whatever he did to get us this original surveillance tape warrants a medal of commendation, especially if he created it himself. We knew Don Fernando Munoz and General Huang were players, but to hear them incriminate themselves while patting each other on the back was extremely satisfying to me. I know that you have used this operative on four or five previous assignments, and I also know that he is a personal friend of yours, so I understand your protective nature towards him. With the exception of myself, no one else knows his identity, including the Director himself, and I can assure you that his name will never appear on any report, be it official or unofficial, nor pass from my lips, so holster your firearm before our special guests arrive. Considering the way General Wilson flew out of the screening room while we were watching the live transmission of this morning's festivities around the swimming pool could only mean that your agent discovered something other than his planned objective. When Randy called me to have this meeting set up STAT, he could have cared less about the contents of the surveillance tape we received this afternoon, so all we can do is wait and see what's got his boxers in a bundle."

The men in the conference room didn't have to wait long. Major General Randall M. Wilson, USMC, currently assigned to Military Intelligence at the Pentagon, came bursting through the double doors of the conference room followed by two civilians in casual attire and his aide, Captain Mitchell Gregg. Without hesitation, General Wilson walked straight to the head of the table and took instantaneous charge of the meeting.

"Gentlemen, in my pocket I hold orders from the Joint Chiefs to immediately cease and desist your operations at Chateau Pacific. A Priority One target has been identified and confirmed to be present, thus rendering all on-going operations secondary to the elimination of this target. As this is of no concern to the Department of Commerce, I must insist that you leave us for a few minutes, Mr. Secretary, then we'll get back to the problem of smuggling. Captain Gregg, please escort Secretary Lawrence to a sterile room and rejoin us with great haste."

As the Assistant Secretary of the Department of Commerce was politely herded out of the room, all the eyes of the men at the table bounced between General Wilson and Special Agent Walker, especially the two new additions. Once Captain Gregg returned and locked the door behind him, Deputy Director McCurdy picked up the phone and dialed a three digit extension.

"This is McCurdy. Sterilize conference room B-5. Security code 11-22-13."

In less than 90 seconds, a red light began flashing on the face of the telephone, then turned green. Once everyone at the table acknowledged the green light, General Wilson placed a DVD in the player, turned on the 37" monitor, and took his seat. The elder of the two civilians approached the head of the table, turned around, and looked straight at Jonathon Jamison Walker.

"My name is Cherfan. Col. Daniel Cherfan of the Israeli Security Force to be exact, Agent Walker. I will be in charge of the mission to exterminate the Priority One target exposed by your operative in Mexico. For his own safety, I must insist you divulge his identity to me immediately."

"With all due respect, Col. Cherfan, you can go fuck yourself. For his own safety, no one knows his name but me, and that's the way it's going to stay. You zealots in the Mossad are too quick to sacrifice lives for a cause, and you'd sell him out in a Tel Aviv minute for the name of a political dissident in your own country, so kiss my ass. His job is done, and he knows how to avoid trouble, but if you don't believe me, I can contact him and tell him to either lay low or pack up and leave." JJ took a quick glance at his superior officer, then sat back and continued, "I understand the need to eliminate every Priority One target, but there's more than one way to play this game."

"Game! This is no game, you fool!" The younger man stood, dashed to the DVR, and pushed play. The image of a young woman with long dark hair and ugly tits disrobing by a pool filled the screen, then the tape skipped to the same woman slipping on a tank top and walking straight into the camera. "This is Fatima Al Washid, more commonly known as Sidiki. She is a cold-blooded killer, currently aligned with the Islamic Brotherhood, and is the prime suspect in the assassination of two Israeli ambassadors, and most recently, the brutal murder of our beloved General Moshi Abraham right here in America."

DEA Agent Frank Yates jumped into the conversation with his Alabama drawl.

"Oh, yeah. Miami Beach, last November. Uniforms called us in because of all the cocaine they found in the room. Forensic tests confirmed he had coke and alcohol in his blood system, and that he'd been sexually active either right before or during his actual murder. Either way, somebody was sitting on his lower abdomen when they partially cut his throat and stabbed him nineteen times in the chest. Once we ID'd the victim, the Mossad took over and we were told to back off."

"Looks like we're there again, doesn't it?" JJ smiled at Yates, then glared at the young Mossad agent. "My operative is already in position, and since we're the ones who found her, who gives you supremacy to eliminate the target?"

"The Joint Chiefs, Agent Walker," replied General Wilson. "Now, give Col. Cherfan the name of your operative immediately. That's an order, Agent Walker."

"Agent Walker is not under your jurisdiction, Randy, and you damn well know it, so cut the crap. If my agent says his operative knows how to mind his own business and stay out of the way, so be it." Deputy Director McCurdy turned his attention to the Israeli commander and tried to calm the growing hostility. "With the exception of the operative's name, I am prepared to share any information we have gathered on the current occupants of the resort, and their activities as of this date."

"That will not be necessary," replied the young officer with a distinct sneer. "We already know who's there and what's going on. One of our finest young officers has been in position to provide us with direct information for months."

"How wonderful," replied McCurdy in a cool monotone. He moved to the DVR and inserted his own disc, pushed play, then watched the horrified expressions of the two guests as they watched and listened to the representative of the Islamic Brotherhood make his presentation to Don Fernando and company. "I take it your fine young officer didn't tell you to be prepared for the arrival of four thousand kilos of pure cocaine, Col. Cherfan? I suggest we take a different approach to this assignment and try to work together. After all, you're not the only Jews in this room."

Surrounded by all the new customized pick-ups, Suburbans, and trendy SUV's, the classic little black Porsche 928S looked as much out of place in the marina parking lot as did the burgundy Taurus driven by Captain

Mitchell Gregg. Even in his cargo shorts, tank top, and sandals, the young Marine officer still felt awkward being out of uniform as he strolled the dock looking for pier 4, slip 13, and his clandestine meeting with his old friend and partner in crime. Snugly nestled amongst the moderate sized sailing vessels, the 38 ft. Irwin named the "Insatiable Sarah" was as inconspicuous as a flea on a black lab, which is exactly what the owner had in mind. "Never stand out in a crowd" were not only words to live by, they were words to stay alive by. After stopping only long enough to knock three times on the hull, Captain Gregg hopped on board and descended into the main cabin.

"Hey, Mitch! Come on in and grab yourself a beer. Mi barco es su barco." JJ shook hands with his good friend, then sat back down at the table with his Corona and maps. "I think we pulled it off today, don't you?"

"Absolutely! I thought the General was going to shit in his politically correct shorts when you told Cherfan to go fuck himself, but it certainly got the job done. We suspected there would be other agents with their eyes on the club, and now we know for a fact that the Mossad has a man on the inside. Do you think we should alert our guys, or just let them play it by ear?"

"I say just leave them alone. First, and foremost, I think you need to change has to had in your next-to-last statement. As visible as this woman is being, their inside man would have alerted his superiors at first sighting, so I think he's dead meat. Your ex-Marine reported that he and my operative have made contact and are working together on a friendly basis, so why fuck up a good thing!"

"I agree, JJ. Our men know they're being watched, so why make the situation any more difficult than it already is. After all, it's not like they're going to blow their covers."

"Exactly!" JJ chugged down the remainder of his beer, then took on a much more serious attitude. "My only concern is how Cherfan plans to take out the hot target. If his team goes in and just starts blowing people away, there could be a bloody reprisal from a number of factions that almost certainly would lead to an international incident."

"I don't like his assault team mentality either, but Cherfan and his hot-headed aide have been given carte blanche by the Joint Chiefs to do whatever they damn well choose to eliminate the target, and all we can do is provide support. Navy divers have already tagged all the vessels anchored offshore for satellite tracking, and by tomorrow evening we'll have enough people in position to seal off the club from the rest of the whole fucking world, so why in the hell send in an assault team and get a shit-pile of people killed!"

"I agree completely," smiled Captain Gregg's gracious host, then pulled a chilled bottle of Sauza Hornitos and a baggie full of cut up limes out of an Igloo Legend 24 sitting next to him, and poured two Burgundy bowls to half full. "Well then, old buddy, since you're the only one of us who knows both operatives, I think it's mighty fucking brave of you to volunteer to be our Official Military Advisor and accompany Col. Cherfan and his hand picked troops on their hazardous mission."

"Go fuck yourself," was Mitchell's only reply, then he reached for the tequila.

LIFE'S A NUDE BEACH

The major difference between the chaos of the morning pre-op party and the afternoon pre-op party was the number of participants involved the chaos. Add Amanda, Kimberly, and Carmen to the naked champagne and swimsuit frenzy going on in the bedroom, and David to the all-guys smoke and joke marathon on the porch, and respectable life as we know it was going to hell in a plain brown wrapper. The only sane person was Chang, because he elected to stay outside in the fresh air and guard the perimeter. The girls were actually having fun getting to know Amanda, and she proved herself to be worthy of all the nice things Terri and I had said about her. Amanda was open and friendly, and enjoyed being included in all the competitive spirit of semi-organized professional modeling. Of course, having the second largest set of breasts in the room didn't hurt her spirit either, especially now that everyone knew for a fact that they were real. Kimberly's scars weren't nearly as horrific as she made them out to be, and Terri found her an electric blue 2 pc. thong that covered the bikini cut on her lower abdomen and forced her to admit that she did, indeed, look fucking awesome in the right suit. As Kimbo swayed to and fro in front of the standing mirror, absorbing her new glamorous image, I thought David was going to come unglued. Beyond a shadow of a doubt, both of them liked what they were seeing. Carmen chose a fluorescent yellow 2 pc.

thong that was so hot looking on her tanned athletic body that she had Jack begging for a rematch after Janinne walked her out to show her off.

The semi-hazardous trek over the mountain to the private beach didn't happen, because Amanda motored us around there on her yacht, then David ferried us across the barrier reef and on to shore in the little wooden dive boat we had brought in tow. Considering all the extra goodies we got to bring along for the shoot, and the volume of plans the girls made for tonight's dinner party at Janinne's, the twenty minute boat ride was well worth the additional time. The atmosphere in the salon was one of celebration and friendship as we sat around sipping champagne, and joked and jousted with one another. Chang volunteered to drive the motoryacht so David could enjoy partying with Kimberly and the rest of us, so everyone was included in the revelry. No one was out to get loaded, except Jack, of course, but the Dom Perignon certainly helped to take the edge off our pending photographic endeavor. Amanda stuck pretty close to Terri, so I got a chance to visualize how the two of them would look together on film in the light of day. Each was structured so perfectly, yet different due to their ethnic heritage, that I could find no reason not to shoot them together. A perfect rose and a perfect orchid in the same photograph are still a perfect rose and a perfect orchid. Terri and Janinne complement one another because of their similarities in structure, but Amanda and Terri together would be more like living proof that opposites do attract.

We beached the dive boat in the sand, and the ladies made poor Jack lift each and every one of them off the boat and onto the dry land so they wouldn't have to get wet. He buried his face in Roberta's massive cleavage when the opportunity presented itself, but even though it was their game, he was polite enough not to drool on the rest of the girls as he performed his strong arm duties. David and I unloaded the camera gear, clothes, and then a special brass trough filled with a case of iced down Dom, compliments of Ms. Tu. When we set up shop around the hut, the first thing that caught my eye was the brand new hammock that had been installed under a new extension of the thatched roof, just like Terri had requested the other morning. The ladies sorted out all their props and other goodies in the hut, and then it was time for something special. Chang had elected to stay on the Hatteras to protect and observe us from afar, but everyone else was going to participate in a group photo. I set the Nikon on a tripod, gathered the troops around the champagne trough, then tripped the timer and ran to my spot between Terri and Amanda. My goal was to repeat this performance at the conclusion of the festivities for a direct comparison of attitude and attire.

As the ladies went about their final preparations, I isolated myself for a few moments to get all my thoughts together. This afternoon session could very easily be another chance of a lifetime to showcase my work for numerous reasons, but mostly because of the subject material I get to work with. All seven women are legitimate candidates for any "Girls of . . . ." pictorial for either Playboy or Penthouse, or both, and if the Count is for real, other publications around the world as well. Carmen thinks she's only doing this for fun, and Kimberly has no expectations because she has no idea how gorgeous she really is, but if I can live up to my end of this deal, each and every one of these ladies has the potential for publication. I've been given a rare opportunity, so now's not the time to get in a hurry or cut corners. Each girl deserves her own special time, and it's up to me to make sure she gets it.

Terri and I had already agreed that she would be both my first and last victim for this afternoon session for three specific reasons. First and foremost, she'd get a chance to show off for the rest of the girls, and give them something to imitate. Secondly, she'd have some down time to think about what we'd done, relax a little, and help the others get ready, both physically and mentally. And last but not least, she'd have the opportunity to step back into the spotlight and blow everybody's doors off one last time before our assignment officially ends and the real party begins.

Terri started out in a bright white 2 pc. thong she pulled out of her hidden stash that molded itself to her luscious body, and by design, the French-cut demi style top both lifted and cradled her breasts to enhance her magnificent cleavage. I had the rest of the ladies follow us around to the various locations I had picked out to watch her perform for the camera, and to emphasize our need for seductive posing. Each girl was going to get two separate sessions this afternoon; one in her favorite suit, and a second in as little as possible, but the locations would probably be the same. I did standing shots around the hut first, then moved to the hammock for a more relaxed posture and some killer views of her glorious posterior. While still at the hammock, I felt it was time to get some of the others involved, so I started by adding Amanda to the frame with Terri, then intermixed the duo so everybody got to play. The mind boggling combination of the afternoon was Amanda laying on her side in the hammock and Roberta doing a semi-reclined pose in the sand next to her. I zoomed in for a tight crop, and was overwhelmed by the two exotic raven haired beauties with big brown eyes and double D assets. I could tell Jack was intrigued by the combination, because he turned into the biggest cheerleader of all while we were shooting, then dropped to his knees and begged them for a chance to join in when the time came to change film.

After the hammock, we all moved to the edge of the jungle for some tight framed shots strictly for the catalog, and then it was time to get Terri wet. I led her down to the beached dive boat to use as a prop and background, and shot a series of her walking into the water, walking out of the water, and then an awesome sequence of Terri crawling and rolling around in the wet sand at the water's edge. Our final stop was the shower where I did a 360 series while she rinsed off in the cool water, stripped for the camera, and got my testosterone running full bore with her trademark sultry innocence. Once finished, I gladly accepted her wet and wild hug and kiss, then escorted her back to the champagne trough for some well earned bubbly, a clean towel, and a seat in the shade under the huge beach umbrella David had set up for the ladies.

Amanda, Roberta, and Kimberly chose to stay with Terri and David in the shade while Jack and I took the other three girls back through the circuit. Bert and Kimbo were really hitting it off well, as were Amanda and Terri, but I think David was having the most fun of all being the bartender, and entertaining the ladies with all the special goodies he had stashed in his shirt pockets. Janinne, Suzan, and Carmen were like the three amigos as they baited and prodded each other into being bold, sexy, and provocative during their tenure in front of the camera. This time, however, it was Carmen who proved to be the least inhibited and most playful, as she teased Jack unmercifully with the promise of another Olympian sexual encounter while exposing herself to him, and the camera, of course. Once we got to the final sequence in the shower, I finished by shooting them as a nude trio, and poor Jack just couldn't take the visual and verbal stimulus any longer. He set the video camera down on a towel, and made an awkward looking mad dash to the Pacific and threw himself in.

Roberta and Kimberly were the next duo on my schedule, and once again, Bert proved to be worth her weight in gold by helping Kimbo relax, and guiding her through the rough spots with her charm, charisma, and cut-the-crap approach to being sexy.

"You're an actress, dammit," she told Kim repeatedly, "Act like you're having fun!"

The golden hues of the late afternoon sun brought out a glow in Roberta's complexion and eyes that further enhanced her exotic image of the ultimate sexual predator. Add her more than suggestive body language to the equation, and even I felt compelled to go throw myself in the ocean. She was toying with me like a lioness eyeing a juicy zebra, but I didn't mind at all. Whatever she was doing mentally to create such an awesome image physically was A-OK with me. Like I've always said, if you're going to hallucinate, might as well have a good one!

Amanda was next on my list and she wasted no time getting in the mood to be at her sensual and sexual prime. Terri pulled out another of her special stash suits I knew she was saving for herself, but with Amanda's coloring and shape, everyone agreed that the glimmering black and white snake print 2 pc. thong looked like it was created especially for the voluptuous little Oriental dynamo. Amanda requested we do her shots on a more one-to-one basis, so I worked her through the circuit without the rest of the ladies hovering around us, and she proved her comfort level with a stellar performance. I changed the sequence to get the catalog shots done first, then turned her loose to crank up the heat and show off the attitude she displayed so well on her yacht. We moved from the jungle to the beach, the beach to the shower, then asked Terri to join in for some wet fun. Their attitude while being playful in the cool water of the shower was light-hearted with lots of smiles and laughter, but when we finished up with both of them wet and nude in the hammock together, the atmosphere turned nothing short of hot and steamy, with heavy sexual overtones. When the cameras finally ran out of film, I was done, too. Enough was enough, I needed a bottle of champagne, something to smoke, and a cold shower!

After my well deserved break, only Roberta, Terri, and Janinne wanted to continue with another session of strictly centerfold style posing. The rest were perfectly content with the photographs we had already taken, and only wanted to sit around, relax, and partake of more champagne and party favors in preparation for our gala event on Janinne's terrace later in the evening. Even Jack begged off video detail to entertain the ladies and be the bartender while David made a run out to the Hatteras for more goodies. Janinne was thrilled to have Terri more to herself, and Bert was happy just to be back in front of my camera as the four of us went about our business of creating both playful and provocative photographs on our very private nude beach. I did a few shots of Terri and Janinne together, but for the most part, we concentrated on taking the most sensual images possible on an individual basis. Not for any catalog, these shots were created for the big boys with the big bucks at Playboy and Penthouse, and ourselves, of course. With Terri around, Janinne was much more comfortable in front of the camera, and her relaxed mood transformed itself into beautiful images through my lens. No coaching was required, just good posing and let her natural glamour do the rest.

While I was finishing up with Janinne, Terri and Bert made a quick trip to the libation umbrella for a little attitude adjustment, then dashed over to the little hut and returned with a bag full of cutesy props and a refreshing silliness to their demeanor. Sometimes the most radiant sexuality comes from simply not trying to force the issue, and now was the time to play. Roberta threw on a gray Mickey Mouse T-shirt that had the sleeves and neck cut out of it and was cropped so short it just barely covered her nipples, a big floppy straw hat, and sunglasses, then started prancing and dancing around at the water's edge. Within minutes, everyone was into the act of being silly, and the fun began. I did my best to become invisible, and simply walked around the festivities and did candids of the girls just being girls, and got some terrific shots. The champagne was really flowing now, but no one seemed concerned that we were all getting pretty toasted because the tight face shots were all over for the day. I snuck up behind Janinne and captured an awesome full length shot of her standing in the sand holding a bottle of Dom in one hand, a crystal flute in the other, and wearing only her Laura Biagiotti sunglasses and a smile as she watched the others playing in the water. When she heard the camera and motor drive clicking and whirring away behind her, she peered at me over her shoulder, arched her back, and started teasing me by shaking her ass in my direction. Suzan caught on to what was happening, and the next thing I knew, both of them were trying to out perform each other in a temptuous and hilarious T&A shake-a-thon.

Before doing the group shot and packing it in for the day, I wanted one last pass at Terri and Amanda, so I asked them to walk down the beach with me for a little isolation from the revelry. In their bottoms only, I photographed them walking away from me both together and individually, then set them down in ankle deep water and did sitting and reclining poses the same way. Totally relaxed and uninhibited, the ladies responded to my request to not create any kind of a facade, and the little girl in each of them came bursting through in their eyes and natural smiles. The Dragon Lady was gone, and twenty-two year old Amanda Tu let my camera reach right into her soul. Wet sandy hair and all, this precious child was a far cry from the boardroom bitch her father was trying to create, or the slut in Christian's wet dreams. When I turned my attention to my beautiful companion and focused in on Terri's mesmerizing eyes, I couldn't help myself from falling in love with her all over again. Beyond all doubt, every fiber of my heart and soul belonged to her, and I wouldn't want it any other way.

The last photograph on our agenda was the remake of our group shot, and by now, everybody was well lit and ready to move on to bigger and better things. The champagne was almost gone, as were any lingering inhibitions, so getting the ladies to completely disrobe for the grand finale was only a matter of dropping a hint. I had three shots left on the roll, so the first one we did topless, the second one nude, and for the third, well, let's just say even the guys participated in the bare-assed festivities. After the last shot was fired, we stood around toasting each other until every remaining drop of champagne had been consumed, then each and every one of our fabulous female companions dashed into the ocean for some serious skinny-dipping while the boys got to clean up the mess. After my camera gear was carefully stowed away, my next concern was getting even for making us do all the domestic chores, so I used all the towels to wrap up their wet suits, packed up everybody's dry clothes in a duffel bag, then joined my fellow conspirators in the dive boat for a non-stop trip to the Hatteras, leaving our naked bathing beauties to make their own way out to the yacht. Well, at least that was the plan. After smoking the last of the Hawaiian, we tied the little wooden boat to the back of the mighty Hatteras, then all three of us chose to strip and dive in for one last wet and wild frolic with our bevy of naked, and beautiful ladies.

THE TASK AT HAND

From anyone's point of view, the solitary couple walking barefoot along the shoreline of the club's infamous crescent beach looked as harmless and carefree as the golden hues of the tropical sunset they were sharing with each other. The man was smiling and at ease with his companion, and the woman looked caught in the grasp of tranquility as she held the skirt of her peasant dress above her knees in a child-like manner to keep the soft fabric from getting wet. They were comfortable. They were unpretentious. They were killers.

"So tell me, my brother, what kind of game are you playing with this fool who calls himself the owner and his whore who lives on the fancy boat? I know why my men and I are here, but I also see there is potentially more at stake than just taking someone's money. It is time for the truth, you devious little boy."

"Yes, it is," replied Mahmood. "Christian is infatuated with the vast fortune that belongs to the family of Amanda Tu, and is willing to do anything to get his hands on it. His plan was to marry her then have her killed, but she only toys with him and refuses his advances, while he continues to fuck everything that walks on two feet. At a time when he was frustrated the most, I confronted him with a new plan. On the night of her arrival, I staged a wedding ceremony using an Oriental prostitute in place of Miss Tu as Christian's blushing bride. We brought in a certain priest from Acapulco that has a reputation for discretion, a weakness for fine wine, and a lust for youthful flesh to perform the vows and make everything legal. We were even clever enough to take a few out-of-focus photographs of the gala event for further proof, and plan to use a computer to transpose her signature onto the marriage certificate."

"So Amanda Tu is officially Mrs. Christian Morea in the eyes of the law, and now you want me to kill her so Christian can inherit her share of the family fortune."

"Exactly, my sister, but the best part is the two hundred and fifty thousand dollars he will pay us for the pleasure of taking her life."

"Has Allah made hummus of your brain? Imbecile! Why should we help a fool to become a richer fool for a mere two hundred and fifty thousand dollars when we can have it all! We don't kill her, you idiot, we kidnap her. Don't you think her family would pay a fortune for her safe return, and we can extort millions out of this resort for not exposing Christian as a conspirator in her murder! Once her family has paid whatever figure we ask, we both know a very cruel man in Syria that would pay handsomely for a woman of her beauty to be a new addition to his harem. She won't live very long, they never do, but we will have collected three times for her instead of just once. The Brotherhood will have millions of dollars to support its efforts to carry out the will of God instead of just a few hundred thousand. You think too small, my brother, and that is why I am here to help."

"Does this change your plans for tonight?"

"Not at all. I will occupy Christian's time while you ply his associates with drugs, whores, and alcohol at the disco, giving my men time to search their rooms and get into position. When the Colombians finally stagger back to their rooms, we will rob them of all their drug money, and then kill them. Tomorrow, we will take care of Amanda and Christian, and then it will be our time to party with the drugs and whores."

Christian Morea had finally awakened from his afternoon nap and staggered into his shower. He was still numb from all the drinking, snorting, and whoring associated with the all night party and morning orgy in the disco, but numb was much better than sick and hung-over like some of his guests with a weaker constitution. As the warm water rinsed the cobwebs down the drain, Christian became more and more impressed with himself and his new found flair for making money. On top of his percentage for just being the host, the thought of nearly one hundred kilos of cocaine locked away in the wine cellar, and the cash he would get from skimming off Don Fernando's payment to the resort made him laugh out loud at his good luck and mental prowess. Add whatever percentage of the Tu family fortune he would receive for being Amanda's grieving widower, and he would be set for life. All that would be left to fulfill his delusion of grandeur would be the death of Unkle Henri, and then the keys to the vineyards would be his to do with as he wishes.

The opening of the glass shower door behind him startled Christian until he spun around and looked into the big brown eyes of the naked brunette that had joined him.

"So, my dear, who are you and why are you here?"

Without losing eye contact, she smiled and then took the wash rag from his hand and started rubbing it on his chest, abdomen, and parts south.

"My name is Sidiki, and I'm going to be your best friend."

THE ULTIMATE PATIO PARTY

The air in Janinne's private elevator was filled with the sensuous and testosterone producing fragrance of Organza perfume that swirled around Terri like an aura of sexuality as we made our way up to the penthouse for what the girls described as the last dress-up affair of our vacation. After tonight, make-up will be held to the bare minimum, and the dress code will be casual beach bum attire at all times. Terri responded to the call of the wild by wearing her tall white heels and an elegant white stretch lace sheath with a modest French cut, but modest had nothing to do with the way the fabric molded itself to her delicious frame and stopped well short of her mid thigh. When she placed her arms around my neck to hug me, as she was doing now, natural reaction was to grab her glorious ass and give thanks to the creator of thong panties, which I was doing now.

"I'm really glad this is almost over, Jeffrey," she whispered. "After tonight, we can just relax and be together. No schedules . . . . no crowds . . . . just us."

"That sounds wonderful, Angel. I can take the last few shots I need of the club on any of our leisurely walks around the grounds."

Terri leaned away from me just enough to nail me with one of her mischievous grins.

"Who said anything about walking, Darling?"

The door of the elevator opened and we stepped into the erotic mayhem of three beautiful women trying to get ready for a party at the same time in the same bathroom. We could hear them laughing and whooping it up the minute we stepped into the foyer, so our natural reaction was to head for the festivities. After a quick stop to pick up a chilled bottle of Mumm and two flutes, I politely hesitated at the bar to let Terri have first access to the bathroom just in case the ladies in occupancy weren't exactly in a lady-like posture, and the room immediately burst into laughter. In moments, my precious angel returned with a distinct blush to her face, tears in her eyes, and fanning herself with her empty hand while she desperately tried to refrain from another outburst.

"Fart jokes," was all she could say before losing it altogether. I held her glass as she did everything but fall to her knees and roll on the floor in laughter, then she regained her composure and drained both our flutes in two grand slams. "Thanks," she said with a cute little smile. "I needed that."

"Obviously! I take it I made the right decision to not follow you into the bathroom?"

Terri looked over my shoulder and replied, "Not necessarily."

I turned to see Janinne standing in the doorway wearing only an ivory lace demi bra and matching thong, and smoking a cigarette. She walked straight up and embraced me like a lover, then kissed Terri on the lips. I passed her a flute, then filled all our glasses for a toast just for us.

"I love your outfit," I said into her hypnotic eyes.

"And I love your girlfriend," Janinne replied, raising her eyebrows. "Wanna trade?"

"I don't think so," Terri answered with another grin. "Just like your breasts, we're a perfectly matched pair that looks better the closer we are together. Besides, after the full spectrum of pleasures we all shared last night, why would you want only me? Limitations can be so frustrating."

"With all the love that flows between the two of you, I doubt the word frustrating could ever be used to describe any part of it," Janinne said in a warm and loving tone of voice. "As for me, I'll take you any way I can get you, Honey."

"Amen," was my only response, then the three of us enjoyed another long embrace.

"Geez, people! Wait for Jack and Roberta to get here!" Suzan walked out of the bathroom in the traditional costume of red Spandex hot pants, matching pumps, and well stocked silver service set. She served Janinne and Terri, then allowed me to be a gentleman and hold the tray while she served herself out of the silver sugar bowl. After another round for all the ladies, Suzan smiled at me and winked, "I want you to take Roberta outside as soon as they get here, because Carmen and I have plans for the big guy in the bathroom. She's lying naked on the black marble counter, and I just spelled out FUCK US NOW in cocaine on her lower abdomen. Do you think he'll get the message?"

"Probably, but what the fuck am I suppose to say to Bert? 'Please come outside while your husband gets assaulted by two horny semi-lesbians in the john!'"

"Silly boy," Suzan replied with her serpentine smile. "It was all Roberta's idea. She told us to wear him down before Amanda gets here so maybe he'll behave himself during dinner. Incidentally, while we have Senor Dong occupied, why don't you try a few snowpeaks off Roberta's awesome tits? We all know how much you enjoy that, and I know for a fact that Bert wouldn't mind in the least, so go for it, Dude."

"Yeah, Dude, go for it!" Janinne was too enthusiastic for her own good, and she knew it. "Well, since Terri and I are going to be occupied perusing my wardrobe for something worthy of this evening's festivities, I see no reason for you and Roberta to just sit around and be bored. After all, why should Jack have all the fun?"

"I thank you for giving me permission to partake of Mrs. Taylor's bodacious tah-tahs, but what makes you think her husband and my soon-to-be wife would allow me to live after such an indiscretion? After all, it's not like I'm the President, or some second-rate eye surgeon."

Before anyone could address the situation any further, the elevator opened and out stepped the breasts in question attached to their tantalizing owner, and closely followed by their personal protector. Gently draped in a miniature red silk cocktail dress with a plunging halter neckline, Roberta was nothing short of dazzling, and when she walked, the angled slit down the front her dress opened just enough to tease any voyeur with the suggestion of black lace, bare skin, and thigh-high stockings. Her long flowing mane had been well brushed for softness, but the bounce in her step emanated from her ominous bustline.

"Damn! If this is going to be a bra and panty party, I'm out of luck because I'm not wearing either," Roberta exclaimed, then smiled at Janinne. "Since I know we're not late, does that make you the appetizer?"

"I don't see why not," replied Janinne. "Terri was going to help me get dressed, but what the hell . . . ."

"First things first," Suzan stated, then served everyone a double dip from her magic sugar bowl. I watched in almost third person omnipotence as Roberta discreetly maneuvered herself closer to me so Suzan could get up close and personal with Jack to begin her seductive game. He hadn't said a word yet, but the glazed-over look in his eyes and the smile on his face spoke volumes about his state of mind. As he bent over the tray to start the second round of cocaine, Suzan whispered something to him that perked up his attention and brought a hint of reality back into his eyes. After serving all the rest, Suzan turned and handed Jack the silver tray, then wrapped both hands around his right biceps, and said softly, "I need to borrow Jack for a few minutes to fix something in the bathroom. If you need us, that's where we'll be."

As they were leaving the room, Janinne moved over to the controls of her state-of-the-art sound system and turned up the volume on Spyro Gyra, then invited us into her wardrobe to play dress up. Having no interest in what was actually hanging on the hangers, Roberta and I took up positions on the antique couch in the study half of the room so we could enjoy the music, sip champagne, and watch the fashion show in both comfort and style. As the subdued squeals from the bathroom began to filter through the sounds of the light jazz, I couldn't help but notice the shit-eating grin spreading itself all over Bert's beautiful face. I refilled both our flutes, pulled a joint out of my shirt pocket, lit it, and passed it to her.

"That's a nice little surprise you arranged for Jack this evening," I said with a chuckle.

"What the hell, Jeffrey, it's his vacation, too!" She filled her lungs with the sweet Colombian smoke, held it as long as she could, then exhaled almost nothing. The shit-eating grin immediately returned to her face, and she passed the joint back to me. "Believe me, Jeffrey, I didn't do them any favors. When Jack is healthy and gets this loaded, he loses all concepts of the fine art of making love and goes straight into attack mode. Don't get me wrong, there is a time and a place for everything, but I'm just not in the mood to get mauled tonight." Roberta took a moment to enjoy a double hit from a one gram vile she pulled from her purse, then continued. "Think about it, Jeffrey, it's the perfect gift for both of us. While they're back there trying to fuck each other's brains out in a meaningless frenzy, I get to sit here, sip champagne, and enjoy some of the world's finest cocaine with a handsome man who appreciates more than just my big tits and wet pussy." She reached over and put her hand on mine, then reached into my soul with her enchanting eyes. "It's not like I don't want you to appreciate them, because I'm very flattered that you find me attractive. I just mean that I'm glad to be sitting here with you, rather than being pounded into submission like those poor girls in the bathroom. And do you know what the best part is? Not only will Jack be worn down and a little more responsive to my wants and needs later tonight, he'll also be eternally grateful to me for giving him two wet lesbians to fuck any way he so chooses, and I didn't really do shit!"

"Like you said, it's the perfect gift." replied Terri, as she and Janinne had temporarily abandoned their search for the perfect party dress and walked over and joined us. The noises coming from the bathroom were getting louder and more pronounced, just as the smiles on all our faces were getting bigger and harder to hide. Terri slipped her new little silver 'cocaine compact' out of her purse and served herself, then passed it on to Bert. "Sounds like they're having fun in there," she said with a giggle. "Do you really think Jack was surprised?"

"Not a clue," replied Bert, "but I wouldn't exactly call what's going on in there fun. I teased him unmercifully the entire time we were getting ready, and made damn sure he stayed good and loaded, so Jack was primed and ready. Hell, I even made him hook up my stockings while I rubbed my ass in his face. They asked for it, but those poor girls will be squirming around in their chairs all the way through dinner."

Janinne stepped out of the room for a split second and returned carrying a silver tray which held two chilled bottles of Taittinger Comtes de Champagne, four new crystal flutes, and a silver ice bucket. She was still wearing her lace thong, but her bra was now a part of the decorations on the silver tray. After setting everything down on the coffee table and passing me a bottle to open, Janinne joined the ladies for another round of party dust, followed by slamming down the last of the Mumm. We toasted love and life with the more opulent Taittinger, then settled back down on the antique couch to enjoy a little time together before the other guests arrived, or so I thought. With Roberta sitting on one side of me, and Terri and Janinne on the other, I got to be the official cocaine holder for their next two rounds, then all three of them rose, moved the coffee table away a few feet, and stood in front of me. Janinne unzipped Terri's dress and helped her slip out of it, while at the same time Roberta reached behind her neck with one hand and unbuttoned her halter top, releasing the full-blown spectacle of her awesome bustline, then stepped out of the little red cocktail dress and tossed it over the back of a chair. Wearing only her black lace garter belt, stockings, and heels, Roberta was the first to bend over and serve herself from the silver compact I was still holding, followed closely by Janinne and Terri, but only after they had removed each other's lace thongs. When she had finished, Terri stood between her two smiling girlfriends for the traditional slam, then looked me right in the eyes and gave me her best Cheshire cat smile.

"The three of us decided you deserve a surprise, too, Jeffrey."

Kimberly and David were the first of Amanda's entourage to arrive for our dinner party, but by the time they showed up, all seven of us were fully dressed and sitting around in the sunken den enjoying a few minutes of relaxation, some light jazz, and the first of another case of champagne. They also had completely missed Andre and his gang turning the patio into an Epicurean masterpiece to delight all of the senses, as well as the mad dash for clothing when the crew walked in through the service entrance in the kitchen without knocking. Although curious, they still set a perfect table for twelve with each and every proper piece of fine china, silver cutlery, and crystal wine glasses in three distinct shapes on long linen tablecloths, then provided atmosphere by lighting the perimeter with torches, and decorating the table with beautiful flower arrangements surrounding elegant silver candelabrums. The reds were breathing, the whites were chilling, so all that was needed were the final elements to arrive for a perfect blending of food, wine, and adult conversation. David's Nordic-German bombshell was wearing an electric blue tube dress that barely stretched from her breasts to her ass, and heels that made her tower over everyone except Roberta and Jack, but David didn't seem to mind at all. He had easy access to paradise, and the time off to enjoy it.

"Amanda will be here shortly," he stated after a toast to their arrival, "but I need to warn you, she's bringing a date."

"Christian knows he's not allowed up here," blurted out Janinne in no uncertain terms.

"Just remember how wrong you were about Amanda," he said with a sly grin, then drained his flute. "You don't need to worry, it's not Christian."

For some reason, I wasn't surprised at all to see Amanda step out of the elevator on the arm of Don Fernando Munoz, but most everyone else was, especially Janinne. I felt her tremble from a foot away, and I could see the waves of uncertainty emanating from her eyes, yet she held strong with a pleasant smile. Followed by the ever-present Chang, they walked straight up to Janinne, and the slick Colombian dressed in the Armani

Tropical over a white silk shirt and endangered species slippers extended his hand to our hostess.

"Please forgive me for intruding on your elaborate dinner plans, but when I stopped to bid a warm good-bye to my favorite child, she insisted I join her this evening, if only for a few minutes. After a very brief conversation, Amanda has also insisted that I repeat what we discussed with all of you. Do you mind, my dear?"

"Not at all, Don Fernando," she replied, almost too quickly. "Mi casa es su casa."

"Thank you very much. Now if I can talk you out of some of that wonderful champagne, I wish to tell you all a story, so everyone get comfortable, please."

"Why not retire to the table, Don Fernando?" suggested Janinne. "Everything is ready, and there's a place already set for you."

The place she was referring to was for Jean Claude, just in case the fowl that flew the coop were to return, but who was I to tell them not to bother? Terri and I were the first to formally greet the odd couple, and walked with them out to the patio to begin the next stage of the evening's festivities. Amanda's blood red micro-mini cocktail dress was a strapless masterpiece made of only the finest silk, and was obviously hand-crafted to establish an immediate impact of the pleasures that dwell within. I didn't see the briefcase Chang was carrying until he set it down between Amanda and her date after seating both of them, then he retired to the perimeter of the light to observe from afar and guard his princess.

"He doesn't get to eat?" Terri asked.

"Chang prepares all his own meals." Amanda was totally relaxed and at ease with both her surroundings and the situation, and that seemed to help soothe everyone's anxiety. "He's my guardian, not my servant," she continued, "and I love him very much for his loyalty and trust. I personally served his meal after our evening prayers, so don't worry, he's fine." Amanda waited for everyone to get settled and quiet down, then she stood, and put her hand on the shoulder of Don Fernando Munoz. "There is method to my madness, and since we all share the common denominator of wanting nothing but the best for Chateau Pacific, I have asked Don Fernando to join us and share his ideas on that subject. Please listen to what he has to say, then hopefully you will understand why fate has joined us here and now."

"I thank you, my child, for the kind words," Don Fernando said after standing, "but I'm afraid my words will not be so kind. Mr. Mason . . . ."

Jeffrey, my friend . . . . before we begin, would you please use your expertise and select for me an excellent red wine for sipping during our conversation?"

"Of course!" was my immediate reply. "I see an aged Volnay that should do quite nicely. The perfect wine for a meaty conversation."

"Excellent! What you have just witnessed is diplomacy in an elementary form. I complemented him, asked for his learned opinion, and complemented him again on his recommendation. Very simple, very easy, and most of all, very easy to manipulate. Had I not agreed with his selection, a simple polite suggestion could have easily allowed me to change his mind, because we had established a bargaining position of equality and balance. This is exactly the way Amanda and I have been able to manipulate Christian. He wanted financial independence from his family, I needed a place to do a little business, and Amanda, well, let's just say she wanted to toy with her mouse for a little while longer. After priming our subject with a three day binge at my thoroughbred ranch in Ecuador, I showed him how to make a few million by hosting some of my business meetings to moisten his greed, then exploited his lust by introducing him to a well versed whore that would say anything I paid her to say. The formula worked to perfection; Amanda teased him with her promises of sexual pleasures, I provided the incentive and the substitute, and all the while, Christian thought he was the one using us! What a dolt!"

"Don Fernando has known from the very beginning that my only goal was to do everything within my powers to add Chateau Pacific to my list of personal possessions, and get rid of Christian. We knew within 48 hours the full extent of his fraudulent claims of ownership, and the intricate legalese that allows Henri Morea to circumvent the import laws and make this resort so unique, as well as provide for a wayward nephew. I used my so-called engagement to Christian as a means of maintaining control while we lined his pockets in the attempt to make him feel important."

"And independent from his family," I added.

"Exactly!" Don Fernando took a deep draw of the opulent bubbly and continued. "Amanda showed him how to invest his new money in art, boats, and other cash markets, but the more money he made, the more bizarre and arrogant he became. Unfortunately, that is also about the time Christian started making a few friends of his own in the inner-workings of underground business who are also very good at the art of manipulation, and now we both agree it is time for Christian to go before the resort is lost to vermin."

"Why not just shoot his sorry ass and deal with his replacement?" replied Jack.

"A wonderful thought, but not a viable option, or our style," answered Amanda. "By rights of succession, the ownership of the resort goes to a niece that is unnamed in the legal paperwork."

"She is also the sole heir to the entire estate of Henri Morea," added Don Fernando, "which includes complete control of the vast holdings of Domaine Morea, vineyards and all. We have researched volumes of family records and no mention of this niece has ever surfaced before Chateau Pacific existed, but we continue to investigate."

"How do you know she really exists at all?" Once Roberta knew she had everyone's attention, she continued on with her legal expertise. "Have you considered she may only be another deception meant to be a buffer between Christian and his family, or the resort and the import laws? After all, as long as a family member maintains a permanent residence here, the free wine can and will continue to flow, and neither government can do shit about it."

"A good theory, Mrs. Taylor, and also an exact assumption, but Henri's brother in Tel Aviv and his cousin in Switzerland have both very recently signed legal documents agreeing not to contest her inheritance or his will." Don Fernando reached down to his waistband to turn off a vibrating beeper, then made eye contact with Amanda and addressed the point of his conversation. "As my time has come to an end, I must point out two things to each and every one of you. First and foremost, my seaplane will be landing soon and I will be leaving this club with my new associate immediately. Shortly thereafter, Ramon will begin transporting my men out to our boats, and we will all be gone before midnight. Predictability is not an asset in my line of work, so Christian will have no knowledge of our departure until we are already gone. As for you, Miss Pavie, I vow never to return to do business here again. I apologize for all the discomfort we have caused you during our five brief stays, but as you now realize, there was a master plan at work. Had we been successful in removing Christian, no amount of money would have prevented us from signing you to a long term contract to continue your roll as General Manager of Chateau Pacific. You are perfect, my dear, and you deserve a great deal of credit for the success of this wonderful establishment. Secondly, I've become very uncomfortable with Christian's public display of a very private lifestyle. I used to travel with only three associates, but now that these parties have gotten so large and out of hand, I needed over two dozen armed guards to feel safe. Beyond all doubt, it is time to move on to a marketplace with less visibility. However, once your coup is successful and a new ownership has been established, I would love to return to Chateau Pacific as a guest, but nothing more. In the meantime, my suggestion to each and every one of you is to be cautious and stay safe. Now, before I leave, it is time to clear my tab." He set the briefcase on the table, opened it, and turned it so everyone could see the neat rows of bundled cash before sliding it over to Janinne. "Maximum capacity of 280 at a thousand dollars a day for three days equals $840,000, and worth every penny."

"I hate to break this to you," she replied, "but maximum capacity of this resort has never exceeded 240 under any configuration. Looks like I owe you some change!"

"How typical. I show him how to make millions and he rips me off for pocket change!" Don Fernando lifted his glass and politely bowed to our hostess. "You owe me nothing, kind lady. Please consider the balance gratuity, and do with it as you wish. As for the rest of you, under the cash you will find a kilo of Amanda's favorite vintage with my compliments. Enjoy as much cocaine as you like while you're here, my friends, but please don't risk trying to take any of it back to the states with you, for that would be illegal."

"One last question before you leave," stated Suzan, then stood up to establish direct eye contact with Don Fernando. I knew in my heart what she was going to say, but the words still made me cringe on the inside. "Have you seen Jean Claude recently?"

"No, my child," he answered, "and that surprises me. I have not seen the young Canadian since early yesterday evening when he joined me at the bar for a bottle of Le Grande Dame, and expressed his desire to leave Chateau Pacific and come work for my organization. Quite honestly, I was prepared to hire him, but I couldn't understand why a man would want to leave a wife as beautiful as you alone in a paradise such as this."

"How did you know we were married?" Now Suzan was starting to tremble.

"That's exactly what he asked, too," Don Fernando said with a queer smile. "I'm very proud of my intelligence group. You'd be surprised what knowledge I've obtained just in the last few days."

"Is that why you're warning us to be so careful?" I asked.

"Exactly, my friend. Now if you will excuse me, I have a plane to catch."

Andre and his staff outdid themselves in the preparation and presentation of the seven course meal that literally did us all in. He started each course with a new wine, brought out the culinary delight to complement the vintage, then reset the table and started the process all over for the next course. We began with a young Macon Villages and a cold shrimp and crab cocktail, followed by a Cote de Beaune to complement an outrageous wild game pate, then blew us away with a opulent Le Montrachet to go with our fresh grilled butterfly snapper and sautéed vegetables. After a garden salad with a French-style chunky bleu cheese dressing accompanied by a delicious Cuvee Pyrenees-Henri for course number four, he killed us with a decadent `66 St. Emilion and rack of lamb with a mild Rosemary sauce that made my palate stand up and cheer. Round six consisted of fresh sliced strawberries and peaches surrounding a piece of home-made cheesecake and the Volnay, then we ended our ordeal with coffee, Port, and an assortment of petit fores. Even though Andre was kind enough to keep the portions appropriate to our sizes, we were all stuffed to the gills, and in no way ready to do anything strenuous. At least not for a while!

As we sat around the table enjoying the last of the coffee, Janinne responded to what sounded like a doorbell by dashing inside and grabbing the portable phone on her nightstand. It was obvious she was pleased by what she was hearing by the huge smile on her face, and she seemed to almost float back to the table after her brief conversation.

"Andre, may we please have a special bottle of champagne for a very special toast," she said, then turned her attention to the rest of us. "That was Unkle Henri. He caught a flight into Miami this morning and has spent the rest of the day helping Mimi, my Godmother and guardian all my life, get ready to move all our belongings to his chateau in France. They were both so happy they were in tears."

"So what's the deal?" asked Roberta. "Are they getting married?"

"Heavens no," she answered with a chuckle. "They're cousins, or something like that. Mimi was part of the family that moved to the United States in 1939 to avoid the Nazis. Unkle Henri's grandmother was Jewish, as were other elements of the family, so parts of them moved to Palestine, and others settled in south Florida. Mimi was my mother's best friend, and since I was only an infant when she died, Mimi legally adopted me and gave me her family's name."

"Out of curiosity, who was your father?" Amanda seemed to focus in on what Janinne was saying more than anyone else at the table.

"I don't really know. I was told he died tragically before I was born. All I know for certain is that Mimi introduced him to my mother, and that they were very much in love."

"What name is on your birth certificate?" asked Amanda.

"Only my mother's, Jennifer Miller. My father was recorded as deceased."

"Now I'm curious," I said. "Where does Henri Morea come into the picture?"

"All my life I was told I had a Guardian Angel that looked after both Mimi and me, and that Angel turned out to be Unkle Henri. Mimi's only job was to take care of me, and Unkle Henri provided all the necessary funds. He paid for everything; my education, our house, our cars, everything. He even helped get me my first job with Air France."

"Why?" asked Amanda. "There has to be a reason."

"Ask him yourself," stated Janinne, then raised her champagne flute. "He'll be here in the morning."

Up in the master bedroom of Christian's villa, a decadent all-night party for two was also in full swing. Complete with heroin-laced cocaine, lubricated toys, and enough Viagra to supply a small fraternity party, Sidiki had promised the best fuck of his life, and she was doing her best to live up to her promise. When he opened his eyes and looked up at the mirror above his king-sized bed, Christian could see the smile on his beet red, sweaty face, but it was the pounding gyrations of his Olympiad fuck-mate that drew the majority of his attention. She was moving and grooving on top of him, and making enough noise to keep him at the peak of his game. He was a stud, and she was going crazy on his rock hard dick, or so he thought. What he had completely missed in his assessment of the situation was the look of pure hatred in her eyes.

DAY SEVEN

I awoke to the sounds of heavy rain pounding against the roof and walls of our little wooden cabin in paradise. Not just your basic tropical thundershower, this was a full fledged tree bending, gully washer of a downpour, complete with high winds that made the huge droplets race from one side of the roof to the other like an old stereo sound effects recording. As I eased out of bed so as not to awaken my sleeping beauty, I couldn't help but take a moment to admire the splendor of her loveliness, and reflect on the joy of spending the rest of our lives together as man and wife. As long as she doesn't get bored with being worshipped, I could think of no reason not to want to be her partner for an eternity of love and passion. I sealed my decision with a gentle kiss on her exposed cheek, and then slipped into the shower instead of jumping her bones. In the real world, making love is much more enjoyable when both parties are coherent.

Our breakfast tray arrived just as I was finished with my bathroom routine, so I wrapped myself in one of the resort's white terrycloth robes and plopped down on the wicker couch to enjoy the coffee, croissants, and fresh fruit. The young man in the electric cart may have been soaked to the skin from the continuing morning monsoon, but our food was warm, dry, and wonderful. I thought about waking up Terri, but decided to let her sleep for as long as possible. As far as I'm concerned, rainy mornings are perfect for quiet, deep thoughts, and today was no exception.

Last night, the pending arrival of Unkle Henri totally dominated the conversation for a solid fifteen minutes after Janinne made her announcement, ending with the agreement that David would fly Janinne down to Manzanillo in the Gulf Stream to pick him up, then Amanda stood and announced that it was time for her to leave. To my complete surprise, and Janinne's chagrin, Terri also made the same statement. Since Kimberly had been invited to stay on the Hatteras with David, the six of us said our good-byes to the remaining guests and made our way down the elevator to the pavilion. The music from the disco was so loud it was shaking the floor, but no one in our group made any mention of wanting to go down there and check out the whore and gangster party, so we continued our trek to the beach bar, then Terri and I wished them well and continued on to our cabana. After she changed into one of my baggy T-shirts for comfort, Terri joined me on the porch for a quick smoke, a glass of champagne, and some serious cuddling.

"Thank you for not wanting to stay," she said softly. "I hope you enjoyed your surprise, but now I want you all to myself. Being pleasured by another woman is certainly an incredible experience, and sharing you with Roberta and Janinne was a trip, but you're the only man I want in my life. I'll always be your lover, but I want to be your wife, too."

"Just tell me when and where, Angel, and we'll have the wedding of your dreams. I can't think of a greater celebration of love than making you my wife."

We kissed softly and held each other for a few moments, then Terri stood up, extended her hand to me, and led me into the bedroom. No cocaine-induced nasty games were necessary, nor were there any pretenses for any kind of an aerobic marathon. The love we shared was passion in its purest form, and when all was said and done, we collapsed in each other's arms and slept peacefully.

As the heavy rain continued to pelt our little dwelling of love, my thoughts drifted to Janinne and her relationship with Terri. My dad told me a long time ago that the last place a man needs to be is in between a woman and what she wants, and beyond any doubt, Janinne wanted Terri. I could be a greedy bastard and take them both, but eventually somebody would get hurt, and that would be unacceptable in any form. The only choice I could make at this time was simply to let them figure it out for themselves, and not force either of them to make a decision one way or another. After all, I'm about to be married to one of the most kind, caring, and beautiful women in the world, who also just happens to love me very much, so who am I to come between her and her friends? We only have two more days left here anyway, then its back to the reality of Houston and trying to make a living. The next time they'll see each other will probably be at our wedding, so what the hell, let them enjoy themselves while they can. It's not like they tell me to leave and lock the door behind me!

As for the rest of today, the mass exodus of the remainder of Christian's special guests should be completed well before noon, then we would literally have the entire club to ourselves to do with as we please. Not like we haven't had free reign to do so already, it's just that now I could turn down the eyes in the back of my head and concentrate more on the woman in my arms. The gameplan for this morning was to let Janinne and Unkle Henri have some privacy to do their personal business, then everyone join them at the penthouse for brunch around eleven. Afterwards, the girls were driving into Manzanillo for their final shopping spree, and David was going to take Jack and I out on the Hatteras for a fishing and smoking expedition, which would leave Unkle Henri and Amanda alone for their business meeting in the privacy of Janinne's office. Until eleven, the only thing on my agenda was getting yesterday's film ready for David so he could make my morning delivery, and making Terri as happy as possible.

"Were you just going to let me sleep all morning?" came the soft voice from behind me, then I felt her arms wrap themselves around my neck. "How much beauty sleep do you think I need?"

"As much as you like, Angel," I replied with a smile. "Considering the results, I have nothing to complain about. How are you this morning?"

"In love with you, Jeffrey."

Terri walked around and laid her beautiful body on top of me for a full length hug, making sure both our robes were open for that personal touch. The soft warmth of her skin and the gentle firmness of her toned body against mine further emphasized the magical energy that flows between us, and fully exposed my ever-increasing need to make her a permanent fixture in my life. Making love to her is magnificent, but being in love with Terri is proving to be a magnificent obsession.

We cuddled and cooed for what seemed to be an endless amount of time, then Terri succumbed to the need for nutrition and made her way over to our breakfast tray. Her short baby blue silk robe didn't quite cover her gorgeous ass, especially from my low angle of view from the couch, so I just laid there and enjoyed her poetry in motion. Luckily, my coffee had gotten cool during our morning embrace, so I had another good reason to join her at the table.

"What would you like to do on this blustery morning?" I asked, after wrapping my arms around her waist from behind, then nuzzled her ear. "It's not like we can go hang out on the nude beach."

Terri arched her back and rubbed her ass into me, then reached back and ran her fingers through my hair, leaving her luscious breasts exposed and begging to be caressed.

"Give me a few minutes to shower and I'll show you," she teased. "Who needs a nude beach when you have a nude bitch, Jeffrey?"

Needless to say, my only option at that point was to volunteer to scrub her back, which I did. Actually, she allowed me to bathe her all over, wash her hair, and then hand dry her with a big soft towel. Sometimes being the male servant has some distinct advantages!

After my chores were done, I left Terri alone in the bathroom to finish her routine and stepped back out on the porch to partake of a little morning marijuana. The gusty winds seemed to have died down, but the rain continued to fall as heavily as ever with no signs of letting up in the near future. My mind was drifting aimlessly between the raindrops and the pools that were forming in the grass throughout our little clearing, when up sped David and Kimberly in a cart that had the cab enclosed in clear vinyl to protect the occupants from the foul weather. For whatever reason, they were both laughing their ass off as they came to a screeching halt right outside our front door, then stumbled inside as I stood there and held it open for them.

"This man is a fucking lunatic," she squealed as she shook the water out of her hair. "He's out there doing doughnuts in the grass around the beach, then tries to hit every puddle at warp speed to wash off the mud. I swear we were airborne at least three times on our way here. Hey buddy, you break it, you bought it!"

"What the hell do I need with a golf cart, Kimbo?" David replied, then grabbed the joint from my hand and took a deep draw.

"I'm talking about me, you asshole!" she laughed, then joined him for a smoke.

"OK, you two, besides picking up my film, are you going to let me in on what's going on here, or do I have to guess?" I said, and offered them some coffee and another joint.

"Janinne is too afraid to fly in this weather, so Kimberly volunteered to go because she knows Unkle Henri, and we thought you and Terri might like to come along for the ride."

"Yeah, come with us. I brought a few of the club's floral outfits so Unkle Henri will be sure to notice us, then Terri and I will pamper him all the way home while you and Captain Knevil fly the plane."

"I don't see why not," I replied, "but we'll have to check with my social secretary first to see if she feels the same way. How much time do we have for her to get ready?"

"The sooner we get started, the more time we'll have to play," Kimberly answered with a peculiar smile and wink. "Terri and I will have plenty of time to dry off and get ready once we're in the air, so there's no reason to get carried away right now, especially in all this rain."

"No shit, so go drag her cute little ass out here and let's get rolling. Think about it Jeffrey, how many times do you get to go play in a totally tricked out GS-5 without the owner on board to get in the way?"

Dragging wasn't necessary because Terri jumped at the idea of going for a ride on a private jet, especially one custom built for Amanda Tu. She threw on a T-shirt and her work-out shorts, tossed her make-up, hair fixings, and white stacked-heel sandals in a nylon gym bag, and she was ready-set-go. I brought along my Nikon and a few rolls of film just in case an opportunity presented itself with the girls, or something equally as scenic, then we climbed into the cart and were off.

David behaved himself during our trip to the airstrip, and we stayed dry in the confines of the covered cart while he deactivated the security system and opened the door to the plane, but the volume of rain still coming down soaked each and every one of us as we made our mad dash up the gangway. At first glance, I was amazed at the size and splendor of the jet's custom interior, as well as the way it was laid out, but considering the owner, I shouldn't have been. The long distance luxury cruiser had four leather recliners that swiveled to form a grouping, a small but well equipped galley, a leather pit-group aft that transformed into a double bed, and a full bathroom complete with a shower, dressing area, and separate toilet. Right behind the cockpit was an entertainment center that housed the sound system, TV, and multiple DVR's on one side, and the smallest water closet I'd ever seen for human beings on the other. It's a good thing David is the pilot, because I seriously doubt if Chang could even fit in there, much less be able to sit and relieve himself on a long flight.

As David went through his pre-flight check list, I was glad to see the sky opening up a little bit and the rain starting to slack up. I didn't doubt his ability to get this bad boy off the ground, but I did have some serious concerns about landing an aircraft of this size on such a small runway under these slick conditions. The ladies seemed to be more concerned with the outfits Kimberly had brought along to please Unkle Henri, the condition of their hair and make-up, and the excessive volume of Dom Perignon in the refrigerator, but I kept my fixation on the conditions of the weather. David fired up the engines, and within five minutes we were taxiing the length of the runway for a final check, then moving back into position for take-off. Once the girls and I had strapped ourselves into the leather recliners, David gave us the old thumbs up signal, then hit the throttle and we were off like a sling dragster. About 2/3 of the way down the runway, David lifted the nose, and the twin power plants shot us almost straight up into the sky at maximum warp. We began a slow spiral to the right while we gained altitude, then he leveled off the aircraft and took us due west, out to sea.

"Hey guys, come forward and have a look!" David exclaimed. "And bring me something to drink! I've got cotton mouth bad enough to choke a big dog."

We unhooked ourselves from the overstuffed loungers, grabbed a few cans of coke from the refrigerator, and moved forward into the cockpit. David had worked us into a clear area between the cloud levels that created a surrealistic visual image of transcending the rings of Saturn, then he raised the nose of the aircraft and we pierced the clouds above us and burst into sparkling blue sky. Kimberly carefully maneuvered herself into the co-pilot's seat, then looked over at David and winked.

"We're going to take the long, slow approach into Manzanillo so Kimbo can get some quality time at the controls," he stated, then looked back and smiled at Terri and I. "Since we're going to be occupied up here for at least thirty minutes or so, why not slip into the back and do something special, like join the Mile High Club."

I don't know who moved faster, Terri or me.

Standing outside customs in the airport terminal, Terri and Kimberly certainly garnished their fair share of attention from both travelers and workers alike. They chose to wear the red floral bandeau tops with matching pareas tied around their waists, and each carried a small cardboard sign that read "Unkle Henri." Not like he was going to miss them, we just thought the signs made the girls look a little more official. After being approached by numerous wanna-be's, and who could blame them for trying, a jovial older gentleman looking a lot like Peter Ustinov's version of Hercule Poirot bowed to the ladies, kissed their hands, then gladly accepted their hugs and kisses in return. After the frivolities subsided, David and I stepped out of the background and introduced ourselves, then I took a few shots of Unkle Henri and the girls while everyone in the general vicinity looked on and drooled. His luggage consisted of a small trunk on wheels perfectly sized to transport two very special cases of wine, a very expensive leather carry-on for his clothes, and a computer sized shoulder bag he refused to allow anyone else to carry for him. With a beautiful woman attached to each of his arms, David and I led him through the terminal and out to the Gulf Stream without incident or delay, except for the curious gawkers that were everywhere. Luckily, the rains had stopped, so our stroll across the tarmac was at a leisurely pace. After stowing his gear and making sure he was comfortable, David and I took our seats in the cockpit and prepared for our quick flight back to Chateau Pacific. Unkle Henri was so engrossed with his female companions, he barely said anything at all to either of us, but there would be plenty of time for conversation with him at brunch, so neither of us felt slighted. After all, considering the awesome spectacle of Terri and Kimberly in their exotic tropical attire, I'm sure all he noticed about us was that we were male.

As we taxied past one of the generic-looking hangars used for service and storage that were separated from the main airlines facilities, something strange caught my eye that caused me to bring it to David's attention. Through the partially opened doors, he confirmed my sighting of at least three military assault helicopters and about thirty uniformed troops milling around that were fully armed. These men weren't just standing around, smoking cigarettes, and looking bored like reservists, they were definitely making preparations for deployment, and soon. David and I looked at each other for a moment, then he just smiled.

"Looks like Don Fernando was right about one more thing," he stated, then increased the throttle. "It's definitely time to get the fuck out of here."

THE BRUNCH BUNCH

Terri and I had the entire main pool and pool bar completely to ourselves as we arrived to swim and float around before our scheduled appointment for brunch up in the penthouse. Unkle Henri had been whisked away by Janinne as soon as he stepped off the plane, and Kimberly and David wanted some privacy before he shut everything down, so we just walked straight to the pool, stripped, and hopped in. With the exception of the waitress who brought us some towels and a bottle of Cordon Rouge, there was literally no one to be seen, but for some strange reason, I still couldn't shake the feeling of being watched. Terri was 100% comfortable and at ease, but I just couldn't let go.

The first sign of life we noticed was when the ATR-42 circled above us prior to landing, and then its subsequent take off in less than five minutes. Since General Huang probably didn't fly commercial, I guessed the passengers were probably the Eastern Europeans and the Koreans. Everyone else would need a more covert method of transportation that avoided customs, metal detectors, and all forms of monitoring. I looked over at my beautiful companion as she turned to soak up some rays on her glorious backside, and said a quick little silent thank you to God for keeping her healthy, happy, and safe on her first, and last, journey into possible danger via JJ and Company. On the positive side, we've made some great friends, produced some awesome photographs, and potentially

305

launched both our careers into the international market and its seven figure rewards, but nothing, and I mean nothing, would be worth the disaster of losing her. I know now that she is the single, most important thing in my life, and I will do everything within my power to comfort and protect her for the rest of my time on Earth. Strange thoughts indeed from a man who's avoided any and all long term commitments with anything female, and sought out confrontation at the deadliest level just for the thrill of victory.

"Hey guys, I see we had the same thoughts this morning," sang out Roberta as she walked up and took over the chaise next to me. "I needed a swim and some fresh air, so I left Jack soaking in the Jacuzzi with his smoke and pain killers. We helped close down the disco sometime this morning, and he's paying for it now."

"You went to the disco!" Terri exclaimed. "Why would you want to go there?"

"Jack got bored with the girl talk pretty quickly after you guys left, and since he wasn't going to get anything from Janinne, he decided it was time to leave. After refilling all our vials with some of Don Fernando's wonderful gift, and himself as well, the disco was our only option. In all honesty, we actually had a great time. Unlike Christian's party, the atmosphere was much friendlier, and since there were a lot more girls than guys by the time we got there, Jack got all the attention he could handle. And I do mean handle!"

"Did you get all the evidence on video tape, like you did in San Francisco?" I asked.

"No need," she replied with a cute little wink. "I let him play around all I wanted until I was ready to leave, then made him an offer he couldn't refuse."

"Dare we ask?" snickered Terri.

"Considering the fact that he's the one that needs the Jacuzzi and pain pills," she beamed, "I think you get the picture! It takes a big girl to put the big hurt on a big boy."

"I don't doubt that in the least," I said to the glow in her beautiful eyes.

"What you and I shared last night was magical, Jeffrey," she answered softly, then changed her tune in the blink of an eye. "What I did to Jack was closer to maniacal. Like I said, I wasn't in the mood to get mauled last night, so I simply turned the tables on him. Damn, it's getting hot around here. Let's get wet!"

Roberta stood up from her chaise and lifted the baggy T-shirt off of her totally naked body, then took five very sexy steps to the pool and slid right in. Terri and I simply smiled at each other and joined her in the cool water.

As requested when we walked her home from the pool, Terri and I stopped back by Jack and Roberta's cabana to pick them up on the way to Janinne's little soiree. We found them both curled up in a hammock in the cool shade of a palm grove, just swaying in the breeze and smoking a joint. As we approached, Roberta rolled out on her feet with no problems, but Jack was a totally different situation. It took both Bert and I to help raise him up, and then pull him out of the hammock and onto his feet. The grimace on his face left no doubt as to the level of pain he was going through just trying to stand up, much less take his first few steps. He did his best to make light of his predicament, but to no avail. Thirteen years in the NFL, and seventeen years with a wild-woman had definitely taken its toll on his muscular, but grizzled body.

"Damn, brother-in-law, I'm going to need another vacation just to recoup from this one," he said to me as I helped him try to walk. "I guess I spent too much time on the dance floor last night."

"And just what kind of dancing were you doing, my friend?"

"The finest kind, Jeffrey" he said with a cruel smile. "The finest kind."

The ladies were walking ahead of us up the trail to the pavilion, and both were whispering and giggling all the way. On occasion they'd glance back to check on us, but for the most part, they were completely engrossed in their conversation. With Terri in a form fitting soft cotton mini-dress and Roberta wearing a killer little gauze shorts set, neither of which showing any signs of undergarments, our concerns had nothing to do with what they were talking about, even if it was us. Jack fired up another joint, then passed it to me and smiled.

"Makes you believe in God, doesn't it?" he said. "The ass on each of those girls up there represents perfection in the art of creation."

"I have to agree with you, Jack. I hate to be politically correct, but I've become a true believer in the Women's Movement, especially when it's walking in front of me."

"Or sitting on your face," he added.

"Amen, brother-in-law. Amen, indeed!"

When we reached the penthouse, Unkle Henri was wrapped up in the company of three gorgeous women, and loving it. Suzan and Carmen were providing the entertainment, and Janinne was providing the visible support as she and the guest of honor stood with their arms intertwined. It was easy to see that both of them had been crying, but the expression on each of their faces emitted nothing but joy. After introducing Jack and Roberta, Janinne reintroduced Terri and I, then Unkle Henri took over the conversation.

"Please forgive an old man," he said to Terri while still holding her hand. "I knew you looked familiar, but in the costume you were wearing, I thought you were an employee of the club, not an International star."

"I'm just a lucky girl with a talented boyfriend," she answered. "I doubt if I'd ever consider myself a star, but thank you anyway."

"A woman of your presence can't help but be a star, my child. Look at the way you lit up this room when you entered, not to mention the glow in everyone's eyes when they gaze upon you. I'm sorry, but as beauty is in the eye of the beholder, I'm afraid you have no choice other than to accept your fate."

"That's what I've been telling her for almost two years, Mr. Morea," I said, "and she doesn't believe me either."

"Please, call me Unkle Henri," he replied, then shook my hand again. "All my friends do. And I should be angry with you, too, Jeffrey Mason, masquerading as a polite, but lowly member of the paparazzi creating a scene at the airport just because of my arrival."

"Old habits die hard, Unkle Henri," I answered with a smile. "I never go anywhere without a camera, especially when Terri is involved. Can you blame me?"

"Not at all, my fine young friend," he responded in heart. "It would be a crime against humanity if you didn't! Now please, I must insist that all of you take your seats while Andre and I prepare the sampling of treats I have brought with me from home. Along with the wine, there comes a story, of course. But if you will indulge me, I favor you'll be too busy sipping to interrupt me too often, so I intend to tell you the story of the families that grew this wine."

Andre and Karin passed out stemmed bowls for both white and red Burgundies, then followed through with the pouring of the white. Unkle Henri did his share by pouring all the red, and finished his task by passing out bottles of both wines for us to read. He grabbed his own glass of the red Burgundy, then Unkle Henri began his tale.

"When my mother married my father, they created the perfect blend of two of Burgundy's premiere wine families. The Moreas and the Pavies had adjoining vineyards all throughout the Cote de Or, and families that stretched from Champagne to Bordeaux, so when my mother fell in love with our neighbors oldest son, a finer merger of viniculture could not have been scripted by any lawyers in either Paris or Hollywood. After surviving World War I, both Andre and Christian Morea were ready to start families and get on with the business of making wine. Andre married my mother and moved in with the Pavies, and Christian married a charming woman from Cannes named Sophia, and brought her to his family's home across the vineyards. I'm proud to say that my father won the race, and I was the first born of the next generation of vintners. The Cote de Beaune that you are holding comes from vineyards that grow on a gentle hillside overlooking my home, and this vineyard was planted by my family in celebration of my birth. My friends, I give you Cote de Beaune-Henri, 2006."

We raised our glasses and tasted a true delicacy of life. Soft, yet still an explosion of delicate flavors, the glorious pinot noir was virtually absorbed by my palate, leaving very little to swallow. The second taste was even better, as was the third, and fourth. Karin passed out glasses of ice water to clear our palates, and Unkle Henri continued his tale.

"In a very short period of time, the brothers Morea had produced five sons, and each was given a specific vineyard to call his own as well as a designated place in the family business. As the oldest, my job has always been managing the vineyards, cousin Francois was groomed to handle the money, my brother Isaac was a natural salesman, and my cousin Pierre and youngest brother Andre were content to be children and just get in the way. In 1939, it became obvious that our peaceful way of life was about to be turned upside down by the Nazis, and since my grandmother was a Jew, my parents decided it was time to make a monumental move. Since the Holy Land was her second most favorite place on the face of the earth, we sent a contingent of family members, including my brother Andre, along with my grandmother to set up residences in both Haifa and Jerusalem. With the help of a Greek merchant who had been a loyal friend of my father's since they were adolescents, we were able to successfully get them relocated, as well as set up another conduit for the distribution of our family wares. With Pierre now being the youngest, he became my protégé and followed me everywhere I went to learn as much as possible about the vineyards. I showed him how to care for the vines, harvest the fruit, and make the wine that now bares his name. Ladies and gentleman, I present to you the 2007 vintage of Meursault Les Pierre."

Again, our palates were blessed with the light elegance of a classic French white burgundy that melted in our mouths. How something so light and delicate could produce so much flavor was beyond my comprehension, but I guess that's the reason I'm a photographer and Unkle Henri makes the wine. After watching the expressions on all our faces, Unkle Henri finally sat down, but his narrative was only getting started.

"In 1943, when both sets of parents were murdered by the Malice over ten cases of stolen wine, I became the patriarch of the family, and Pierre inherited my role as heir-apparent to the vineyards. In the years following the war, however, it became obvious that Pierre needed to spread his wings and get a broader education of life, so we sent him to Paris to attend college and experience a different style of people. From college, he went straight into law school and graduated with honors in two short years. With me managing the vineyards, Francois handling the money, and Isaac doing the wheeling and dealing, we now had a fourth partner in Pierre that could travel in the more polished circles of the French aristocracy and lead us into the future with a broader perspective. It was from one of those polished circles of society that Pierre met his wife Laeticia. She was an elegant young woman from a very powerful old Parisian family, but unfortunately all of her beauty was superficial. She had been raised to believe she was a superior being because of her heritage, and looked down on our family because we worked with our hands in the dirt. It was only after her father confirmed our net worth that she agreed to allow Pierre the privilege of her company. As you can imagine, their marriage was the social event of the year, with enough fluff to choke a large horse, but their problems began as soon as they returned from their Caribbean honeymoon. Laeticia refused to leave her family and friends in Paris to join her husband on his trips abroad for the domain, and even though our wines supplied the funds for her exorbitant lifestyle, she considered the rest of Pierre's family beneath her, and never once graced our chateau with her presence. Poor Pierre was caught right in the middle between all her tantrums and rigid social calendar, and our family business that required him to travel all over the free world. As I was his mentor, we spent many an hour on the telephone trying to soothe his pain, and many times he would come home to our chateau for the simple pleasures of walking through the vineyards and tasting the latest vintages. This precarious lifestyle lasted for a number of years, and then Laeticia began to sour as her beauty began to fade and her mental capabilities diminished due to years of non-use. To make matters worse, she blamed the stories of her sexual indiscretions on Pierre's neglect of her needs and lack of compassion for her social standing. After all, her father was worth millions and he never had to work, so why should her husband? It was at this time in his life that Pierre moved his residence back to the chateau, and left Laeticia and all her little demons to dwell in their Parisian townhouse. With divorce being out of the question, separation was his only option, and I welcomed him home with opened arms."

"In June of the following year, less than two months after my brother Isaac and his wife were murdered by a Palestinian hit squad because of a very lucrative arms deal he had masterminded with Israel, our cousin Mimi wrote that she was coming to France on holiday from her home in Miami, and asked if she and a friend could spend a few days at the chateau with us. As we hadn't seen her in over ten years, our answer was an immediate yes. Mimi and another contingent of our enlarged family had fled to southern Florida to escape the Nazi occupation, just as our grandmother and her group had gone to the Mid-East, so we were anxious to see how the States had changed our cute little cousin. What neither of us expected was the impact her visit would have on the rest of our lives. But it was not Mimi that caused the change, it was her friend. The young woman that accompanied Mimi to our home was a statuesque blonde with big green eyes and a sincere love of life. She was the breath of fresh air that Pierre had needed for a number of years, and even though he was fifteen years her senior, he was the sophisticated, romantic, and handsome Frenchman she had dreamed about all her life. I never believed in love at first sight, but the spark that occurred between them when their eyes first met changed my mind for the rest of my life. Well, needless to say, their love for each other put a wooden stake through the cruel heart of Pierre's marriage to Laeticia, and even though he was up front with his beautiful American about his situation, her only concern was pleasing him. They frolicked around the chateau and vineyards like children at play during the day, and spent every night together for the length of her extended stay. At a small dinner party on the evening before the ladies were to return to Miami, Pierre confirmed his love for Jennifer to everyone who was in attendance, and proposed marriage. The rest of the evening was filled with tears of joy, and many toasts to their happiness. When they left for the airport the next morning, all full of love, the last thing I expected was to never see Pierre and Jennifer again. When confronted face to face with divorce, Laeticia's choice was to put a gun to the back of Pierre's head, then turn it on herself. Needless to say, the paparazzi turned the tragedy into a major scandal, and both families were dragged through the sewers by both the press and the court system for months. Right in the middle of all this insensitivity, Mimi confronted me with the fact that Jennifer was pregnant with Pierre's child. As I was a coconspirator to the beautiful love-affair that created this precious child, I pledged my full support to Jennifer, but asked if she would please use discretion about the father until the waters calmed. Unfortunately, Jennifer died from pneumonia less than three months after the birth of their child, leaving Mimi as legal guardian. We gave her my mother's maiden name, and raised her in Miami as one of our own, which she truly is. Now it is time to set the record straight and hand over control of her father's estate to his rightful heir. In legal documents that will be signed with all of you as witnesses, I now present to you the heir-apparent to Domaine Morea, and owner of Chateau Pacific, my niece, Janinne Pavie."

Even though she already knew the punch line, Janinne was glowing with pride, and ready to burst with excitement. We all gathered around her and filled her moment with lots of hugs and kisses, then followed Unkle Henri into the study for the signing of the documents.

"This is going to come as quite a surprise to Christian," smiled Roberta. "I assume you have made provisions for his lawsuit that is sure to be filed the instant he reads these documents?"

"Certainly, Mrs. Taylor," replied Unkle Henri. "The equivalent of one-fifth of our family wealth, his father's fair share, has been set up in a trust fund to take care of Christian for the rest of his life. Any attempt to force his way back into the family business, or contest my will, would cause him to forfeit all rights to this trust fund. My brother Andre and my cousin Francois have both signed legal documents agreeing to Janinne's inheritance, and keeping Christian away from the money-making elements of our family business. As you have probably ascertained, being president of Chateau Pacific is only a figurehead position, requiring little or no actual participation to draw a full salary. Even if the new owner decides to fire him on the spot, which she certainly has every right to do, another puppet job can be created for him, so Christian should have nothing to complain about except losing a home he doesn't deserve in the first place."

Once the ceremonies were concluded, Andre moved us out onto the patio where he had replaced the banquet table from the night before with two adjoining circular tables, each with a huge umbrella to provide shade and comfort, and had set up a Euro-American style buffet under the canopy for our pleasure. Karin served the beverages, Andre worked the portable grill and made the omelets, and the rest of us consumed it all. It's amazing how quickly a bite of this, and a taste of that, can fill up an entire plate, leading only to the necessity of a second plate for all the important items. I did my best not to be a complete pig, but somewhere between the Eggs Benedict and inch thick grilled pork chops stuffed with shrimp and pico de gallo, I lost all concepts of moderation. I'd like to say the marijuana, wine, and champagne had no effect on my appetite, but that would be a lie, too. My only salvation was that everyone else was misbehaving in the exact same manner, and having just as much fun. It was only after the majority of the eating had been done that the conversation turned away from the culinary delights on display in front of us to the business at hand.

"Unkle Henri," Roberta began, with a coy little smile and a bat of her big brown eyes, "I had the pleasure of tasting some of your vintage Bordeaux's that had hand written labels with dual family names. I've heard a few tales, but if I may be so bold, would you be so kind as to explain the conspiracy behind these labels?"

"A woman of your beauty can be as bold as she pleases," he replied, "and it is only my age, and the size of your husband, that limits my degree of kindness. The story of the labels holds no conspiracy, only contempt for the elitist Parisian bureaucrats that originated the phrase about death and taxes. You see, the creation of our many wines is taxed on each and every step of the process. We pay taxes on the land, the vines, the amount of grapes we harvest, the bottles, the corks, the amount of wine we produce, and even the French oaks that are felled to make the barrels and casks for aging and storage fall under the watchful eye of the taxman. Add the ungodly sales and export taxes we pay into the equation, and even a schoolchild can see that we are being squeezed unmercifully by the extortionist politicians to support their lifestyle." Unkle Henri took a moment to swirl his Cote de Beaune and have a relaxing sip, then continued. "Vintners have been trading wine back and forth since the dawn of time, and the government has always wanted its fair share. In the early twenties when our economy was at its worst, the first place they looked for more revenue was the vineyards, of course. Instead of paying additional taxes on wines that were produced for private consumption and trade, my grandfather joined a group of his colleagues and created the labeling system that allowed us to continue our free trade system under the disguise of family gifts. Since both names were on the bottle, both families shared in the vintage without being taxed again on a product that had already been taxed numerous times. A few of us old-timers still continue the practice to this day, and it's a good thing, because not only is it the legal basis behind the concept of Chateau Pacific, it also allows me the ability to bargain and spar with my fellow vintners. Believe me, lawyers, Hollywood agents, and even old horse traders have nothing over a couple of old negociants deliberating whose wine is better, and which vintage has a greater value. I have an old friend at Mumm that loves my Volnay and gives me a 3 cases to 1 advantage when I trade for that Cordon Rouge you're enjoying. On the other hand, my own flesh and blood in Margaux only gives me a straight 1 to 1 exchange for my Nuits St. George that she adores. It would cost me less to simply buy her Bordeaux's at wholesale, but what would be the fun in that? To coin a phrase from Mr. Mason, old habits do indeed die hard."

"And what about the stories that try to link your family and certain smuggling conduits to the escape routes used by refugees during the Nazi occupation?" I asked. "According to certain historians, you're a hero to a great number of escapees with questionable Jewish ties, and yet elements within your own government claim your family to be illegal profiteers."

"The stories are true, but I would never consider myself to be a hero," he replied. "The same people that forged our shipping documents for a few exports that bypassed the heavy handed tax collectors also served us well by providing immigration documents for our friends and associates who chose to leave France instead of facing torture and murder. As payment for our services, many of them signed over the deeds to their vineyards and other properties in exchange for their freedom. For those who had neither money nor property left for payment, we offered our services for free, and my family would provide them with food, clothing, and even a little operating capital for their journey. The same bourgeois politicians that fattened their bellies by dancing with the Nazis were the first ones to cry foul after the war when what was left of my family began to reap the rewards of our endeavors, and it is their heirs that continue to disrespect and accuse us to this day. To them, my only comment is silent disregard."

"Good for you," I answered. "I'd love to talk more about the war years, and life in general at the chateau, but unfortunately, Jack and I have an engagement to go deep sea fishing while the girls hit the shops in Manzanillo. I hate to break up the party, but if we're going to keep to our schedule, it's now or never."

"I have to agree with you," Unkle Henri replied with a smile and a raised glass. "Schedules are important, especially when they allow an old man time for a nap before my business meeting with Amanda Tu. There will be plenty of time to finish our conversation over the next few days, so please, go and enjoy yourselves while I take a moment to close my eyes and relax."

While everyone else was standing around in the sunken den preparing to embark on their afternoon endeavor, Terri led me into Janinne's bathroom and closed the door. She walked over to the raised black marble counter, turned and let me set her on it, then pulled me close for one of her patented Charmin kisses. They're very soft, very absorbing, and most definitely get the job done. She leaned back for a quick moment, opened her eyes and looked deep within my soul, then pulled me towards her and kissed me again.

"I love you, Jeffrey," she whispered as we held each other tightly. "I never want to be without you. I hate to be selfish, but to hell with our friends, I want you all to myself. Knowing Bert and Suzan, we'll all be drunk by the time we get back from Manzanillo, so be prepared. I don't care what anyone else has planned for us, my intentions are to spend the rest of our day making love to you."

"What about tomorrow, Angel?"

"I promise to make every tomorrow even better, Jeffrey."

LADY IN WAITING

Unkle Henri took a brief moment to check out his appearance in Janinne's full length Cheval mirror, adjusted his tie, then stepped into the elevator and pressed the number 2. The hour of sleep had refreshed his little gray cells, and he was now as ready as possible to confront the mega-wealth of the Tu family's only daughter. He knew in his heart that her so-called engagement to Christian was a ruse the instant Janinne said the words, but the necessity of a private meeting signaled him to be both leery and cautious. Whatever Christian had gotten himself into this time, money would not be able to expedite the situation when dealing with people worth billions. Along with more than half of the shipping that circumvents Hong Kong, the Tu family also owns the exclusive distribution rights to the entire selection of wines from Domaine Morea for all of Southeast Asia; so once again, Christian may have put the family business in jeopardy with his decadent personal life.

As he stepped out of the elevator onto the soft carpet of the business office lobby, Unkle Henri was glad to see the entire floor vacant of all personnel. He took a moment to admire the interior architecture, then tapped lightly on the French doors to Janinne's office, and stepped inside. As Amanda Tu stood up from one of the wing-back chairs and stepped to greet him, the sight of the buxom woman-child tightly draped in classic Oriental fashion nearly took his breath away. Although covered from her neckline to her ankles in orange floral silk, a man would have to be blind not to notice the way her body moved inside the soft fabric, and Unkle Henri was not blind.

"Bon jour' Miss Tu," he said with a pleasant smile, then politely kissed the back of her hand and indulged himself in the splendor of her perfume. "I am Henri Morea, but please, call me Unkle Henri."

"It would be a pleasure," she replied, then stood her ground so he could continue to absorb the beauty of her image. "Do you like my dress, Unkle Henri?"

"What's not to like? Please forgive me for staring," he smirked, "but I do find your choice in fashion worth admiring. Miss Clark said that you were stunning, but I was not prepared for this!"

"Terri said I was stunning!" she exclaimed, acting more her age. "Wow! When I'm standing next to her, I think she makes me look like dog food."

"No dog could ever be that worthy, Amanda," he laughed. "Now, it is my understanding that you have a proposition for me. When a man reaches my age, that usually means a business deal, so shall we sit and get down to business?"

"Absolutely." Amanda offered a wing-back chair to Unkle Henri, then curled up on the couch across from him, taking full tactical advantage of the waist high slit down the side of her floor length skirt. Chang set down a silver tray containing an elegant tea service for two in Janinne's finest china on the coffee table between them, then moved back behind her glass desk and assumed his position of silent observer. Amanda poured the steamy beverage into a cup over a lemon wedge, then passed it to her guest. "I believe you like your tea up with a squeeze," she said with a smile.

"Very good! I can see you've done your homework."

"In more ways than one, Unkle Henri," she replied, then poured herself a cup, and settled back into a comfortable posture on the couch. "First and foremost, I must congratulate you on this magnificent resort. I fell in love with Chateau Pacific on my first visit, and my feelings have gotten stronger with every return."

"Merci! Our concept has always been to appeal to the creature comforts of our clientele, and I think Miss Pavie has done an excellent job of adding her personal touch to the total ambiance of our establishment." Henri took a moment to sip his tea, then in his own subtle way, got right to the point. "So, does this mean that it is my club that you are in love with, and not my nephew?"

"Absolutely!" she laughed. "And everyone knows it except him! Unkle Henri, I saw through his deception of ownership the instant the words left his mouth, and it took less than 24 hours to prove the full extent of his fraudulent claims, but that only made me work harder to achieve my goal."

"And what is your goal, Miss Tu?"

"Possession," she replied, in a cool monotone. "My goal is the possession of this resort."

"Amanda, a woman of your wealth doesn't need to marry for property, so why the charade? Since you obviously know that Christian will never own or control Chateau Pacific, or any other holdings of Domaine Morea, why bother to continue the facade of engagement?"

"Insight, Unkle Henri," was her response, "and leverage, of course. Once I learned of the unique circumstances that allow the unrestricted flow of wine from France, I knew I would never be able to buy this resort outright, so I wanted to find a way to keep an insider's view, as well as the ability to manipulate Christian at will. His proposal of marriage provided an instant solution to both scenarios, and moved the game to the next level. Unfortunately, the game is now over, and it's time for me to get down to business. It's true that I'm here to make you an offer, but not for the resort. Well, not all of it. I want to enter into a partnership that will allow me the ability to build my own residence and live here, on a part-time basis, of course. My second offer is simply to buy Christian's villa as part of the partnership and live there."

"And what about my nephew?"

"In either option, he has to go."

"I agree," Henri replied, then stood and began to walk around the room. "Christian has gotten himself involved with the wrong kind of people his entire life, and now his exploits jeopardize the resort we built to help save him. According to my sources, over a million dollars in cash is being deposited every week into a bank in Manzanillo, and then transferred by wire into an account in Switzerland. An audit of the excellent books kept by Janinne proved beyond all doubts that the money wasn't generated by Chateau Pacific, and since his salary and profit-sharing checks are deposited directly into a separate account, simple logic dictates that Christian is once again involved with something illegal. I was only going to talk to him, but now I see it is obvious that Christian must go for Chateau Pacific to survive. I see no reason not to accept your offer, Miss Tu, but I must confer with my niece as to which option she would prefer, and what percentage she wants to relinquish for the partnership."

"I'm not asking for a large percentage, Unkle Henri, just the ability to say I'm a part of the ownership. I also want it to be made perfectly clear that I will be a silent partner, and support Janinne Pavie as General Manager with complete control over the day-to-day operations and decisions. I do have a few ideas I've already shared with Janinne, like putting in an exclusive boutique filled with our own designs that can be custom fitted by our own family of tailors, and using my money to buy either a large sailboat or motor yacht for cruises and parties. Once Christian is gone, the guests will be allowed to enjoy the cigarette boats he supposedly bought for the club, so throw in a few catamarans and wave runners, and our water sports options will be first class. Now that she knows I'm on her side, I think Janinne and I are well on our way to becoming good friends."

"I certainly hope so, Amanda," Unkle Henri replied with a smile, "because as of two hours ago, she is now recognized as the legal heir to Domaine Morea and the owner of Chateau Pacific and all its properties."

"She's the niece in your will?" Amanda exclaimed loudly. "That will come as quite a shock to Christian! He told me she's nothing but a burned out stewardess that gives good head. I'd love to be in the room when you tell him!"

"And so you shall," he replied, "and then I think we should let the burned out stewardess have the pleasure of firing him in front of both of us. My brother has always said that Christian needs a good dose of reality, so I think I'll send him to enjoy the Spartan life of being an Israeli. I'm sure Andre can find something constructive for him to do to earn his keep."

The doors to the office opened and in stepped Christian and his pet Arab. Mahmood's eyes were clear and focused, but his master's face was flushed and contorted as he was in obvious suffering from the massive hangover from hell associated with a near overdose of Viagra, cocaine, and way too much champagne. Christian did his best to evaluate the surprising encounter he just walked in on, but found it to be too much of an effort, so he simply reverted back to his usual asshole self.

"I see you've torn yourself away from your precious vineyards to come meet my bride," he said with a distinct sneer. "I hope you like what you see."

"What I see is far more pleasing than what I've been hearing, Christian. Perhaps you should join us and answer a few questions."

"What lies has this bitch been telling you, unkle? She's only jealous because I've found a new slut to comfort me until our wedding day. My whore of the Nile kept me up all night long with her magical ways, and wouldn't let me rest until after the sun had come up, so forgive me if I'm a little rough this morning."

"It's after one o'clock in the afternoon, you worthless peasant, so to Hell with your rough edges," Unkle Henri burst out. "I want to know who is supplying you with the cash to make such outlandish deposits on a weekly basis?"

"No one you would approve of, Unkle Henri, but I assure you it is a very profitable relationship. The money is being wired into an account that will always be there to supply our family with an abundance of operating capital for whatever opportunity we choose. Be it new vineyards in Oregon for a transplant of our most productive vines from the Cote d'Or, or a cash buy out of existing vineyards, I intend to move us into the Pacific Northwest within the next year. If we can pull off the same scam, I propose we build the next Chateau Pacific on the Oregon coast as close to our new vineyards as possible. If we lower the overall capacity to less than half, and charge three times as much, we'd make a killing! Americans love to flaunt their wealth, so if we made our new coastal villa with an over abundance of sexuality and luxury, there is no telling what an average six-figure a year executive would pay for a three or four day tryst in an exclusive 'let's fuck' environment. Add a little enticement, like some good smoke, a well placed three gram vial, and a cadre of well endowed starlets for comfort, and the business at hand can be concluded with profitability for everyone, and no casualties. As long as we maintain a secure environment that guarantees discretion, I see no reason not to move forward with my idea."

"Idiot! The only scam around here is you!" Unkle Henri was livid with anger. "No one gives away that much money without strings and conditions, especially to someone with your level of incompetence. You are being used in a money laundering scheme, and now you have the resort involved by allowing the use of its name on the bank account. Have you learned nothing in your life about honor?"

"Honor is an old-fashioned ideal that no longer applies," Christian replied boldly. "With the amount of money I've got stashed away, I can buy all the honor I need."

"Before you start spending money that isn't yours, which you've done all your worthless life, perhaps you should make sure it really exists. Once the illegal cash is converted to transferable assets, it is clean and can be sent anywhere. Since you obviously weren't smart enough to set up the Swiss account personally, what makes you think that other people don't have access to the funds?"

Christian made eye contact with Mahmood, then walked directly to Janinne's computer and turned it on. After banging on the keyboard for a few minutes, he stormed towards the door.

"I hate her fucking computer," he uttered, then stopped in the doorway. "Come into my office and I will prove the funds exist, and that they are mine."

Unkle Henri winked at Amanda and offered his arm, then escorted her across the lobby and into Christian's office. With Chang right behind them, Henri and Amanda took the two leather chairs across from his desk, and watched with pleasure as Christian and Mahmood jumped through all the hoops necessary for doing on-line banking. After a few frustrating minutes that bordered on sheer panic, Christian slammed his fist down on his desk and spun around to face his uncle.

"How did you know?" he screamed. "My money is gone, and you're laughing!"

"It was never your money," Henri replied calmly. "If you would like, your Unkle Francois can assert his influence and find out where it's gone, but I think your new associate can answer that question much more quickly. My grandfather taught me that a major advantage of being an honorable man is the ability to read deception in the eyes of your opponents, so perhaps your partner in crime can explain the smirk on his face to all of us."

"You think you're so fucking smart," bellowed Christian, "but your days are numbered, old man. Sooner or later you'll be gone, then all that you've worked so hard for will be mine, and I can do with it as I damn well please. Be careful how you talk about my friend, or I'll have him throw you off my property!"

"This isn't your property, darling, and it never will be," interjected Amanda. "I've known that from the very beginning, but I doubt your friends in the Islamic Brotherhood have figured it out."

"The Islamic Brotherhood!" screamed Unkle Henri, then stood and confronted his nephew face to face. "Are you truly ignorant enough to trust the same people that killed your mother and father? It's time for me to send you to your Unkle Andre, so you can learn more about your new associates and experience first hand their terror and lack of compassion for innocent civilians. As of this very second, you are dismissed as president of

321

Chateau Pacific and should prepare yourself to vacate your residence here immediately. We will fly to Miami tonight, where I will put you on a plane to Israel, and then I can return to the peace and quiet of my vineyards."

"Vineyards! You have no vineyards!" replied Christian in an arrogant tone, then unlocked the bottom drawer of his desk and removed a large briefcase. "I'm holding 20 million dollars and a letter of intent from a gentleman in Syria as deposit on the future sale of your precious vineyards. I've already sold them, Unkle Henri, now all you have to do is die."

From the briefcase, Christian pulled a Walther PPK-S, pointed it at his uncle's chest, and pulled the trigger three times. The impact of the .380 hollow-points lifted Unkle Henri off the ground, and the Grande Negociant of Domaine Morea was dead before his body hit the floor. Amanda sat frozen in fear at the carnage she had witnessed, but Chang and Mahmood immediately went into action when Christian turned the gun towards her. Even before Chang had his .44 Mag drawn and leveled, Mahmood jumped between Christian and Amanda and raised both hands.

"No, my brother!" he screamed. "Do not threaten this woman! She is too valuable, and he will kill us both, so please, give me the gun. You have what you want! The club . . . the vineyards . . . everything! Please give me the gun so you can live to enjoy everything you have always wanted. You have it all, my brother, so please, don't threaten this woman or you will have to die!"

Christian's eyes darted between Amanda, Unkle Henri, and Chang's two-eyed aim down the barrel of his weapon. He felt confused, totally and completely confused, yet his mind was racing with ideas of survival. As if on instinct, he smiled a childish admission of guilt, and passed the pistol to his friend. Mahmood held the gun between his two enclosed hands and returned the fake smile, then turned and faced Amanda's primed guardian.

"Please, my friend, the danger has passed, so put down your weapon and be calm. My friend only wants to live, and poses no further threat to your mistress, so please, lower your weapon, and we can discuss what just happened."

"Drop the fucking gun," was all he said, and that's all that was needed. Chang kept his gun leveled at Mahmood's face, then took two giant steps forward and put his left hand on Amanda's shoulder. Without diverting his attention from the two targets standing in front of him, Chang spoke one word, "Come."

Before she could move, Amanda heard a peculiar whiffing noise, and Chang collapsed like a sack of rocks. She knew he was dead without looking, but worst of all, she knew she was alone.

"Thank you, my brother. I find this game much more to my liking." Sidiki stepped into Christian's office from the lobby holding a Beretta clone with a silencer, and admired her handiwork. "Do not worry, my precious one, he did not suffer. A warrior deserves a quick death, and that's what he received. Now the problem is, what do we do with your fiancée? He's not a warrior, and as you already know, he's not much of a lover, so what shall we do?"

Amanda sat with both hands gripped tightly around her clutch purse, manipulating her stress levels by squeezing the leather, and watching the murderer of her beloved guardian strut her stuff to a captive audience. She had faced death before, but never without Chang. Sidiki walked over and picked up the Walther, removed the clip, then set it down on the desk next to Christian.

"Sit down," she began, then turned to Amanda. "Allow me to show you what to expect if you don't cooperate. Watch closely!"

She then spun around and pointed her gun straight at Christian's genitals.

"I can offer you only two choices, lover boy. Since you're not a warrior, either you pick up that gun and blow your brains out, or I will start with your dick, and blow you to pieces from your waist down. Your choice. Death by your own hand, or death by mine with lots of bleeding and suffering. Ten . . . nine . . . eight . . . seven . . . six . . . five . . ."

Christian reached for the pistol, but Sidiki put a shot into his shoulder that threw him back into the chair, then emptied her fourteen shot clip into every part of his body that wouldn't kill him immediately.

"A fucking Jew named Christian," she said to his slumped body. "How pathetic. Did you really think I would let you touch me and live!" She slammed a new clip in her automatic, pointed the muzzle at Amanda's face, then smiled. "Stand and walk, or stay and die."

40

THE PEACEFUL PACIFIC

David, Jack, and I were an hour north, and at least three joints into our pleasure cruise on the bridge of Amanda's mighty Hatteras when the beeper attached to a belt loop on David's cut-offs started going berserk. He was nonchalant about responding until he read the message, then made an abrupt U-turn and hit the throttle. David grabbed the telephone attached to the dashboard, dialed the numbers as quickly as possible, and waited impatiently for an answer after hitting the speaker-phone button.

"Hi, baby!"

"Hey Kimbo," he began, "the princess is jumping up and down on her panic button. Where are you and what's going on?"

"I just finished restocking the pool bar, and I'm sitting here with Andre and Karin discussing tonight's menu for Unkle Henri over three of my special frozen Martinis. With the exception of that strange new girl we saw yesterday at the pool and two of her bodyguards, I haven't seen anybody other than staff since you guys left. Andre says he only served lunch to six men, and they showed up in two groups of three."

"How do you know they were her bodyguards?" he asked quickly.

"Oh, you know," she replied. "The usual paraphernalia; Uzis, pistol belts, flack jackets."

"Holy fucking shit! I need you to do me a favor right now this very second. Amanda and Unkle Henri are supposed to be having a meeting in

Janinne's office as we speak. Go stick your head in the door and check on them first, then go into Christian's office, turn on his computer, click on the security system icon, and then turn the illumination off on his monitor. We're on our way back, but we're a solid hour away. Be careful, baby, and call me back as soon as you check things out."

David made a quick disconnect, dialed another number, and was not pleased that he didn't get an answer. He took a key out of his pocket and unlocked a cabinet under the dash board, then reached in and handed Jack a pair of high powered Zeiss binoculars.

"Something peculiar is going on back at the club, so we've got to haul ass. Amanda activated her panic button, and Chang didn't respond to my call, so something is definitely wrong. I want you to drive the boat while Jeffrey and I go downstairs for a few minutes. Just follow the coastline, and keep your eyes open for anything unusual."

I followed David down the ladder and into the salon, then waited as told while he disappeared to the lower deck. In my gut I knew what he was doing, I just didn't want to admit it to myself. When the phone rang on the bar, I took a long refreshing breath of air, and picked up the receiver.

"This is Jeffrey."

"Oh my God, Jeffrey," Kimberly said in a shaky voice, "they're all dead! Unkle Henri, Chang, and Christian have all been shot to death in Christian's office. Tell David Amanda's not here, and I did what he asked with the computer. Oh Jesus, whoever did this must be some sort of maniac because they shot poor Christian at least a dozen times."

"OK Kimberly, get the fuck out of there and go back to your normal duties at the pool bar. I'll have David call you back in a few minutes, but for now, try to stay calm, keep your eyes open for Amanda, and please, don't tell anybody about what you just found. When the girls get back from Manzanillo, take everyone up to Janinne's penthouse and lock yourselves in until we get there."

"OK, I can do that," she responded, trying to bolster her courage. "And tell David not to worry, I'll have my two best friends with me."

"Andre and Karin?" I asked.

"No, Smith and Wesson."

I'd barely hung up the phone when David showed himself in the stairway and motioned for me to join him below. I followed him in silence until he led me into the communications room and showed me what was on the computer screen.

"We're in deep shit, buddy," he said, pointing to the bodies lying motionless on the floor in Christian's office. "Looks like somebody cleaned house and took the Princess with them. I'm doing a scan of all the security cameras to try to find her, and see who we're up against."

"I think we both know who," I answered. "Now we need to know numbers. Kimberly would have noticed a helicopter or airplane, but with four or five Scarabs at their disposal, getting Amanda offshore to an awaiting boat, or just away from the club should be fairly easy. At this point in time, why is irrelevant, but I just can't convince myself that she is their only target."

"She's not," he replied, then made solid eye contact with me. "We're on that list, too. Me for being her bodyguard, and guilt by association for you and Jack."

"I agree, but not for the obvious reasons. With both Christian and Unkle Henri dead, maybe their target was the club itself, and getting Amanda was only secondary. With no living witnesses, except Amanda of course, all they have to do is sink this boat, and everything can be blamed on a tragic accident. Either way, we have to die for them to get what they want. I just wish there was a way to contact Terri and the girls to keep them from returning to the club before we get there. Kidnapping isn't the only way to make money with a beautiful woman, and there are five of them in that Suburban."

"Sorry Jeffrey, but I can't be concerned about anybody other than Amanda. Her family pays me to protect her, and if she dies, I die, too. I know it's not part of my written job description, but I guarantee you my ass is history if anything happens to her."

"Well, excuse the fuck out of me! Whether I help you, or you help me is irrelevant if we don't get back to the club alive. If their tactics are only hit and run, then they've already got what they want and they're gone, but if they want it all, whoever is behind this will either be coming after us, or preparing a surprise for our return. Either way, we'd better be ready to work together or nobody's going to walk away from this alive."

"OK, OK! I know you're right, I just wasn't prepared to . . . . Bingo! There she is!"

David quickly typed in a code, and the screen stopped flipping from one camera to another, and maintained the image of Amanda, Sidiki, Mahmood, and a well armed soldier in battle fatigues all standing in the main living room of Christian's villa. By manipulating the zoom, angle, and focus of the surveillance camera, David could see that Amanda was unharmed, but it was crystal clear that she was scared shitless, and her assailants were making the most of her situation.

"Sound," I said to David. "Turn up the sound."

"I wish the fuck I could. All the audio is run through the AV room in the villa, and I can't control it from here. When I set up the link to Christian's security system, I didn't have time to tap into the audio lines without getting caught, so I took what I could get and got the fuck out."

"Been there, done that," I replied, thinking of my encounter with Christian's AV room. "It would just be nice to hear what they are saying so we could get a better idea of what we're up against. The good news is that she's OK, the bad news is they don't look like they're in any kind of a hurry."

"I guess they're waiting for us," David said. "Or waiting for something to happen to us."

"I just hope they're not waiting for the girls to get back from Manzanillo!"

"Amen, brother," he responded, then stood to leave the room. "Either way, you're right about us being prepared. Come on with me, Jeffrey, and we'll go check out the prop closet."

I followed David back into the salon and watched as he opened the hidden compartment that contained his arsenal. I could taste the adrenaline as my mind raced through different scenarios of engagement, but the grim reality of Terri's situation helped keep me calm and focused. Killing is not a sport, it's a job, and if her survival requires me to slip back into that mindset, I can do that job very well.

"Everything in this cabinet comes in two's," he began, "so pick what you want. Clips and ammo are in the drawers underneath the rack, and the vests are in the very bottom drawer. Look Jeffrey, I know you know how to handle yourself, but what about Jack? If we get into a firefight, and there's no reason to believe we won't, what do you think he's going to do?"

"If Roberta is in danger, he'll do whatever it takes to survive and protect her. Just because he's never been in the military doesn't mean he won't fight, but we need to be direct and to the point about what we're heading into. As long as we tell him the truth, I'm sure Jack will let us know in no uncertain terms what we can expect when push comes to shove."

"Pushing and shoving doesn't bother me," David replied. "It's the killing and dying that has me concerned."

"What you're saying is my choice is really no choice," Jack said as he looked into the computer screen. The view of the corpses from the security camera in Christian's office, and the sight of Amanda being held at gunpoint in the villa only strengthened his resolve to be an active part of the solution. "Three people have been murdered, Amanda's been kidnapped, and now you think these people are going to try to kill us, too!"

"That's it," replied David. "They know I'll be coming after her, and they know I'll be armed and dangerous, but they're in no hurry to leave, so that makes us believe there's more to this than just the princess."

"Nobody wants Bert to be a widow, but chances are pretty strong that we're going to have to defend ourselves," I added. "On the other hand, if we don't get back to the club and resolve this situation before the girls return from Manzanillo, they're going to be right in the middle of it, too."

"I'd rather Roberta be a widow than a victim," Jack answered, then locked eyes with David. "Just because I've never been in the Army doesn't mean I can't handle a gun."

"Just because you have doesn't mean you can, either" laughed the former Marine, then got deadly serious with Jack. "What's important for you to understand is that these people mean business. There's no refs, no rules, and when you go down in this game, you're out for good. It's winner take all, with no chance for a rematch."

"I get the picture," he replied. "No fear."

"No, brother-in-law," I said to his face. "Fear is good. Fear keeps you alive."

Jack didn't trust himself with anything automatic, so he chose a Smith and Wesson Model 29 .44 Magnum for his handgun, and a short barreled Winchester 12 gauge pump loaded with 00 buckshot as his close range party toy. Chang's Kevlar vest was a little big on him, and David's spare was almost to small for me, but any protection is better than nothing, especially considering the alternative. After Jack went back to the bridge to retake manual control of the boat, David and I loaded ourselves down with his new .40 caliber weaponry, got both M-16's primed and ready for action, then rejoined Jack for one last joint to calm our nerves while we waited for whatever the fuck was about to be coming our way.

"So far, so good!" thought Amanda as she sat down on one of the antique couches in the recently late Christian Morea's villa. The request was made of her politely, and with dignity as Sidiki escorted her over to the sofa, then sat in a chair directly across from her. Mahmood brought over a bottle of Dom Perignon, two crystal flutes, and a plain manila folder containing documents he set down on the coffee table, then opened the bubbly and served both ladies.

"Do not be afraid, my precious one," she said to Amanda, then slid the golden bubbly down her own throat. "See, there is nothing in this bottle other than champagne. I have no intentions of harming you, or letting any harm come to you, so drink this in celebration of your wedding."

"My wedding?"

"Exactly! You see, a few nights ago, Christian Morea and Amanda Tu were married in a very private ceremony here at Chateau Pacific. The bride was an impostor, of course, but one Oriental girl with big tits looks like any other to a well paid drunken priest with lusty habits of his own. Since I can promise you being his widow will be much more fun than being his bride, all I need from you is your legal signature on the marriage certificate and one additional document, and the business portion of this meeting will be concluded. We could use a computer and forge them, of course, but I would much prefer your legitimate signature as a showing of your good faith and cooperation"

"He's dead," Amanda replied calmly. "What good would it do to perpetrate this fraud if the mark is already deceased?"

"Simple," was Sidiki's smug little response. "As his widow, you now own controlling interest in this club, which you will sign over to us. Mahmood will take over Christian's position as president, the money will continue to flow, and life will go on as usual."

"You really don't know, do you?" Amanda stated without expression, then got down to priorities. "Look, I have no problem signing your documents as long as I get to walk out of here alive. I don't give a shit about this club, anybody in it, or the money you're going to steal from it, but what promises do I have that you're not going to kill me as soon as I sign my name?"

"Have faith," replied Sidiki, "and my promise that I will shoot you if you don't."

Amanda picked up the cheap ball point lying next to the opened folder, signed both documents, then slammed her champagne and held her glass up for more. After being refilled and sharing another slam with her congenial captor, Amanda began to get light-headed, then found herself floundering in the downward spiral of a heavy narcotic. She tried to resist, but her whole body seemed mired in the adhesive nature of the furniture.

As she slumped over and faded into unconsciousness, the last things that registered in her mind were a cacophony of laughter, and two big hands ripping open her dress.

"Damn, I'm sweating like a fucking pig," exclaimed Jack from the helm as he maintained thirty knots on our trek back to the club. "Even in all this fucking sea breeze, my vest is soaked and I can't keep my hands dry."

"Me, too, brother-in-law," I answered. "Waiting and not knowing is always the toughest part, no matter how many times you've been through it. Fate is a cruel mistress that loves to fuck with your mind while she spins her web, and there's not a fucking thing we can do about it except concentrate on the job at hand. We're only about fifteen minutes away from the club, which means they've had at least 45 minutes to plan and execute whatever they have in store for us. As long as we stay this far offshore, we won't have to worry about surprises, but the closer we get, the sooner they have to play their hand. We have two trump cards to play; the amount of firepower we're carrying, and the fact that they don't know we're aware of what's really going on. Unfortunately, once we start shooting back, both advantages will be gone, so we have to make damn sure the first ones count."

"Thanks, buddy," he said with a cruel smile, "just what my wet underwear needed, more pressure."

"No extra charge, brother-in-law."

Something caught my eye as I made a sweep of the coastline, and I quickly focused the powerful lenses on two scarabs heading northbound at high speed. Without hesitation, I picked up the phone and dialed the two digit extension of the communications room.

"Two boats coming up fast from the southeast," I said to David. "They're still hugging the coastline, but I guarantee you they've seen us. Anything new downstairs?"

"Same old shit," he answered. "So far the count is three. I just hope she's too out of it to remember what they've done to her. Hell better have lots of room, because payback is going to be a mother-fucker!"

"Agreed! If they'd do that to her, given the chance, they'd do it to Terri and Roberta, too. Whatever it takes, they have to pay for their actions." I took a quick moment to check on the boats in question, then continued, "OK, we've been made. The two scarabs have slowed down for a little pow-wow . . . . I count two uniforms in each boat, and . . . . yep, they're showing weapons, so we're on the menu for today."

"Good! Here's our chance to cut down the odds, so keep our weapons out of sight, stay on our present course, and I'm on my way."

"Try to hurry, David," I answered. "They've cranked it up and are heading our way."

The three of us watched from the bridge as the two powerboats raced closer towards us, bringing confrontation and death right along with them. David kept a low profile with the binoculars so as not to alert the in-coming soldiers of our degree of readiness, and I made one last check on our equipment before the shit hits the fan, but the waiting period was finally over. Within a few brief moments, the three of us would be thrown face-first into the logical terror that is mortal combat.

"Look!" exclaimed Jack. "They're waving at us like we're a bunch of idiots!"

"As far as they're concerned, we are," was my answer. "Two can play that game, brother-in-law, so let's wave back."

And we did! Like a couple of drunks on a pleasure cruise, Jack and I jumped up and down and waved at our assailants as if they were long lost drinking buddies.

"That did the trick," David said. "They're laughing their ass off while they're getting their weapons ready. All four guys are in uniform, so everything is a target. I can see only small arms with limited range, but they have more speed and maneuverability so we still have to let them get close for the first pass. I'm going to ram this bitch right down their throats, causing them to split, then each of you will have only one boat at a time to deal with. The reinforced hull of this vessel can take anything their weapons can dish out, and all the glass is bulletproof, but we're wide open from the ass end, so as soon as they pass, I'm going to make a hard left and angle for another run. With the two of you on the back deck firing from both sides, and me laying down coverfire from the cockpit, we should do some serious damage, if to nothing else but the boats. This bitch causes a hell of a wake at full throttle, so expect their scarabs to roll and leave their underbellies exposed. Everything we've got should blow holes in their hulls, so pour it on. I'm going to keep both MACs up here with me, so you guys take the M-16s. Your shotgun only has five shots, Jack, so let Jeffrey give you the 30 second crash course on how to shoot one of these genuine US military bad boys. The custom rounds we staggered in those 30 round clips are designed to do a number on second generation body armor or explode on impact, which means neither the boats nor their occupants will be able to withstand a few good direct hits. After the first pass, though, it's going to be a dogfight, so just keep firing short bursts until we're the last ones afloat. Remember, their job is to kill us."

"And our job is to survive round one so we can help the girls," I added.

"Amen, brother-in-law," Jack said in a cool monotone. "Let's get it done."

David took over the controls and began a leisurely turn towards the oncoming scarabs as Jack and I went over the fine art of how to make an M-16 shoot. I showed him clip in, clip out, the charging handle, the full automatic switch, and how to sight in on a target, then it was time to put that knowledge to use. We both scampered down the ladder and got into firing position by the back walls of the salon, with me on the starboard side and Jack to port. At our feet, each of us had a nylon gym bag holding our extra pre-loaded clips, speed-loaders for Jack's revolver, and a back-up handgun, just in case.

"Come on in, you sorry mother-fuckers!" David was screaming at the top of his voice so Jack and I could hear over the rumble of the twin diesels. "Get ready, get set, go baby go!"

He rammed both throttles to full, and the mighty Hatteras lurched forward into battle speed. In seconds, I began to hear the impact of small arms fire bouncing off her hull, then the staccato fire of David's twin MACs.

"Now!" I screamed, then laid out a wall of fire that raked my opponent's scarab as it raced through it. As if in slow motion, I watched down the sights as the rounds ripped through the wood and fiberglass, and inundated the occupants of the cockpit. The driver made a hard turn to the right which took them right across our wake and caused the scarab to become airborne, and I emptied the remainder of my first clip in their exposed underbelly. David made the hard left he promised while I was changing clips, but I didn't have to hurry because my target was sitting dead in the water. I put burst after burst into the bobbing hulk for good measure, then turned my attention to Jack.

"Are you OK?"

"They're running away," he shouted in between shots. "I hit them with a few rounds and they took off!"

"Not for long," I replied, then slid back over to my side of the boat for a better view as we crossed their wake.

The scarab made a wide sweeping turn well out of range, then using its advantage in speed and mobility, maneuvered itself for a direct assault on our exposed stern. Like a Messerschmitt on the tail of a B-17, the scarab followed our every turn and made long range, high speed passes in an attempt to pick us off with the high volume of rounds they were firing at us. For the most part, they were ineffective, but the occasional splattering of soft lead against bullet-proof glass certainly kept everyone's attention focused on the dilemma at hand, until David pulled an old pilot's trick. He put the Hatteras into the tightest turn and circle it would maintain, forcing the Arabs to move well within our effective range if they wanted a kill shot, and they most certainly did. After their first pass that peppered us pretty good without any return fire, I raced up the ladder to the bridge for a better angle of fire on their next pass, and was startled to find David standing in a pool of blood.

"Shell fragments from ricochets," he shouted. "I never felt the impact, only the burning and stinging in both legs. Take care of these assholes, Jeffrey, so I can lie down!"

"Go right ahead!" I replied, then reached over and pulled the throttle back to less than half speed. "Stay down until you hear me start shooting," I shouted to Jack, "then pour it on."

Smelling blood, the Arabs thought we were disabled and raced straight in for the kill. I waited until they were well within pistol range, then cut loose with a barrage of shells aimed straight down their throats. I saw the head of the driver explode like a watermelon hit with a sledge hammer, and Jack dissected the cockpit and passenger with a prolonged burst that ripped both of them to pieces. Within seconds, smoke started pouring from the engine compartment, and the cigarette boat exploded into thousands of tiny fragments.

THE PASSION OF PERSUASION

After making a quick stop at Boca del Rio so Carmen could pick up a change of clothes and her car, the ladies were finally on their way back to Chateau Pacific. Their shopping spree had taken longer than planned due to the high degree of celebrating they were doing, the amount of money they were spending, and the amount of attention they were receiving everywhere they went. Stories from their previous visit earlier in the week must have circulated all throughout the marina, because they were inundated by worshipping males within minutes after stopping at the cantina to start off their afternoon, and continued to have an entourage of admirers that followed them as they meandered through the shopping district. Roberta even received a proposal of marriage from a caballero that supposedly owned a two thousand acre horse ranch and had one of the largest "vessels" in the marina. Needless to say, the drunker they got, the raunchier the "vessel" jokes became until all five girls had no more laughter left in them. Privacy was restricted to dressing rooms and toilets, so Janinne was glad when Roberta and Suzan decided to ride with Carmen in her Z-28 convertible, leaving her alone with Terri for the remainder of their trip.

"I'm glad it's finally just the two of us, because there's something I want to talk to you about," she began, then reached over and held Terri's hand. "You know how I feel about you, so now that I'm the official ruler of my little domain, and no longer have to deal with Christian, how would you and Jeffrey like to live here? I know we joked around about the possibility, but now it can become a reality. Houston's not exactly the hub of creation, and yet both of you have succeeded in getting established in the national marketplace, so why not continue here? I love Amanda's idea of having a boutique at the club of our own tropical fashions, so having you and Jeffrey around to do the images for our website, as well as anything else you can contract out from your existing clientele, should keep the two of you busy and do nothing but further establish your careers. Throw in the added income Jeffrey could make by offering his talents to our guests, and you'd have it made!"

"Sounds like you've got this all figured out, girlfriend," Terri replied with a smile, then leaned over the console and kissed Janinne on the cheek. "Being here, and being with you, has certainly been an incredible experience for me. Living here would be like living in the ultimate fantasy, and I know for a fact that Jeffrey would feel the same way, but there's one thing you need to understand from the very beginning. I love Jeffrey with all my heart, and I'm going to be his wife. Most of the guys I've met have fallen into two basic categories; those that wanted to possess me, and those that just wanted to fuck, but he's different. Not only is he my lover, he's my best friend. He cares about me on the inside even more than he does the packaging. Jeffrey says he wants to spend the rest of his life being in love with me, and I feel the same way."

"Me, too," Janinne answered. "I'd never try to replace him, nor would I ever want to come between you. You're just so precious, I can't help but love you, too."

"Thank you," said Terri. "Between you and Jeffrey, I've never felt, or been, so well loved in all my life."

"Between me and Jeffrey is exactly where I'd like for you to wake up every morning of every day you're here," she replied. "I hope that doesn't sound too tacky of me."

"Quite honestly, as long as Jeffrey doesn't mind, I think it sounds wonderful."

The road along the mountainous coastline hit a straight-away long enough to make a safe pass, so Carmen and crew zoomed around the Suburban like it was standing still and took the lead. With Roberta riding shotgun and Suzan in the back, they were both doing shots of Hornitos straight from the bottle with one hand, and holding their hair with the other, while Carmen kept both hands on the wheel and her foot to the floor.

"Either somebody has to pee, or Jack's in for trouble again," Terri laughed.

"Or both," exclaimed Janinne. "It's a good thing we're almost there!"

"I agree," Terri replied with a sly little grin. "Jeffrey deserves a healthy dose of TLC, and I can think of no better time to discuss our future living arrangements."

Within minutes, both vehicles slowed and made a left turn down the unmarked jungle road that led to Chateau Pacific. A steel security gate hidden by the dense foliage closed behind them to keep out any unwanted visitors, and a light flashed in the security office alerting the guard on duty of their pending arrival. A hidden video camera activated by a motion sensor flashed their image on his screen for proper ID, but the four men in the security office didn't even bother to look. They knew who was coming, they knew their job, and they were ready.

Janinne drove the Suburban around the convertible and through the large archway that opened into the circular courtyard, and parked in her usual spot next to the security office. Since staff would not be returning until tomorrow, and the first people to be sent away by Christian before one of his parties was always her security personnel, she was surprised to see activity inside the brick and glass structure, but gave it no further thought after recognizing Mahmood standing there like an idiot staring out the window at her. Carmen parked in the adjoining space, then all five girls congregated at the back of the Suburban to retrieve their spoils of the day. Their plan was to open something bubbly and chill in the hot-tub until the boys return, then Terri was going to take Jeffrey back to their cabana for a little convincing and a lot of romance. At least that was the plan. As they walked past the security office towards the lobby entrance, Mahmood and three of his associates stepped out and stopped them in their tracks.

"There's been a slight incident here at the club while you were away," he began, "so I think it would be best if you let me and my men escort you up to your penthouse."

"Not in your wildest dreams, asshole," Suzan replied.

"Oh, but I must insist," Mahmood answered. The charm in his voice and the 9mm automatics on display in all four men's hands made for a convincing argument. He led them to Janinne's private elevator, punched in her secret code, then held the door and smiled as all five women filled the small car. "Don't worry," he said, "we'll be right behind you."

When the elevator door opened, the ladies were greeted by the sight of Sidiki standing in the foyer with a soldier at her side carrying something small, dangerous, and fully automatic. Their gasp of surprise created a pause that seemed to last for an eternity until Sidiki finally spoke.

"Please come in," she stated warmly. "You are in no danger now, so please just relax, and I will try to explain what has happened. I have very little time, so please hurry."

They did what they were told, and went straight to the sunken den, but no one sat down. Instead of joining them, Sidiki and her associate stayed at the edge of the foyer to talk down on their captives.

"There are two things you need to know," she began. "The Korean faction that attended Christian Morea's business meeting made an attempt to kidnap Amanda Tu earlier today that ended in the death of her bodyguard. My men killed the Koreans, and we now have Miss Tu safely in our custody. She was not harmed, but remains emotionally upset about the tragic loss of her guardian. Second, and most important, the family Morea is no longer involved in the operation of this resort. I am Head of Security for the new owners, and until I turn over control to the new management, I am in charge. You should feel lucky that my men and I were here to save you. White slavery is very popular these days in the Far East."

"That can't be true," Janinne replied. "Unkle Henri said nothing to me about any of this during our morning meetings. Where is he? I need to see him!"

"He is no longer available," she answered in an eerie tone. "We made our deal with Christian, and he was dying to please us."

"So why are you holding us at gunpoint?" asked Bert.

"We are holding you for your own protection," Sidiki replied. "Until I am certain all the terrorists have been eliminated, you are far safer up here under guard."

"This is bullshit!" exclaimed Janinne. "Who are these new owners, and what have you done with Unkle Henri?"

The elevator doors opened, and Mahmood stepped out with the rest of his goons. He remained standing in the foyer with Sidiki, but his men walked through the girls to the glass doors, then turned around and faced the party. Everyone with a gun could see that the initial shock was wearing off their prey, and that fear was setting in deeply in its place.

"I have told them about the evil plot of the Korean's, my brother, and also about the change in ownership. What I neglected to tell them is that you are the new President and General Manager of Chateau Pacific, and that their services are no longer required."

"Sad but true," he stated, but said nothing else because of the look in his sister's eyes.

"Now, before we leave to continue our duties, I must be rude and to the point. Since two of my men have already had the pleasure of making the acquaintance of the princess, I will leave them here with you for your protection. However, I must warn you that their understanding of your language is limited, and that their orders are to keep you here at all costs. Do not make any sudden moves, and make no attempt to leave this flat. These men are soldiers, and we're in a combat situation, so in plain English, don't fuck with them if you value your life. As soon as it can be arranged, I will provide all of you safe passage away from here, but until then, I must insist that you cooperate."

"I don't know who you are lady," Roberta said boldly, "but Janinne was right. This is bullshit! We just drove in here with no problems, so why the fuck do we need your safe passage to get out? Tell it like it is, sister. We're hostages."

"Only until I can get you on my ship," Sidiki responded. "Then you will be my prisoners."

"Do you really think my husband is just going to let you walk out of here with me?"

"If your husband was aboard Amanda's yacht with her other bodyguard and the photographer, then I have nothing to fear, because you no longer have a husband. Four of my best men were dispatched to exterminate the occupants of that yacht, and return it for your transport out to my freighter. Your husband will not be coming back, Madame. You are now a widow."

Sidiki nodded her head and all but one guard moved to the elevator. The soldier who had been standing with Sidiki in the foyer stepped to the side and let everyone else enter, then cracked a smile at her final orders.

"Behave yourself, Ahmed," she stated softly. "And don't handle the merchandise. There will be plenty of time for that once they've been transferred to the boat and sedated for their journey. Just like the princess, they won't be able to put up much of a fight, but I guarantee their pussy will be just as sweet."

"Oh my God," Jack exclaimed, the image of his wife being held at gunpoint filling the frame of the computer monitor. "What the fuck do we do now?"

"We kill every one of those sorry mother-fuckers, then send the dogs after the goombahs that cut the orders," David answered. "Now we know there are only four soldiers left to guard two operatives, five hostages, and the princess. We've got to get them out of there, that's what the fuck we're gonna do now!"

"We all know that," I intervened. "The question is how."

"Two targets, two teams," David answered. "Since I've been in and out of that villa at least a dozen times without getting caught, I know what I'm going to do. My question is how do I get you on that roof without getting everybody killed?"

"I appreciate the thought, and so do the girls," I said, "but unless you've got a matter transporter, I can't see them letting us get off that long straight pier. One guy with an automatic weapon sitting in the boathouse could make our lives pretty fucking miserable until his buddies arrive for the grande finale."

"Why can't we just pick up that phone and let the police handle all this?" Jack stated. "There's a lot more cops than there are of us, and they've got a lot more experience."

"I could call our friend," I said to David. "He said we could be picked up in fifteen minutes if we ever needed to escape."

"Sounds good to me, but that could get the hostages killed just as easily. As long as the Arabs think they're still winning, the girls will probably be safe, so that's why we have to be quick and decisive in our first assault. If those assholes start seeing helicopters and uniforms, there's no telling what they'll put those girls through before everybody dies. Yeah, call him, but don't be surprised if he puts the ball back in our court. We're here, he's not."

The open-line priority call to JJ took less than 45 seconds to connect, and I told him everything. In turn, he told me the crazy bitch was a hot target and that people had already been dispatched to do away with her. He estimated their arrival in less than an hour, and promised he would inform them of our current situation as soon as we disconnected, then told me in no uncertain terms that I was not to let anything happen to the most beautiful woman he'd ever met. After apologizing, he assured me that whatever decision I made would be the right one for the time and place, and wished me luck.

"So what the fuck are we gonna do?" asked Jack again. "According to this diagram, the only ways we can get up to the penthouse consist of two elevators and a stairway, but steel doors and secret codes limit our access to only the main elevator from the lobby. That's no choice, that's suicide."

"That's exactly what those assholes are supposed to believe," answered David, "but there's got to be at least one more way. That penthouse was built for a Saudi prince, so there has to be an escape route planned, just like the tunnels coming out of the villa. If there are main stairwells on both sides of the building that go to the third floor and stop, and a single flight that goes up to the service elevator landing outside Janinne's kitchen on four, my bet is there's a duplicate set of stairs on the opposite side of the building for a quick exit. If those stairs don't exist, our only other options suck pretty bad."

"Those stairs are a pipe dream, and you know it! I'd be better off trying to climb up the side of the building than wasting my time looking for something that doesn't exist." I was losing my cool and couldn't stop myself. Not a good sign, but better now than later!

"My only decision to make is do I want to climb four stories of glass or brick?"

"Why not just use the fucking fire escape?" Jack burst out. "Since they probably don't have one, my other thought is how do people get to the air-conditioner units on the roof for service?"

"That's it!" David started banging away on the keyboard, and up popped the original building diagram showing fire escape routes. There on the screen, in 3-D animation, was not only the hidden stairs that lead into the back of the large walk-in closet next to Janinne's powder room, but it also illustrated a ladder built into the exterior bricks that connects the corner of the patio with the ground. Under the Utilities and Maintenance menu, we found a ladder that parallels the main elevator shaft up from the third floor to a trap door in the roof for access to the refrigeration units. "So the good news is that there really are viable options to get up to the penthouse," he said, "but the bad news is still everybody dies if you get caught."

"Looks like the key to this puzzle is the third floor," I said to myself out loud. "What's up there besides the bottom of Janinne's pool?"

"Half of it is storage, and the other half is the biggest temperature controlled wine room I've ever seen. Kimberly and I did the dirty deed on a dozen cases of Dom Perignon the first time she showed it to me, and it remains one of our favorite spots."

"Nothing like a cool place for a quick fuck on a hot day," Jack replied.

Each of us looked at the other, the subject was immediately dropped, and I had to leave the room. Back on the bridge, I took over manual control of the boat, but was still having doubts about my ability to do the same with myself. We were getting close enough to see the beacon that marks the opening of the bay, but the coastline seemed to be just creeping by. The most precious entity of my entire world is being held at gunpoint, and completely at the mercy of over-zealous thugs that thrive on killing innocent people in the worst ways, and I can't do shit about it until we get there. The twin diesels were giving us every ounce of power they could, but with the purpose of our mission looming directly in front of us, even a scarab would have been too slow.

The phone rang on the dash, but the voice took me by surprise when I answered.

"This is against all the fucking rules, so don't identify yourself," JJ began. "The containment personnel are in position around the perimeter as we speak, so the crazy bitch ain't going anywhere by land or air. The ATL refuses to delay his engagement, no matter the circumstances, and orders you to stand down. As long as he gets what he wants, he doesn't give a shit what happens to the girls, so you've got less than thirty minutes to get them out before all hell breaks loose. Nobody moves before the ATL arrives, and I promise you everyone is aware of the hostage situation, but we both know what's going to happen. The choppers are on the pad, so get it done, amigo. I only wish I was there to help. Good luck."

ASSAULT 101

Kimberly made a quick stop at the beach bar to make sure there was no one hiding in there, and then continued her stroll down to the pier and boathouse. Inside the folded beach towel cuddled in her arms was David's cellular phone and her compact Smith & Wesson 9mm. automatic. She breezed through the abandoned shop with a feeling of relief, then continued her trek into the sea cave to check out the boat docks. The only other occupant of the facilities was bent over the back seat of David's camouflaged cigarette boat and shoulder deep into the engine compartment. Rocking out to some classic Doobie Brothers blaring from the stereo system, Antonio Diaz was enjoying not only his work, but the privacy it allowed him. An educated, but grizzled old man of 33, Saint Anthony shared his home with his lovely wife, six children, and two grandchildren in a sleepy little village up the coast, so going to work was a pleasure. He was the best engine mechanic within a three hundred mile radius, but more than that, he was honest, trustworthy, and Ramon's favorite uncle.

"Hi Antonio," Kimberly said after turning down the music. "Sorry to bother you, but where is everybody?"

"No bother, Miss Kimberly," he replied with a big toothy grin. "I'm almost finished installing the new injectors, so I deserve a break. Mahmood told everybody to take today off, so I'm enjoying my holiday working on David's hot-rod. I've still got to find out what Christian and his friends did to those other two boats, but I will save that for tomorrow. That hija de puta who claims to be Christian's new partner stole the only two boats that are still running for her bodyguards, then demanded I make all boats ready for an offshore run this afternoon. She may think she's the boss, but the only way she'll make it offshore today without those other boats is if she's a good swimmer!"

Kimberly just laughed, then made her way up the stairs to the watertight door that accesses the stairwell up to the villa. She entered four different six-digit codes, and couldn't contain the smile beaming from within when nothing she entered would open the door. Kim entered a final ten digit code that confirmed the priority lock-out, then made her way back through the boathouse and walked out to the end of the pier. After taking a good look back for any movement of any kind, she sat down and made a call.

"It worked," she said boldly. "That door won't open for anybody but you, lover. Wow, a bad ass dude with a hard dick, and a computer hacker to boot; what more could a girl want? Sorry, I'll behave myself. Anyhow, there's nobody in the beach bar, boathouse, or cave except Antonio, and he's just finished working on your boat. He said that fucking cunt told him that she was Christian's new partner, then sent four of her men out in the only two boats left running after the three-day party."

"Great! That means they're cut off," answered David, "but that also means we've got to move fast before they find out. Take a quick swim just for show, then herd everybody you see into the kitchen for safety. We'll be visible from the penthouse in just a few minutes, so stay loose and be quick. Disable the freight elevator on the ground floor so they won't be able to use it as an escape route, then just hang out and wait. When Jeffrey and Jack get there, help them any way you can. I love you, Slim. Be careful."

"I love you, too, David," she said softly. "I know where you're going, and I know why. Don't worry about me, I'll be here when you get back."

David kept the peddle to the metal as we rounded the beacon and made our stretch run up to the pier. I was carrying a MAC .40 equipped with a Sionics noise suppresser, a Beretta Centurion fitted with a brush silencer, and all the pre-loaded .40 caliber clips I could carry in the designated compartments of my military-style web belt and suspenders. Jack had taken a liking to the M-16 that saved his life, and held on to the magnum revolver as well, so I was the stealth, and he was the power. Our goal was simple; get to the kitchen without getting killed, then up to the penthouse in the shortest amount of time. Once there, all I have to do is kill two trained soldiers in front of five scared girls before they can retaliate. Easy enough, now if I could only breathe.

"OK, according to the surveillance cameras, there are two guards in the penthouse, two with Amanda, Mahmood, and Sidiki in the villa, and nobody else showing anywhere I looked," David said to Jack and I. "I've engaged a top priority lock up of all the security doors in the villa to limit their avenues of escape, and then initiated a full diagnostic back up and restore maintenance program for the entire security system that will take it off-line for about an hour, so now we can't see them, but they can't see us either."

"There's just too much open ground that's visible from the penthouse for us to use any of the main trails that lead past the pools, so Jack and I will pick up the royal pathway behind my cabana and work our way up to the opposite side of the pavilion, then make a dash to the kitchen. What I'm worried about is you, David. You can't hardly walk, much less run or climb, so how are you going to get up to the villa?"

"Straight up the main trail, my friend," he answered. "I've got a few alternatives once I get there, but you're right, there's no way I can make a run through the jungle, so I've got no other choice. Besides, it's the quickest route, even with gimpy legs."

"And I thought I was the only crazy fucker here," Jack said with a laugh. "Getting ready for the Cowboys was never like this."

Running parallel to the pier, David took the Hatteras as close to the boathouse as possible, then Jack and I hopped down onto the wooden planks and tied her mooring lines as quickly as we could. Wasting no time, we helped David down, then made our move towards the beach bar. Using the rockface as cover, we stayed along the inside edge of the walkway, and did the same with the border of the jungle until we got to the main trail.

"Take care, Marine," I said to David as we shook hands.

"Give 'em Hell, Army," he replied, then exchanged high fives with Jack. "Watch your ass, big guy. These people don't know how to play fair. They'll kill you any way they can, so remember, no mercy. They sure as shit won't show the girls any."

As he hobbled up the trail towards the villa, I couldn't help but drift away for a moment to other times and other places when I said good bye to other comrades-in-arms, and never saw them alive again. No matter how strong a warrior's spirit of survival may be, sometimes the odds are just in the other guy's corner. Jack tapped me on the shoulder, then looked me in the eyes and said,

"No mercy, brother-in-law. Let's get to it."

Moving as quickly as we could, I led us past our cabana and up the small trail to its intersection with the royal pathway. After waiting a moment to listen for any human sounds, we made the right turn that took us past the point of encounter with Jean Claude, and uphill to the pavilion. Jack emulated my every move and posture, but I could tell he wanted us to move faster than caution would allow. If our foes are strangers to the club, then they wouldn't necessarily know about this trail and we could run right down the middle of it. On the other hand, Mahmood has been here long enough to obtain complete knowledge of the entire system, and easily could have taught his associates how to use these trails to their advantage. Either way, us getting killed down here in the dirt won't help the girls in the penthouse one damn bit, so I chose to be cautious rather than careless, and we still reached the pavilion in less than five minutes.

I left Jack at the edge of the jungle trail and crept up the stairs to make sure the pavilion was deserted, then we both ran on our tip-toes across the concrete floor to the doors entering the kitchen and stopped. Rather than bursting through the doors and scaring the shit out of a bunch of already scared shitless people, much less get shot by Kimberly, I hesitated, and again took the cautious approach. I could hear someone talking, but cared neither for his tone of voice nor heavy accent. I cracked open the swinging doors for a quick peek, and my heart dropped into the pit of my stomach. Standing with most of his back to me was a man in green battle fatigues, holding his prisoners at bay with one of those new 9mm. submachine guns I'd seen the other night at Christian's business meeting. Kimberly and Karin were on their knees trying to render aid to Andre who was unconscious on the floor, but all the rest of the small group of employees were standing motionless in fear of their assailant. There were two people standing behind him in my line of fire, so I passed my fully automatic weapon to Jack and drew the Beretta.

"I can see you in the door," the soldier screamed. "Whoever you are, come in or I will shoot these people! Come in now!"

He turned his face to see who'd stepped through the door an instant before the .40 caliber round ripped through his throat and ended his miserable fucking life. I knew he was wearing a vest, so I had to aim high, just like he would have done to me. The loudest noise to be heard was the tinkle of brass bouncing around on the tile floor, then a cry of relief from his hostages.

"Jeffrey! Oh, thank God it's you!" Kimberly scrambled over to me and threw her arms around my neck, then did the same to Jack. "He saw me from the penthouse and came down to recruit me for their little party, then decided he wanted Karin and Rosie, too. Poor Andre tried to object and that asshole hit him in the face with his gun."

"That means there's only one guard left upstairs with the girls," Jack said in a calm demeanor. "Let's get up to the third floor and find that secret staircase so we can sneak up on that mother-fucker before he gets suspicious."

"That staircase isn't much of a secret," replied Kimberly, "but you'll never get through the door. Both back doors are steel and only open from the inside, just like the one on three."

"OK, that means I'll climb up the service ladder and go over the roof," I answered.

"I don't think so," she said. "There's a huge padlock on that door and Janinne is the only one with a key. You have to remember, she's been stalked by Christian since the day she got here, and takes her privacy very seriously."

"So how do you explain the security camera in her penthouse, and the view we were getting through the computer?"

"That's easy, Jeffrey," she answered. "Although she doesn't know it, David is the one who installed the electronic kill switch for Janinne, so he and I are the only ones who know the command codes to override it. David recommended our current security software program because he knows how to manipulate it so well, and Amanda insisted Christian have it installed or she would never return again."

"Wonderful! I guess that means I'm climbing up the side of a four story building totally exposed on a fire ladder."

"Only if you're Spiderman," Kimberly replied. "Janinne had that ladder removed when she was redesigning the penthouse for herself. Like I said, she wanted to deny Christian any avenue of access."

"Now I know why she always wanted us to stay with her," I remarked, then had to smile at the look in Kimberly's eyes. 'OK, so safety was only one of the reasons."

"That leaves us only one option," Jack stated coldly. "We've got to use the private elevator."

"Not we, brother-in-law, only me. I want the two of you on the third floor in case he tries to move them down the stairs. If he gets that far, you'll have to take him out because I won't be around. No matter what, promise me you won't let that asshole walk out of here alive."

"No matter what, Jeffrey," Jack replied. "I promise."

I stopped at the dead soldier only long enough to pass Kimberly his submachine gun, and Karin his automatic pistol, then it was time to go. He carried no communication devices, but that doesn't mean the guy upstairs isn't wired to the others. Kimbo reminded me of the not-so-secret code for the elevator as we embraced, but for some reason, she held on for an extended amount of time.

"David's out there all alone," she whispered. "I promised him I'd help you, so get this over with so we can go help him."

"I agree," was my reply to her, then slapped high-fives with Jack, rechecked my weapons, and moved out through the swinging doors.

The elevator door opened as soon as I put in the code, so at least it didn't have to come back down and alert the guard. Expecting the worst, I prepared myself for my assailant to be standing in the doorway ready to cut me to pieces with his automatic weapon, so I had to be ready to do the same. I thought my heart was going to pound right out of my chest as that sorry-ass little elevator took its sweet fucking time getting to the penthouse, then it stopped, and the doors opened onto a vacant foyer. I dropped to one knee and made a quick glance out the door, but again saw nothing. There were no noises to be heard, no motion to be sensed, and worst of all, no one to be seen. I locked the elevator so it couldn't get called downstairs, then crawled into the foyer to search out the girls and their captor.

When I reached the stairs leading down into the sunken den, I caught my first glimpse of the girls, and my heart soared. They had been moved outside and were sitting around the table where we had enjoyed brunch with Unkle Henri only a few hours ago. Their hands were tied behind them, and those assholes had put duct tape across their mouths, but they were all alive, and none the worse for wear. The remaining soldier was walking the perimeter of the outer railing, which would have made my four story climb nothing but suicide, but he seemed to be enjoying the view more than he was paying attention to his captives. Like David said, as long as they think they're winning . . . .

Remembering how limited his view of the penthouse would be because of the dark tinted glass, I took a peaceful moment to decide on a plan of action, then moved cautiously to the door in the kitchen to let Jack and Kimberly join the party. I had to get through the glass doors and closer to my target without jeopardizing the girls, which meant I needed a distraction, and what better way to distract an Arab than blonde hair and bare breasts.

"He's expecting his partner to show up with Kimberly, so that's what we're going to give him," I said to them both. "Sorry Kimbo, but I'm going to need you to be the bait, so rip open your shirt to attract his attention to you, instead of the guy hiding behind you. Once outside, we're going to walk straight at him, then drop to our knees and start shooting. Jack, I want you to stay low in the shadows until we make our move, then stand in the door and pour it on. You're our ace in the hole, so if anything happens to us, it's going to be up to you to take care of the girls. He's gonna catch on pretty quick once we hit the sunlight, but that should still give us a few extra seconds to get close enough to take him out."

"I don't mind being the bait," Kimberly replied, "but don't expect me to walk out there unarmed. I'm a damn good shot, so let me help."

"I'd never ask you to risk your life without a way to defend yourself. I'm going to slam you into the glass wall to get his attention, then act like I have your arm pinned behind you for leverage as I manhandle you towards him. You should be able to keep a pistol concealed behind your back for those first few steps, then it won't matter any more."

"Amen, brother-in-law," Jack replied, "because he'll be dead."

We all made one last check of our weapons in cold silence, then Kimberly turned to Jack and smiled.

"Do me," she said, and sacrificed her silk shirt to a greater cause. He ripped it up real good to show a struggle as well as her bountiful assets, then leaned forward and kissed her cheek.

"David's a lucky man," he said softly to her. "You've got guts, kiddo."

We moved down into the sunken den and waited for the guard to move himself into the proper angle of fire, then started our little facade. Kimberly bounced herself off the glass wall to gain his attention, then let me slam her against the door for effect. Keeping her body between me and the guard, she opened the patio door and stepped outside. I had my MAC in the ready position at my waist, and I could see Kimberly's automatic was cocked with the safety off, so now it was only a matter of seconds before our moment of truth. The guard was smiling at Kimberly's exposed breasts as he started to walk straight towards us, but his expression changed the instant we stepped out from under the canopy and he got his first real glimpse of me, but then it was too late.

"Now," I screamed, then dropped to one knee and opened fire. My first burst caught him flush in the chest and threw him back into the railing, then the three of us hit him with enough firepower to lift his body up and over the edge. His vest may have saved him from the bullets, but the fall splattered his brains all over the roof of the pavilion.

My ears were still ringing from the booming of Kimbo's pistol right next to me as I set down the MAC and ran over to free Terri. Tears were flowing from her eyes as I removed the tape from her mouth, then kissed her before she could speak. Jack and Kimberly wasted no time cutting loose the nylon straps that held the girls down, and Terri latched on to me like a baby Koala bear on a eucalyptus tree.

"They told us you were dead," she cried. "Oh, Jeffrey, never let me go!"

"Everything's going to be OK, Angel," I whispered. "Nobody can hurt you now."

"What the fuck is going on around here?" asked Roberta, fully wrapped up in Jack. "That little bitch told us they have Amanda under their protection because some Koreans tried to kidnap her, then she tells us that she and Fuck-face are the new club managers, and we're her prisoners."

"Delusions of grandeur, Bert," I answered, then turned to Janinne. "I'm sorry to be the one who has to break the bad news, but Unkle Henri and Christian have been killed, and Amanda really has been taken prisoner. We don't know why, but one of their goals is to take over control of this club, and Sidiki is definitely in charge. The good news is that we were able to contact the authorities, and they're on their way."

Janinne did her best to maintain a stoic image, but the tragic loss of her Guardian Angel was more than she could endure, and she collapsed in tears. All the girls did their best to console her, as I did too, but my thoughts were still on the living and the job that remained to be done. Kimberly broke away from the scene and made direct eye contact with me, which meant it was time for us to go. David and Amanda both needed and deserved our help, so I had no choice but to leave the arms of my lover and embrace the danger at hand. There were still four vicious adversaries out there that not only had Amanda captive, but were now alerted to our presence because of the gunfire. I pulled Terri away from the others, and held her tightly in my arms.

"I've got to go help David," I whispered. "Without him and his toys, we never could have pulled this off, and now it's time for me to reciprocate. I promised not to leave him out there all alone, and the government troops will probably only make Amanda's situation even worse, so if we're going to get her out alive, it's now or never."

"Please stay here with me," she said in a shaky voice. "I never want to lose you again, much less twice in the same day."

"I'm not going to get lost, Angel," I replied. "This is almost over, but I can't let it end here. I owe David your life, and that's one debt I intend to repay. Please understand."

"I understand, Jeffrey," she pleaded. "I just can't make myself let go of you."

LAST DANCE

I worked my way back down the royal pathway in full stealth mode, fully focused on staying alive, yet putting myself in harm's way with every step. Getting Terri to let me go was easier than it was to get Kimberly to stay and help Jack guard the girls and remaining employees. After an earful of words even I found offensive, she finally agreed to let me do my thing all alone, and promised to bring the guys up from the kitchen so everyone would be safely locked up in the penthouse. I appreciated her spirit and intestinal fortitude, but I was going to have enough problems looking after my own ass, much less hers, too. A sophisticated weapon is still a sophisticated weapon no matter who's pulling the trigger, and I would hate to see the effects of one on her Olympian body.

I had already passed the trail leading down to our cabana when the gentle breeze and natural sounds of the jungle erupted with the spatter of automatic gunfire in near proximity. I heard two distinct weapons firing short bursts as I raced forward, then one long sustained volley, then nothing. Rather than take the trail around the ravine to the hidden back door of the villa, like I did the other night, I chose to take the more direct route down through the ravine, then up the other side to the base of the big tree Jean Claude had recommended the night of the fuck party. The underbrush was heavier than I expected, but none the less it provided excellent cover as I made my way to my designated vantage point.

I'd heard no more firing in the two minutes it took me to get into position, but when I peered over the edge and looked down on the patio, I fully understood why. David had himself propped up against the column at the end of rock wall, his right arm and right leg both bloodied by the recent exchange, yet still had his weapon trained on Mahmood. One soldier lay dead at his feet, but Christian's pet Arab stood his ground defiantly because he was using Amanda as a human shield. He had his left arm around her chest and was using her right breast as a handle, while at the same time kept his automatic pistol rammed in the small of her back. Her beautiful Chinese dress was ripped all to shit, and we'd all been witness to the physical abuse she had endured, so I wasn't surprised to see her so out of it he had to jerk her around like a big rag doll, but she was everything he needed at the moment. It was a stand-off in no uncertain terms, and Mahmood definitely had the upper hand. There was no way David could use his MAC without killing them both, and the Arab was doing his best to take full advantage of the situation.

"~~Drop your fucking weapon,~~" ~~he screamed,~~ "~~or I will blow her in~~ half!"

"Go right ahead," David replied, trying to lure him closer. "You kill her, I kill you, or what the fuck, I'll just kill you both. Either way, I'm a dead man, so what difference does it make! If she dies, I die. Get the picture, asshole?"

I knew what was coming, so I had no choice but to get ready. Sooner or later, Mahmood was going to make his move on David, and I would have the only angle for a clean shot. This damn Beretta may be a great combat weapon, but a target pistol it's not! I've had to make tight shots before, but not with a gun I'd only fired once in my life. I unscrewed the silencer for the believed purpose of greater accuracy, rested my two handed grip on the rocks in front of me for support, cocked the hammer, and tried to stay calm as I watched the scenario unfold down the sights of the pistol.

"You have been defeated," Mahmood yelled. "We have everything. Drop your weapon or you will be the cause of her death!"

In my peripheral vision, I caught the glimpse of two figures racing out of the hidden back door and into the jungle, but I couldn't let my eyes stray from the situation in front of me. Sooner or later, it had to end in death, and my guess was sooner. As if on cue, David lowered his weapon, and spoke.

"Come on asshole, take your best shot."

Mahmood snatched Amanda off to his left side, and leaned forward while raising his pistol, leaving his full profile in my sights. The Beretta boomed one time, and Mahmood's head exploded like a beefsteak tomato colliding with a 34 oz. Louisville Slugger. Both he and Amanda landed on the ground in a pile, and I couldn't stop myself from running down to their bodies to make sure she didn't get hit, too. Amanda's face was covered with blood as I cradled her in my lap, but I found no wounds as I wiped her off, so all of it had come from Mahmood.

"Thanks, Jeffrey," David said as he knelt next to me. "You were the only chance we had to walk out of here alive, and you did it."

"It was my shot to take," I answered. "I'm just glad I didn't hit her."

"You not only took it, mother-fucker, you made it!"

Amanda began to stir and move around a little, so David took over the role of caretaker while I let my respiration get back to normal. She moaned a few times, then opened her eyes and tried to speak.

"David . . . . Chang's dead," she said. "She killed him."

"It's gonna be OK, princess," he replied softly, while still trying to comfort her. "The bad guys will all be dead soon, and Chang can rest in peace."

She looked up at David and smiled, then caught a glimpse of Mahmood lying dead in the dirt next to her and started kicking what was left of his head.

"You held me down . . . and laughed . . . while people raped me," she screamed, then began to cry. "They raped me, David. They all raped me!"

Another outburst of multiple automatic weapons fire close by brought our attention back to survival, so I helped David and Amanda move to better cover, then headed towards the action at maximum speed. We were the only armed antagonists facing the Arabs, so unless the containment troops had gotten involved, something was wrong. Very wrong! I was past the ravine and almost to the beach bar when the sounds of helicopters approaching made the situation even more desperate. Sidiki was their target, too, so if I wanted to take care of her personally, I had to find her before they took over and disarmed all us civilians.

I broke into the clearing where the trails merge, and the sight of the carnage surrounding the bullet-ridden beach bar kicked me right in the gut. Suffering from a minor head wound herself, Kimberly was on both knees in the sand holding Suzan's motionless body, and Carmen's bloody remains lay in a heap not two feet away. Judging by the ferocity of her numerous exit wounds, whatever happened was at extreme close quarters, and Carmen took the brunt of the action.

"We only wanted to help," Kimberly cried, as I knelt down next to her and checked Suzan's carotid pulse. Hit twice, she was still alive, but not for very long without immediate care. "They caught us by surprise, Jeffrey. We never had a chance."

At the sight and sound of two Huey assault helicopters zooming in from over the south rim of the bay, I ran out onto the open beach and started waving my hands over my head like a crazy person trying to get their attention, but it was the soldier standing on the bridge of the Hatteras that saw me first. The beach all around me began erupting in deadly little explosions, and even at this range, the impact of the 9mm. round against my vest knocked me off my feet and face first into the sand. I felt someone pulling on me as I tried to fight off the shock waves rippling through my body, then two big hands lifted me up like a sack of potatoes and ran with me back to the safety of a clump of palm trees.

"That was pretty fucking stupid, brother-in-law," Jack said, then smiled at me. "I promised Terri I'd take care of you, and look what you've done. This used to be a perfectly good vest."

"It still is," I answered. "If I'm still alive, it must be."

"You are," Kimberly replied, "but Sidiki and the guy that shot you are getting away on Amanda's boat. Can you walk?"

"Help me up to my feet, and I can run! What's up, Kimbo?"

"I've got the keys to David's scarab," she answered, and we all took off running for the boathouse.

The mighty Hatteras was heading towards the mouth of the bay at flank speed by the time we pulled out of the sea cave in the camouflaged cigarette boat. Both helicopters had already landed on the beach, and I could see the assault troops scurrying around to their appointed duties, but we were certainly getting our fair share of their attention. Since there was no way to make direct contact with them, Jack and I emptied our hands of weapons and waved our arms over our heads as a sign of friendly intent. Maybe it was our actions, or the sight of a tall slinky blonde driving the boat, but for whatever reason, instead of shooting at us, they reloaded a handful of soldiers into one of the helicopters and took off after us. Now that we knew the assault troops weren't going to gun us down, we turned our attention to the real enemy trying to make their escape.

Kimberly kept the hammer down on David's hot rod as the sleek craft quickly closed the gap between us and the lumbering fishing yacht.

Having just been in the opposite situation, I certainly didn't want to repeat the mistakes the Arabs made when they assaulted us on the Hatteras, so I instructed Kimbo to stay directly behind them, then told Jack to use his magnum pistol and concentrate his fire on the exposed driver on the bridge. I picked up the M-16 and tried to do the same thing with volley after volley of three round bursts, but at this range, our fire was only harassment. The death blow would probably come from the soldiers in the helicopter, but we still had to try.

The pilot of the helicopter buzzed our speedboat for a better ID, then made his first pass of the Hatteras to do the same when four submachine guns opened up on him. The driver was firing one in each hand, and Sidiki was doing the same thing from the open stern as they peppered the low flying craft, causing it to swerve violently to escape the hail of bullets. Now that the enemy had defined their capabilities, I doubt the pilot had any intentions of ever getting that close again. We held our fire as the helicopter made three high speed criss-crossing passes in an attempt to pick off the two occupants of the boat, but each time the return fire did much more damage than was induced. The only positive factor to their failed attempts was that it provided us with enough of a distraction to get much closer to our prey, and then it was our turn.

With the helicopter faking an assault from the bow, we slid up their ass and cut loose a barrage of automatic weapons fire that riddled the exposed bridge of the Hatteras and made minced meat of the driver. He bounced and staggered from all the impact, then did a header over the railing and into the water. Unfortunately for us, then it was Sidiki's turn. She popped up from Jack's old position at the stern wall and sprayed the bow of our boat with enough lead to create another anchor, then tossed a hand grenade our way. Kim made a hard turn to port and hit the gas only seconds before the detonation that could have blown us in half. I cut loose with my MAC to at least make her duck, but we were in such a hard 360, I would have been lucky to just hit the boat. Hers, preferably.

Our designated driver completed her masterful turn at full throttle, and took us right back up to firing range in a matter of seconds. With us on the port side, and the helicopter coming up hard and fast on the starboard, we had all the elements in our favor, except luck. Sidiki laid a long burst into the helicopter that started at the feet of the pilot and worked its way up and through the entire passenger compartment, then turned her guns on us and laced the cockpit twice. Nobody was hit, but all three of us were praying our asses off in gratitude.

Although her occupants were jumping around trying to avoid all the flying lead, the scarab managed to maintain a steady course, so we had the perfect angle of fire when Sidiki made her move up the ladder to take control of her boat. As if in slow motion, I watched as the rounds coming from my MAC danced across her twice before she grabbed her chest and fell backwards onto the back deck. Splattered blood on the back wall under the ladder proved I had hit her, but only the helicopter could confirm the kill, and they were too busy trying to save their own ass.

"I gotta get on that boat," I shouted at Kimberly. "Can you bring us up along side?"

"I can try, but are you crazy enough to make that jump?"

"No choice," I answered. "Somebody's got to do it."

"Fuck the boat," Jack stated. "Let the Navy sink the mother-fucker and be done with it! There's nothing on that boat we need!"

"We need confirmation, brother-in-law. If she's not dead, we're still in trouble."

Whether he agreed or not, our course was set, and I had to do it. Kimberly fought the strong wake, and guided the scarab close enough along side the Hatteras to where they were banging against one another, and now it was up to me. Just as I was stepping up on the sidewall to jump, however, Jack grabbed me by the back of my shirt and shorts and flung me onto the back deck of the Hatteras like yesterday's garbage. My landing was neither pretty nor painless, but at least I made it in one piece. Sidiki wasn't moving, but I still grabbed her guns, then dashed up the ladder and throttled down the mighty beast. After making a U-turn in the mouth of the bay, I locked the wheel on course back to the club, and slid down the ladder to make sure my companion wasn't going to rise from the dead and suck the blood from my neck. What I found was a woman in her twenties, with two massive exit wounds in her chest and little chance of survival. Drowning in her own blood, and with the taste of death on her lips, she still had enough hate left in her heart to try to fight me as I placed her right hand over the gurgling hole that used to be part of her sternum.

"Make your peace," I said to her glazed eyes. "Your war is over."

The group of soldiers waiting for me on the pier may not have been the friendliest people I'd ever met, but at least they were on the right side. As expected, the first thing they did was disarm me, then they put Sidiki on a litter and we were escorted over to the command center and aid station set up by the helicopters. She was still alive, and by their prompt actions, my initial impression was that they wanted her to stay that way. What they do with her later on is their business, but for now, I was glad to see them put forth the effort to save her. The fighting was over, and the good guys won, so why not extend the hand of mercy to a wounded combatant that would never be a threat again. After all, even if she just partially recovered, she'd either be executed or live the rest of her life in prison.

In the shade of a palm grove right off the beach, a team of medical personnel were dealing with their wounded soldiers from the helicopter, and our casualties as well. Although Kimbo's head wound was really just superficial, one young medical officer went to great lengths to make sure the wound was properly cared for and that his patient was comfortable. The fact that her torn, wet, and tattered shirt left the majority of her breasts exposed probably had nothing to do with his level of commitment, but he sure was enjoying his work. The two men working on Suzan, however, had completely different expressions on their faces. They were doing everything within their power to keep her alive, and even though they were winning, their struggle with death was still intense.

Walking slowly our way from the direction of the villa came two soldiers carrying Amanda on another litter, and David, walking with the assistance of a familiar face. I'd met Mitchell Gregg through JJ a few years ago, and he even dropped by the studio once while in Houston for a conference, but all that was before Terri entered my life. I helped him set David down on the cool grass, and the young doctor so engrossed with pampering Kimberly had no choice but to disengage himself and treat the new patient.

"Looks like you two took care of business without us," Mitchell said, as he smiled and stuck out his hand. "JJ told everybody what you were up against, so tell me first, how'd you pull it off? Divide and conquer, or just good luck?"

"All the right kinds of toys," I answered. "Without David's bag of tricks, we'd be nothing but fish food right now. We were lucky they didn't know we had assault weapons, or things would have been a lot different from the very beginning."

I was going through all the details of how and why for Mitchell, when up marched the Assault Team Leader and his entourage of Royal Guards. At least that's the way it appeared to a civilian like myself. They marched straight up to us and then the ATL's Clown Prince put his bad breath right in my face.

"You were ordered to stand down and let our men take care of this," he shouted. "All these people are dead and wounded because of you. Who the fuck do you think you are?"

"He's the one that got the job done," Captain Gregg replied, "And that's the way my report is going to read. The hostage situations were resolved, and the majority of the enemies were destroyed by these unnamed guests of the hotel in self defense before we arrived, so back off Lieutenant. Hell, he even brought you back the target."

The two Israeli Officers stormed over to the litter where a doctor was working on Sidiki and shoved him away.

"She is alive?"

"Yes, Col. Cherfan," replied the doctor.

The old dog nodded at the young pup, and the proud junior officer pulled his pistol and pumped three rounds into the heart of the helpless woman lying at the feet of his beloved commander.

REUNION

The reunion under the pavilion was bittersweet with the joy of survival mixed with the tragic loss of good friends. Jack and Roberta looked like they would never let go of each other again, but it was Janinne who was hit the hardest and needed the most comfort. She slipped back and forth between periods of crying and grieving over the death of her family, both new and old, and then just totally lost it. The fact that she was now the inheritor of a multi-million dollar family business only seemed to make matters worse for her at this point, but I had no doubt that in time her strength would resurface and she would grasp the reality of her new situation with both hands. For now, the only thing she wanted to grasp was Terri. All of us, including Karin and Andre, were doing everything within our power to console Janinne in her time of need, but her point of focus remained fixed on my lover.

When I noticed Mitchell Gregg walking up from the pool area, I disengaged myself from all the sadness, and moved to meet him around the main bar for some privacy. Even though all our actions were done in self-defense, as far as everyone is concerned, I'm still just a photographer on assignment, so why compromise whatever future I may have by a slip of the tongue now?

"Are they still down there pounding their chests and patting each other on the back?"

"Oh, fuck yes," he answered. "Cherfan thinks they've just cleansed the Jewish nation of Public Enemy Number One single-handedly. The fact that you delivered her to them alive means nothing."

"Good! I don't want any credit for anything. The only reason I brought her back alive is because I'm a lousy shot."

"After what David and Kimberly told me, I think there are a few dead terrorists that might disagree with you," he replied with a smile. "And speaking of dead, so far we've found two separate groups that were killed execution style. The Koreans had their hands tied behind their backs with nylon straps and were shot in the head at point blank range, but the Vietnamese were simply herded into a bedroom and riddled with gunfire. General Huang must have been forced to watch, then tortured, because he was shot at least a dozen times below the waist before being tossed on top of the grizzly pile to bleed to death."

"Sounds like their style," I answered. "Now you know why we weren't going to wait for the cavalry to come charging in and save us. We're just lucky they wanted to keep the girls alive."

"I doubt if they would have felt very lucky once they were prisoners on one of those freighters," Mitch said. "All things considered, you did exactly what I would have done in your shoes. Win, lose, or draw, you had to take your best shot, and you did."

"My best shot didn't do Carmen and Suzan much good."

"According to Kimberly, they chose to get involved and slipped out while Jack wasn't looking. They made their own decision, and unfortunately paid the ultimate price for it. Suzan will be evacuated in the first helicopter with the Israeli casualties, but her condition doesn't warrant much hope."

"I didn't think so," I replied, shaking my head. "So what happens now?"

"My orders are to stay and take care of the clean up with the containment forces, but you've got to go. JJ wants you and David out of here ASAP for debriefing, and since Amanda needs the services of a quality hospital, my suggestion is to get your people together and let David fly all of you back to Houston. We'll get all the bodies and evidence bagged and tagged for transport back to San Diego, then do our best to just disappear. I need to talk to the witnesses and emphasize the necessity of their silence for fear of international repercussions, but you can just get your gear and head to the airstrip. David says he should be ready to leave in about 30 minutes," Mitchell looked over at the group of survivors, then smiled and shook my hand. "You did a great job down here, and I think you deserve more than just a kick in the ass out the back door. If there's anything I can ever do for you, all you need to do is ask."

I thanked him for the kind words, but when I described my encounter with Jean Claude so he'd know where to retrieve the body, I could see the tension levels rise in his face. After confirming that absolutely no one else was aware of our deadly confrontation, he rushed off down the appropriate trail leaving me to talk to our group, and numb with the knowledge that I had signed my own death warrant by killing an agent of the Mossad.

The very familiar arms that wrapped themselves around my waist brought me back from the ozone to the here and now. Terri had been watching my conversation with Mitch, and curiosity had gotten the better of her.

"You don't look so good, Jeffrey. Is there something wrong?"

"Yes and no," I replied, then turned and embraced her with all the love I could muster. "According to that officer, we've just been involved in another chapter of the Arab-Israeli conflict, and he's worried about our future safety. It's important for all of us to keep silent about what happened here today, or there might be repercussions from certain factions on both sides. David is going to fly Amanda to a hospital in Houston, and I've been ordered to go with them for a debriefing by the State Department. I wish we could finish our vacation, Angel, but I'm afraid it's time for us to go pack."

"You go do what you have to, but I'm not leaving," she said softly. "Janinne needs me, and I'm going to stay."

Cruising at 35,000 feet high above the Sierra Madres, the Gulf Stream V was almost too quiet for all the noise going on inside my head. Amanda was asleep in the comfort of her custom bed, and even though I knew exactly where we were going and why, nothing could change the fact that I was going there alone. I had left the most precious element of my life standing in the pavilion with tears in her eyes, and her arms wrapped around the friend she decided needed her more than I do at this time. Roberta and Jack had chosen to stay so they could help fill the void left by Suzan and Carmen's misfortune, but Terri's decision was based solely on the emotional needs of Janinne. As I kissed her good-bye, I told her I understood, but that still didn't change the lump in my throat or the churning in my stomach. Understanding was easy, letting go was the problem.

Adrift in the abyss of my loneliness, I barely moved when David eased into the recliner across from me. He fired up one of his famous Thai-Hawaiian combo joints and passed it my way after taking the first hit.

"I hate to admit it," he said after exhaling as little as possible, "but I miss my lady, too. We may not be planning a wedding like you and Terri, but nothing worth a damn can take the place of a woman that loves you. Who would have ever thought a couple of old whore-dogs like us could get so mesmerized by a pair of pretty faces?"

"If that's all they really had going for them, I doubt if we'd feel this way. At least we know they're going to be safe while we're gone."

"No fucking shit. We just took on some bad mother-fuckers and kicked their ass. With Christian gone and their key players dead, I doubt if they'll ever be interested in Mexico again."

"Probably not, but you never know about crazy mother-fuckers that think everything is God's will. Armed conflict is usually over possession, not religion, no matter what spin the leaders try to put on it."

"They can blame whoever they want," David sneered. "We still kicked their fucking ass. Antonio can fix the damage done to our boats, and if not, fuck 'em. They're only toys, and toys can be replaced. The bottom line is we're still standing, and they're all dead. As for now, we've got priority clearance straight into Ellington Field for our little get-together with your buddy, then it's off to a VIP suite at Methodist Hospital. Once the princess gets cleaned up and thoroughly checked out, I imagine we'll be stopping by your studio for a visit before heading off to God knows where. I'd like to think we'll be going back to Mexico so she can finish her deal with Janinne, but until she tells me where to point this plane, I won't have a fucking clue."

"Since there's no reason for Amanda to go to France anymore, I guess our trip to St. Tropez is off for now. I need to spend a few days sorting and editing slides, then I can promise you I'll be on a plane back to Terri."

"Wait for me, my friend, and I'll take you there myself. You having all her pictures ready is another perfect reason for Amanda to make an immediate trip back to Mexico. If I tell her you're going there one way or another, how can she refuse the man who saved her life? By the way, I hope you realize the Tu family is going to be very generous to the people who saved their little girl. Chang's family will receive their honorable blood money, and you and I could see a six or seven figure blessing for our good work. We took out some nasty mother-fuckers, so why not reap the rewards of our conquests? Nobody wants to work forever!"

Amanda started to stir around a little, so we moved back into the cockpit to keep from disturbing her. No matter how rosy David painted our future, what he wasn't saying was the fact that we were both marked men for the rest of our lives. Intelligence is a cheap commodity these days, so if we really just killed some key players in an Arab-backed multi-million dollar scam, our chances of remaining anonymous were less than slim to none. Like they say, money talks, and since neither of us leads a very low-profile lifestyle, finding either of us shouldn't be too much of a challenge. Taking a few candid photos of drug dealers for JJ was easy to accomplish and well worth the risk, but this was a whole new ballgame. Two hours behind us, one of the world's most beautiful and loving young creatures was safely enjoying another colorful sunset over the bay at Chateau Pacific, but on my horizon, all I could visualize were deeper and darker shades of gray.